THE ROOM IN THE GROUND

OTHER TITLES BY JOHN AJVIDE LINDQVIST

The Writing in the Water

Let the Right One In

Handling the Undead

Let the Old Dreams Die

Harbor

Little Star

Let the Old Dreamer Die

I Am Behind You. The First Place

I Always Find You. The Second Place

X. The Last Place. I Am the Tiger

Our Skin, Our Blood, Our Bones

Fail Again, Fail Better. Notes on Horror and Writing

Border

The Kindness

Alternative Facts and Birds—illustrated by Mia Ajvide

The Reality

THE ROOM IN THE GROUND

A THRILLER

JOHN AJVIDE LINDQVIST

TRANSLATED BY MICHAEL MEIGS

Previously published as *Rummet i jorden* by Ordfront publishers in Sweden in 2024. Translated from Swedish by Michael Meigs. First published in English by Amazon Crossing in 2026.

Published by Amazon Crossing, Seattle

www.apub.com

Amazon, the Amazon logo, and Amazon Crossing are trademarks of Amazon.com, Inc., or its affiliates.

EU product safety contact:
Amazon Media EU S. à r.l.
38, avenue John F. Kennedy, L-1855 Luxembourg
amazonpublishing-gpsr@amazon.com

ISBN-13: 9781662525063 (paperback)
ISBN-13: 9781662525056 (digital)

Cover design by Jarrod Taylor
Cover image: © Katharina Brandt / ArcAngel Images

Printed in the United States of America

THE
ROOM
IN THE
GROUND

PROLOGUE

July 2

On his first day in his newly purchased villa, Kim Ribbing stepped outside and caught sight of a small reddish-gray deer. Its head was up as it watched him from the bushes beyond the fence. The roe deer didn't flinch as Kim slowly descended the stairs and crossed the lawn to put his hands on the bars of the metal fence.

They stood motionless, fifteen feet apart, man and deer, eye to eye. Kim had never been particularly enamored of animals, but this moment of silent "contact" fascinated him, as if he and the deer were wordlessly exchanging the stories of their lives. For a bewildering moment Kim lost all sense of self and saw himself through the deer's eyes.

Then a veil descended between them. That mystical contact broke, and he was Kim Ribbing again, standing on his property and contemplating an astonishingly unintimidated deer. The deer also sensed the change. It snorted and withdrew, unhurried, its white rump bobbing as it went.

They had the same encounter the next morning, and the morning after that. Kim came out on the landing with his morning coffee to find the roe deer waiting for him. He put the cup down, went downstairs, and crossed the yard to the fence. He and the deer communed for a minute or two, and during that time Kim felt vividly alive, at one with the secret pulse of nature and the wide world beyond. Then came the disconnect, and their surroundings were ordinary once more.

On the fourth morning he was awakened by a sharp, flat report echoing outside. Julia Malmros had spent the night with him and lay slumbering. He got up, concerned, and turned on the coffee machine. When the coffee was ready, he poured himself a cup. He stepped out onto the landing.

Just as he'd feared—the deer was in its accustomed spot but crumpled on the ground. Kim descended, hurried across the lawn, and saw its throat had been torn open by a bullet. Its dark eyes stared up at a dead sky.

Kim grasped the fence and looked around. No hunter to be seen anywhere. Someone had shot the roe deer for fun or in anger because it had nibbled the wrong strawberry bed. Kim's knuckles whitened. His eyes felt an unfamiliar prickling sensation.

Beautiful, innocent things existed in the world despite all its ugliness. You could commune with them without fear. But some people wounded and killed those beings just because they could and because that was how they were inclined.

There and then, as Kim stood staring into the roe deer's gleaming dead eyes, he finally decided to kidnap Dr. Martin Rudbeck.

I

JULY 2–9

1

July 8, daytime

Kim Ribbing pulled the heavy steel door shut behind him. The subbasement room's soundproofed walls absorbed the crash as it hit the metal frame. He leaned over Martin Rudbeck to say, "I want to *understand.*" Strapped onto a cot and clad only in his boxer shorts and T-shirt, the doctor tried to respond, but Kim held up an admonishing index finger. "Hold on. Let me rephrase that. It's true, I want to understand. But more than that, I want *you* to understand."

"What am I supposed to understand?" Martin Rudbeck's voice was reedy and hoarse after a day without food or water. Kim had long ago lost count of the number of times that Rudbeck had strapped down a teenaged Kim Ribbing this same way for yet another senseless electroshock treatment.

"Understand what? Who you are!" Kim wrinkled his nose at the doctor's piss-soaked boxer shorts. Urine had trickled along the cot's webbing and dripped onto the floor, but the man hadn't shat himself. "You want to use the toilet?"

Martin Rudbeck nodded. Kim picked up an open shackle fastened to a weighty fifteen-foot-long chain welded to a heavy ring in the concrete wall. He set the shackle around the man's neck and secured it by clicking a padlock into place before releasing the leather straps. The doctor groaned as he struggled up to a sitting position. Kim indicated a door at one end of the room. "The toilet's in there. The chain's long enough."

Kim pointed to the shackle around the doctor's neck. "Just so you know: I don't think you have a chance against me, but let's suppose you try to attack me with the toilet tank lid and you succeed." Kim made a sweeping gesture. "This room is completely soundproof. You have no way to get free of the chain, and I don't have the key on me. Result: You die in here."

"Am I going to die here anyway?"

"No. I'm going to let you go. Eventually. When I feel like it. Subject to a few minor conditions, but we can discuss those later. Now go. Take care of your business."

Rudbeck pushed himself off the cot and almost collapsed. When he turned and staggered toward the toilet, Kim saw a brown stain on the seat of his boxers.

"Water . . ." gasped the doctor before opening the door.

"There's a sink," Kim said. "Drink from it. Or from the toilet, if you want."

Kim left the doctor taking care of his needs and went back upstairs. When he returned, Rudbeck was huddled on the floor halfway between the toilet and the cot. His face was in his hands, and his long, graying, "elegant physician" hair hung in disorder.

Kim tossed him a pair of old boxers. "Here. In case you want a change."

The doctor turned his back and pulled down his soiled shorts. Kim looked away from the sight of the man's loose, pale buttocks, shaggy with white hair. It was just as well he was holding the doctor prisoner on ethical grounds instead of aesthetic ones.

"Aren't you fine," said Kim tonelessly after the change of clothes. The black boxer shorts stretched tight across the man's potbelly and made him look like an elderly tourist on a charter vacation. "Lie back down on the cot."

"And if I refuse?"

Kim waved at a table in the far corner, beyond reach of the chain, where a tray with scalpels, tongs, and a surgical saw was in plain sight. "Found that stuff in a storeroom. God only knows what they were up to down here. I've got a Taser too, from Shanghai. And a blowtorch, in case I feel like using one."

"And you'd use those on me?"

Kim's eyebrows rose. "Of course. I wouldn't enjoy it much, but I would."

"You're mad. And I mean *mad* in a clinical sense."

"Yep. Sounds like you, all right."

The doctor stared defiantly at Kim, who calmly returned the gaze. Martin Rudbeck looked down, sighed, and awkwardly got up to lie on the cot. Kim secured the straps before taking a key from his pocket to open the padlock. The neck shackle opened, fell, and hit the floor with a clang.

"Thought you said you didn't have the key," the doctor said.

"I lied. But I won't carry it on me from now on."

Kim went to the table and hung the key on a hook in the wall. He evaluated the distance between the cot and the table. "How much are we talking about? The chain's short by about ten feet, if you stretch it out all the way. Pretty frustrating if you ever find yourself permanently stuck in here."

The doctor stared at the trayful of instruments. "You're planning to torture me?"

"Depends."

"Depends on what?"

"On how good you are at *understanding*."

"And when I . . . understand? Then you'll release me?"

"Exactly. But on certain conditions."

Kim went to a bench, picked up a laptop, and turned it on. He double-clicked a video file and showed Rudbeck the screen. Martin's eyes opened wide. "But . . . what the hell, that's . . . it's my living room? How did you . . ."

"Took control of the camera on your television. Couldn't get into your computer, amazingly enough. What kind of firewall do you have?"

"Guess."

"Maybe TokenSoft, military grade. Doesn't matter. I have the computer itself now."

"It's locked too."

Kim smiled. "I'll crack it, don't you worry. I'm sure there are lots of goodies on it, but for the time being we have this." He pointed to the screen. "From July 3."

Martin Rudbeck's eyes twitched to the left as he tried to remember what he'd done five days earlier. His lips quivered.

Kim nodded. "You remember, don't you?" He tapped the space bar, and the screen showed Martin Rudbeck entering the living room and seating himself on the sofa with his open laptop. Kim fast-forwarded so the doctor could be seen tapping something, then resumed normal playback speed. Rudbeck was balancing the computer on his right palm, the way a waiter carries a serving tray, while his left hand was rubbing his crotch. He shuddered and his lips twisted into a grin, then he relaxed and continued kneading himself.

The doctor lying on the cot shut his eyes. "This is, of course, extremely unpleasant to watch, but it's hardly enough to blackmail me."

"True," Kim said. "If that's all I had, I'd have to keep you locked up. Or maybe I wouldn't have bothered to pick you up. But I happen to have borrowed . . . a really clever program called Clean Sweep. Developed by a certain Ali Abbas of the Stockholm police. It searches the internet for stored and streaming videos of abuse, and guess what?" This time when Kim looked at him, Rudbeck immediately broke eye contact and his lower lip began to quiver. "Okay," said Kim. "You guessed it. But maybe we should take a peek? Here's the video that was streaming at the exact time you were enjoying yourself in your living room."

Kim clicked and brought up a video of a little girl screaming and crying. He muted the soundtrack and fixed his eyes on the wall. He'd seen this video and had no desire to see it again. It showed a ten-year-old

Asian girl, two grown men, various types of whips, and an oversized dildo. It was one of the most stomach-turning scenes Kim had ever seen, and he'd seen more than enough a few months earlier while documenting a pedophile ring.

Rudbeck didn't want to watch it either, at least not in his current circumstances. He averted his eyes and stared at the ceiling. "I don't understand what you're trying to prove."

"I thought you'd say that, so I arranged a split-screen version." Kim coughed and rubbed his eyes. "I had to watch it repeatedly to make them sync, and that . . . was not pleasant."

Kim clicked a third video file. The upper half of the screen played the abuse video while the lower half showed Martin Rudbeck watching it on his sofa. In real life, the doctor kept his eyes fixed on the ceiling. *"Watch it!"* Kim shouted in a voice harsh with disgust. "Otherwise I'll fix your eyelids open. I'm not joking; I'll staple them in place. You want that?"

Martin Rudbeck glanced at the screen, where it was clear his own ecstatic reactions coincided exactly with certain "high points" in the torture of the girl. Martin Rudbeck swallowed hard. His voice quavered. "That . . . proves nothing."

"I believe, in fact, that it does," Kim said and stopped the video. "The videos are watermarked with time codes . . ."

"Those can be manipulated," the doctor said. "That's your profession, isn't it?"

"It certainly is. But you and I both know these haven't been altered. And I shudder to think what I'm going to find when I manage to unlock your computer."

"You'll find nothing except what I need for my research."

Kim stared at the doctor for quite a while before replying. "I don't understand how you were able to hoodwink the appeals court and explain away the torture you subjected people to, including me. But this time you're going to find it a lot harder."

Kim fast-forwarded through several minutes of video showing the doctor's frenetic masturbation. They made the man look like a jumping jack with a broken, twisted sex drive. Kim slowed the image to normal speed when the doctor sat up on the sofa and set the computer down on one side of the coffee table. The screen of the man's laptop was plainly visible.

Kim froze the image. "Look. There she is. You see that little girl? The blood? You want to listen to her scream when they—"

"That's enough," said Martin Rudbeck. "That's enough!"

Kim folded up the laptop. "Clearly, it wasn't enough for you. You took a little break, that's all. Then you went back at it for another eight minutes and twenty seconds, till the girl was completely torn apart. I literally cannot find the words to describe the type of person you are."

"This is my profession," countered the doctor, who was perspiring heavily. "I have to see, so that I—"

"So you can *understand*," Kim finished. "Right, I've heard that before. And how does this *understanding* arise from sitting and jacking off to the torture of a child?"

"I . . . I . . ."

"Enough!" said Kim. "Just stop. You know I've got you dead to rights. When I eventually turn you loose . . . if you so much as get within an arm's reach of any youngster again, I will release this video. And if anything happens to me, I have a friend who'll do it for me. Understand?"

"You must—"

"Shut your mouth. Now. *Do you understand?*"

Martin Rudbeck panted and wheezed before finally nodding. "Yes. I understand."

"Good. So now we can get started."

2

July 8, daytime

After attending the funeral for Astrid Helander's parents at Hope Chapel, Julia Malmros wandered aimlessly around the grounds of the Skogs church cemetery. They were vast, and she knew that about a hundred thousand persons had their last resting places there. It was difficult not to contemplate one's own insignificance in the wide world, the years one had left, and the question of how to use them.

Another aspect of the funeral began to nag at Julia as she moved toward the cemetery exit: Despite everything, she was still walking the earth, one of the living. The sun had dried up the previous evening's rain, but the scent of fresh grass was strong, and Julia's body felt several pounds lighter than usual. It was wonderful to be alive, at least for the time being.

Her lips twitched in a faint smile as she remembered how Kim had sat drumming his fingers on the tabletop while she drank her coffee. He had a strong tendency to act on his own unrevealed wishes and unannounced schedules, and Julia enjoyed teasing him a little from time to time. He'd been abrupt and mostly unresponsive that morning. Something was on his mind, but Julia knew it was useless to ask about it. He'd let her know when he decided to do so.

They'd gone to bed together immediately upon returning from Norway the week before. Julia hadn't had time to comment on Kim's crazy choice of a new residence before their lips met and they'd melded through most of the night. They'd made love three times. Julia had gone to sleep afterward in a haze of bliss, completely exhausted.

Walking across the grassy lawn illuminated by momentary sunbeams despite light cloud cover, she found she was . . . happy. Not in a profound or orderly way, but in a strong, superficial sense, a dizzy elation. An agitated, fleeting joy of the sort that a rabbit might express with a high, twirling leap.

Screwing like rabbits.

Yes, indeed. That too. It was wonderful to be sexually active again, and even more lovely that it was with Kim. After the excesses of that first night, their lives together had settled into comforting routines, even if their physical encounters still had the thrill of new lovers. Julia didn't dare ask if Kim felt the same way. For the moment, he wanted her, and that would have to be enough.

But that's not what I want.

No, and that was the obstacle to achieving an established, stable happiness. No matter how much she and Kim rolled around in bed and reached out to one another, she didn't know where she was with him. He could lie in her arms as she caressed his scarred skin, yet Julia sensed that he was somehow escaping, slipping through her fingers like water or sand.

Oh well. She wasn't lying under a gravestone yet, and she'd keep going and hoping for the best as long as she could still put one foot in front of the other. Julia exited the cemetery and took a taxi to the Frihamnen cruise port.

3

July 8, daytime

TV4's fall premiere was the series featuring Åsa Fors, eight one-hour episodes based on Julia's novels. Filming was finished, the first episode's rough cut was ready, and she was on her way to view it. Her expectations weren't particularly high. She'd seen a few scenes and thought the settings had been unrealistic, unnecessarily cleaned up, as if police work were somehow romantic. Oh well, maybe the final edit would be closer to the truth.

Julia entered a vast lobby and walked up to an equally imposing reception desk. It could have accommodated ten persons, but only two were stationed there. Julia approached a thirtyish woman whose hair was put up in an elaborate knot. "Hi. I have an appointment."

The woman looked up from her computer screen. Her rigid posture relaxed and she smiled. "Oh, hi! I've read all your books!"

"Oh, really," Julia replied. "I hope you enjoyed them. I'm supposed to meet Ylva Strandberg."

"Could I please see your ID?"

Julia still wasn't used to that. For years now it hadn't been possible to enter Swedish Television, Swedish Radio, or TV4 unless you presented an ID. The woman had recognized Julia, but even so . . . what had they imagined? That she'd whip a revolver out of her bag, commandeer the place, and start transmitting Islamic State propaganda?

Julia knew it was useless to complain. She took her wallet from her shoulder bag and put her driver's license on the counter. The woman inspected it, turned to her computer, created a visitor's badge, handed it to Julia, and waved toward a sofa arrangement. "If you'd please have a seat and wait, Ylva will be here right away."

Julia nodded and almost asked which Åsa Fors novel she liked best but decided that might be construed as fishing for a compliment. It would be embarrassing for them both if the woman couldn't recall a title because she really hadn't read any of them but had merely recognized Julia. So she walked across the reception area and settled on a stiff, hard sofa, her hands in her lap.

She was a bit nervous. She'd become much more sensitive about people's opinions of her since the debacle with her Millennium novel. Today, though, she wasn't the one being judged; she would be asked to evaluate someone else's work. But she still felt just as uneasy. Maybe it was simply that the situation was so like all those times she'd sat waiting to be called into the school principal's office. *So, then! Miss Malmros has started smoking? That behavior is not acceptable here.*

Julia shivered. No one here was going to contact her parents. No scolding was forthcoming, and her papa wasn't going to ground her, considering that he was currently bedridden and barely capable of remembering who she was.

Julia saw Ylva Strandberg's sleek figure beyond the revolving glass doors to the building's interior. The Åsa Fors series had been contracted to Bluefish, an independent studio, but TV4 was the lead production company, and Ylva Strandberg was the in-house producer. Julia wasn't entirely sure how the whole thing was structured. Lots of names and faces had flickered past her, and she had no idea what half of those people did.

Julia rose and went to meet Ylva. They'd met several times before and had no reason to dislike one another, so greeting hugs were called for. Julia had nothing against that, but Ylva Strandberg was very thin and four inches taller, so Julia always felt like a tree hugger during the quick embrace. Ylva's neck smelled of perfume—was it Gaultier? A little hint of rebellion, maybe.

"How are you?" Ylva asked as they separated.

"All right," said Julia. "A little tense, to tell the truth."

"No need. It'll be super good."

Ylva loved hyperbole. "Super," "great," and, unusually, "aces!" During a discussion with a foreigner likely to underwrite a project, Julia had heard Ylva use the obligatory cinema-industry expression "super excited." It sounded entirely natural when it came out of Ylva's mouth.

Ylva's heels clicked over the marble floor as they approached the revolving doors. Julia wore her comfortable black Skechers with padded soles. She felt no need to project a business attitude. That was certainly one benefit of being older. If she'd been wearing Ylva's shoes, her calves would have cramped in fifteen minutes.

Julia followed Ylva upstairs and through hallways. She quickly lost track of their location within TV4. Each time she published a novel, she'd been invited to TV4's morning-program sofa, and she could find her way to that studio, but today she might as well have been in the labyrinth at Knossos.

They walked the length of a wider hallway. Ylva slowed her pace so they were side by side. "That was really something, what you did on Malou's program, wasn't it?"

"That's one way of putting it."

"Everyone here was talking about it, I'll tell you! But it's a super boost for the series, all that attention."

When her proposed text for the continuation of the Millennium series was turned down, Julia had made the mistake of ranting about it to Malou von Sivers on her program *Malou After Ten*. That had caused a hell of a storm in the media, prompting threats of lawsuits, and Julia had felt forced to retreat to her cabin on Tärnö to escape intrusive reporters.

"Glad to be of assistance," said Julia.

Ylva opened the door to the projection room. The place was a nanocinema with eight armchairs facing a seventy-five-inch LED screen. Ylva went to a computer and pressed some buttons. The screen lit up: "Åsa Fors—Gentle Steel." She gestured toward the screen. "We're preparing a proper intro. I've seen some of the initial versions. It'll be super fine."

"Okay," said Julia. "And 'gentle steel'—is that . . . a temporary title?"

"Oh, no," Ylva said with a little frown. "We really like it. A series needs a subtitle, part of the marketing, you know. Showing she's a woman police officer. Gentle but hard at the same time. Gentle steel."

Julia nodded and wondered what "gentle steel" could possibly be used for. Maybe the same as hard cotton? She didn't want to be a sour-puss who complained "no good!" unless she could come up with something better. She needed to think about it. The risk was that the "gentle steel" was already up there, which looked ominous.

"Okay," Ylva said and tapped the space bar. "We can discuss that later. I'll leave you alone with Åsa."

"I'm used to that," Julia said.

Ylva turned off the overhead light. The door closed behind her with that institutional sucking sound. Julia settled back into the acceptably comfortable armchair and watched the screen, where a counter had appeared in the bottom corner. The numbers were a bit annoying at first, but she soon got used to them.

The cut was fifty minutes long. Julia viewed it with increasing distaste. There was nothing wrong with Carina Skytte, who was playing Åsa Fors, even though she was unnecessarily good-looking. The settings were well chosen, the cinematography was captivating. The problem was that the episode wasn't . . . good. It took Julia a while to put her finger on it, but it was basically the same quality she'd disliked in earlier clips. This was nothing like real police work. It had been romanticized.

Not only was Åsa Fors better looking than the version in Julia's novels, her life was far less complicated. In the novels Julia detailed Åsa's many shortcomings and self-doubts, her mood swings and her egotism. The television-series Åsa seemed to have been 3D printed and proceeded through her investigations with hair impeccably in place on a head also always firmly in place. In brief, she was a supercop, a type Julia had never encountered in real life. She didn't even have the literary counterpart's problems with tinnitus resulting from a gun fired too close to her ear.

It ended, the images disappeared, a blue screen was left. Julia remained in the armchair, wondering what in the hell to say. She wished Kim were there; he had no problems expressing his opinions. It wasn't that Julia *abhorred* the series; she found it mediocre, certainly nowhere near the quality of her novels.

She'd been sitting there for a couple of minutes when the door opened and the ceiling light came on. Ylva Strandberg looked expectantly at Julia as she settled into the adjoining armchair. "Well? What did you think?"

Take the money and run was the sign flashing in Julia's mind. If Ylva had had a bag stuffed with the nearly one million kronor Julia would collect for the broadcast rights, she would probably have swept up that bag and taken to her heels.

"In fact," Julia said, "it was . . . very good-looking."

"Right?" said Ylva and lit up. "That scene out on the ice . . . only natural light and, even so, it was aces! And what did you think of Carina?"

"Right, she was good. And good-looking."

"You mean *too* good-looking?"

"Maybe a little. Yes."

Ylva's disappointment showed in a little pout. "Yes, well, that's hard to adjust now, of course you know that. But in a series like this, you need some eye candy too."

"Excuse me," Julia said. "When you say 'a series like this,' what do you mean?"

"Excuse me for pointing it out," replied Ylva, "but this isn't, like, *The Wire*. Don't get me wrong, I think the novels are tip-top, but they work best by offering a bit of escapism."

"Now I'm the one who doesn't understand," said Julia. "If there's one thing I've been congratulated on, it's the realism of my novels."

Ylva nodded. "Absolutely, everything touching on police work. But as for the intrigue, the plot twists . . . excuse me again, but take *The Key to Paradise*, for example. A businessman with the key that winds up a cuckoo clock and the cuckoo has a USB flash drive in its beak. That's not something that would really happen, it's . . . how to say it, it's *heightened* reality. Like something from a fairy tale. Nothing wrong with that; on the contrary!"

Julia felt a slow grinding deep inside. She could say a thing or two about how they'd transformed even the boring slog of an investigation into an unpredictable adventure like "Jack and the Beanstalk." In their telling, the clues came to light thanks to Åsa Fors's brilliance rather than as a result of dogged application of police techniques.

Julia could have made plenty of bitter, even accusing comments, but she merely said, "Yes, I see. I suppose that's what it is."

"Right," said Ylva. "That's what it is."

They batted a few meaningless comments back and forth. Julia steamed with stubborn, suppressed indignation. Then Ylva escorted Julia back through the labyrinth and they parted at the reception. No goodbye hug. Julia went down the stairs to the street, thinking, *Heightened reality. A bit of escapism. Oh, you producer monkey, you!*

She needed to discuss this with someone who understood, or, rather, she had to gripe to a sympathetic ear. Maybe drop in on Malou for a quick visit? Been there; done that. Wouldn't fly. But Julia had a tried-and-true solution: talk to Irma.

Irma Ryding had been a detective-story novelist thirty years longer than Julia and had even seen a couple of her novels adapted into pretty crappy films. And she was Julia's best friend, so if anyone would understand, she would.

Irma answered in her sharp, thin voice on the second ring. Julia said, "I've just been at TV4 to see the Åsa Fors series—"

"Oh, my!" Irma interrupted. "And I can tell by your voice they were mean to you. Come on over, won't you? Wish I could meet you in town, but my hip's still giving me trouble."

"I'll be there in fifteen minutes."

4

July 8, daytime

The case against Frode Moe now was one of tracking down digital evidence, so Jonny Munther's investigating team had been dissolved. Christof Adler had returned to his assignment, consisting for the time being of office duty and following up on phone inquiries.

Christof had had the rank of assistant investigator for only two years and was still considered a rookie. That's why it had been a bit of a surprise when he received the news he'd been requested for the group investigating the Knektholmen murders. Had he somehow caught Detective Superintendent Jonny Munther's eye? Christof had no idea.

Christof Adler had never cherished any exaggerated notions of a police career—car chases, shoot-outs, hostage situations. During the Knektholmen investigation his assignments had consisted mostly of tedious, unpleasant searches of residential spaces, but even those had been more entertaining than sitting at a desk and taking the phone calls the dispatcher didn't immediately redirect to patrol cars in the field. When his phone rang this morning, Christof Adler hoped it would be something at least a *little* bit more interesting than a report that someone had seen "some shady character."

"Thanks for calling the police. You're speaking with Christof Adler. How can I help you?"

Noises of someone clearing a throat on the other end, then a man's voice. "I'd like to report a disappearance."

Not terribly unusual, but more interesting than a shady character.

"And what's your name?" asked Christof Adler.

"My name's Wilmer Syd and it's about my former professor, Martin Rudbeck."

Rudbeck. Rudbeck? . . . That name sounded familiar, but Christof Adler couldn't place it.

"Okay," Christof said. "And why do you believe he has disappeared?"

"We had a meeting set for yesterday afternoon, but he never showed. A few hours later I got a text saying he'd left for Thailand."

"And that text was from his phone?"

"Yes. But believe me, that is completely out of character. He would never do such a thing, never leave without a word."

"And you're sure about that?"

"Absolutely sure. He's the sort of person who makes his plans months in advance."

"Have you tried phoning him?"

"Yes. He doesn't answer."

"Can you provide me his telephone number? And his national ID number, if you happen to have it."

"Just a moment, I'll . . ." The noise of pages turning. Wilmer Syd gave him the phone number and said, "I have a registration number here. It's 550321-0154. Will that do?"

"Certainly. And what do you think might have happened?"

"No idea. I went by his house, but no one's there. I texted back and emailed but got no answer."

"You'll understand, I hope, that I must ask this question. Has he ever exhibited any sort of . . . suicidal tendency?"

"None whatsoever. And I know he was looking forward to our meeting. It was for the two of us and a former student of his who . . . oh, well, that's irrelevant. But no. He would never take his own life.

Or go to Thailand just like that. That's unthinkable. Something must have happened."

"Okay, I'll see what we can do."

Even though Christof Adler didn't daydream about car chases and shoot-outs, he could still wish that cyber searches were more like *Mission: Impossible.* Tap a button on the keyboard, sweep a hand across a screen image, and behold! All the information you need.

Instead, what Christof had was an acquaintance who worked in the passenger information unit. As soon as someone flies into or out of Sweden, each airline is required to record and share the individual's ID information with the unit. This was instituted principally as a measure against terrorism. The ID info is linked with the airline route and with the checked bags.

Johan Åkerman had enrolled in the Södertörn police academy with Christof, but he'd dropped out after six months to study data security. He regarded his job at the passenger information unit as temporary, something to do until he could enroll in a program on forensic information technology. He'd helped a couple of times earlier, and Christof hoped this would be one more that would settle the matter quickly. He rang and Johan picked up immediately. They exchanged some pleasantries, then Christof said, "Listen, I'd like to ask you for a favor."

"Again? When are you going to do a favor for me?"

"As soon as you ask for one."

"I'll have to think of something," said Johan. "What's it about?"

"I just need to know if a person has traveled out of the country."

"Does this have a possible connection with terrorism?"

"We might be able to construe it that way."

"Hmm. Got a passport number or ID registration?"

Christof gave him Martin Rudbeck's information. That name again echoed somewhere in Christof's mind, but he still couldn't connect it to a time or place. A keyboard rattled for a few seconds, then Johan said, "Yep. He's out of here."

"Okay. Was that yesterday?"

"Yes."

"I know that this is sensitive, so can you just . . . let me put it this way: Did he go to Asia?"

"Hmm. Yes."

"Great. Thanks."

"I have a dog," said Johan Åkerman. "A Labrador. Named Musse."

"Oh, yeah?"

"Sometimes I tell myself, *Walking him can be real boring sometimes.* And then I think, *Wouldn't it be great if someone came by and took Musse on a really long walk?*"

Christof laughed. "All you have to do is phone me."

They said goodbye and ended the call. It was obvious this Wilmer Syd guy didn't have a real notion of his former teacher's character. But Wilmer had been extremely insistent, claiming it was *unthinkable*, so Christof decided to double-check. He got up, went to Carmen Sánchez's office, and rapped on the doorframe. Carmen looked up from a folder she was studying and beckoned him in.

Christof had spent quite a lot of time with Carmen during the Knektholmen murder case, and he'd found her approachable. Not that he was infatuated with her or anything; he was attracted instead by the way she tended to her duties without complaint and remained focused. He liked her, that was all.

"I was just wondering," said Christof. "You have a contact at Telia, don't you?"

"Sure," said Carmen. "Why?"

Christof held up his notepad. "Got a phone number here, a Telia account. Is it possible for them to check and find out where the corresponding phone is located? There's a person who's been reported missing. I mean, no formal complaint has been registered, but . . ."

"What kind of person?"

"Uh . . . Rudbeck. Martin Rudbeck."

"Martin *Rudbeck?*" asked Carmen Sánchez as she took the note from him.

"Yes? Does that name say something to you?"

Carmen didn't reply but peered at the number as if it might be concealing some secret message. "A court order is required to search for a phone's location."

"Yeah, but I thought that maybe, you know . . . and this Rudbeck guy, what's with him?"

Carmen picked up her phone. "Go google him while I'm phoning my guy."

Christof Adler went to his desk and did what Carmen Sánchez had suggested. He found that Dr. Martin Rudbeck was the so-called Shock Doctor who'd treated—or, rather, mistreated—Kim Ribbing and a number of other youths with procedures verging on sadism. The doctor hadn't been sent to jail, but his license to use electroshock treatment had been revoked.

Ribbing. Again.

Christof Adler had met Kim Ribbing only briefly, when Kim came in to provide his written testimony about the events on the Henrik Ibsen oil rig. Christof had found Ribbing reticent but intelligent. The guy had a particular knack for irritating Jonny Munther, who got surly just having Ribbing in the building.

Carmen Sánchez appeared in his doorway. "Thailand. He's in Thailand."

"Aha. That's what I'd found also. *Case closed!*"

Carmen nodded toward the phone Christof was holding, which displayed an article about the trial of the Shock Doctor. "Given that background, I'm sorry to hear that he's running around in Pattaya. But that's outside our jurisdiction. Unfortunately."

5

July 8, morning

After kidnapping Martin Rudbeck twenty-six hours earlier, Kim Ribbing had done everything necessary to cover his tracks. While the doctor was still groggy and apparently not understanding what was happening, Kim strapped him to a cot in the basement room and pressed Rudbeck's index finger on his phone to unlock it. Then Kim left.

He changed Rudbeck's phone settings so it wouldn't go to sleep, then copied the contents to his own phone. He turned on his laptop, searched for last-minute trips, and found a TUI charter departing to Bangkok in three hours. He took out Martin Rudbeck's passport, which he'd brought from the man's house, used the information, and paid for the flight with the doctor's credit card. He checked the man in online. That was the easy part.

He glanced at his watch. Unless the flight was delayed, the first passengers would be arriving at the airport, and Martin Rudbeck had two and a half hours to register as a passenger. Maybe Kim had been unduly optimistic about times when he'd chosen an impending departure, but he wanted to get the doctor out of the country, so to speak, as quickly as possible, before anyone noticed his absence.

Kim tossed the things that he needed into his backpack, then straddled his Honda motorcycle and drove to Arlanda Airport. He didn't need to be there to carry out the necessary steps, but if they didn't work, he'd be obliged to take a riskier, more hands-on approach.

Kim Ribbing got to Terminal 5 fifty-five minutes later. He found a niche with a couple of benches from which he could watch the TUI check-in desks. Registration for the Bangkok flight had just begun. He settled in and opened his MacBook Air. Its relatively limited computing power might pose a problem.

For more demanding tasks he usually borrowed a device from someone in HackPack, preferably Moebius's monster laptop, but that would require a better connection than he had via his phone. The free Wi-Fi service was worse. Of course, Kim could hack into the airport's own Wi-Fi, but that would leave him less time for his more important errand.

He started Sniper and let the program chug away in the background, searching for weak points in the system. He then opened Jack the Ripper and went to the log-in interface for airport employees. Strolling past the TUI counters, he'd memorized the names on the badges of the three stationed there. He tapped "Malin Malmberg" and set the Ripper loose with a dictionary attack on her password.

As Jack the Ripper tested Malin's account with a list of the ten thousand most common passwords, Kim checked Sniper's progress. Not great. The program hadn't zeroed in on a single point of access so far.

Fuck.

The brief time—two months—Kim had been in Cuba without access to the internet had been enough for security systems to update against known threats. Sniper was used commercially to identify possible vulnerabilities. Kim's modified version did the same. Airports were particularly attentive to data security because of the danger of terrorist attack, and Arlanda was obviously no slouch in that regard.

The lengthy check-in queue wound through the stanchions. The counters would be open for one more hour, and Kim's backup plan depended on the presence of a crowd. Jack the Ripper signaled that its search had ended without locating the password.

Fuck.

Kim bit one nail. Maybe the staff had been instructed to come up with hard-to-crack passwords that would never appear in even the most obscure lists. Something like Lr&h5?6Gs7. If so, it would be useless to try with the other names Kim had memorized.

He pondered for a moment and unleashed Jack the Ripper for a brute-force attack on Malin's password, a randomly generated search of all possible combinations. This was where his MacBook Air's limited computing power became a factor. Instead of generating a few hundred thousand combinations, there were several billion to be tested. Given the Apple computer's capacity, only by pure chance would it come up with the password in time. It was looking like he'd have to employ the more hands-on method to get Martin Rudbeck onto this plane.

That method depended upon luck, and Kim was beginning to wonder if his luck had deserted him. Had poor planning become his downfall? Well . . . if this try failed, anyone looking for Martin Rudbeck would still have one other false trail to deal with, and Kim hoped to have set the man free by then. The game wasn't over yet.

The Ripper ground away for another quarter of an hour before Kim gave up. He turned off the laptop, put on a baseball cap and a pair of sunglasses, then picked up his bag and joined the queue at the check-in desk. He stepped a bit to one side and scanned clients' faces, pretending to be reading something on Martin Rudbeck's phone.

He found his target among the travelers at the head of the line. A gray-haired man looked around, and Kim got a good look at him—a wearier version of Martin Rudbeck, flabbier, less attentive, with cold, dead eyes. Kim avoided thinking about what the man might be intending to do in Thailand. For now, he suited Kim's purpose.

Kim waited until his target stepped up to the check-in counter. He made his move, timing his steps to reach the counter just as the man put down his passport. Kim slammed Martin Rudbeck's passport on top of it and exclaimed breathlessly, "Sorry, I'm in a rush! My plane leaves in twenty minutes!"

The woman behind the counter frowned. "Where are you going?"

"Bangkok! Quick!"

She looked down at her workstation and Kim switched the passports as the man tapped his shoulder and said, "Hey, you, what do you think you're doing?"

The clerk smiled. "That flight leaves in *one hour* and twenty minutes. Everyone here is checking in for it, so you should just get in line."

"Oh! Aha!" said Kim, picking up the man's passport. "Oh, my goodness!" Kim moaned. Squatting as if to put it in his own satchel, he let it slip down his arm so that it landed in the man's travel bag.

The man ignored him and dealt with his—or, rather, Martin Rudbeck's—check-in. Kim turned to one side, judged the distance between the man's carry-on bag and others in the queue, then straightened up while slipping Martin Rudbeck's telephone into the empty outer pocket. He left the counter in feigned embarrassment, again proclaiming, "Oh dear!"

His mark looked like an experienced traveler, a bit blasé, so probably wasn't one of those nervous types who checked his boarding pass five times before approaching the gate. If he did, he'd see that the name on it was wrong. He might get stopped at passport control. Kim had done the best he could under the circumstances, but obviously plan B had some notable weaknesses.

Kim glanced back over his shoulder to see that the first phase had worked, at least. The man left the counter with a boarding pass inserted in the passport as his checked bag disappeared down the conveyor belt to be put aboard the Bangkok flight. Dr. Martin Rudbeck had just set out on a well-deserved vacation.

6

July 8, afternoon

No matter how much Kim Ribbing hated the fact, the man strapped onto the cot before him had essentially shaped Kim into the man he was today.

Martin Rudbeck had presided over the six-month electroshock regime that had turned Kim's brain into a cloudy mush. Kim had been emerging from childhood into adolescence, trying to understand his place in the world. The first shock treatments had jolted his black depression, allowing light to filter in, but as the voltage increased, a different type of darkness descended upon him, a black, burning hatred. That was the person Martin Rudbeck had created.

Kim came into Martin Rudbeck's clutches after he'd triggered the bomb aboard a cabin cruiser that killed his parents and grandfather. No one ever suspected what he'd done, but his subsequent depression, apathy, and self-destructive behavior had eventually resulted in commitment to an institute for electroshock treatment. Or, put more bluntly, for torture.

Kim hated the man before him as only one who has been deformed and had his understanding of life distorted can hate. Perhaps Kim could better understand himself if he could just understand this man's evil.

A day after Kim created the temporary Rudbeck avatar at Arlanda, the real doctor told him, "People will come looking for me."

"Not for a while," said Kim. He pulled a chair over next to the cot and sat down. "You're in Thailand right now."

Kim ran Find My Device for Rudbeck's phone with the data he'd copied. His tactic had succeeded. The phone was currently in Pattaya, a mecca for child prostitution.

"Thailand?" asked Martin Rudbeck. "What do you mean—"

"Shut your mouth," Kim interrupted. "Not important. What you need to grasp is that nobody's coming to rescue you. The only way you'll get out of here is if I decide to let you walk out."

"Why are you doing this?"

"I told you. I want to understand how a human being like you can even exist. We can start with that video you sat and jerked off to. How can you take pleasure in watching a child being tortured?"

"I already explained," Martin Rudbeck said, twisting on the cot. "My work—"

Kim held up one hand—*halt!*—to silence him, then picked up the wooden base of an old table lamp from which he'd removed the shade and shattered the Bakelite bulb holder. The sharp, bare electrical leads were exposed. A long cord ran from the lamp to the electric socket. Kim stood up and pressed the leads against the doctor's belly just above the navel. Martin Rudbeck screamed, and his body spasmed, trying to hunch up in pain, but the leather straps held it in place.

"Like I said," Kim told him, "unbelievably enough, I really don't want to torture you, but I will, if that's what's needed to get honest answers. I'll try again. What's the pleasure in watching two men rape and torture a child?"

Martin Rudbeck moaned and writhed, but eventually his body sagged. He stared at the fluorescent light overhead. "It's hard to explain."

Kim showed him the broken lamp. "Try."

Rudbeck tried to clear his throat. Twice. Finally, he said, "There's a strong light within the darkness."

"Philosophic crap," said Kim and lifted the lamp.

"Wait!" said Martin Rudbeck, instinctively tightening his arm muscles, trying in vain to protect his belly. "Try imagining extreme abuse, like . . . yes, like in that video. The darkness is so overwhelming that there's light at the same time. Everything that's extreme contains its own antithesis."

Kim lowered the lamp. "Abuse, it's called. It's torture. Of a child. And it turns you on."

"It's not sexual excitement, but more like . . . an ecstasy."

"So, you're saying that there's a *religious* dimension to it?"

"Yes. You could say that."

Kim stood up and walked a circuit around the room. He picked up a scalpel and tested its blade against his thumbnail. Martin Rudbeck's eyes followed him, wide in alarm. Kim could do *whatever he wanted* with the man, and the doctor knew it. The scalpel clattered as Kim dropped it on the tray. "You talk about *ecstasy.* For example, take those Christian mystics who lived in random grottos in the desert and ate grasshoppers. You believe they sat and jerked off as the Good Lord's angels descended upon them?"

"They must have," the doctor said. "Even if the painters didn't depict them that way. There's a sexual aspect to the spiritual, just as there's a spiritual aspect to the sexual. Have you ever experienced—"

"Shut it!" said Kim. "We're not talking about me, and you're starting to theorize in a manner that I find . . . irritating. You may recall that I become unpredictable when I'm annoyed."

"Yes. You're sick, Kim."

Kim stepped forward and leaned over Rudbeck. "You have forfeited *all* right to label anyone as 'sick.' You get horny when you see a child hanging in chains while two men stick all sorts of things up her . . ."

To Kim's surprise and disgust, he noticed how the lump that was Martin Rudbeck's penis inside his boxers twitched and rose a bit at the mention of the pornographic child abuse video. Reacting as if burdened with the tiresome task of taming an unruly hound, Kim gave Rudbeck a lengthy electric shock just *below* his navel. The doctor squealed like a wounded dog and the erection disappeared.

"Don't you dare get horny, lying there," said Kim. "Answer my questions. What. Do you get. From it?"

"The same thing," Rudbeck panted as sweat trickled down his brow. "The same thing. Defiling the innocent," the doctor said, nodding emphatically. "Dirtying something that's pure. There's rapture in doing that."

"Have you *groomed* girls?"

"What?"

"You know what the word means. Have you? Made little girls take their clothes off in front of a web camera?"

Martin Rudbeck's features quivered. Kim went to collect the scalpel. He ran the blade along the contours of the head of Rudbeck's penis, obvious through the fabric of his shorts. "Don't forget: I have your computer. I'll be able to see all your despicable little secrets, so think carefully before you answer. If you lie, the blade is waiting." Kim tapped the point of the scalpel against his captive's member. "Freeing you from this thing would be doing a good deed."

The doctor yelped as the scalpel point penetrated the cloth and touched his genitals. Then he said, "Yes."

"Yes, what?"

"What you were asking. I have done that."

Kim had to resist the impulse to carry out the threat he'd just made. He envisioned himself ripping open those shorts and making the world a better place with one quick slash. Only the risk that the doctor would bleed to death restrained him. Oh well, he could always heat up an iron and cauterize the wound. An option for later. The thought brought the imaginary smell of burning flesh billowing up into Kim's nostrils, and a black madness surged through his mind.

"Okay," he said and removed the blade. "So that's why you've got such strong protection on your computer. Because it holds . . . what? Photos? Videos of young girls as they . . . ?"

"Yes."

"Give me the password. That will save us some time."

"No."

"Excuse me?"

"No. I don't intend to give you the password."

"But my dear man," said Kim, throwing up his hands, "do you still not understand the situation you're in?"

"You can say what you like. You won't get it from me."

Kim rubbed his face with his hands and lowered his voice an octave. "Don't let the fact that I've been speaking in a normal tone mislead you. You're no more than a pile of shit to me, a sack of stinking guts with the ability to speak. You cannot deny me *anything*."

"I refuse. You were already sick when you were a boy, Kim, and I don't plan to—"

The word "boy" made Kim see a dense curtain of red. This was the very man who'd prevented him from ever becoming a normal boy, who'd robbed him of his early teenage years to satisfy his nasty need for so-called *research*.

Kim jammed the contacts of the broken lamp against the man's penis through the fabric of the shorts. The doctor screamed and bucked wildly on the cot, tears gushing from his eyes as his scream dwindled to dry croaking. Five seconds of this, and the doctor's groin spasmed and his shorts turned red with blood. The stink of burning flesh rose to Kim's nostrils. Martin Rudbeck's thrashing head fell to one side and he vomited onto the floor.

Something within Kim urged him just to let the current pulse until Rudbeck's cock was a blackened hunk of flesh. Rage and madness possessed him; an iron taste filled his mouth. Only Kim's aversion to losing control of himself saved the doctor. Kim threw the lamp aside and rubbed a wrist across his eyes.

Be still. Stay in control. You're not a child. Calm down.

Kim waited until the doctor's screams had subsided, becoming no more than a sniffling, broken confused plea in a whisper. "God, Gawwwd . . ."

"God's not listening, Martin Rudbeck," said Kim. "And if he is, he's tooting a plastic horn and shouting 'hooray.' You're alone here with me, and I'm telling you: I'm going to shock you till you vomit up that password. Test me if you dare. This is *nothing* compared to what you did to me."

The doctor hacked up a shining green bubble of slime and spat into the vomit on the floor before reciting in a quivering voice a long, intricate combination of capital letters, lowercase letters, and numbers, a code that would have taken weeks to break. Kim memorized it instantly.

"Good," he said. "Keep this in mind from now on: The word 'no' means 'pain.' Understood?"

The doctor nodded weakly and whispered, "I thought we were supposed to talk about . . . about you. About your . . . experience when I . . . when I treated you."

Kim snorted. "Treated? You never *treated* me. No more than I'm *treating* you right now. But we'll talk about that too, eventually. Don't worry, we have plenty of time." Kim went to the door. He pulled and it rumbled along its metal track. "Now you get to be alone with your foul thoughts. See if you can come up with an explanation that's a little less abstract for next time. Otherwise, I might get irritated again."

"Can . . . can I have something to eat?"

Kim nodded at the pool of vomit on the floor. "Why don't you see if you can find some chunks in that? Oh, no, you're strapped down. Uncomfortable, isn't it? Just imagine how it feels when you're fifteen years old."

Kim extinguished the fluorescent tube. The room was left in total darkness. He hauled the door shut and padlocked it.

7

July 8, afternoon

Astrid Helander sat aboard the number 69 bus headed toward the center of Stockholm shortly after she'd visited Kim Ribbing and he'd offered her a room in his enormous villa. Astrid was still wearing the black tulle dress from her parents' funeral that morning. She was in emotional turmoil. It felt like a cockfight, conflicting emotions attacking one another so violently that feathers flew.

On one hand, the funeral had been horrible. Astrid hadn't gotten along with her parents for years, but it was still a terrible, numbing experience to see the people who'd brought her up reduced to inanimate objects, each in a wooden box ready to be cremated. Astrid's ears had begun to throb when she entered the chapel at Skogs church and saw those flimsy coffins, as if she'd suddenly been plunged deep underwater. The throbbing had continued throughout the ceremony.

It subsided only when the assembly was allowed to approach the coffins. Astrid was the first to move forward. There was audible sniffling in the pews of the crowded chapel at the sight of *that poor little orphan girl* standing before simple caskets containing the bullet-riddled remains of her mama and papa. The caskets were closed, but Astrid knew all too well what the bodies inside looked like, for she'd been there when it happened. She'd escaped slaughter by a hair's breadth.

The sniffling in Hope Chapel turned to sobs when Astrid placed a rose on each coffin. She did not weep. She seemed to see herself from a distance and knew that a fourteen-year-old girl saying farewell forever to her parents was just about the most miserable sight imaginable. But the pressure lessened as she ascended from the depths.

Maybe this was what people called *closure.* Ever since the hail of bullets on Midsummer Eve two weeks earlier, her parents' deaths had seemed abstractions, a haze to live through rather than an ending. Living with her uncle offered no solace. Her whole existence was temporary, a provisional arrangement while waiting for something else. There was something *final* about the two wooden boxes and the roses Astrid set upon them, something she could wrap her mind around and hold tight.

In the time that had passed since her parents were murdered, there were only two things that stood out in the haze. Both were connected to Kim Ribbing. The first was Kim's rescue of Astrid from Vamlinge Hospital, spiriting her away behind him on his motorcycle and returning some semblance of life to her. And now his offer of a room in his villa, a refuge from her undefined existence.

Those were the origins of the emotional cockfight deep within Astrid as she sat on the bus. She still felt heavy and wordless after the burial, which she'd fled when the long line of well-meaning attendees had become too much. On the other hand, she felt relieved and hopeful at the prospect of sharing a house with Kim Ribbing, whom she admired. Maybe she was a little infatuated, even though Kim had sternly insisted she forget such feelings.

Astrid got out at Kungsträdgården and walked toward the shore at Strandvägen. One of the tedious aspects of living with her uncle was that he didn't entirely trust her. After her twelfth birthday, Astrid had been given free use of the subsidy the government provided for child support, but he'd put a stop to that. Now, instead of having 1,250 kronor a month to use as she wished, she had to depend on her uncle for any spending money at all. For the moment she had a grand total of 92 kronor. She was the heiress of who-knew-how-many millions, a whole island in the archipelago with an architect-designed villa, a six-room apartment on Strandvägen, and a Tesla. And more. But not until she turned eighteen. Until then, she had only her 92 kronor.

Astrid Helander had two superpowers. First, she could hold her breath until she passed out, a tactic she used to escape occasional panic attacks. The other was falling. Thanks to her training as a gymnast, she could fling herself headlong onto the ground or even down a staircase, appearing unconscious, without hurting herself too much. It was a cool trick for scaring her classmates and, in addition, extremely *useful* in situations of the sort that Astrid was planning.

In her black dress Astrid felt like a bird of ill omen as she walked along Kungsträdgården past the people in thin, light-colored summer clothes licking ice creams or roller-skating in the sunshine. The heavily funereal mood weighing her down didn't make things any better. She was a black cloud in a world of brilliance.

Astrid emerged onto Hamngatan, turned to the left, and walked toward the Galleria. She was perspiring heavily beneath the nonwicking fabric of her dress, so stepping into the air-conditioned shopping center was a relief. She headed for Clas Ohlson.

At the display of reading glasses, she examined frames priced at 89 kronor and chose the ones that looked much more expensive and had the weakest lenses, rated only +1. She'd shoplifted for a while when she was twelve, but the thrill had quickly died. Not long after that she'd been allowed to manage her own child support, so she'd stopped stealing things.

It would have been simple to let the spectacles slip down below her neckline and lodge between her breasts, but she decided it wasn't worth the risk. If everything went as she was planning, her financial woes would soon be resolved.

Astrid paid for the glasses and found an unsurveilled nook between two shops. She raised the spectacles over her head and dropped them onto the floor. One lens broke. She did it again and damaged the other, after which she tucked them into a pocket with her phone, went outside, and crossed the street.

She was only fifty yards from the main entrance to the Nordiska Kompaniet, Stockholm's famous department store. Astrid went through the vast NK lobby and took the escalator to the food hall—or, rather, "the gastronomic hub," as NK had dubbed the place. Then she set out on her hunt.

Astrid strolled along shelves and displays packed with delicatessen items from all over the world, piled in such profusion that any reasonable person would be revolted. Astrid was, at least. She got a vaguely queasy feeling seeing small packets of cookies priced at more than a hundred kronor and two hundred varieties of "artisanal cheeses" at breathtaking prices. All this was deeply disgusting, given the state of the world.

Ten minutes of ambling brought Astrid a candidate. A man in his sixties wearing boat shoes and a bright white Lacoste polo shirt was leaning over the fish counter to inspect a lobster. Astrid glanced around to make sure no one was watching, put on her glasses, and sidled up behind him.

When he straightened up, Astrid rapped the back of his head and threw herself backward, flinging the glasses from her face. She screamed, made a half somersault backward, and collapsed on the marble floor, clutching her forehead and moaning, "Ohhhh!" Too bad she didn't have any fake blood with her, but she hoped her performance was convincing enough without it.

She sneaked a look at the man through half-closed eyes and saw he was frozen in shock, his hand to his mouth. He rushed to Astrid. "My dear girl, how did this happen?"

Astrid whispered a pitiful reply. "Wondered what was so special about the lobster, so I looked, too, and then . . . I don't know." She squeezed her eyes shut and rubbed her forehead. "Ohhhh . . ."

"Are you all right?"

"Hurts. It hurts!"

The man offered her his hand. "Come, let me help you get up. There's a bench over there, you can . . ."

"Thanks," whispered Astrid. Before she took his hand, she groped around for her glasses. Still clutching his hand, she crawled to the spectacles, picked them up, uttered "no, no, no . . ." under her breath and started crying. Another minor superpower of hers. "My glasses . . ."

Still on the floor, she held up the shattered lenses. Remembering her black dress, she had a sudden inspiration and sobbed, "They were brand new, for my grandmother's funeral. Ohhhh . . . Mama will be *furious.*"

Some other shoppers had gathered to see what was going on between the man in sailor togs and the little girl in mourning black. The manager came around the fish counter. "What happened here?"

"I don't know," said the man in the Lacoste shirt. "I straightened up and somehow her forehead collided with the back of my head. I don't see how . . ."

Before the man could try to unravel the unlikely series of events, Astrid wailed in desperation. Holding her smashed glasses, she looked down at them, bereft as a girl grieving a dead baby bird. Tears were streaming down her cheeks when she looked up. She saw several shoppers giving the Lacoste man hard looks. He rubbed the back of his head and said, "But I can just . . . I'll make it up to you somehow, then."

"But . . . but how?" sobbed Astrid.

"Of course, well, I'll pay for new spectacles. How much did they cost?"

Astrid pretended to try to remember. "They're progressive lenses. Mama said . . . she was really upset when she told me . . . she said four thousand five hundred kronor." Astrid wailed again and finished, "As if it was *my* fault my eyes are so bad!"

Some of the spectators crowding around made sympathetic sounds. Astrid heard someone whisper, "Oh, you *poor* little thing."

"Hmm," the man said, looking suspicious. "Four thousand five hundred? Hmm!"

Astrid examined the frames. "But, of course, all I need is new lenses, so maybe . . . three thousand?"

That trick seldom failed. Three thousand had been Astrid's goal from the start, but people were always more inclined to open their wallets when they thought they were getting off easy. The man looked a bit less skeptical, and when someone in the crowd muttered, "Listen, you, go ahead and pay," that did the job.

"I don't have any cash," the man said. "So how can we . . . ?"

"You can use Swish," said Astrid.

The man nodded and took out his phone. After Astrid gave him her number, a woman in the crowd spoke up. "What was that number? I'll round it up with another five hundred since some people prefer to pinch pennies."

"Me too," said a man. "What's the number again?"

Samaritan benevolence spread through the onlookers, and when all was done, a total of five thousand kronor had come fluttering into Astrid's account. She gingerly got to her feet and put on the shattered eyeglasses before addressing them in a quavering voice. "Thanks *ever so much*, all of you. I will never forget this." Maybe it was pushing it a bit too far, but Astrid ended by saying, "Grandmother is smiling down from heaven."

8

July 8, afternoon

Irma Ryding lived in a two-room flat up four flights of stairs at the far end of Stockholm Old Town. "The king's next-door neighbor" was the way she put it. There was no elevator. After climbing two flights, Julia had to stop for a break. She'd probably never been less fit. Only a year earlier she'd been able to climb the whole way, two steps at a time. She needed to get back into shape, and soon; her Itrim gym membership was still current.

Irma and her husband, who'd died ten years earlier, had lived in a rented three-room place on Kungsholmen. After Irma's spouse passed away, the Author's Fund had found the Old Town apartment for her, a charitable action Irma callously called an "accelerated posthumous award."

Once Julia had recovered somewhat, she climbed the last flights and rang Irma's doorbell. Dragging and thumping sounds came from inside, and Irma was leaning on a crutch when she opened the door. She'd broken her hip quite recently but refused to discuss it, since, in her own words, she had no intention of becoming "a tiresome, complaining old woman."

Julia leaned over, hands on her knees, to take a couple of deep breaths. Irma gave her a skeptical look. "Respiratory troubles?"

"You might say that," Julia replied. She held up a paper sack. "Brought some sticky buns."

"Do tell," said Irma. "Thought I'd lost my taste for those. Come in."

Julia didn't know anyone who possessed as many books as Irma Ryding did. Literally *all* the walls in her apartment were occupied by floor-to-ceiling bookcases, and the hallway was a narrow passage with books shelved on either side. The living room walls, except for a single window looking out onto a blind alley, were completely filled with bookcases. The sofa, the armchairs, and a small television protruded a couple of feet into the central space. The window provided little light, thick carpets covered the floor, and tobacco smoke had penetrated everything. If Julia had had the slightest susceptibility to claustrophobia, she wouldn't have entered. She didn't, so she didn't mind, but she still felt like a dried bloom in a flower press.

"Coffee's almost ready," said Irma. "Come out to the kitchen."

The only objects in the kitchen other than the oven, the fridge, and the sink were a small table and two chairs. And more books. Lots and lots of books. Irma read omnivorously: detective novels, thrillers, classics, poetry, nonfiction of all sorts. She even knew her Harry Potter and her Stephen King. The only literary works she couldn't tolerate were the kind that usually won the annual August Prize for literature. *Pain-in-the-ass* novels, she called them.

The percolator gurgled away on the counter—sounding suspiciously like it was in its death throes. Irma had owned that antique model over the ten years of their acquaintance and probably long before. Julia nodded in its direction. "Always sounds like it's about to draw its last breath."

"Aha," Irma said as she carefully settled on a chair with the help of her crutch. "Not yet. It'll outlive me. I'll put it in my will for you, if you want."

"Well, no, I'm pretty satisfied with my espresso maker."

"The books, then. Want those?"

Julia surveyed the shelves in the kitchen that held only a fraction of the books in the apartment. She shook her head. "No room for them."

"Not *these* books," Irma said. "I mean my own. The publishing rights. When I die. Want to have those? I have no living relatives, and the backlist still brings in a fair amount in royalties every year. Just so you know."

Julia plopped onto the chair across the table and put down the sack with the buns. "I don't want to talk about that, Irma. You're not going to die."

Irma raised her thinning eyebrows and said, "Of course I am! Who do you think I am, Methuselah? Even he had to kick the bucket at last—though, granted, it took, what? Nine hundred and fifty years?"

"I think you should try to beat his record."

"God help me, I'd rather jump off a cliff. Or fling myself off the roof of the stock exchange, land right on one of the beautiful people."

"Can we talk about something else, Irma?"

"Of course. Let's discuss you."

The percolator gave its last painful gasp, and a red light signaled that coffee was ready. Julia got cups and poured, put a splash of milk in Irma's cup, set it in front of her, and sat back down. Irma put her chin onto her folded hands. "Okay, baby. Spill it."

Julia described her impression of the television series and its cleaned-up image of the slog of ordinary police work. Their brilliant, snappy repartee for Åsa Fors. She ended with Ylva Strandberg's summation of her novels: "Heightened reality. A bit of escapism."

"Hmm," said Irma, and scratched her nose with her index finger. "Hmm, hmm."

"What do you mean, 'hmm, hmm'?" said Julia. "That's what you think too?"

"Meh," said Irma. "It's true, there are some things . . . like that flash drive in the cuckoo clock . . ."

Julia threw up her hands. "Well, what the hell? Ylva used the same example! Am I never going to hear the last of that cuckoo clock? It was a *comic touch*!"

"Sure. And some people might think it inappropriate in a novel with graphic depictions of evil and sudden death. Some could consider it a little . . . fanciful."

"Okay, and do you know how many copies it sold?"

Irma's look was accusing, or maybe, actually, disappointed. "Hey there, girl. Take it easy. That's not what we're talking about."

Julia looked down and rubbed her suddenly sweaty neck. "Hey there, girl" was Irma's standard reproach when Julia began taking things too personally. It was intended to bring her back to earth, and it worked every time. Julia felt a shiver of embarrassment. "Sorry, I just . . . I'm such a fool."

"You are, in some ways, yes. But not most of the time. You simply must understand that people want to enjoy getting away from the ordinary. There's hardly a single bestseller that's not a fantasy on some level or other. Mine definitely are. Though they're not bestsellers. Not anymore."

"But I aim to write as realistically as possible."

"Then you need to choose subjects that are more realistic than stuttering Chinese mafia bosses who hide things in cuckoo clocks. Nota bene: That's not a criticism. I like your stuff, but realism? Not a hundred percent."

Julia slumped. Irma was probably right. And so was Ylva. In search of consolation, she worked a cinnamon bun out of the paper sack and took a bite. The bun was stale, and she suddenly wanted to weep for herself. More than anything, she felt pathetic. She gave herself a mental slap, chewed, and swallowed. Her mouth felt dry as dust. "I did have an idea, actually. About the True Swedes and sniper shootings in a suburb. That's probably more . . . realistic, don't you think?"

Irma shrugged. "Depends entirely on how you write it, but yes, the idea's certainly more believable. Contemporary, even."

"The problem is that I don't know very much about the True Swedes."

"You'll need to do some research then, as usual. I can give you a hand."

"You?" said Julia, surprised. She sat up. "Don't you have your own novel to write?"

Irma's face twisted in disgust, and she ran one hand down along her side. "This damned hip makes it impossible to concentrate. Don't feel like trying either. But I can manage a little research."

"Oh dear," said Julia, "I didn't know you were finding it so painful . . ."

Irma waved that sentiment away. "It's no problem, don't worry about it. I've started smoking grass. That helps."

Julia's jaw dropped as she stared at her eighty-one-year-old friend. Irma put her cup to her lips and calmly sipped the cooling coffee. Of course, she knew exactly the effect her comment would have, but no one feigned indifference better than Irma.

"Okay, seriously," said Julia. "You smoke *weed?*"

"Grass, ganja, call it what you like," said Irma, putting her cup down. "No choice if I'm going to make it down those stairs to buy groceries. Though they are starting to give me funny looks in the shops."

"But, really . . . how do you get hold of it?"

"Don't worry. I have my dealer."

"And how did you meet this . . . dealer?"

"Friend of a friend." Irma gestured as if shooing away a fly. "Enough about that."

"Okay, just one last thing."

"Uh-huh?"

"Are you high right now?"

Irma laughed at that. "Nope, right now I'm straight as an arrow. I was planning to go shopping later, so that'll require a few puffs."

Julia held up a hand to stop her. "Okay, so here's what we'll do: You draw up a list and *I'll* go shopping. You're not going to turn into Old Town's junkie grandma just for some milk and a sausage or two."

"Don't need much more than that."

"The list can be as long as you want."

"And a couple of puffs will be pleasant, anyway."

Julia put her hands to her temples. "Seriously, Irma? Are you going to end your career sinking into a swamp of narcotics?"

"Now you're exaggerating, Mommy. It's not as if I'm shooting *horse.* And it really does help."

"Uh-huh, right. It's your life!"

"It is that. For a while, anyway."

Irma picked up a little spiral notebook from the windowsill and started writing out a shopping list. Julia just watched, shaking her head. Irma had never been an alcoholic, though she'd always appreciated her wine and booze, but this was different. Or was it? Some people claimed marijuana was less dangerous for the body than alcohol, and it did seem that Irma was handling her substance abuse with discretion. Julia wasn't going to quarrel about it.

Irma finished her list and chewed on her pen as she studied it. Then she took the pen out of her mouth and asked, "How's it going with that bloodstorm of yours? That Kim fellow?"

"No change. We get together. We talk. We go to bed. But I have no idea what I mean to him."

"And how about you? Are you in love?"

Julia sighed. "Yes. No doubt about it."

"You've got a hard row to hoe. Should bring him by here sometime, so I can get a look at this boy wonder."

"I'll try. I'm going to his place tonight."

Irma scribbled one more line before she folded the note and handed it to Julia. "And we'll take ourselves a look at the True Swedes. I can devote some time to checking out his videos. The ones of that party leader, Schwarzkopf."

"You know how to do that?"

"Well, good God," exclaimed Irma, tapping her temple with a fingertip. "You think I was born yesterday? I know how to use YouTube as well as anybody."

9

July 8, afternoon

After shopping for Irma and carrying back two bags of food, forced to stop at each and every landing on the way up, Julia went by her own apartment to put in a bit of time on research. She was going to Kim's place that evening, but that business with the True Swedes had roused her curiosity, had made her want to get to work. There was something intriguing about it. As Julia worked her way through the streams of tourists along Västerlånggatan, she reviewed what little she knew so far.

Since the Sweden Democrats had become the new normal, the previously tiny True Swedes party had gotten a lot more supporters. It now polled at about 2 percent, halfway to the minimum for parliamentary representation. Julia suspected there was a lot of hidden support, people who were reluctant to express favor for a party so crudely opposed to foreigners.

The big difference between the True Swedes and, for example, the Nordic Opposition Movement was their charismatic, eloquent leader Claes-Göran Schwarzkopf. That name of German origin, if translated literally into Swedish as "black head," roughly "fuzzy-wuzzy," was as offensive as the N-word. And no one had failed to notice the irony of the last name of the man who claimed to be "the only *svartskalle* who loved Sweden."

Their ideology was ill defined. Leaked meeting minutes had shown that they were even more extreme than they made themselves out to be. They seemed to have ties with criminal organizations and motorcycle clubs, and the party leader's background was remarkably vague. The True Swedes were on the upswing in some municipalities in southern Sweden, where one of their candidates had proclaimed his intention to "blow up all the monkey houses"—in other words, the refugee camps. That was just about all Julia knew; she'd need to learn a lot more. It was entirely possible her project might be physically risky.

Her apartment was stuffy when she got there, so she opened the window facing Järntorget before sitting down to her computer. Julia decided to start with the most interesting and therefore most dangerous part: rumored links between the True Swedes and the Apostates motorcycle club. The Apostates' star was rising, as was the party's, and it was assumed the bikers were now in control of most of the trade in illegal drugs in north Stockholm. Add to that their protection rackets, kidnappings, social services frauds, and good old-fashioned burglary. The Apostates were active and ubiquitous—in their own territory, at least.

Julia found it a bit ludicrous that ill-intentioned forces had the tendency to gravitate toward one another. The True Swedes had dreadful views and the Apostates did dreadful things, and they acted like birds of a feather. The only thing lacking was some creepy cult to join the alliance.

The Apostates had, in fact, come from a bunch of Christian bikers who called themselves the Converters. Those guys had devoted time to rolling around with Bibles in their saddlebags and evangelizing. Some members had gradually lost interest in the word of the Lord and had turned to criminal activity instead. They were expelled, and as rejects, they formed their own club, the Apostates. There might well be a touch of satanism in their activities and rituals. A photo from one of their parties showed their leader, Dennis Hamberg, posing with a rack of goat horns on his head, imitating the demon Baphomet.

A photo from the same event showed a couple of True Swedes leaders hoisting beer steins toward the camera with one hand and making the sign of the devil with the other. That proved nothing in and of itself. The gesture of extended index and little fingers had roughly the same origin as a V for victory and signified hard rock more often than devil worship. Still . . .

Julia called up the Facebook pages of some Apostates members, segued to pages of their friends, and so on. What she really wanted was to find a thread or photographic proof linking Claes-Göran Schwarzkopf to the long-bearded bikers in patch-covered leather vests. She came up with nothing. She shut down her computer toward eight o'clock and took a taxi to Gärdet.

10

July 8, evening

Bottles clinked in the shopping bag as Julia unlocked the gate to Kim's villa. She crunched her way up the gravel drive. There was a light in the kitchen window. As usual, Julia had no clue where she'd find Kim or what his mood would be, which was equal parts suspenseful and frustrating. At least she knew she wouldn't be bored.

After passing through the empty office space on the ground floor and mounting the stairs, she found Kim sitting at the kitchen table in front of his computer. He had a sour expression and barely glanced at Julia when she greeted him.

"Something not going right?" asked Julia, putting a bottle of white wine into the fridge before picking up a corkscrew to open the bottle of red.

"Computer's hung up," said Kim, irritated and tapping on the keyboard.

"Maybe you're hitting the keys too hard?" said Julia. She filled a glass and held it out to Kim.

He waved it away. "Not tonight. Give me a beer."

Julia opened the fridge and took out a Brooklyn pale ale. She opened it and put it next to him as he banged his keyboard again and muttered, "Come on, you piece of crap!"

Julia pulled up a chair and sat across from him. "Hard disk?" she suggested. "I used to have a computer that—"

"It's solid state," said Kim. "No moving parts. It just wants to aggravate me."

"Mm-hmm, that's probably it," Julia said. She took a swig of wine and stopped trying to converse. Her role in Kim Ribbing's existence could go from alluring lover to annoying hanger-on in the span of five minutes. She left Kim to mistreat the keyboard a while longer, then asked, "Do you know anything about the True Swedes?"

Kim heaved a sigh, rubbed his eyes, and slapped the computer again before answering. "The extreme rightists? Yeah. Why?"

"Started looking into them. For a novel."

"Planning to write nonfiction?"

"No, but somebody said my writing's a little . . . fanciful. Trying to come up with something more realistic. More present day."

"I don't think your stuff is so fanciful. It's more like . . . fables."

"What do you mean? Fables are just animals that—"

"That was a joke," said Kim, deadpanning.

"Aha. Okay."

They sat in silence, drinking. One difficulty with Kim was that when he got into a certain mood, Julia couldn't do a damn thing to change it. He was ruled by some personal interior mechanism. Rarely did exterior events intrude. Julia was almost always the one obliged to cater to *his* feelings, *his* needs. Even so, she decided to make another try. "Know anything about the Apostates, then? The biker club?"

"Heard the name, that's all."

"The leader, that Dennis Hamberg. It'd be a stretch to call him an *intellectual*, but he seems a good deal smarter than your average biker."

"What makes you think that?"

"He gave some interviews, and his verbal ability is . . . he thinks things through, that's all. Even has a sort of life philosophy. Tends toward nihilism."

"Probably a requirement for a real criminal," said Kim. "Believing in nothing at all."

"Maybe. But in his case, it's a more reasoned ideology."

"I see."

Julia saw Kim was losing interest, so she decided to approach it a different way, one that involved her personally.

"I was looking for possible links," Julia said, "between the Apostates and the True Swedes. Dennis Hamberg has a cousin, Birk Hamberg, who runs a printing shop where the True Swedes order their material. Do you think it might be possible to . . . you know . . . take a little closer look at it?"

Kim rubbed his eyes again and said, "I'm not in the mood for private investigation right now, Julia. Got no time either."

"Guess not," Julia said. She then asked, even though she wasn't expecting an answer, "What are you doing there?"

"A . . . project."

"What kind?"

"Peace of mind."

Kim wouldn't say anything more, and he looked around the kitchen as he finished his beer. He slapped the bottle down onto the table.

"How did things go with Astrid, then?" asked Julia.

"Went fine. She has her own room here."

"Oh, my. How do you expect to—"

"Sorry, I have to ask you to leave," said Kim. "I have some things to do."

Something cold and quivering, like a dying fish, squiggled through Julia's chest. For a moment she was frightened to death, and she had trouble keeping her voice steady as she said, "Are you breaking up with me?"

"What?"

"Yeah, well, you just asked me to leave. I just got here, and I brought wine, too, and . . ."

Kim shook his head so hard that it flung his black hair across his face. "Asking you to leave and breaking up with you are completely different things."

"Mm-hmm. Sure. But . . ."

"Figure it out for yourself. But I want you to leave."

"Okay. Right, yeah." Julia drained her wineglass, got up, and put it on the counter, Kim drumming his fingers on the table the whole time. Julia felt limp. Rejected. She needed to say or do something to explain her reaction, but she knew that would irritate Kim just that much more. If she'd had a tail, it would be stuck between her legs.

Goddamned Kim Ribbing.

Julia managed to maintain her last trace of dignity as she left the kitchen, back straight, without another word. When she got as far as the landing, she heard Kim's voice in the kitchen. "Julia?"

"Yes?"

"See you later."

"Yes," said Julia. "Sure." She hurried down the stairs to keep from adding a devastatingly humiliating *thanks.*

11

July 8, evening

After the outer door had closed and Julia Malmros's footsteps had retreated down the gravel drive, Kim Ribbing shook his head in disbelief. He'd never understood why people had such difficulty taking things at face value. He'd asked Julia to leave, and she'd interpreted that to mean he didn't want to see her ever again. How could she even associate those two ideas?

Dr. Martin Rudbeck had claimed, and maybe was still claiming, that Kim suffered from paranoid schizophrenia. Physicians who weren't intent on categorizing him as a total nutcase to justify continued electroshock treatments would have favored some variety of "neuropsychological dysfunction," which was the current jargon. Asperger's, maybe, with a touch of idiot savant syndrome. That might partially explain Kim's inability to understand and react to ordinary social behaviors. He himself tended to favor the attitude of *They're the weird ones, and I'm totally normal.* He'd said she should leave. Julia heard, "I want to break up with you." Who was it that had *dysfunctional* hearing?

Kim put the empty beer bottle into the trash under the counter, took out a can of beef ravioli from the pantry, and opened it. He briefly considered pouring it into a bowl and heating it in the microwave, but enough was enough. He found a plastic fork in a kitchen drawer and went down to the basement. *Not going to be using a blowtorch with this stuff.* Probably not, anyhow.

Of course, Martin Rudbeck lay exactly where Kim had left him. The blood spots on his boxers had coagulated. *Went a bit overboard with the electricity there.* Kim wasn't inclined to regret his past actions—*what's done is done*—but he needed to maintain control of himself.

The doctor's pupils contracted as Kim turned on the light, walked to the table, and put down the can of ravioli. Rudbeck watched him and licked his dry lips. Kim went to him, picked up the lamp base, and said, "You're probably beginning to realize that the cavalry's not going to come riding to your rescue. Maybe that's going to make you feel desperate enough to do something stupid." Kim waved the bare contacts at the doctor's crotch. "Don't do it. Next time I'll roast you longer."

After fastening the neck shackle, Kim used his left hand to loosen the leather straps. His right hand was ready with the lamp socket. Rational analysis should make it clear to the doctor that it would be no use to try to knock Kim down, but men aren't always rational in extreme situations. On certain nights in Vamlinge, especially after a "treatment," eyeless shapes had materialized around Kim in the dark, and true madness had threatened him.

Once Kim had loosened all the straps, he backed away from the cot. "Now go do what you have to do."

The doctor didn't move, and there was something vacant in his expression. Kim recognized that behavior, especially from the early days in Vamlinge when he'd been on psychiatric drugs. Some days he was struck by an apathy so profound he couldn't move a single finger. Maybe that's where the doctor was, now that he'd given up all hope of rescue.

Kim approached the cot and held the lamp leads six inches from the arch of the man's foot. "Up with you now. I don't want to clean up your shit. Need a zap to get you started?"

Martin Rudbeck slowly shook his head and hauled his legs over the edge of the cot so he came up into a sitting position. "Maybe it wasn't right," he said in a slurred voice. "What I did to you."

"Everyone knows that. Except you," said Kim. "And don't even think about asking for forgiveness. Get yourself up. Now."

The doctor made his way to the toilet, dragging the chain, and closed the door behind him insofar as that was possible. He gave out a long moan above the splashing in the toilet. "There's blood," he whined. "In my urine."

"Dear me," said Kim. He fetched the can of ravioli and placed it on the cot with the plastic fork. He set the chair just outside the reach of the chain and sat down, crossing his arms. He didn't care what the doctor had in his urine, provided it wasn't a key to the neck shackle.

Rudbeck took his time. Maybe he wanted to hold himself in a different position for a while. Lying stretched out motionless for hours could make you think the world around you was tilting.

"Come on out," said Kim. "Otherwise maybe I'll change my mind about giving you food."

The Martin Rudbeck who came limping forth looked about ten years older than the one Kim had abducted thirty-six hours earlier. His hair seemed to have gotten grayer, and his skin was even paler than when he'd gone into the toilet. Maybe it was the sight of blood that had caused that shift of hue. A light came on in his dull eyes when he saw the can of ravioli, and he shuffled forward a touch more quickly.

Kim looked at the floor as the doctor shoveled the contents of the can into his mouth and ended with an uncomfortable belch. Kim looked up to see the doctor sitting and studying the empty can and its sharp edge. "Throw it in the corner," said Kim. "And lie back down."

"Can't I sit here for a while?" pleaded the doctor.

"No. If you had listened to me *even a single time* when I begged not to be shocked again, then maybe. But now? Lie down!"

The doctor threw away the can and moaned in self-pity as he curled up on his side, then turned on his back and stretched out. "Don't remember you begging," he said. "You didn't say anything."

"No," said Kim. "Before then there was a brief time when I thought mercy was possible. I stopped believing. Then things were better."

Kim yanked the straps around the doctor's ankles. When he threaded the strap across the man's chest and pulled it through the buckle, he said, "Do you remember how you used to pull these straps tighter when you decided I was being disobedient? Shall we see how tight I can make this one?"

Martin Rudbeck reached out and grabbed Kim's wrist. "Kim, please. I'm not healthy. My heart . . . there's a risk that . . ."

Kim snatched away his hand, nodded toward the broken lamp, and said, "Touch me one more time, and you won't have any urine at all, just blood."

A nasty glob of meat sauce jolted out of Martin Rudbeck's mouth as Kim pulled the chest strap as tight as he could. Kim clearly remembered the horrible discomfort of not being able to take a proper breath, breathing only in short gasps, that continuous stifling sensation. Martin Rudbeck was no different from the two men in the video he'd watched. He enjoyed torturing children.

"Kim," gasped the doctor as Kim secured the man's hands, "I . . . can't . . . breathe."

"How many times did I say that to you when I was still trying to communicate? How many times did I ask you to loosen the restraints because it felt like I was drowning? And what did you do?"

Kim moved his chair next to the cot after immobilizing the doctor. Martin Rudbeck was breathing in short wheezes. Kim said, "So. Where were we? Oh, yes. Your treatment of me. We were discussing that already, so we might as well take up the subject again." He held up the lamp. "Since I'm not planning to give you any carrots, it'll have to be the stick."

The doctor glanced at the broken lamp. His cramped breathing prevented him from speaking in long sentences. "Kim. You *injured. Me. That time.*"

"You injured me. For life."

"Treated. Is this. Revenge?"

"Partly. If they'd locked you up and thrown away the key for what you did to me and the other boys, you probably wouldn't be lying here. But you got off. Plus, you were back in Vamlinge and pawing Astrid. This cannot go on."

Martin Rudbeck opened his eyes wide and managed to put an injured tone in his voice. "I. Didn't. Paw. Her."

"You know what I mean. Your very presence constitutes abuse. You stink of smut and always will."

"I. Have never—"

"Shut it! I'm not interested in your lies. What I want is to understand. That's what's important. Revenge is the cherry on top. So. You tortured me for two years. Why?" Kim waved the lamp at the doctor's crotch. "And every time you call it 'treatment' or 'for your own good,' that's going to hurt. Bad."

The doctor gulped. His eyes rolled about as he tried to reshape the claims he'd made both publicly and probably to himself to justify his behavior. He gave Kim a pleading look, but that was no use.

Kim remained stone-faced. "Seems that's hard for you to do. Let me rephrase. What did you get out of torturing me?"

"Power?"

"Obviously. But how banal! You already had authority over me. The question is why you needed to *torture* me also."

"You. Defied. Me."

"A professor of psychiatry let himself be provoked by a fifteen-year-old boy? Sounds unprofessional, if you ask me."

"You are. Special. You Refused. To Bend."

"Mm-hmm. I wouldn't yield. And that's why I had to be tortured?"

"I liked. To. . ." The doctor's eyes glinted stubbornly as he glared at Kim. "Tame. You."

"Aha," said Kim. He got up and moved the lamp closer to the doctor's groin. "Your fingertips are tingling, I bet."

"Please . . ."

"However," said Kim as he pulled away the lamp, "you don't have to worry, provided I like your answers. I'm a *tamer* too." Kim held out his arms and gestured at the surroundings. "This is how it goes, isn't it? *A Sadist's Downfall—The Story of My Life, featuring Martin Rudbeck.* And why was it so important to dominate me?"

"I was. Attracted. To you."

"Thought so. But I must give you a little credit. You never laid a hand on me. How did that come to be?"

"Different. Attraction."

"And that was?"

"Iden . . . tification."

"Now I'm getting a whiff of your psychiatric mumbo jumbo. You're saying, then, that you *identified* with me, a helpless teenager? And that's why I was being tamed? How does that fit together?"

Martin Rudbeck's breath gurgled deep in his chest, and his lips twisted into a grimace as he forced out the answer. "By. Taming you. Tamed. Myself."

Kim rubbed his chin. "Now that's interesting. Maybe you're just cooking up something to keep me satisfied. But if so, that's a good one. I'll have to think about it. And you can, too, if you're ready to stop making up fantasies."

Kim put the broken lamp on the floor and stared at the doctor, who lay there fighting for breath, his mouth gaping, opening and shutting like a fish out of water.

"And just to show you that mercy is real and does exist . . ." Kim released the chest strap and reset the buckle one notch looser, which gave the doctor about an inch more room to breathe.

"You never did that for me," said Kim, walking toward the door. "So there's only one explanation: It's evidence of the existence of *mercy*, right? Good night."

12

July 8, evening

After Kim Ribbing sent her packing, Julia Malmros went back to the Old Town to drink away her cares at her usual haunt, the Angel Pub. The summer evening was warm and every table on the terrace was occupied, so Julia went inside, which was as good as empty. Petra, the bartender, stood between the bar counter and a wall of bottles, looking at her phone. Petra was a couple of years younger than Julia and had worked at the Angel for as long as Julia had been a regular customer. Chatting casually over the years, sometimes briefly, sometimes at length, they'd become buddies, though not friends. When Julia took one of the barstools, Petra held out her phone. "Look at this disgrace!"

A video in slow motion showed Ronaldo being fouled. He writhed in pain as if his foot were being amputated without anesthetic. Julia knew nothing about soccer. Petra often mentioned La Liga, but Julia had no idea if she was referring to a club in Spain or one in Italy. At least she recognized Ronaldo, so she nodded in agreement. Petra put down her phone and asked, "What'll it be?"

Julia studied the shelves where all sorts of alcohol awaited, though single-malt whiskys predominated. She chose an eight-year-old Lagavulin, knowing that it would taste like a distillation of charred peat. She was looking for a real slap in the face. Petra poured half a tumbler and held it up. "Will that do?"

"Could be better," said Julia. "But I'll take it."

The scent was pungent. Julia took a sip, and her tongue curled up, resisting the one-hundred-proof alcohol. Her palate reacted to the initial taste of old leather followed by a burst of smoky flavor. Exactly what she'd been needing.

Julia leaned on the bar and remembered that in winter this had been the exact spot where she'd described to Irma her bloodstorm, that sudden flaming passion for Kim. Now here she was again, unwanted, dismissed by the very same Kim. Julia took another sip and shook her head.

Get hold of yourself.

Julia had known nothing would be easy as soon as that burning attraction landed on her like a ton of bricks. Loving Kim was like trying to embrace the wind. You could never tell from what direction it'd be blowing or whether it was going to blow at all. *Just take it as it comes, be happy when it turns into a storm, and wait it out when it stops blowing. Here's to that.*

"What's on your mind?" Petra had noticed Julia's twitch of a smile. "Something nice?"

Julia nodded toward her bartender friend's shiny ring. "How long have you been married, Petra?"

Petra stretched her back, straightened up proudly, and proclaimed, "Twenty-five years come fall."

"And did you ever . . . question it?"

Petra ran a hand across her forehead and pretended to wipe away sweat. "Ugh! Lots of times! Especially at first. But you know, time passes and you, well . . . intertwine. And finally, you can't imagine anything different. I don't know if you remember, but Palle had problems with his prostate . . ."

"I seem to recall you called it his 'hermit crab.'"

Petra laughed at that. "Exactly. But he was in a lot of pain for quite a while. Chomped down the painkillers but was still miserable. I was annoyed at first by the way he whined and staggered around. And, you know, we weren't getting it on, if you know what I mean."

"Understood."

"Mmm. But you know, eventually, after maybe a couple of months, there was a kind of . . . tenderness. Okay, Palle was a wreck, but he was *my* wreck, and it was my responsibility to stick with him. My *duty*, maybe I should say. My assignment. My task in life. Listen to me, going on!"

"I want to hear it. Please."

It looked as if Petra was perspiring for real. She wiped her brow with her sleeve. Julia had never heard her talk like this, and maybe that's what was making Petra uncomfortable. She wiped her hands on her apron. "Well, anyway, once that had sunk in, things were a lot simpler, and we actually got closer to one another than ever before. A deeper relationship. And afterward . . . well, he got better. Since then we've been rolling along as usual, like before. But those new feelings are still there."

Julia lifted her glass. "I'll drink to that."

Petra went back to watching her soccer match, and Julia finished her whisky, pondering whether Petra's comments could serve as counsel. Was it her *duty* to love Kim Ribbing, no matter what he might say or do? Perhaps. Nobody else was doing that, at least as far as Julia knew, and every one of us probably needs *someone*. She could think of it like that . . . at least it was one way of viewing the situation.

She hadn't needed to drown her sorrows, since they weren't really sorrows. Julia put down her empty tumbler and paid. "Say hi to Palle," she said. "And thanks for the lovely story."

"Yeah, sure," said Petra. "But don't ask me to tell it again, that's all."

Back in her apartment, Julia took out bread, Bregott butter spread, cheese, and ham to toast herself a croque monsieur that she intended to eat while reading Denise Mina. The queen of Scottish detective fiction was a new favorite. She'd just settled into her armchair when her phone rang. Caller ID told her it was Irma.

"Hello there," Julia answered. "How are things with the YouTuber?"

"I hope you're joking," Irma said.

"Not at all. Why?"

"A YouTuber is someone who *posts* to YouTube, not someone who looks at it. Weren't you the one who wanted to be more up to date?"

"I was joking."

"Hmm, I wonder. Anyhow, that Schwarzkopf guy's videos are a whole chapter unto themselves, and we'll talk about that some other time, but I've come across somebody interesting. Do you know a Jocke Bäckman?"

"The name sounds familiar, but—"

"Spokesman for the True Swedes when their support surged, and he was closely associated with their successes."

"Did I hear you say *was*?"

"Correct, and that's what makes him interesting. He left them six months ago and seems to have gone underground."

"And you think that . . ."

"Indeed, I do. That you've got someone there with insider information, and he might be willing to share it. If you can dig him up, that is. He gave the *Aftonbladet* some interviews, so maybe they can put you in contact."

"How about if you have a friend of a friend? Now that you've gotten linked up with the underworld?"

"What are you imagining?" asked Irma. "Clandestine meetings in pedestrian tunnels, parking garages? Nothing of the kind! I make an appointment, a package tumbles through the letter slot, I push out a wad of bills. Done deal. I've never even seen the man."

"Uber weed."

"What?"

"Nothing," said Julia. "A *contemporary expression*."

"Huh. A little knowledge is a dangerous thing; don't you get your ass in a sling. Kissies!"

"Love you too!"

Julia looked at her croque monsieur and then at her computer. No, that was enough internet surfing for now. She'd had a tough day and could indulge herself a little. She took a bite of her warm sandwich and opened *Garnethill, A Novel of Crime*. She was fascinated by Maureen O'Donnell, the protagonist, a young woman who'd spent long stretches of a horrible childhood in mental institutions, was accused of a murder she hadn't committed, and now had to solve it. Did that remind her of anyone?

13

July 8, evening

The frilly black blouse with pearl embroidery from Filippa K cost 1,299 kronor at the Boozt website. No problem after her performance at NK, so Astrid Helander filled in her bank card information and paid. Then she brought up the blouse in full-screen view again. The computer her uncle had lent her was slow. It had to grind away for several seconds before producing the image.

It didn't look like something Astrid's contemporaries would buy for themselves. It was more suitable for an older woman or, perhaps, a lady-in-waiting from the 1700s. Astrid hadn't been planning to buy anything, but when she saw this blouse, it had practically *screamed* at her and she'd obediently responded.

There was something odd about Astrid's reasoning and tastes. An acquaintance of her parents had once called her "an old soul in a young body," and Astrid had adopted that motto because that's exactly how she felt—as if there were something inside that was older than she was.

When she'd looked up "old soul" online, she'd found that the concept was a given in teachings about reincarnation. For example, Taoists believed that someone lived through five incarnations before ascending into the cosmos. During her final incarnation the believer was often an empathetic but somewhat introspective lone wolf feeling the urgent need to share her knowledge with others. That description fit Astrid exactly. She was always being told that she was a bit too old for her age, which was a sign of an older soul. Like appreciating things and clothes from bygone times. *Check, check.*

Subsequently Astrid seriously considered whether she had gone through previous incarnations. Certain images would come to her mind. For example, she saw herself lying in a blizzard with a woman in crinolines leaning over her. Okay, that *might* be an event from *Gösta Berling's Saga*, her favorite book, no more than that. But she didn't think so.

In another image that kept presenting itself, she saw her hands dragging a *klåra* through a potato field. Astrid knew that the device was called a *klåra* even though she'd never heard the word and couldn't find it on the internet. She'd never harvested potatoes.

Astrid folded her seventh paper airplane and sailed it through the window that stood open to the summer evening. Her uncle had declared ten o'clock "time to hit the hay." Fortunately, Astrid had no need to go to sleep that early, but he stipulated that her bedroom door had to be closed and she was not to "get up and run around." Despite whatever age her immortal soul was, Astrid was being treated like an eight-year-old.

Kim Ribbing had said to come back the day after tomorrow, but Astrid planned to try her luck by returning to the villa the following day. She was fed up with her uncle's rules. His gloomy voice and mannerisms constantly reminded Astrid of her parents' funeral. She didn't want to be in this place. She wanted to be with Kim.

It would probably take a very long time for Astrid to get over the loss of her mama and papa, those who knew her best. Or to lose that empty feeling around her heart and the shudders that frequently occurred when she thought phantoms were watching her. But she would try.

Astrid folded a sheet of paper into a swallow shape, went to the window, and cast it into the darkness. She watched it grow smaller and smaller as it sailed down toward the Karlberg Canal. Tomorrow she was going to cast herself out of this place. Her life would begin again tomorrow.

14

Christof Adler stored his exercise clothes and his bandy stick in his locker. That morning's match against the IT department's "Crackerjacks" had ended with a 6-4 victory for Christof's team, the "Bandy Badasses," all drawn from the criminal investigation group's day shift. The name was already in use when Christof joined, and no one knew where it had originated. The two teams generally met once a week, and it was usually the more athletic, better-trained Bandy Badasses who carried the day. Christof did two training sessions a week at the gym.

Christof was generally viewed as a dependable person, stable verging on boring. Some of them found it a bit intriguing that he'd been living for several years with Cecilia, a woman six years older who had a seven-year-old daughter named Matilda. Christof didn't want to abandon his city bachelor lifestyle entirely, and he stayed part of the time at his rented efficiency apartment on Inedalsgatan. But he remained faithful to Cecilia, of course.

Christof was a foodie, particularly interested in cooking Asian dishes, and he couldn't be beat when it came to sushi rice. He and Cecilia worked on huge jigsaw puzzles or binge-watched television series or went on long walks. Despite his job with the police, Christof was perpetually surprised to find people making life difficult for themselves and for others. Life was so simple if a person kept calm and enjoyed it.

The only thing you might find a bit off-putting about Christof Adler was his deep interest in all types of fantasy. He'd read all the *A Song of Ice and Fire* books and watched the TV series *Game of Thrones* three times. He was an active participant in an internet group that discussed the most obscure details of *GoT*, and he'd even gone so far as to write some fan fiction. No one at police headquarters knew that.

His obsession began when thirteen-year-old Christof read *The Lord of the Rings*. After that, accessing alternate realities had become something of an addiction. Maybe his stable character was due in part to the fact that he lived part of his life in far more thrilling parallel realities. He also played video games, especially those from Nintendo.

Christof crossed the open office space and nodded to various colleagues before settling at his desk. Someday he would surely be promoted from assistant all the way up to inspector and have his own room, but until then he was perfectly happy with the way things were.

Before Christof was brought into the team investigating the Knektholmen murders, he'd spent several weeks with the intervention group. Working in the field, in other words. He still had various reports to finish, sign, and submit, ranging from descriptions of burglaries to arrests of marijuana growers. He began work with his mind feeling scrubbed clean by that morning's physical activity.

Christof's phone rang just as he began sketching the burgled dwelling to accompany his report on seizing stolen goods. It turned out to be Wilmer Syd, who was insisting on speaking directly to Christof. The man's voice was shrill and dissatisfied. "Dr. Rudbeck is not in Thailand. Not at all!"

"All indications point that way."

"I don't know what kind of *indications* they can be," said Wilmer Syd, not bothering to hide his scorn. "But I now know that they do not point that way at all."

"And how do you know that?" Christof asked, his equanimity disturbed by the man's patronizing tone.

"Because I was able to call his phone."

"Oh, really? I assume that was a good thing."

"It would have been good if Martin Rudbeck had answered, but I assure you it was not."

"You must explain that a bit more."

Wilmer Syd sighed, as if everything should have been clear from what he'd already said. Then he said, "The man who answered had found a dead phone in his bag, so he charged it. It had been charging for several hours when I called."

"And what is this man's relationship to Dr. Rudbeck?"

"Didn't you hear me? No relation at all! But somehow Martin's— that is, Dr. Rudbeck's—phone had gotten into his bag."

"How did that happen?"

"How should I know? It's the police's job to investigate. And another thing. When that man went to check into his hotel, it turned out that he also had Dr. Rudbeck's *passport.*"

"I don't understand. How had he gotten it?"

Silence on the other end. The next time Wilmer Syd spoke, his tone was formal, no longer sarcastic. "May I speak to one of your supervisors?"

"That's not necessary. You can speak to me."

"It appears that you do not understand the seriousness of this matter, and I would prefer to speak with someone who . . . how old are you?"

"That's neither here nor there. I'm sitting here now, and you're speaking with me. If I find it necessary, I will take up the matter with my *supervisors,* but until then I'm the one you speak to."

Christof Adler nodded. *That's the way to tell him.* Even out in the field there'd been individuals who questioned Christof's competence, referring to his relatively young age; he'd had to put his foot down and make it perfectly clear that a man with the rank of assistant was no mere intern but a fully authorized representative of the forces of law and order.

Wilmer Syd groaned but gave in. "Yes, all right. But try to understand that some person or persons have set this up to make it appear that Martin is in Thailand."

"Which means?"

"For God's sake, man! He's been taken, kidnapped! Maybe murdered!"

"That's quite a leap, to say—"

"For his whole life," interrupted Wilmer Syd, "Dr. Rudbeck has striven to rehabilitate people, principally young persons with severe psychological problems, or *dysfunctions*, to use politically correct parlance. Since such individuals very rarely understand what's best for them, many of them have developed a dislike, even a *hatred*, for the person who treated them. Over the years, some, I don't know how many, have threatened Martin with the most horrible things. Now maybe someone has done something."

"It's a little too early to draw such—"

"Draw whatever conclusions you want when you, no, someone more knowledgeable than you, has investigated this. The essential thing is that some person or persons have made serious efforts to lay down a false trail, and this is as carefully thought out as it could possibly be."

There was some more bickering back and forth with Wilmer Syd, whom Christof Adler found just about as annoying as a person could be. Even so, you couldn't deny that he had a point. It *was* inexplicable that the doctor's phone had gone traveling on its own, eloping with the man's passport.

Christof promised to call back as soon as he had something, and they hung up. The criminal investigation assistant sat there for a while, drumming his fingers on his desk. Then he looked up Rudbeck's number, checked the address, and began calling the neighbors.

The first one was at work and knew nothing about it, but he struck pay dirt with his second call. A woman by the name of Elisabeth Svanström, eighty-three years old according to the registry, had some things to report.

"Rudbeck?" she said after Christof explained his reason for calling. "Ah, yes, he lives just across the way, we say hello from time to time, and those newspaper articles about him were horrible. You couldn't find anyone politer, and I refuse to believe a word of it."

"I see. Do you have any idea where he might be right now?"

"Poor fellow must be in the hospital."

Christof's eyebrows went up. "And what makes you think he's in the hospital?"

"Well, after all, an ambulance came and took him away."

Quite a few people had the misconception that all social services were somehow magically linked, and that firefighters, police, and medical attendants always knew exactly what others were up to. This was not the case.

"An ambulance, you say," said Christof, taking out his notepad. "And when was that?"

"Now, let's see, it was . . . the days tend to blur together when you're alone at home . . . It wasn't yesterday, because that's when I . . . day before yesterday, must have been. That's right. Two days ago."

"So, July 7. What time of day?"

"If you tell me that the seventh was two days ago, it was. Yes, what time could that have been? I'd just gotten out of bed, and I was waiting for the coffee to finish perking when I noticed that ambulance outside his house, so it must have been . . . just after eight."

"Eight in the morning, then?"

Elisabeth Svanström chuckled. "You mean you think I get up and make coffee at eight o'clock *in the evening*?"

"You never can tell; everybody's different. Do you have any idea what hospital it took him to?"

"No, but that can't be so hard to . . . Danderyd Hospital's the closest to here."

"Thank you very much for the information. I might need to contact you again."

"That'll be just fine. I don't have much to do, and it's nice to have a little conversation."

July 7, ca. 8 a.m. Ambulance.

Christof tapped his pen on the pad. It couldn't be excluded that Martin Rudbeck himself might have laid the false trail. Let's say that an ambulance picked him up because of some illness or condition he wanted to keep from people. The man who'd answered the physician's phone might have been an acquaintance doing him a favor. But that was pure speculation, not appropriate at this early stage.

Stage! Christof heard himself thinking. He shook his head. If this really were an investigation, the whole thing would seem absurdly simple. But that detail about the passport . . . that was harder to explain. Maybe there'd been some sort of misunderstanding.

Christof called Danderyd. The operator called him back via police headquarters' main number, and he spoke to someone who confirmed that, yes, Martin Rudbeck had been admitted for care. Specifically, to the isolation ward of the contagious diseases unit. Christof asked for more information and was told that nothing was available, due to confidentiality of medical records, unless there was written authorization for a criminal investigation. Christof couldn't assert that was the case. He said thanks and rang off.

The business about the infectious diseases unit fit nicely with his own hypothesis. Contagious diseases serious enough to warrant extended quarantine carried a stigma. It was like people who went to jail but were said to have departed on a long trip.

Christof picked up his phone, intending to call Wilmer Syd. He wasn't looking forward to hearing the man's shrill voice again, but at least he could take satisfaction in shutting down the little know-it-all for a bit.

15

July 7, morning

Kim Ribbing's first step in what would become the kidnapping of Martin Rudbeck was to obtain some tools from Moebius. Then he sat down to go through Facebook. He'd drawn up a list of ambulance drivers working out of Danderyd and studied their posts.

Social media users' tendency to post photos of what they ate, completely incomprehensible to Kim, was apparent in some of the drivers' Facebook accounts. He focused on those with overnight shifts who didn't eat breakfast at home. After skimming past cats, children, sunsets, books, and flowers, he finally came upon Kenneth Klint, who worked the night shift. Once off duty in the morning, Klint regularly had breakfast at the Espresso House in central Mörby before returning to Danderyd. Indisputable proof: the countless photos of breakfast sandwiches and cappuccinos glistening with heart-shaped swirls.

Danderyd Hospital's security system was relatively up to date. Kim made a few changes in Jack the Ripper's source code that instructed the program to use the computer's maximum processing power for a brute-force attack on the log-in credentials of one of the employees at the reception desk, while Kim used his backup laptop to search Facebook.

It took Jack several hours to break the moderately difficult password, and during that time Kim's MacBook Air overtaxed itself. It had worked without stopping, the fan running almost the whole time. The device had burned out; it was busted and would never work properly again. *Fuck.* He should have gotten Moebius to let him use that monster laptop.

But what's done is done. At least he'd gotten in. Kim studied some of the medical records to see how they were phrased, then he filled out a blank form with Martin Rudbeck's information. He came to the field where he was supposed to specify the contagious disease for which the patient was being admitted. In a moment of frivolity, Kim chose Ebola.

They'd be scratching their heads over that one, wondering how the good doctor had managed to contract a devastating disease completely unknown in Sweden, but since Ebola cases were held in absolute quarantine, there was little risk someone from the outside would come to check. For safety's sake, Kim wrote in the "special remarks" section that the patient should be kept isolated and any medical personnel coming in contact with him must take every possible precaution. Double-layered hoods and face shields. Impermeable coveralls. Full-length gloves. His fictitious Rudbeck wasn't going to be pleased to be handled by techs who looked like astronauts. Kim completed the form and saved it where it would be ready when the time came to "admit" the doctor.

At 6:00 a.m. on July 7, Kim Ribbing packed the instruments he needed into his Honda bike's top case. The only thing that didn't fit was the two-foot-long metal pipe that he strapped along the side. He looked at the sun just climbing above the treetops, put on his helmet, and rolled off toward central Mörby.

As he wove his way through the morning rush along the E18, he mentally reviewed the details of what he would be doing over the next few hours. The best plans were always the simplest. Unfortunately, he couldn't claim that this one fit that category, even though it did have a certain elegance.

Kim's personal rule was that action plans should include no more than two points of uncertainty. This one had at least three. Even if it failed, he was practically certain his own involvement wouldn't become known, leaving the possibility to try, try again. The doctor was going to wind up in Kim's clutches one way or another; he was determined about that.

At twenty minutes to seven, Kim parked his bike outside the shopping center and sat monitoring the entrance. At five to seven, an ambulance swung into the parking lot fifty yards away and Kenneth Klint got out. He was clearly a creature of habit. This was the first moment of uncertainty. The signal blocker in Kim's hand was no larger than an ordinary car key, and when he pressed it, a blue light turned on.

Kenneth Klint's routine could be regarded as an advantage in these circumstances. People with deeply ingrained habits assume that everything is just as it should be. The man stepped away from the ambulance, dug in his pocket, found his remote, and pressed the button to lock the vehicle. He didn't verify that the ambulance really had locked. After all, it *always* did. But not today, because Kim's tiny transmitter blocked the signal.

If Kenneth were to go back to make sure the vehicle was locked, Kim had an alternate approach and the electronics necessary to clone the key, but that would have been riskier and would have taken extra time. Kenneth Klint went to the mall entrance, and Kim took a circular route through the lot to get to the ambulance. He pulled on a pair of single-use plastic gloves, opened the door, and slipped into the driver's seat.

He'd studied this model of ambulance on the internet and knew that the onboard diagnostics port was in a niche beneath the steering wheel. That connection was used by mechanics' shops to monitor the electrical systems. This time, however, Kim connected an OBD scanner to identify the vehicle's locking code. The most adept car thieves could do that in twenty seconds, but Kim wasn't familiar with the menus, so almost five minutes passed before he could start the engine.

Wanting to avoid fumbling around in the ambulance's equipment at this early stage, he'd brought his own surgical mask and a cap in his backpack. He put them on. Then, finally, he added a pair of sunglasses in case a traffic camera picked him up en route.

Kim assumed that the vehicle had a GPS tracker so the operations center could monitor its location, a connection contrary to his goals. He plugged a small but powerful transmitter into the cigarette lighter; designed to block GPS signals, it was reserved for military purposes. But this campaign could be seen as *war*, couldn't it?

He adjusted the seat, then rolled out of the parking lot and headed for Täby.

Kim had already driven several miles north on the E18 when he thought to look at himself in the mirror. Here he sat, swathed in cloth like the Invisible Man, driving a stolen ambulance. Only a week earlier he'd thrown himself off an oil platform in the North Sea, holding a rubber dinghy overhead to slow his fall. Did he have an unhealthy need for kicks? Or was it true, as some people claimed, that there was something wonky with his brain?

He was immensely talented at concentrating and teaching himself. That was probably the hitch. When Kim had drawn up his plan to kidnap Martin Rudbeck, he'd picked over every single moment and detail with laser precision without taking time to consider the *overall* implications—in other words, the staggering choices that would make any other human being cry out, *But what in holy hell am I doing?*

Kim slammed a hand against the wheel, snorted through the surgical mask, and said aloud, "What in holy hell am I doing?"

He was perfectly aware that everything had gone like a charm and he had the ability to think outside the box. Your ordinary kidnapper whacks his victim on the head and tosses him into a van, *wham, bam, thank you, ma'am.*

The problem was that those kidnappers were usually arrested, and Kim had no intention of getting caught. Besides, he wanted a few days to work unhindered. His idea was to release the venerable doctor before anyone even noticed he was gone. That required unconventional methods, so here he was, sitting in an ambulance, outfitted with a mask and all the rest of it. No wonder.

Dr. Martin Rudbeck was the last loose end from Kim's past, the one he hadn't dealt with, and that bothered and annoyed him. When this was done, he would . . . well, okay, what would he do? The truth was that he could just go beachcombing for the rest of his life, the way he had in Cuba, but he assumed that would eventually drive him mad. He would have to teach himself to cook or devote himself to some serious diving. Update his programming skills. Or *something*. He could think about that later.

When the vaulted facades of Grindtorp came into sight ahead of him along the E18, Kim turned off at Täby and drove toward Lievägen, where Martin Rudbeck's modest red villa with white trim lay among a scattering of houses. Kim had walked that street virtually with the help of Google Maps. Rudbeck had neighbors but not many, and the front of his house was hidden by a hedge. Not perfect, but not bad either.

He stopped in the Ellagård Tennis Club parking lot, a couple hundred yards from Rudbeck's house. He located the button that released the back door of the ambulance, then took off the sunglasses, got out, and went to the back. He needed to check a detail of the ambulance's equipment. He made sure nobody was around before pulling on a white plastic single-use coverall. He'd paid ninety kronor for a package of three at Byggmax. He might have left textile fibers in the front, but he wasn't about to change from his current clothes. He pulled open the back door of the ambulance and got in.

He already knew the standard equipment for an ambulance, so there were no surprises. What *did* surprise him was that the interior seemed more spacious than it looked from the outside. Kim advanced to the back wall and checked the respirator. He'd studied that gear online, but he wanted to be sure he knew how to operate it. Once satisfied, he emerged and closed the doors.

He took a thick marker from his pocket and, with a few quick strokes, altered the license number from FGH 371 to EGH 874. He didn't know whether traffic cameras were programmed to signal alarms if they captured the plates of a stolen vehicle, but that seemed entirely possible. He put away the marker and returned to the cab.

A drop of sweat oozed into his eye. At nearly eight o'clock in the morning, it was still fairly cool, but his impermeable coverall didn't breathe, and the gloves, cap, and mask made him feel sealed in cellophane. He put on the sunglasses anyway, since people might well have closed-circuit cameras trained on the streets. It wasn't easy to remain anonymous these days.

As he drove out of the lot, a boy, maybe twelve years old, walked by toward the tennis courts carrying a racket case. The kid stood gaping in astonishment when he saw Kim's figure behind the wheel. Kim waved; after a moment of hesitation, the boy waved back. Kim drove on toward Lievägen.

He parked in front of the villa at ten minutes to eight. Having studied Martin Rudbeck's habits through the television camera, Kim knew the man usually left home at eight and was away for half an hour, presumably on his morning stroll.

Kim maneuvered the ambulance so he had good sight lines toward the front door and the porch. Then he rolled the window down a bit and pulled out the metal pipe into which he'd inserted a capsule of tetrodotoxin, a venom derived from puffer fish. The capsule was a finned dart, a miniature syringe under pressure. Striking its target, the dart would inject its contents through the leading needle. It was customarily used to subdue animals—literal animals—rather than Dr. Rudbeck.

That approach was also unconventional and probably belonged to the category of *What the holy hell am I doing?* But Kim had been careful in his calculations. At the trial Martin Rudbeck had pleaded for leniency on various grounds, including his weak heart. Kim didn't know if that was true but didn't want to take any risks, and that's why a Taser had been out of the question. A violent electrical shock could dispatch the doctor straight to hell well ahead of schedule.

Nor did Kim want to get too close to the man. As a result of his long years of professional practice in service to evil, the doctor had plenty of enemies, and Kim had watched via the TV camera as the doctor sat on his sofa cleaning his pistol. Maybe the doctor packed his gun whenever he went out.

Kim needed to capture Rudbeck quickly, from a distance, in a way that wouldn't risk killing him. It came down to the simple Teledart blowgun that Moebius had ordered for him without asking any questions. There was, however, *one* problem with tetrodotoxin, and that was why Kim had made sure he knew how to use the respirator.

At exactly five minutes to eight, the front door opened and Martin Rudbeck stepped out onto the porch. The front path ran directly to the gate, so he didn't notice the ambulance. He was wearing a pair of light-colored jeans and a white short-sleeved shirt. Kim wondered if he was carrying his pistol and, if so, where it was holstered.

Kim's neck knotted with the rage accumulated over all the years. The doctor had let his curly graying hair grow out and had shaved off the pathetic little goatee that had made him look like a caricature of a psychiatrist. He *was* a parody of a shrink, and Kim hated him with all of his young man's heart.

Kim focused, clenched his jaws, and took a deep breath through his teeth, then put his lips to the pipe's mouthpiece. As the doctor turned back to lock the door, Kim exhaled with a sudden, quiet *ptui!* and the envenomed dart flew at its target. Kim had set up a shooting gallery in the basement of his new house and practiced until he could hit a matchstick from twenty feet away, so stinging the doctor's ample posterior posed no difficulty.

The dart penetrated his right buttock. The doctor jumped as if he'd been stung by a wasp and turned to look. When he saw the dart dangling from the rear of his jeans, he frowned and then looked around. His eyes met Kim's for a couple of seconds. Maybe he recognized Kim behind the cloth mask, maybe not. In any case he turned quickly to unlock the door.

Fuck.

Kim dropped the blowgun. His hands clutched the steering wheel. He'd used a dose of only a hundred grams to avoid stopping the man's respiration, enough, in theory, to kill a large dog but sufficient to paralyze a human being. In theory. But the son of a bitch was still up and moving.

He had no plan B other than to think up something later if this failed. The doctor turned the key and opened the door, still with the dart's orange fins dangling from his butt. Kim ground his teeth. If Kim had misjudged the dose, making it too strong, and the doctor managed to get inside and lock the door, he might very well die when the poison kicked in. That would be *one* way to solve the problem of his continued existence on this earth, but not the one Kim had wished for.

But no—something was happening. Before the doctor managed to step back inside, he grabbed the doorframe and his head slumped. He tottered as his body bent lower and lower, then he lost his hold and collapsed into the hall.

Quick now, quick as you can.

Kim threw open the ambulance door and raced around it, opened the rear, and pulled the collapsable gurney out onto the pavement. He unfolded the legs, seized the handles, and walked backward, pulling the gurney after him. He saw a pale oval face appear across the street in the gap of a curtained window. Nothing to do about that. At least he was masked.

Kim opened the gate and went up the path through the yard, the gurney wheels rattling and jolting on the flagstones. The ambulance made him look credible, and the gurney added to it. Kim was sure that he couldn't have managed to haul Martin Rudbeck all the way from the porch to the gate to stow him into a waiting car; that scene would surely have made the neighbor call the 112 emergency number. *There's somebody dragging somebody away here. That can't be right, can it?*

But now he had the gurney and a touch of good luck. The porch was just high enough for Kim to crank the gurney to the same height. Martin Rudbeck lay flat on his stomach with his face on the rag rug just inside. Kim stepped over him and took a couple of moments setting things up inside, then returned to Rudbeck. Kim grasped his shoulders and turned him on his back. A pair of frightened, reproachful eyes met his.

"Hi there, Martin," said Kim, raising his sunglasses and pulling down his mask to reveal his face. "We're going to take a little ride."

Tetrodotoxin paralyzed but its victim didn't lose consciousness. Martin Rudbeck was fully aware of what was happening but unable to move. Kim's plastic coverall rustled as he leaned over and checked the doctor's respiration. It was shallow and irregular, and the man's lips had already started to turn blue. *No time to lose.*

The rag rug under him was an unexpected bonus. Kim dragged both the rug and the doctor out onto the porch. The doctor's head bumped over the door sill and struck the wooden surface of the porch. A stifled groan came from his throat.

"Sorry," said Kim. "But we're in a bit of a hurry."

The doctor and the gurney almost fell over as Kim struggled to position him on the plastic mattress. He didn't dare fasten the strap across the doctor's chest, which would have further impeded his respiration, so Kim left him there and went to lock the front door. He took the keys with him.

"Here we go," said Kim, pushing the gurney ahead of him to the open gate. "This is just about as much fun as you and I used to have, isn't it?"

The doctor lacked the breath to reply, his eyes merely staring accusingly as Kim trundled him out to the street. He unlatched the top of the gurney from its wheeled support, grasped the stretcher rails, and pushed it into the ambulance. He retrieved the undercarriage, climbed in, and shut the doors behind them.

Martin Rudbeck's face was deeply flushed. A pitiful squeaking came from his throat as he shuddered and tried to inhale. Kim unhooked the oxygen mask, put it over Rudbeck's face, and opened the valve. The balloon feed expanded and contracted with a hissing sound, and Martin Rudbeck's torso mirrored those movements.

"See?" said Kim. "I'm not planning to kill you. Maybe that's a consolation. But we'll just have to see . . ."

Kim didn't know how long the effects of tetrodotoxin would last, and he hadn't brought anything to tie the doctor down, since he'd assumed something appropriate would be found inside the ambulance. And there it was. Kim came across a roll of gauze in a drawer and used surgical scissors to cut off sufficient lengths. He knotted the doctor's wrists and ankles to the stretcher frame. "I understand this feels uncomfortable, but there's worse to come, believe me. Oh, yes, indeed, but now we're on our way. See you later."

Kim climbed out and slammed the doors. When he checked the other side of the street, he saw the pale oval face watching from behind the curtains. Kim grinned behind his mask and gave the face a thumbs-up.

16

July 9, morning

At exactly ten o'clock, just as Christof Adler was calling Wilmer Syd, Julia Malmros stood at the Sveavägen crossing to Tunnelgatan. A single rose lay upon a bronze plaque embedded among the paving stones: *Swedish Prime Minister Olof Palme was murdered here on February 28, 1986.*

It seemed a strange place for a meeting, but Julia's appointment was with a strange person. Jocke Bäckman had been the True Swedes' press and media spokesperson for just under a year when he quit and went underground six months earlier. Julia's acquaintance at the *Aftonbladet* daily newspaper had succeeded in tracking him down for a reluctant, unrevealing interview. The journalist had kept Jocke Bäckman's contact information and gave it to her.

Like many of the party's leaders, Jocke Bäckman had a police record. He'd started out as a counterfeiter and con man. Given that it was almost impossible to make credible copies of current Swedish banknotes, Jocke satisfied himself with muddy imitations he sold to credulous customers for 20 percent of their proclaimed face value. When the notes would later turn out to be unusable, the purchasers weren't likely to go to the police to complain, "Look, I bought this counterfeit cash and got cheated."

It was Jocke's charm and convincing manner that succeeded in duping his marks, not the quality of the banknotes. Eventually, a couple of those arrested for trying to pass Jocke's bills squealed on him. He went to prison for two years. He used that time to study the media, and when he was released, his knowledge and personality made him the perfect candidate for the post of spokesman for the True Swedes. He was handling media when the party first caught the public eye. His departure had not been explained.

Julia didn't recognize Jocke Bäckman when he emerged from the Hötorget underground station. He had his hands jammed into the pockets of his bomber jacket, he'd cultivated a beard, and he wore sunglasses. Only when he walked up and gave Julia a short nod did she realize who he was.

Jocke had been reluctant to meet when she phoned to explain her aims. He didn't want to "blab to a bunch of inkslingers," as he expressed it. Julia had explained she was doing research for a novel and this was just for background. She promised never to mention Jocke's name and to pay him five thousand kronor for his trouble.

A long silence had followed. Finally Jocke had said, "I don't have very much to tell you."

"Let me be the judge of that."

With a sigh and a groan, Jocke had agreed to meet, but only briefly, and now here he was, looking like a somewhat less-than-cutting-edge version of Joaquin Phoenix in *I'm Still Here*.

"Jocke?" Julia asked. She held out her hand.

Jocke Bäckman kept his hands in his pockets, tilted his head to the right, and said, "We'll walk through the tunnel. Then that's the end of the conversation."

Julia glanced in the direction he indicated and saw the opening to the pedestrian tunnel gaping like a dark open mouth between the sunlit building fronts. Julia knew of the existence of the 750-foot tunnel, more than a century old, but although she'd lived most of her life in Stockholm, she'd never traversed it. Without waiting for a reply,

Jocke walked toward the pedestrian crossing between Norrmalm and Östermalm. Julia fell into step with him.

"Why did you give up on the party?" Julia asked.

"Personal reasons."

"That's not a very informative answer."

"That's the only one I have to offer." Jocke heaved a sigh, evidently something of a specialty of his, and added, "So, listen. I felt that as a press spokesman, I didn't have any real insight into what I was supposed to be saying."

"And that was?"

"The party line, of course. What do you think we're discussing here?"

"When you say you didn't have insight, do you mean ideological? Practical?"

"All of it. I didn't have a clue."

They reached the tunnel entrance. The doors opened automatically. The temperature inside was much cooler. The tunnel wasn't as dark as it had appeared from outside. Green metal plating covered the vaulted walls, and hidden lamps reflected from the white ceiling. When they'd gone a few steps farther, perspective seemed to distort, and Julia had the brief illusion she was in the middle of a wide green meadow. She turned to Jocke. "Which members had the insight you lacked?"

"There was an inner circle. Claes-Göran himself, of course, along with three or four more."

"Have any names?"

Jocke exhaled noisily through his nostrils. "You can look them up yourself. Forget about getting names from me, I'm not a . . ."

Jocke let the unspoken word die away in the faintly echoing tunnel. *Squealers got no friends*, no, but something told Julia that Jocke Bäckman's circle of acquaintances was limited in any case.

"If I understand correctly," said Julia, "you found the party has an agenda that's different from the one they tell the public?"

"I don't see it that way. It's just a fact. When we had meetings . . . there was never any talk about what we wanted to do, just about how things would be *presented*, what story we were going to sell, if I can put it like that. And I was usually the one whose job was to sell that story, even though I knew it was fake."

"But what did they really want, then?"

"Like I said. No idea."

"None at all?"

"Nah. But I promise you, it's a lot worse than what they were saying in public. That's all I can tell you."

Jocke started when a bicycle bell dinged behind them. He was obviously very nervous. Julia assumed the True Swedes, like criminal gangs, didn't look kindly on those who dropped out, especially any who spilled the beans to the media. A human rocket in the form of a cyclist in biking tights whizzed past them and continued along the straight pathway through the tunnel.

"As press spokesman," asked Julia, "did you have any contact with Birk Hamberg?"

"Why do you ask?"

"I mean, because he prints the press material and flyers and all that. And you were the spokesman . . . say, is it true they call him Bimbo?"

Jocke Bäckman's lips twisted in a faint smile for the first time. "Just don't say that where he can hear you, that's all."

"I won't. And?"

Jocke Bäckman pressed his lips tight and plunged his hands deeper in his pockets. He shook his head slowly and said not a word. They'd gotten halfway through the little-used tunnel. There was something oppressive about finding yourself beneath a mountain on a bright summer day with Jocke Bäckman hunched over as if the enormous weight overhead really was pressing down upon his shoulders. Julia realized that she was in the company of a deeply unhappy person.

"I know," she said, "that Birk is the cousin of Dennis Hamberg, leader of the Apostates, and I thought . . ."

Jocke Bäckman looked over his shoulder and lowered his voice to say, "If I were you, I'd be damned quiet about that, if you're concerned about your health. Go digging into all that, and you'll be the one who winds up buried. I've heard things. I'm not saying any more."

Jocke Bäckman's attitude and posture made it clear he was drawing the line there, so Julia changed her approach. "Claes-Göran Schwarzkopf, then? What do you think of him?"

"Two-faced."

"Excuse me?"

"The same as the party. One face he shows in the spotlight and another that . . . yeah, well, I don't know when he shows that one. But it's there. I know that much."

"What makes you think so?"

"I know human nature. You don't get to be a con man unless you can read people, and I promise, that guy is a psycho."

Julia didn't comment that Jocke hadn't been such a brilliant con man. No reason to contradict him. They were nearing the tunnel exit onto Birger Jarlsgatan and their conversation was almost done. Julia said, "You haven't come up with anything more than hints and guesses, and I don't see any way those are worth five thousand."

She knew she was taking a chance. The chat had given her some food for thought, and if nothing else, Julia's opinion had been reinforced: There was something fundamentally rotten with the True Swedes.

When they reached the east exit, Jocke stopped; he looked out into the street and back into the tunnel. "Okay. Here's something for you. I was at the print shop once, supposed to check on . . . something or other. But when I got there, the office door was open and inside I saw . . ." Jocke glanced around again before finishing his sentence. "Dennis Hamberg and Claes-Göran Schwarzkopf. Discussing something. When they saw me, Hamberg shut the door in my face. After he gave me a look warning what would happen if I ever did what I'm doing right now."

"Understood," said Julia. "I didn't get it from you."

"You got *nothing* from me," said Jocke Bäckman and pushed open the door. "Send me the cash by Swish. You have my number, right? And then you delete it."

Julia stood inside for a while, watching Jocke Bäckman's hunched-over figure disappear up Birger Jarlsgatan and turn toward Stureplan. Julia took out her phone, called up a photo of Claes-Göran Schwarzkopf, and zoomed in on his eyes. She saw no indication that the man was a psycho.

"What kind of oddball are you, really?" Julia addressed the screen. "We need to take a closer look."

Claes-Göran Schwarzkopf had started out as a relatively successful stand-up comic. A lot of his routine was devoted to mocking people from other cultures. He kept it just barely this side of the line, but as social attitudes changed, he slipped over to the dark side without even realizing it. Jokes about Somali food that had earned him applause were greeted by stony silence.

Claes-Göran tried to talk his way out of difficulties by claiming that he was simply "making fun of people's prejudices," but few people swallowed that. Those prejudices were his own, disguised in comedy patter that was no longer funny. His engagements dwindled and soon only xenophobic and anti-immigrant groups wanted to book him. With them at least he could let himself loose and slather on bitter comments about the hypocritical *establishment* and *cultural elite*.

He disappeared from live performances for a year, and no one knew where he'd gone. He returned with a YouTube channel called Project: Sweden analyzing "real" Swedish customs and traditions. Claes-Göran hiked in the mountains, fished for herring from a rowboat, joined sing-alongs of Evert Taube hits, and enjoyed crayfish parties. He also scrutinized common habits like chowing down on grilled sausage and mashed potatoes at Sibylla fast-food joints or Friday TV nights eating cheese puffs.

Not a hint of racism or disparagement of other cultures; his videos were totally focused on *what's authentically Swedish*. And most important of all: Claes-Göran was *entertaining*. Everybody cracked up when Claes-Göran popped up with a smear of mashed potato on his nose singing praises of grilled sausage as a symbol of national unity or had a dialogue with the herring he'd just fished up.

His channel became very popular. It wasn't streamed under the name Claes-Göran Schwarzkopf but instead under "A True Swede." He even wrote about Swedish customs on his blog *Where in the World Do Folks Drive Kids Around in a Tank?* His posts were always signed *A True Swede*.

When Claes-Göran Schwarzkopf declared that he intended to establish a political party, the name was entirely predictable: the True Swedes. Finland already had its True Finns, so why couldn't the Swedes do the same? A comedian heading up a political party? No problem! Just look at Italy's Beppe Grillo and his Five Star Movement. Claes-Göran was off to the races!

With a YouTube channel and more than a hundred thousand followers, Claes-Göran certified himself as a true lover of Sweden intimately acquainted with the souls of his countrymen. When the time came to publish a party platform, he played the magician, pulling the drape off the metaphorical cage to reveal a metaphorical Swedish tiger. No more fooling around! All the manifestations of Swedish culture that Claes-Göran had been extolling were *under attack* and in danger of extinction. Attack by whom? Immigrants, of course.

Claes-Göran's first tactic was to emphasize his group's differences from the Sweden Democrats. Yes, the party had done one or two good things, but without realizing it, they'd become part of the hated establishment, veering right and veering left. *Regulated immigration?* Nothing but a screeching halt was acceptable if the Sweden we know was to survive.

Claes-Göran said that if there was anything he loved even more than Swedish culture, it was nature. He'd hiked in the forests, rowed on the sea, and wandered in the mountains. If there was an inner sanctum of the Swedish soul, that sacred space smelled of salt water, fir needles, and mountain air. Immigrants were seeking to usurp and vandalize even that space.

Claes-Göran came up with a graph that showed the projected growth of the national population and the corresponding effects on the environment if Sweden continued to accept immigrants. This couldn't go on. The establishment was shamelessly conspiring to dominate the country and destroy the proud souls of Swedish folk.

And so on.

The most evident difference between Claes-Göran Schwarzkopf and other opponents of immigration was that he had both charisma and a sense of humor. His career in stand-up comedy had inspired his use of social media to target people who shared his views, folks who thought it hilarious when he called Islamic prayer "sticking your ass up to God" or claimed Afghans treated their hair with the Swedish equivalent of WD-40.

He reined in his worst gibes and over time began to pick up more adherents, but he never changed his fundamental demand: zero immigration. Ideally, immigrants already established in Sweden should be repatriated or excluded. Swedes shouldn't mix with them at all. Integration had failed, so it was time to try the alternative: isolation.

One of Claes-Göran's most striking ideas was that of "Year Zero." *Year Zero is right now, time to put an end to foreigners' desecration of Swedish culture.* True, Swedes had—unfortunately—accepted pizza and kebabs, but it was time to put a stop to it! Right now! *From now on, it's Year Zero, and not a single foreigner or alien practice will be allowed into Sweden.*

The future starts now, and it would belong to Claes-Göran Schwarzkopf and the True Swedes. So-called evolution had proved to be a thoroughly un-Swedish abomination. Enough of that fraudulent "progress"—it was time to reverse course and hit the throttle!

17

July 9, morning

Astrid Helander exited the bus at Gärdet. She saw the Kaknäs telecommunications tower stretching up toward heaven and was tempted to walk there and take the elevator to the top. She'd never visited it. Her fifth-grade class had made a field trip to the tower, but Astrid happened to be out sick that day. If you're a Stockholm resident, you're practically obliged to have been to the Kaknäs tower at least once, right? Though it was probably closed these days. Oh well, Astrid hadn't splashed around in the Sergelstorg Fountain either, and anyhow, she was aware that her sudden desire to become a tourist wasn't real. It arose because she was nervous.

Yesterday Kim had said *the day after tomorrow*, and Astrid didn't know what he'd think when she turned up a day too early. Astrid was just so incredibly eager to get started with a new, totally authentic life. She didn't have a clue what it would be like, but she knew full well that it wasn't going to happen at her uncle's place.

She hoisted her bag up on her shoulder and started down Lidovägen. Birds twittered in the leafy treetops. The rustling branches cast pleasantly waving shadows along the gravel path. It was huge that Kim could live in such a place in the heart of the city. Astrid knew enough about house prices to see that he must have a *vast* fortune to be able to afford this neighborhood.

And that villa! Astrid stopped outside the gate to admire the two-story structure with its yellow stucco walls and the two columns of the front porch supporting the wrought-iron balcony. *Thirty million, at least.* She tried the gate handle and found it locked.

Astrid checked around the gate but there was no doorbell or intercom. She probably should call Kim's mobile phone, but Astrid was scared he'd tell her to wait until tomorrow. She thought her best chance would be to present him with a fait accompli. On the other hand, Astrid had the impression that Kim Ribbing wasn't going to be a pushover.

Whatever. She decided to chance it. Astrid was slim and short, and her head was similarly proportioned, so she grasped a couple of the vertical bars and succeeded in working her head through the gap. *No turning back now.* She shrugged her bag off her shoulder and pulled off her thin jacket. She wriggled and twisted and arched her body. It took a couple of minutes, but then she fell onto the gravel path inside the fence, her chest and breasts aching from the effort.

Her bag wouldn't fit through the gap, so she spent an additional five minutes emptying it one item at a time and pulling the things through the bars. Last of all was the empty bag. She repacked it, got to her feet, and slung it over her shoulder. *Ta-da!* She was through and ready to go.

Without stopping to wonder whether she should, Astrid hurried up the drive and the front-porch stairs, then rang the bell. She'd resolved *not* to try to get inside the villa if Kim didn't respond. *Moderation in all things.* In that case, she'd sit and wait for him. When she heard steps inside, her misgivings intensified. She realized she'd already intruded. Trespassed, even.

The door opened. Kim wore only a T-shirt that reached to his knees. It was printed with the slogan "Anything you can do, I can do bleeding." His eyes opened wide when he saw Astrid.

Her brave greeting: "Hi!"

"What are you doing here?" Kim asked gently. "How did you get in?"

"Through the gate."

Kim looked over Astrid's shoulder. "It's locked."

"Yeah, well, like, literally *through it.*"

Kim glanced at Astrid's slim figure and nodded. Then he said, "You should come back tomorrow. I have things to do."

"For real? I can just stay in my room."

"Not possible. Tomorrow." Kim started to shut the door.

Astrid's eyes flooded with tears. It wasn't manipulation, really; it was autosuggestion. Just as when she'd flung away her glasses at the NK department store, Astrid imagined how horribly sad the situation was and tears burst forth. "Please, oh please!" sobbed Astrid, letting them gush. "I can't stand it. I can't bear staying in that apartment. He's so mean to me!"

Her uncle was stiff and a bit distant, but in that moment Astrid convinced herself he was really hard on her and she was the most pitiful victim imaginable.

Kim paused, the door half open. He stared intently at Astrid. "What does he do?"

"He's just *so mean,*" moaned Astrid, wiping her cheeks. "All the time."

Kim stared at the floor. Finally, he opened the door. "Come in, then."

"Thanks ever so much," Astrid said and stepped inside the downstairs office area, her mental picture of her uncle changing from that of a leering devil to that of his usual self. She followed Kim. As they went upstairs, she asked, "Do you have something I can eat? Didn't have breakfast."

"Check the fridge, take what you want. Anytime."

"Okay, thanks."

"One thing," said Kim. "Stop saying *thanks.* Puts my teeth on edge. Either do something or don't. No reason for thanks."

"'Kay, got it."

"Good."

Kim settled into an armchair and took out his phone as Astrid went into the kitchen. Four chairs were set around an old-fashioned wooden table that had seen better days. Two were plastic and two were wood. Didn't really go together. She opened the fridge, where there wasn't much more than butter, cheese and . . . *what's all this?* Astrid scowled and checked the freezer compartment. It was full of kebabs, pizzas, and beef pierogi.

"You shouldn't buy this crap," she called.

"What?"

"I said you shouldn't be buying this shit. You know where the beef in those pierogi comes from?"

"Doesn't bother me."

Astrid slammed the freezer shut, went back into the living room, crossed her arms, and took a stance before Kim. "You're telling me it *doesn't bother you* where that meat comes from? Are you aware how they treat the animals in those damned slaughterhouses?"

"Yeah, I have an idea. I saw your videos."

"And it doesn't bother you?"

"Right."

"How is that even *possible?*"

Kim shrugged. "I don't care. They're animals."

Astrid saw red. Literally. She wanted to give Kim's leg a swift kick but held herself back. "*They're animals?* What is wrong with you? Are you out of your mind?"

Kim lowered his phone and smiled a little. "Maybe. According to some people."

"According to me, too, if you keep saying that."

"Take it or leave it."

Astrid clenched her fists and hugged herself hard. She was burning with anger, even though there was a voice of reason inside whispering that maybe she should ease up on Kim. He'd broken her out of Vamlinge and was offering her refuge, so she just waved her fists and shouted *"arrgghhh!"* She stalked into her room, slammed the door behind her, and locked it.

18

July 9, morning

Kim Ribbing remained in his armchair, contemplating the door Astrid had just slammed. As soon as he'd seen Astrid swing out of the window of her room in Vamlinge, Kim had thought, *That girl's got heart,* and he hadn't been wrong. Astrid had attitude. *Maybe a bit too much, that's all.* And so here Kim sat, like a teenager's clueless daddy.

No. That didn't bother him at all. He hadn't the least intention of trying to make peace with Astrid. The girl was welcome to her attitude and her foul mood. Those weren't Kim's problems. He didn't care about animals, that was a simple fact, and he wasn't about to start caring now.

Just before Astrid turned up, Kim had been in the underground room, dealing with Martin Rudbeck, who'd gotten a can of beef stew this time. Kim wondered which would upset Astrid more—the fact that he'd taken the doctor prisoner or that he fed the man meat? Probably the latter.

They hadn't had much of a conversation in the basement. Kim still hadn't fully evaluated that business about *by taming you, I was taming myself.* Maybe that was just pseudopsychiatric mumbo jumbo the doctor came up with to placate Kim, but the notion had something to it, suggesting he was less a practicing sadist than an inverted masochist. In which case, it was a manifestation of clinically aberrant egotism to use a fifteen-year-old boy to restrain one's own impulses. The man was an ass, but maybe of a different stripe than Kim had supposed.

Kim pulled on his other biker outfit. It was thinner and of red leather that would offer less protection in an accident, but light enough to wear in the heat, since it breathed. He knocked on Astrid's door before leaving. "I'm going now. I'll be away for a few hours."

He thought Astrid was in such a snit that she wouldn't respond, but then he heard her voice through the door. "What're you going to do?"

"Buy a new computer. You can have the old one if you want. It's here on the table. It's slow but it still works. Your keys are next to it."

"Save the receipt."

"What did you say?"

"Save the receipt when you buy the new one. Or, no . . . send it to me. With your phone."

Kim shook his head. "Whatever for?"

"Can't you just do it? Then maybe I won't be mad at you anymore."

"You can be as mad as you like. That's up to you. But sure, I'll do that."

"Good."

No *thanks* this time. *The girl learns fast.* Kim descended the stairs, pulled on his biker boots, and got his helmet. He stepped out onto the gravel drive but felt the need to check. He went to the gate and eyed the distance between the bars. *Looks impossible.* Kim put his own head to the gate, but it was too big for the gap.

Clever girl.

He turned and saw Astrid watching him from the kitchen window. Kim threw out his hands to signal, *How the hell?* and Astrid dismissed the question with a wave. *Who cares?*

Kim returned just over an hour later with a brand-new MacBook Air. He found the door to her room open and the girl nowhere to be seen. Kim unpacked the MacBook and started setting it up with help from the cloud. A pop-up advised him that the job would take about two hours. Kim had several programs that required a lot of memory.

He left the laptop loading itself and went to the kitchen. Kim had no regular mealtimes; he ate when he got hungry. He was hungry now. A pizza prepared with meat from tortured animals would do just fine, so he opened the freezer.

Puta madre, as Hector the parrot would have said.

The freezer compartment was empty. And the package of ham slices in the fridge was gone. Kim checked the trash bin under the counter and found it had been emptied. Astrid had even taken the trouble to go outside and dump Kim's food into the garbage. *Puta madre!*

He found a note on the counter: *I left the cheese, but if you knew anything about the dairy industry, you wouldn't want it. Or maybe you would, because you're wicked ♥ Astrid.* Kim stood staring grimly at the note for several seconds.

Then he laughed out loud and made himself a cheese sandwich.

19

July 9, afternoon

Julia Malmros was worried. She'd rung Irma Ryding's doorbell three times without getting a response. Either her friend had gotten high and gone out to see the city or . . . Julia found Irma's lighthearted attitude toward her own increasing fragility hard to take, especially when Julia couldn't bear imagining anything drastic. So, it was an enormous relief when she called Irma's number and her friend answered on the third ring.

"Where are you?" asked Julia.

"At home. Why?"

"Because I'm standing outside your door, ringing and ringing. Why aren't you opening?"

"Aha!" said Irma. "Just a minute."

Bumps and dragging sounds came through the door, and Julia grimaced. She'd once happened to ask Irma if she could have a key so her elderly friend wouldn't have to toil her way to the door each time. "Not on your life," Irma had answered. "I'd rather lie here and rot with my privacy uninfringed." Julia had felt a lump in her throat and never mentioned the subject again.

The door opened. Irma stood there hale and hearty but with fatigue in her eyes. The fear Julia had felt was transformed into great tenderness, which made her exclaim, "You idiot! Have you gone deaf?"

"Huh?"

"I said—"

"Joking! My hearing's fine, thank you very much. But not when I'm wearing headphones. So, who's the idiot around here? Come on in, you."

Julia stepped inside, took off her shoes, and asked, "Headphones?"

"Correct. The walls are thin here, and I didn't want the neighbors to think . . . I was watching that Schwarzkopf fellow's videos, and they're anything but comic, I can tell you that. It doesn't bother me a bit if you think I'm a junkie, but *this* stuff! Let me show you."

A laptop stood open on the living room table, headphones plugged into it. On the screen Claes-Göran Schwarzkopf was on a little stage, holding a microphone. Irma made her way onto one end of the two-seat sofa and beckoned Julia to sit next to her. "You know about *The Truth Barrier?*"

"The poetry collection? By Tranströmer?"

"Maybe that's where they got the name, but no. It's a feed with alternative news, where they claim to have overturned the barriers and explain what's really going on, especially when it comes to immigration."

"Okay," said Julia, taking her seat. "I understand the premise."

"Right. And on their site . . ." Irma pointed at the screen. "Several years ago, they sponsored a festival where Claes-Göran did his routine. That was just when he was starting to lose bookings and was quite bitter. You can stream his entire appearance on the site. It's not on YouTube, for example, because it's so . . . well, see for yourself."

Claes-Göran had a goatee and dark hollows under his eyes. He wore a Hawaiian shirt, maybe to offset his wretched appearance. He appeared in front of a banner printed with the words "The Truth Barrier" and the image of a fist smashing a glass window.

"And here's the special part," Irma said and clicked so that the video snapped to eighteen minutes into the performance. She hit the space bar.

Schwarzkopf stalked back and forth across the stage, waving his hands in a manner probably inspired by the comic Richard Lewis. The subject under discussion was *places* and what should be done with the monkey houses that Stockholm's suburbs were becoming.

Claes-Göran's solution was simple: poisoned bananas. Dump a load of cyanide-soaked bananas on every marketplace out there and watch the problem solve itself. And this was the point: The poison was useful only to do away with the survivors. Most of the monkeys would murder each other fighting over the bananas.

Julia Malmros didn't know which was more horrific, Claes-Göran's imitation of an angry monkey jabbering in fake Arabic while waving its arms or the audience's delighted laughter and applause. Irma hit the space bar and froze Claes-Göran in a loose-lipped monkey grimace. She pointed at him. "Quite a guy, huh?"

"Really," said Julia. "That's a performance he certainly wouldn't want people to see now. Bull's-eye. And some of his supporters wouldn't be happy to see it, even if they agree with what he's saying." Julia shook her head in disappointment. "And, say, are there really people who honestly think like that?"

"You heard them laughing."

"But that's not the same as wanting to *do* such a thing. To poison all immigrants."

"It's a simple solution," said Irma. "There are people out there who can't comprehend anything except the simplest of solutions. Did you learn anything from that Bäcklund guy or whatever his name was?"

"Bäckman," Julia said. "Jocke Bäckman. Yes, according to him, *that*"—Julia pointed at Claes-Göran—"is the real party platform, even if they tell the public otherwise. Only the innermost circle knows what they really stand for. I was able to get a couple of his opinions about persons who might be insiders."

Irma closed her laptop and leaned back against the sofa cushions. She stared sternly at Julia for a couple of seconds before saying, "I hope you're aware that looking into all this isn't without personal risk?"

"Oh, I doubt that."

Irma squinted at her. "You really want to risk your life? Because some flunky on TV4 says that you write fantasies?"

"That's not what it's about."

"Oh, no? Then what *is* it about?"

Her meeting at TV4 had certainly been the starting point, but now there was a more important goal to her project. Julia wanted to show Kim she was fully competent, in hopes of making him willing to share more over time. She wasn't about to confess that to Irma, since she'd only just become aware of it herself.

"Okay, then," she said. "Let's say that's it. I must go now."

20

July 9, afternoon

Astrid Helander had no firm statistics, but the evidence of her own eyes had led her to conclude that Karlavägen was jammed with more Teslas and Audis than any other street in Stockholm, which said something about the income of the people living there.

Astrid's tendency to target the wealthy was more practical than altruistic. Somebody living on the margins would find it terribly hard to cough up a thousand-kronor bill, while a Tesla owner would see it as chump change, something to get rid of as soon as possible. And *certainly*, Astrid would never take it into her head to cheat some single mom with a kid. Unless forced to, that is. That hadn't happened so far, since Stockholm was crawling with nitwits with more cash than they knew what to do with.

She'd chosen to post herself on the stairway to the house at 61 Karlavägen, between Wiberg's Photo and the Östermalm Glove Shop. Several luxury vehicles were parked along the street: Teslas, Audis, and the latest-model Volvos. She sat with Kim Ribbing's old laptop open on her knees, tapping away, making up nonsense rhymes so she would look busy.

The horse stands on the field and munches
Cows wander around in bunches
One steps on a mine and kinda
Gets herself blown to China

From the corner of her eye, Astrid saw a man approaching a shiny silver Audi A5. The door unlocked with a distinct clunk. Peering at him, she saw a middle-aged guy in an expensive-looking pale blue shirt, rolled-up sleeves revealing a pattern of tiny flowers. High-quality shoes and famous-brand jeans. The Audi door sighed softly as the man pulled it open. He slipped behind the wheel.

The operation Astrid was about to undertake wasn't without risk, but hey, *no pain, no gain*, right? She quickly made the calculations. His car was boxed in by two others. He'd need to go back and forth at least twice, adjusting the angle each time before he could get out into the street. His last maneuver would have to be a reverse; otherwise, her scheme wouldn't work.

Astrid waited until he'd rocked it back and forth twice, then she slipped behind him and curled up behind the car. The man advanced again and turned the wheels. He'd be out after the next reverse. Astrid closed the laptop and stuffed a plastic capsule in her mouth. As he reversed for the last time, she jumped to her feet and slammed a fist on the trunk, screamed at the same time, and threw herself face down onto the street.

As she fell, she twisted her right hand to aim the computer screen and keyboard at the street and slammed the laptop into the pavement with a deafening sound of breaking glass. This was the moment of greatest danger. She'd thrown herself into a corner where she *shouldn't* get run over even if the man didn't stop, but you could never be sure. As a precaution, she pushed her feet and lower legs under the parked car next to her. Then she bit down on the capsule.

Luckily, the Audi driver wasn't the hit-and-run type. Astrid heard him kill the engine and open the car door. She pressed her forehead against the street and wailed.

"Oh, God, dear God! How did this happen?" a voice cried behind her as a hand touched her shoulder. "Hello? Miss? What happened? I didn't see you, how could it . . . hello? Please say something!"

With a groan, Astrid turned over and let the fake blood dribble from the corner of her mouth. The man clutched his head in his hands, horrified. Astrid coughed up more blood, then spat the red lump of the capsule beneath the parked car. The man pulled out his mobile phone. "I'm calling an ambulance."

"No, don't," Astrid pleaded in an unsteady voice. "I just . . . bit the inside of my cheek." She spat out a smaller splash of blood onto the pavement before she repeated her routine from NK and burst into tears over her ruined laptop. The screen was badly cracked and the keyboard was in pieces. *Brand new! It was only a few hours old. How unlucky can a person be?*

By this point Astrid had gotten to her feet, and the man had recovered from his initial panic after seeing she wasn't badly injured. Kim's MacBook Air had a lot of scratches and wear and tear on the underside from regular use, so the man wasn't buying it yet. "New? It looks to me—"

"I have the receipt right here. You don't believe me?" She fumbled with her telephone and finally held it out to show the receipt Kim Ribbing had sent her a couple of hours earlier. MacBook Air purchased that same day for 14,495 kronor at the Apple Store. The man looked back and forth between the ruined laptop and the receipt, reluctant to accept the contention, but at last he had to give in.

"Really?" he said. "What can we do about this now?"

"I *must* have a computer," said Astrid. "I just have to!" Astrid had taken a sharp dislike for him during their short exchange. He had a cynical, knowing look, almost contemptuous, even though he'd just run over a fourteen-year-old girl. As soon as he saw Astrid wasn't badly hurt, he'd turned to check his own vehicle. No, she was going to stick him for the full amount, even if it took a little longer.

"You think I should pay you fifteen thousand just because you walked behind my car?"

"You didn't even get a *scratch*," sobbed Astrid. "While I . . . I saved up for it for a whole year!"

"Okay, sure, but fifteen thousand . . ."

Astrid waved her phone. "I'm calling the police! I'm not joking. You didn't look, and you ran over me! Here I go!"

The man waved at the street. "Now, now, calm down a little."

Astrid used her phone's camera to snap the smashed laptop, the car's license plate, and her own bloody mouth.

"What are you doing?" He'd lost some of his haughty attitude.

"Collecting evidence," said Astrid. She aimed the camera at him, but he held up a hand to block her.

"Cool down a moment here. We can . . . we should settle this. How can I . . ."

"By Swish," said Astrid.

"I can't . . . it's not possible . . . that much, all at once."

"Raise the permitted amount," said Astrid. "You can do that in the settings."

"Aha, I can't believe you knew that!" the man said and poked his phone. "Will this work, do you think?"

His sour attitude lightened considerably as he made the necessary adjustments to his account. His voice was almost gentle when he asked for Astrid's number. Her position of advantage made her bold, so she said, "And I want another thousand for pain and suffering too."

"Pain and suffering?"

"Yes. I got *hurt*, in case you didn't notice."

Muttering a bit, he accepted, and a *ping!* from Astrid's phone signaled that the sixteen thousand had arrived. The man didn't bother with farewells. He got into his car and drove away.

Astrid crossed the street and tossed Kim Ribbing's old laptop into a trash can. Now she had the cash to buy herself a new one. She didn't need as fancy a model as Kim's, so she'd have a few thousand left over.

Astrid went down to the ICA on the esplanade to buy vegetarian food to replace what she'd trashed. Maybe she'd take pity on Kim and get a couple of vegetarian pizzas from Anamma. Then she'd go home and prepare dinner.

Home?

Yes, that was as close to a home as Astrid could manage, for the moment. She hadn't really considered the matter, but in fact, she was a kind of live-in companion for Kim Ribbing. Not so bad.

21

July 9, early evening

I want you to leave.

Julia Malmros stood before the open window of her apartment, looking over Järntorget where people in summer-weight clothing strolled through the bright summer evening. She remembered the cold and the slush that had covered the plaza when she'd found Kim Ribbing outside her door. And how they'd hurled themselves into her bed, rarely getting up for the following two days. That seemed so long ago now.

I want you to leave.

Julia knew Kim well enough to be pretty sure he hadn't meant it as harshly as it sounded, but even so, it hurt so damned much to be abruptly dismissed. To know that your presence wasn't desired. Julia ran a fingertip along the dusty window frame and considered: There was an alternative, after all. She could break up with Kim once and for all. Their relationship was probably doomed to failure anyway, so why prolong the suffering? Julia's belly quivered as if she were standing on the edge of a precipice rather than in front of her second-floor window.

I just . . . can't.

Julia didn't understand it, but there was something inevitable and irresistible about her relationship with Kim. Something that couldn't be avoided, at least on her side of it. She knew exactly when and where that had happened: When their hands had joined a few feet above the

North Sea. When she'd pulled him up from the raging sea and into her arms. That had sealed it, and so it remained in Julia's heart, no matter how unreceptive Kim might be.

Julia sighed, stepped away from the window, went to her desk, and rolled up her sleeves before opening the laptop and clicking her mailbox icon. A message from Stockholm's central court had two attachments, sentences concerning two of the True Swedes who were probably part of the inner circle.

The first was Gustaf Lanegren, responsible for environmental policy. His interest in that sector consisted principally of opposing immigration. Overpopulation of the country hindered sustainable development.

Gustaf Lanegren's own contribution to sustainable development had been placing a bomb under the car of a leftist municipal politician in Huddinge. The man's party was constantly proposing resolutions in favor of increased immigration, and Gustaf Lanegren's patience had finally given out. Using instructions and material from the dark web, he had fabricated a bomb and attached it to the vehicle's ignition.

Gustaf got something wrong, and the bomb didn't go off. It was discovered during a routine vehicle inspection a few months later. The police bomb squad was called in and defused a device covered with Gustaf's fingerprints. He was charged immediately, and when his confiscated computer revealed every step in the process, Gustaf was sentenced to eight years for attempted murder.

His counsel had appealed, and an explosives expert testified that the bomb almost certainly wouldn't have killed the politician if it had functioned. The verdict was altered to a questionable "attempt at grave bodily harm" and the sentence reduced to two years.

And then there was Carl Zetterblad, specialist in economic and political affairs, who in fact had studied business for two years before giving up to devote himself to internet scamming. He'd set up about a hundred accounts on Tradera that gave each other 100-percent-positive seller feedback. He then picked up countless digital images from

Blocket that he "sold" to the highest bidders. Before complaints could be lodged, he moved the funds out of the accounts.

And it was Carl, again, who nosed around the dark web and purchased several thousand pirated email addresses. He discarded those obviously belonging to women and then sent a mass email from "Anonymous Sweden" claiming he'd taken control of the addressee's web camera and if a specified amount wasn't paid into this or that account, the recipient's wife would receive video proof of what he'd been up to. It was a shot in the dark, a totally random con, but to Carl's astonishment, twenty-four individuals obeyed his instructions. And not one of them reported him.

Finally, he'd downloaded photos of a Ukrainian porn star named Lizaveta and created a fake profile on a dating site. Several men took the bait, and he strung them along in awkward English and put up ever more audacious photos. When the conversation got around to invitations to come visit Sweden for a *smoking hot* encounter, Lizaveta didn't have the money, of course. What could a poor girl do?

Lizaveta collected enough cash to cover both the trip and the hotel, but one of the men recognized the photos and went to the police. They froze the account with the payments and impounded Carl Zetterblad's computer. It proved a simple matter to recover deleted files related to earlier con jobs. It was, however, difficult to prove that Carl was the perpetrator. He claimed he'd been hacked, that he'd lent the computer to someone, and the judge contented himself with a sentence of only fourteen months.

And those two were the crème de la crème of the True Swedes. Julia downloaded headshots of Gustaf and Carl and studied them. Gustaf Lanegren was the person Julia had seen celebrating with the Apostates, but Carl Zetterblad was a new face. He looked like someone from a good family gone to rack and ruin. Hair combed back, buttoned-down pink shirt, but his eyes had a ravaged look. On the silver chain around his neck dangled an odd symbol, a sort of eye with a cross through the center. Julia drummed her fingers on the desktop. Where had she seen that symbol?

It was just past six, and the heavy feeling in Julia's chest wouldn't go away. She went to the kitchen to pour herself some boxed wine, drank half a glass, and replenished it. It was stupid to seek solace in alcohol; maybe she should go ahead and have a smoke with Irma some evening? That thought amused her, and she lifted her glass to toast the people strolling through the streets below.

To your very good health. Skål!

Julia pounded one hand on the counter and rushed to her computer to pull up Facebook photos from the Apostates' gala. She scrolled through them until she found the one of Gustaf raising his beer stein in a toast. *There. On his right arm.* Julia enlarged the image. Gustaf's shirtsleeves were pulled up to his elbows, and just below the bend he had a tattoo of the eye with the crisscrossed pupil.

Julia googled *Claes-Göran Schwarzkopf* and the screen populated with images. She went through them, searching for a corresponding piece of jewelry or tattoo but found none. She called up an image unloaded from the *Almedalen Weekly* six days earlier, where Schwarzkopf was holding forth from an improvised speaker's stand outside some venue. Carl Zetterblad was clearly visible in the background, holding up both hands and applauding whatever Claes-Göran had just said.

Julia zoomed in, methodically examined every part of the photo, and finally got a hit. On Claes-Göran Schwarzkopf's right hand, which was clutching the microphone, she spotted a signet ring. When Julia enlarged it, she saw it bore the eye symbol. What did that signify?

She googled *fascist* and *Nazi symbols* and got a display of the Othala rune and the Hagal rune, the sun wheel, Thor's hammer, and even Pepe the Frog, but nothing that remotely resembled the image used by the True Swedes. They'd hardly want to flaunt something that revealed the far-right convictions they were trying to hide. Julia googled *nationalist symbols.* The Othala rune and the others came up, as well as some more closely related to Swedish traditions. Scrolling down, she found what she'd been looking for. "Odin's eye," it was called, representing the eye that Odin sacrificed at Mimir's well to be able to view everything past and everything yet to come.

Searching for Odin's eye, she got references only to Norse mythology and the story of Mimir. It wasn't unusual for Scandinavian nationalist movements to turn to mythology, but what, specifically, did it mean for the True Swedes?

I want you to leave.

Julia winced. Kim Ribbing hadn't been in her thoughts while she was searching the internet, but now, as the evening came on, he crept back in, as always, a menacing lynx climbing up the curtains of her consciousness to sink its claws into her heart.

Goddamned Kim Ribbing.

How many times had she thought that? More than she could count, and even so, she came running back whenever he called. It was pathetic how relieved she'd been by the last little "see you later" that had indicated there would, in fact, be a continuation. Because there *had* to be more.

22

July 9, early evening

"I can't decide if I'm willing to buy that," Kim told Martin Rudbeck. "That stuff about *taming*, it seems just too . . . elegant. Symmetrical. I think you're just lying here in the dark, cooking up things you hope I'll want to hear."

After the doctor had used the toilet, Kim allowed him to sit on the cot for a while, keeping the shackle around his neck. Kim had noticed bedsores developing and decided he could afford to be a bit indulgent. The truth was that Kim was beginning to tire of this little game. Martin Rudbeck had gotten a taste of his own medicine, and two nights strapped down in the dark had been enough to break him. His gaze was hesitant, his hands trembled, and as soon as Kim had come down and turned on the fluorescent light, he had burst into tears.

The doctor mumbled something Kim couldn't hear from fifteen feet away. He moved his chair forward to be in earshot of his former tormentor. Kim didn't feel threatened by his listless, passive prisoner.

"Can you say that again?" said Kim.

"So much life," was the doctor's slurred reply. "So . . . much . . . life."

"I don't get what you're saying," Kim said. "But there's something else that's been bothering me. All this that you did to me—did you treat *lots* of other boys that way to . . . tame them?"

The doctor's head swayed heavily from side to side. "Just you."

"And what was so special about me?"

"What I said. So much life." The doctor moved off the cot and staggered to the wall where the chain was anchored, then sank to the floor. He looked up and stared at the empty room beyond Kim's shoulder before continuing. "Almost no one's inner life is perceptible. You can't tell how aware a person is. But with you it was different, unlike anyone I've ever known. Even with all that darkness and stubbornness, you were the most *alive* person I had ever met. You defied me with white-hot resistance."

"But it's a hell of a contradiction that I've never felt as *dead* as I did all those years with you."

"That was your own choice. If you'd opened up and been willing to converse, we could have created something entirely different together, mutually beneficial."

Kim shook his head, reached for the makeshift shock stick, and stood up. "Don't you shrinks ever analyze yourselves? Can't you hear the pathetic *rationalizing* in that? Persuading yourself you had fine, noble motives for torturing me? Can you possibly believe that?" Kim advanced on Rudbeck and brandished the broken lamp. "Get your sorry ass up. Go back to bed."

The doctor struggled to his feet with a long groan, the slack chain rattling behind him on the concrete floor. He nodded toward Kim's foot. "Why are you wearing those?" Kim glanced down at his basketball sneakers and instantly realized that Rudbeck was distracting him, but it was too late. The doctor grabbed the opportunity to act.

In his right hand, hidden behind his back, the doctor had gathered a loose length of chain that he whipped toward the broken lamp Kim was holding. The metal links slammed Kim's hand between the thumb and wrist. His arm jolted in blazing pain and the lamp went flying.

The doctor's sluggishness and impaired reactions were fake, meant to get Kim to drop his guard. A second vicious cast of the chain sent it twisting over Kim's head and around his neck. Rudbeck yanked hard with both hands, tightening the loop and choking his captor.

"I wasn't rationalizing a fucking thing," the doctor snarled in his ear. "I knew *exactly* what I was doing. Because you were an obstinate little punk who needed to be taught a lesson, and I enjoyed it. Just as much as I'm enjoying *this*!"

Red blotches filled Kim's vision as the oxygen supply to his brain was blocked. The metal links dug into his vulnerable neck tissue as the doctor twisted the chain as hard as he could. The hot spittle of his triumphant declaration burned in Kim's ear.

Kim tried to work his fingers under the chain, but it was drawn too tight around his neck. The red blotches expanded and melded with one another, and the blackness of his peripheral vision began welling toward them. His kicks couldn't reach the doctor's naked feet. He tried to pull back enough to plant a heel in the doctor's groin, but that feeble maneuver failed.

Fuck.

The doctor panted in Kim's ear as a curtain fell, blurring and obscuring everything. Kim's mouth opened and shut but couldn't get any air. He made one last desperate thrust, turned his body a quarter circle, and saw the white wall just inches away, rapidly turning black.

Seconds from unconsciousness, Kim felt his limbs slackening as his brain dimmed. His strength and will were being violently squeezed to extinction.

One last chance. Kim grabbed the chain with his fingertips as tight as he could and pulled his knees up to his chest. His own weight intensified the strangulation, and the black curtain fell even faster. When no more than a tiny dazzle of illumination remained in all that darkness, he gathered his legs and kicked both heels into the wall.

The doctor staggered a couple of steps backward and then fell on his back with Kim on top of him. The pressure let up slightly, and Kim got half a breath of air. The blackness lifted slightly. Kim managed to throw himself to one side, gaining space between the two of them, then jammed his elbows into the man's gut.

Martin Rudbeck gagged as if starting to vomit, and the pressure eased enough for Kim to get his fingers under the chain and tear it off. The doctor coughed and gasped for air, stretched full length on the floor. Kim sat on his chest. A choking gust of stinking sweat and heat emanated from the doctor's body. Kim smashed his jaw with a right cross. And then a left cross. Rudbeck's head was knocked from side to side and his spittle splashed across the concrete.

"You think," Kim croaked, "you have the *right* to kill me, huh? That's what you think?"

The sounds from the doctor's mouth were incomprehensible. Kim's knuckles ached, and his punches had probably broken the doctor's jaw. He deserved it. Nothing but foul talk and lies came out of that stinking mouth.

Kim's throat sucked and wheezed as he avidly gulped down air. The shapes around him cohered at last and stood out in sharp relief. He coughed, his throat burned, and he could hardly swallow for the pain. Throbbing and aching, he worked his way across the floor and wrapped his fingers around his shock stick before pushing himself to his feet.

All the fight seemed to have gone out of Martin Rudbeck, who lay limp on his back, staring up at the ceiling, pitifully trying to catch his breath. Kim pressed the leads of his improvised Taser against the doctor's feet and sent him flopping and convulsing like a flounder hauled aboard a trawler. "Lie on the cot. Now."

Kim didn't believe the man's limp submission was feigned this time. With violently shaking limbs the doctor made his way up onto the cot and continued staring glassily upward.

"At least we know where we stand," Kim said. "Strap down your legs and then your right hand."

Martin Rudbeck did as he was told, with a sigh from his innermost depths. Kim couldn't comprehend what the man had been thinking; without the assistance of his captor, the doctor would have starved to death. Maybe he'd hoped that he'd be able to wrench the chain's anchor out of the wall. Kim didn't believe that was possible. He'd just saved Martin Rudbeck's life, but he wasn't expecting any thanks for that. *Idiot!*

Kim fastened the strap across the left wrist and tightened the belt across the chest, then walked across the room and fetched the Taser he'd purchased in Shanghai. Its two long filaments, positive and negative, had come tipped with sharp darts, but Kim had snipped those off and replaced them with alligator clips. The doctor yelped when Kim clamped one onto the left earlobe and the other onto the little toe of his right foot. Kim showed him the box with the charged battery. "Two thousand volts. A proper kiss, as a certain gentleman commented to me."

Martin Rudbeck shook his head. His eyes filled with tears. "You'll kill me, Kim. My heart . . . I won't survive . . ."

"That's as it may be," said Kim. "I suggest you come up with a more convincing answer. Tomorrow we'll end this."

"You mean I'll die tomorrow?"

"Remains to be seen. You just lie there and think about it."

Kim turned off the light and pulled the heavy iron door shut behind him. This was going nowhere fast. Tomorrow he'd set the doctor free. But before that, the man could spend a night lying in the dark, contemplating his own demise, connected to a device that would do the job. Let the doctor reflect upon his mortality. That would do him good.

As soon as he started up the stairs, Kim heard rattling and clattering and caught the scent of food cooking. When he got to the kitchen, he found Astrid Helander busy agitating a frying pan containing a quantity of golden-brown balls.

"Hi," said Astrid, without looking up from the pan. "We'll have vegetarian meatballs with mashed potatoes. That okay with you?"

"What—you're *cooking*?" asked Kim, perplexed.

"Well, someone around here has to," said Astrid. "And I threw your food out, as you might have noticed."

"Yes, I . . . it came to my attention."

Astrid glanced at Kim and her eyes opened wide. She gestured toward his neck. "Well, shit! What did you do to yourself there?"

"Work accident," said Kim and dismissed the subject by pointing at a covered pot emitting steam around the lid. "What's in there?"

"Potatoes, obviously," said Astrid. "For mashing. You have a potato masher?"

"A *what*?"

"Masher." Astrid clenched a fist and made a couple of pounding motions. "To mash the potatoes."

"Not a clue," Kim said. "I thought mashed potatoes came from flakes."

He couldn't understand why Astrid thought that was so funny.

23

July 9, evening

It was almost nine o'clock when Julia Malmros shut down her computer and rubbed her eyes hard, trying to erase the disgusting images from her memory. She'd spent much of the evening going through Claes-Göran's YouTube channel, Project: Sweden. There was nothing particularly remarkable about the individual videos, but taken together, they left you feeling overwhelmed.

The Sweden he showed was so *incredibly* wonderful, its culture was so developed, and its history was so brilliant. An ideal, flawless country. There was none of his earlier ranting against other cultures, foreigners, and immigrants. Those themes were nowhere to be found, either in his words or in the images. He created a world that was purely, ethnically Swedish. Not even in the huge crowds enthusiastically singing Evert Taube songs was there a glimpse of dark-skinned individuals or anyone with black kinky hair. If you studied the images closely, you found that some of the faces were suspiciously blurred, as if they'd been edited in postproduction.

You couldn't help being impressed by the long-term perspective embodied in Claes-Göran's project. First, you devote a couple of years projecting the picture of a flawless Sweden without a trace of anyone foreign-born, and only after that do you establish a political party warning of the threat from those foreigners, a party and threat that seemed to have leaped out from nothing and nowhere. The man was despicable, but he was anything but stupid.

Julia had watched for the signet ring with Odin's eye while reviewing the videos but didn't see it, so it must have gone onto Claes-Göran's finger sometime later, maybe when the True Swedes party was established. She had no time to check that just now.

Julia got up from the desk, her joints cracking, went to the kitchen, and looked down toward the Gyldene Freden. None of the Swedish Academy's noble spirits was visible, and she remembered Kim sitting at the kitchen table the first time he'd entered her apartment and her life.

I want you to leave.

Julia pressed her hands to her chest. An uneasy feeling was stirring in there, heated and restless, like a wounded little animal scurrying around looking for a way out as its blood seeped into her lungs. The tingling in her fingertips and feet wouldn't go away. She had a feeling she was going to lie awake tossing and turning all night. She sighed and rubbed her cheeks.

After wandering aimlessly around the apartment for several minutes, unable to find anything with which to distract herself, she picked up her phone and called Irma Ryding.

"Hey, girl," Irma answered. "How are things?"

"*Comme ci, comme ça,*" Julia said. "Hmm . . . I was just wondering . . . do you have any grass?"

"Yes. Why?"

"Goodness, you know, maybe you'd like to . . . smoke a little?"

The silence on the other end lasted a couple of seconds. Irma gave a snort. "What happened to that little prude? The one talking about the *junkie granny?*"

"She . . . she's not here just now. I gave her some time off."

"Aha, I see. Okay. Awfully nice of you. I usually smoke purely for medicinal purposes, so to speak, but I can probably make an exception for you."

"Meaning . . . ?"

"Meaning get yourself over here right away. Besides, got some things to tell you."

Julia felt a little better as she quickly donned her thin summer jacket. Now she'd at least have a definite direction, a straight line to a goal instead of randomly wandering. She hoped the grass would exorcise the images of Kim Ribbing and allow her to sleep. She prayed it wouldn't make her even *more* paranoid.

When she came out onto Västerlånggatan and padded across the cobblestones, she realized that she was feeling an entirely new sort of apprehension. To put it simply, she was *nervous*. Her experience of recreational drugs was limited to a single puff of a sweet-smelling cigarette her last year in high school. She hadn't felt anything except a bit of disorientation. Julia assumed that the experience that evening would be different and was afraid she'd make a fool of herself in front of Irma. Oh well, make it or break it; she was hoping for at least a bit of *peace*.

The thumps of Irma's crutch were audible from inside the flat after Julia rang. She still thought her friend should swallow her pride and give her a key. After all, her father didn't mind that arrangement. That reminded Julia, as the thumping approached, that she really should visit him again soon to make sure he didn't forget her entirely.

Irma had a mischievous smile on her face as she called out loudly, "Well, lookie here! Here comes Speedy Gonzales to snaffle up a bit of weed!" Her voice echoed in the stairwell.

"Shh, Irma! Think of the neighbors!"

"Stopped doing that when I turned eighty. Come in."

When they seated themselves on the living room sofa and armchair, Irma pointed to a wooden box on the coffee table. "Before we fry our brains, I want to tell you what your volunteer *researcher* has come up with lately. You remember Bente? Bente Möller?"

"The psychologist?"

"Mm-hmm. I had her as a consultant for some things in my novels. We've called each other a couple of times a week since she retired."

"Okay."

Julia felt a pang of melancholy. She did have friends other than Irma, but she was terrible at staying in contact, and then the bloodstorm had overtaken her and she hadn't spoken to any of them, even though she'd missed a couple of their calls. Irma was better at managing her own friendships.

"Bente asked what I was doing these days, and I told her about you and how I'm looking into the True Swedes, and especially how I was trying to trace that Schwarzkopf fellow's background. Bente got really quiet for a while, but then she said a single phrase. Know what it was?"

"No idea."

"Tractorball."

"Tractorball?"

"Mm-hmm."

"What on earth is that? A tractor ball?"

"That's what I said too, but Bente told me it was a single word and she'd already said too much. Professional confidentiality, stuff like that."

"But I don't understand—"

"Hold it right there," said Irma, lifting a hand as if directing traffic. "Of course, I googled it as soon as we finished. The only hit on 'tractorball' was a Norwegian handball league. So, 'ball' isn't a formal dance, it's just the round thing, a ball. But 'tractorball' sounds really strange, doesn't it? Makes me think of polo, but not with horses, played on tractors instead, with a gigantic ball. And really long mallets. Hmm?"

Julia tilted her head. "Seems maybe there's been some smoking going on here already?"

"No way, José. Just lively fantasy. But that's when, you see, *that* is when I got my sudden inspiration. Flashback, I said to myself. Sounds like a typical username for Flashback!"

"Good Lord, Irma. You use Flashback as well?"

"Of course. Best site for research if you want to keep up with the times. You should give it a try. There's a thread about you, but I do *not* recommend that you read it."

Julia promised she wouldn't, knowing it was the first thing she'd do when she next turned on her computer.

"So," said Irma, "I type 'tractorball' in the search field, and *voilà*! A user with that name was very active for several years."

"Okay, but what meaning does that have—"

"The *meaning*," said Irma, holding up that admonishing index finger, "is that I am almost one-hundred-percent certain that Claes-Göran Schwarzkopf and Tractorball are one and the same. Ages and locations match. He says he's twenty years old and lives with his mother in Upplands Väsby. I couldn't verify his mention of his mother, but he does come from Upplands Väsby and was twenty when Tractorball wrote several of the posts."

"Okay. And what do we get from that?"

"That Claes-Göran Schwarzkopf is, or at least was, a psychopath. An amateur psychologist would probably put him down as, say, a hallucinating paranoid with a touch of OCD."

"What did he write that would lead to that?"

Irma ran a hand over her forehead. "Ugh, I'm getting all heated up, just sitting here and telling you all this. Want a sip of wine?"

"Wine and weed? I'd probably have to crawl home afterward. No, thanks."

"Doesn't work that way. In any case, *I* want some."

Irma reached for her crutch, getting ready to rise, but Julia stopped her. "Sit, sit; I'll get it."

"All right, then," Irma said. "Just this once, since I've been your star investigator and all that. Get a move on, I'm dry as a bone."

Julia went to the kitchen and took a half-full box of white wine from the fridge and poured a few ounces into a wineglass, thinking about Tractorball and wondering what people might have written about her on Flashback. Sometimes she'd google herself once, twice, or even three times a week, but Flashback had never occurred to her. She felt like using her phone to check immediately, but that would be pathetic.

Besides, Irma would be suspicious if she was slow. Julia returned to the living room instead.

"Tsk-tsk," said Irma as Julia put the wineglass before her. "What were you thinking? Just wetting down the bottom?"

"You said *a sip* of wine."

"Are you familiar with the expression 'figuratively speaking'? People say they're going out 'for a beer,' but how often does that mean a single beer?"

"Can we get back to Schwarzkopf?"

"Okay, sure," said Irma. She took a sip and made a face as if the inadequate volume had adversely affected the taste. "Where was I? Ah, yes, his posts on Flashback, that was it. He uses the N-word pretty frequently."

"Well, that's distasteful. Go ahead."

"Right, Claes-Göran was obsessed by an irrational fear that 'they' would invade the house and kill him and his mother."

"Did he have any cause to fear that—"

"No, no! And when I say 'irrational,' I really mean 'completely mad.' Nuts! For example, he felt obliged to make sure that the stoppers in the washbasin and the sink were in place, since if not, *they* could get in through the plumbing."

Julia couldn't hold back a laugh. "Seriously?"

"Yes. And all the electrical sockets had to have plugs in them, since otherwise they . . . yeah, I can't remember exactly how he tried to explain it, but somehow they could get inside that way too. Maybe by taking control of his thoughts. That's why I call it OCD. Came up with plenty of absurd rituals he believed were necessary to keep them out."

"But that's complete madness! How can he even present himself as a normal human being?"

"What do I know? On Flashback he writes about medicines that *they* secretly try to feed him and he only *pretends* to take. Maybe there was a time he started to accept drugs and he became more . . .

functional. But at the root of it is that overwhelming fear. That might be good to keep in mind."

Julia snapped her fingers. "All this actually explains something I was wondering about. Those videos, on Project: Sweden, all those squirrel images . . ."

"I looked at them too, but I don't remember any squirrels," said Irma, draining her glass with a dissatisfied grimace.

"Well, if someone's making a documentary, or even filming a story, he'll insert, you know, here and there . . . ordinary images to create a pause or a mood. Maybe a few branches, a seascape, or just a squirrel."

"I see," said Irma. "To set the tone."

"Exactly. And many of those intervals . . . this occurred to me when you mentioned his delusions . . . many of those intervening images show an *intrusion* or at least something getting into somewhere."

"What do you mean?" asked Irma, setting down her glass with a baleful look, as if it had offended her.

"Well, you see, in the middle of a report about something, up pops a picture of wasps crawling into their nest, a mouse slipping into a hole, beetles chewing their way into a rotting tree trunk, or just a squirrel wiggling its way into a birdhouse. Pictures that are like, what d'you call them . . ."

"Subliminal messages," Irma said. "Messages the brain accepts though one's not consciously aware of them."

"Yes!" said Julia. "And there are so many images like that, it can't be mere coincidence. It's like Claes-Göran Schwarzkopf is intent on implanting the idea that there's a constant intrusion going on."

"Hmm. I thought it was a bit weird, but I didn't see that. Cool. You're not as dumb as you look."

"Thank you. Can a person have a little puff now?"

"Indeed, a person can," said Irma, reaching for the wooden box. "Just have to roll a joint."

"Good God, Irma, who are we? Cheech and Chong?"

"Maybe yours truly wasn't a hippie back in the 1970s, but that's no excuse to be ignorant of the terminology. Quiet now. I must concentrate."

Irma opened the box and took out cigarette papers, a package of John Silver rolling tobacco, and a transparent plastic bag with fibrous brownish-green contents Julia recognized from her years on the beat. She'd removed similar packets from the pockets of agitated or distracted individuals, delivering her useless warning about the dangers of drugs. And now here she was.

Irma stuck the tip of her tongue out of one corner of her mouth as she concentrated. With great care she licked and joined two papers, filled them with tobacco and sprinkled onto it some marijuana, then rolled it all into a tapered shape and licked the edge shut. She examined the joint with a frown. "Not my best, but good enough to get the job done." Irma patted the sofa cushion next to her. "Come sit here. Don't want this to get messy."

Julia obeyed. She studied the joint. Its end was twisted tightly shut. "Goodness me, Irma. We're really doing this."

"Yes, ma'am," said Irma, taking from the box a Zippo lighter etched with the image of a skull. "Here we go, into the purple haze."

The twisted end flamed up when Irma put the lighter to it. She took a puff. A sweet odor reminiscent of marzipan filled the room. Irma sent the joint Julia's way.

She took it gingerly between her thumb and index finger, hesitated just a moment, then took a deep drag and held it in her lungs as she returned the joint.

To and fro, back and forth. Julia had taken four drags and still seemed to feel nothing, but her eyes were drawn to the skull-decorated lighter sitting on the table. A silver cranium on a dark background, black hollows instead of eyes, and grinning teeth. Was it leering at her? What strange thoughts were bubbling inside that bare, silvery forehead? The skull seemed to grow and come nearer, or maybe it was becoming more evident, even three-dimensional. She imagined the skeletal body that the skull would be fastened to, how it emerged from the lighter, and then she and Irma were following it. Into a valley, like somewhere in the Alps, with summer flowers in lush grassy meadows . . .

"How are you doing?" Irma asked.

Julia broke away from the skull's stare. "Good, thanks. No problem."

"Just wondered. You've been sitting, staring at the lighter for at least five minutes now."

"Oh, my. Right, maybe it has gone to my head a bit."

"A *bit*? You're high as a kite, girl."

Julia realized that she was slumping in the sofa like a sack of potatoes. She straightened up, trying to recover her dignity. "Hardly! I was thinking. About him, that guy . . . what's his name, the one on Flashback?"

"Tractorball?"

Julia couldn't help it; she exploded in laughter and threw herself back against the sofa cushions. She laughed so hard her belly hurt as she whinnied, "Tractorball . . . tractorball . . . !"

So much for regaining my dignity.

Irma shook her head, ground out the joint in the ashtray, and said, "No more for you, girl."

Once her giggles had subsided, Julia took a couple of deep breaths. "But, really? I was . . . thinking—why? . . . Why hasn't anyone, um, discovered that? Some reporter? You can't be the only one—"

"Actually, there's a whole thread on Flashback," said Irma, "discussing whether Claes-Göran wrote those posts. But no one has suggested he's a . . . never mind, if I say it, you'll probably laugh yourself to death. Claes-Göran insisted to an interviewer that he's never had a profile on Flashback."

"So if I were to reveal that, then . . ."

"You'd be in *really* hot water," Irma filled in. "I strongly advise against it. No! I *forbid* you to do it. I have the distinct impression the man in question is extremely dangerous."

Gloom suddenly descended upon Julia. She wasn't a particularly courageous person, and maybe her True Swedes project was wrong-headed, even meaningless. She was such an idiot. An idiot and a coward. Obviously, Kim could never love such a person. She was old, and ugly as well. *Damn and double damn.*

Julia realized what she was doing, what she was thinking. She twitched all over, slapped her thighs, and cried, "No! I want to listen to music!"

"Aha," said Irma with a little smirk. "Bob Marley, will that do?"

"No! Peps! I want to listen to Peps! Do you have a record by Peps? Peps Persson?!" The way the name popped out of her mouth was so funny that Julia had to say it again. "Peps!"

"Thank you, I heard the first time," said Irma and opened her laptop. "And who needs records when we've got Spotify?"

As Irma tapped on the keyboard, Julia threw out her arms and cried, "You're completely unbelievable, Irma! With your YouTube and Flashback and now your Spotify too! Is there no limit to your, what d'you call it, your . . . being *up to date*? You're an outright digital genius!"

Irma had called Peps up on Spotify. "Your boyfriend leaves me in the shade. What do you want to hear?"

"Uh-uh, nope!" said Julia, waving an index finger. "No talk about Kim. Let's go with Peps. The one about the apartment and the *tittle-tattle.*"

Irma pointed to the list on the screen. "That one? About the tenement flat and the nosy neighbors' 'tittle-tattle'?"

"Yes, that's the one. Play that one!"

Irma double-clicked the trackpad and reggae music began streaming from a little speaker in a bookcase that Julia had never noticed, and she began swaying in time as Peps sang in his broad southern Swedish dialect.

Julia glanced at Irma and saw her friend watching her with an amused little smile. Julia was all too excited—okay, too *high*—to be affected, so she just slapped Irma's knee and roared, "Come on, then, mama! It's *swinging* now!"

Irma raised an eyebrow, but she did what Julia wanted. She began to rock from side to side in time to the music. Maybe only to indulge her, but Julia didn't care, for here they were, together, swaying to the beat while Peps sang. She didn't even think about Kim. The realization she wasn't thinking about Kim made her think about Kim, but she pushed away those musings and sang along.

Keeping the motion and the rhythm, Irma joined in.

A great evening. *Without* Ribbing.

24

July 9, evening

Astrid Helander logged out from the Animal Action forum and shut down her computer. She'd participated in a thread debating demonstrations versus direct action. Most members favored protests and performances—for example, posting themselves costumed as bloody rabbits across the street from a market hall. Some of the hardcore participants advocated violence and threats against, say, pig farms and dairies. Astrid was starting to lean that way. After all, the movement wasn't achieving any *results*.

She and Kim hadn't said much during the meal, and Astrid had the impression Kim was finding the situation uncomfortable. Well, Astrid didn't intend to *move in* yet, but on this first evening she wanted to see what spending the night in the villa would be like. Afterward, she changed into the nightgown she'd brought and crawled into bed.

The villa was quiet. The only sound was the clattering of Kim's keyboard in the living room. Astrid had left the window open just a bit, and through it came the low rustling of the wind in the treetops. She blinked her eyes and yawned.

The emptiness that had held her in its grip since her parents' deaths had started to fade and allow her spirit to stir. Astrid had even felt a sharp touch of her former self during the online discussion. She had a hollow throbbing deep within, but that was beginning to let up too.

There was something she hadn't mentioned to Kim. Arriving that afternoon after conning the man with the Audi, she'd noticed Kim's shoes in the hall but found no trace of him. Her cautious investigation of the property had eventually taken her as far as the closed sliding door in the basement. Putting her ear to it, she'd heard Kim talking to someone.

Since Kim hadn't said anything about this, Astrid assumed he was keeping something hidden, which could be related to the vivid red marks around his neck. Astrid curled up in bed in a fetal position. She'd have to be careful, but she intended to find out the next day just what Kim Ribbing had down there in his underground room.

II

JULY 10–11

25

July 10, morning

The sun was high in the sky at half past ten that morning, but Martin Rudbeck, strapped down in all-encompassing darkness, knew nothing of that. Only when completely immobilized had he realized how much a person moves every day. Pinches his nose, rubs an eye, scratches an itch. He was incapable of that now, and a prickling sensation over one nostril was driving him mad. He tossed his head, trying to create enough air movement to affect it, but that provided no relief. Nor did it loosen the alligator clip fastened to his earlobe.

Ribbing. Goddamned Ribbing.

Still, it wasn't as if he didn't understand Kim Ribbing. His treatment of the teenage Kim had been . . . dubious. One decisive difference was that, as a physician, he'd been dead sure the young man needed to be calmed and protected from himself. Granted, perhaps Ribbing was right to insist that his explanation was a rationalization, but he'd been convinced of it nevertheless. And he was doing vital research into the use of electroconvulsive treatment for adolescents.

This kidnapping, however, was nothing more than revenge, and Martin Rudbeck was equally convinced of that. Ribbing's blather about "understanding" wasn't worth two cents. Rudbeck himself had often used the expression, but after a long career in psychiatry, he had come to the discouraging conclusion that there was no way to understand another human being, at least not in any profound sense. One couldn't even fully understand oneself.

Did that make him evil? Perhaps, but that's the personality he had to manage and the life he had to live. A life that might be about to end at Ribbing's hands.

Tomorrow we'll end this, Kim had said.

After Kim had left, Martin spat a wad of bloody slime toward the ceiling in a pathetic effort to leave some trace of himself, and he'd spent hours that night going through possible scenarios. Not a pleasant exercise, but he couldn't defend himself against the images that materialized in the black void like famished ghosts. More than anything, of course, he feared the electric shock that would pulse from his toe to his ear, probably shutting down his heart on the way, though that wasn't *guaranteed.*

The more the terrified Martin Rudbeck contemplated his fate, the more he saw suffocation as his most likely end. Nothing could be simpler than blocking his airway, for he was unable to defend himself. Tape his mouth and block his nostrils. Martin Rudbeck began hyperventilating as he imagined himself struggling to breathe nonexistent air.

He did not know where the idea had come from, but at some point he became convinced that Ribbing intended to place a plastic bag over his head and secure it at the neck. The plastic would be pulled into his mouth as he gasped for air; carbon dioxide would replace the oxygen inside the bag. His brain would shut down. He'd die.

Martin Rudbeck didn't want to die, but he didn't know how to keep it from happening. Though naturally eloquent and a good judge of character, he didn't believe he could talk his way out of this, especially not after attacking Ribbing. He'd seized that final, desperate opportunity and failed.

There was a creak on the stairway beyond the door. Martin Rudbeck pissed his boxer shorts. His heart raced, his hands clenched and opened. Forgotten were the itching nostril and the pinched earlobe as his executioner approached. Was that the rattle of a plastic bag?

Dear God, get it over with quickly.

He sobbed and hot tears ran down his cheeks. He'd never been so frightened in his life. He emitted an involuntary squeal when the iron door was pulled aside, and he whimpered when the light came on. Steps came across the concrete floor. The doctor's eyes opened wide when Astrid Helander came into view.

"You?" said Astrid. She wrinkled her nose. "What are *you* doing here?"

26

July 10, morning

Half an hour earlier, Astrid Helander had been lying in her bed when she heard the outer door open and close. The motorcycle started a few seconds later. She lay motionless until the engine noise faded into the distance. Then she got up and dressed.

She started by making a full review of the schizophrenic decor of the rooms. Kim's bedroom was one of the more extreme examples. A pair of jeans had been slung onto a large antique seafarer's chest featuring an elaborately painted *1814*. Next to it was a globular red chair of 1970s design that looked like it had come from *A Clockwork Orange*. Between the chest and the chair was a floor lamp that appeared impossibly futuristic.

Astrid sniffed the unmade bed and recognized faint traces of some woman's perfume. She'd gotten the impression Kim had an on-and-off relationship with that Julia Malmros woman. Astrid had no particular opinion of Julia other than the fact she'd really appreciated the thousand-piece puzzle Julia had given her when she turned ten. Anybody who respected Astrid's intelligence got brownie points. The presumptive relationship with Kim, however, resulted in significant demerits.

She went through the pantry and living room, encountering a bit of everything, including lots of electronics for which she couldn't imagine any use. Kim seemed to be something of a techno-nerd. In a coffee can in the kitchen, she came across five vials with labels that identified them as tetrodotoxin, a substance that mystified her.

Once that was done, she went to the unoccupied main floor and the door to which she'd pressed her ear. Not a sound. The padlock was a simple one, and Astrid spent some time looking around for a key. She pulled out the drawers in the desks scattered around the room, checked beneath lamps and behind folders with titles in French. Nothing.

If Kim wasn't carrying the key with him, he'd probably hidden it somewhere nearby. Astrid jammed her hands in her pockets and stared so intently at the padlock that her sheer willpower should probably have popped it open. She went up on tiptoes and ran her fingers along the top of the doorframe. *Ka-ching!* Her fingertips closed around a little key that proved to fit the padlock. *Kim isn't as clever as he seems,* she thought.

Astrid removed the padlock, left it hanging on its hasp, and pushed open the door. A narrow stair directly inside led down into the darkness. Astrid turned on the light. There was something ominous in the way the stairway ended on a naked concrete slab, so before descending, she went back to the kitchen to collect a deadly looking carving blade from the knife block. Then she crept down the stairway. Not a sound was to be heard. The stairs creaked; she stopped and listened. Nothing. She went the rest of the way down to the concrete floor and looked around.

To her right an open wooden door showed a space that was probably a boiler room, and other doors looked like tool closets. Something much more interesting was on the left: an impressively heavy steel door secured with a padlock. Astrid sighed. She doubted she'd be lucky a second time. That disappointment lasted a couple of seconds, but then she spotted a key on a hook next to the door. *Double ka-ching!* What kind of slovenly security was this? Well, there'd been no expectation Astrid would be on the premises, and he couldn't know that she was a born snoop. Astrid's view was that she merely wanted to keep herself informed.

She unlocked the door and held the knife ready in her right hand. She had to apply her whole weight with her left hand to get the door to budge. She heard a muted squeal.

Rats?

Despite Astrid's ardent defense of animal rights, she didn't care for rats, and she hadn't had any truly profound objections when her father had set out traps on Knektholmen after rats had crossed the frozen bay to invade their place. She had, however, stopped him from putting out poison, since that was torture. Were there rats in Kim's cellar?

That he talks to at night? Huh. Not likely.

Astrid found the switch for the overhead light. The room beyond the doorway was generally bare. The only things she saw were a table with a computer and some small surgical instruments. A cot stood in the middle of the room, and a chain fastened to the wall led to it. Astrid saw a head of gray-streaked hair. Where had she seen that kind of haircut recently?

With all senses heightened and knife held high, she circled the room, slowly nearing the cot. She saw the profile and immediately recognized the man strapped there. She took a couple of steps forward and looked down into Dr. Martin Rudbeck's wide-open eyes.

"You?" she said. "What are *you* doing here?"

So there was a rat in the basement after all.

Martin Rudbeck glanced toward the door to see if anyone was with Astrid and then whispered, "Set me loose. He's planning to kill me."

"Who is?" asked Astrid in her normal tone of voice. "Kim?"

"Yes. Is he in the building?"

"Nah. He went out for a while. Why are you lying here?"

"Just free me, that's all."

Astrid took her time examining the clamps on Rudbeck's little toe and earlobe. Filaments led to a yellow box with a couple of buttons. It was marked with a lightning-bolt symbol. Astrid surveyed the leather straps around Martin Rudbeck's wrists, ankles, and chest. "Seems to me that if you're lying here like this . . . there's probably a good reason for it."

"He's a psychiatric case, that's the reason."

Astrid remembered very clearly how in Vamlinge the doctor had sat across from her bed and touched her foot, how he'd *intruded* into her private space, so she didn't give a damn for his diagnosis. Astrid walked to the table and poked through the surgical instruments. She put down the carving knife and picked up a scalpel.

"He *tortured* me," Rudbeck whispered shrilly. Astrid walked back and gave him a chilly look.

"No sign of that," said Astrid. She pointed the scalpel at him. "Don't see any injuries."

Martin Rudbeck nodded frantically toward the broken floor lamp by the wall. "With that thing."

"He tortured you with a *lamp*?" Astrid taunted, though she understood perfectly well when she saw the exposed filaments and the cord plugged into the outlet. "All due respect, but that doesn't exactly sound like standard practice. Why did he do that?"

"I already told you. He's ill."

"And, like, that's no explanation. I have a diagnosis too, but that doesn't mean I don't know what I'm doing."

"I know you have a diagnosis," Martin Rudbeck replied, assuming a more professional tone. "And everything indicates that you are still suffering post-traumatic stress, which prevents you from making rational decisions. What happened with your mother and father—"

"Don't you talk about my parents!"

"See? All indications are that you're still in denial and need professional help to work your way through the trauma you suffered."

"And who's supposed to give me that? You?"

"I have many years of experience working with traumatized youth. And if you'll just undo the straps—"

"Not a chance. Not before I understand why you're lying here."

The doctor cleared his throat. His voice became stern. "Astrid! Unless I'm mistaken, you feel guilt, both emotionally and physically, for what happened to your parents. Many persons of your age have strained relationships with their mother and father. For example, I've seen that girls especially are often crushed by feelings of guilt when a parent becomes ill or suffers an accident, because they had such a difficult relationship."

Astrid poked the doctor with the scalpel. "Shut up."

"Ow." Martin Rudbeck winced at the barely perceptible pain. "I'm not saying that's your case, Astrid, but there are some young girls who choose suicide over living with those feelings. *What could I have done? Should I have been nicer? Did I love them at all before they died? Did they love me?* Those questions weigh terribly upon young minds . . ."

Astrid put down the scalpel and picked up the yellow box. One of the buttons bore a lightning-bolt identical to the one on the box itself. Astrid ran a thumb across it. Rudbeck coughed sharply and cried, "Don't do that! You want to become a murderer?"

"Maybe," said Astrid. "If that's what it takes to make you shut your trap."

The doctor was a dirty old man, but he'd managed to touch Astrid's most sensitive point. It was true that her conscience kept accusing her of not fully loving her parents. They were dead now, and that would never change.

"You can threaten as much as you want," Rudbeck said. "But you must understand that all you're doing is defending yourself against a reality you'll have to deal with sooner or later. And the sooner, the better. Your reaction leads me to believe that my guess about your relationship with them is correct. You need help, Astrid. Otherwise, you'll grow up and become a person unable to give or receive love."

The only thing that kept Astrid from shocking the old creep, fatally or not, was the knowledge he was right. To prevent herself from doing something stupid, she walked over to the computer on the table and opened it.

"Don't touch that!" said Martin Rudbeck.

The computer desktop was almost empty, populated only by a few video files. Astrid double-clicked one of them.

27

July 10, morning

Julia Malmros opened her eyes just after ten in the morning, and her mind filled instantly with agitation and a reggae beat. Dim images from the previous evening filtered through her brain. It hadn't been until after one in the morning that Julia had wobbled her way home from Irma's place, and by then she'd been wild and loose. Half as much weed would have been enough.

Puffing on a second joint, she'd sprawled out on the sofa and told the whole story of her miseries with Kim Ribbing, the torments that lived within her. Then things changed, and she wanted to sing more reggae. Julia screwed up her face as she lay in her bed. Unless she was remembering it all wrong, she'd even *danced*.

A great evening. *Without* Ribbing.

Julia huddled up and whimpered a little, feeling sorry for herself yet despising herself for self-pity. She'd made her own choice, after all, and surely weed wasn't *that* dangerous, was it? The most humiliating part was that Irma had been cool, calm, and collected the whole time Julia was going wild. That nasty old lady probably remembered every painful detail. That sweet, beloved nasty old lady.

Julia reached out and stroked the pillow where Kim's head had rested during the days of their bloodstorm. That was the only time he'd been in her apartment. They'd been together at her summer cabin and in his new villa and, for heaven's sake, in a helicopter over the North Sea. Julia squeezed her eyes shut and recalled their devouring kiss beneath the thump of the helicopter's rotors.

Good Lord, Julia. You're turning into a cheap romance novel.

She pushed her legs over the edge of the bed and sat staring for a while. Her head felt twice as heavy as usual. She slowly sank to the floor. She had a bird's-eye vision of herself as Donald Duck on a camping vacation. If only Mickey Mouse could press a button on the camping trailer wall to lower her into a bathtub and instantly serve up a piping hot breakfast.

Ugh. No, not breakfast. Her stomach felt incapable of it, and her guts were choked with old smoke. But coffee, yes, real coffee. Julia clutched the bedpost, pulled herself up to her feet, and put on her morning robe. She found her mobile phone on the coffee table in the living room. No missed calls, no messages. She sniffled, then opened Spotify to play "Two Dark Eyes" by Sven-Ingvars. She hadn't tapped any more than the *Two* into the search field when she slapped the back of her hand and put the phone down. She could hear Irma's voice in her mind: *Get a hold of yourself, girl!*

The chugging of the espresso maker had a calming effect on her, as it usually did. As the coffee gurgled into the cup, she realized she was standing there humming the lyrics about not saying no but rather maybe.

Julia sipped her coffee, staring down toward Järntorget. A woman tourist, probably Japanese, stood with her arm around the shoulders of the statue of Evert Taube as three others snapped photos. What could the Japanese possibly have in common with Evert Taube?

The haze in Julia's brain was beginning to fade, and she was able to take a more sober view of her situation. She hadn't the slightest doubt the previous evening's excesses were related to Kim. Forgetting her preoccupation with their relationship for a moment had been so liberating that she'd flipped out.

Enough of this. A quick shower, another espresso, and then she'd go to his place and make him speak. How did he feel about her, really? Did he want them to be a couple? No matter what he replied, she'd then know what she had to face.

She thought about the lyrics again, about saying maybe rather than no.

Wrong. Say *yes*.

28

July 10, morning

Kim locked the gate, rode his Honda slowly up the gravel drive, and parked it by the front stairs. He used a plastic-enclosed chain to secure the front wheel to the cast-iron railing. He opened the Honda's top case and took out a bag with fresh-baked breakfast bread he'd bought at the Fältöversten shopping center. That purchase was unusual for him, but he'd felt the need for a motorcycle outing.

He wasn't sure what to do about Astrid. Maybe he hadn't been thinking clearly when he offered her the room. Kim had a strong need to protect his privacy. He appreciated Astrid, but her mere presence had a disturbing effect on him. Oh well, maybe he'd change his mind. In any case, they needed a proper discussion.

Kim had a feeling something was wrong as soon as he opened the front door. Something about the villa's atmosphere—it seemed to be holding its breath. He heard the tap running in the kitchen as he went up the stairs. He found Astrid at the sink, splashing water on her face.

"Hi," said Kim. Astrid jumped. "What are you up to?"

Astrid was pale, and her hand was trembling as she turned off the water. She dried her hands and face with a kitchen towel and sagged onto a stool, completely abject.

"What is it?" Kim asked. "Has something happened?"

Astrid released a shuddering sigh and gave Kim a miserable, fearful look. She whispered, "Sorry. Really sorry."

Martin Rudbeck's head was flung back so that his blank eyes met Kim's as soon as he and Astrid stepped into the basement room. The doctor's mouth was frozen in a silent scream and his tongue hung out. The Taser lay on the floor beneath the cot.

It wasn't hard to figure out what had happened.

It took a lot to make Kim Ribbing lose his composure, but this time he stood there with his arms dangling, stunned that his carefully prepared plans had gone up in smoke. The doctor was supposed to be released, to be a free man in an hour or two. Now he was difficult to deal with, considering that he was stone dead.

"Sorry," Astrid said again behind Kim. "*Really* sorry. I opened that video, saw what they were doing to that child, and how he, that guy there . . . everything went black. I don't remember how it happened, but I guess I must have . . . pressed the button."

"Fuck," said Kim. "*Fuck.* You understand what you've gotten your-self into?"

"Yeah, I understand. I didn't mean to."

"How did you even get *in* here?"

"I, like, happened to . . . find the keys."

Kim put his hands on his hips and drilled his gaze into Astrid's eyes. Her lower lip quivered, but she didn't back down. "Astrid," Kim said, "from now on you and I must be completely honest with one another. There's not a chance in the universe that you *happened* to find those keys."

That did it. Astrid looked away, her eyes jumpy as she stared around the floor. "Okay. I looked for them. Heard you talking with someone down here, and I got . . . curious."

Kim shook his head and detached the alligator clips from Martin Rudbeck's ear and little toe, picked up the Taser box, and reeled the filaments back into it. Here it was—the murder weapon. Kim ran his eyes over the doctor's body. Even in death it gave off a foul, sweaty odor. He rubbed his eyes. "Damn. Hell. Shit!"

"Really sorry," said Astrid. She shuffled across the floor toward him, looked up, and met his eyes. "But I'll help out."

"Help out . . . with what?"

"Well, we gotta get rid of him. Somehow. Don't we?"

Kim circled the cot, staring down at the body of the person he'd probably despised more than anyone else in the world. He was unmoved by the fact that the doctor was dead; in Vamlinge he'd spent a good deal of time imagining execution methods significantly more drawn out and painful than a single jolt of electricity. No, his objections were purely pragmatic. It was horribly *impractical* to have a corpse on his hands. Not to mention the fact that any potential prison sentence would be tripled or quadrupled by the crime of kidnapping.

Astrid looked at him timidly. "What are we going to do? Any ideas?"

Kim put a hand to his forehead. "Listen, you—I don't know! No matter what you may assume about me, I've never found myself in a situation like this. Why the *hell* would you do this, Astrid?"

"I said, didn't I? I blacked out. And, besides, why did you have him here anyway?"

"I had questions."

"Did you get answers?"

"No. And I sure won't get them now."

They stood there for a long time, staring at the corpse, as if holding a wake or observing a minute of silence. Astrid's hand tentatively grasped Kim's. He let it happen. He had no moral objection to the fact that Martin Rudbeck had died in his underground room, but now they had to focus on Astrid. What would happen to her if this became known? Psychiatric confinement was the most likely outcome. As for him, he'd rather die than be locked up again.

Astrid wrinkled her nose as she surveyed the convulsed, strapped-down body. Then she said, "Maybe we should cut him up?"

Kim could hardly believe his ears. He looked down at Astrid, who was still holding his hand, and said, *"We?"*

"Yeah," Astrid said. "I think I know a whole lot more about butchering than you do."

29

July 10, morning

Jonny Munther's participation in the Knektholmen murder investigation was mostly done. He'd sat in on the many long interrogations of Frode Moe and Bruce Li. Between them, the two had accumulated an impressive number of charges, including conspiracy to murder, illegal threats, attempted murder, and illegal incarceration. Add to those the business dealings under investigation by the financial crimes unit as attorneys and prosecutors prepared for what would inevitably be a lengthy trial. There was lots of digging to be done, but those excavations were not assigned to Detective Superintendent Jonny Munther but to others. Meanwhile, he sat at his desk and contemplated the Marc Chagall poster of the embracing couple hovering above the rooftops.

First-time visitors to Jonny's office might be taken aback by the sight of that poster, since it seemed so out of sync with his character. In fact, it was a vestige of an earlier time and earlier life, from the very first years of his marriage to Julia Malmros. Back when Jonny still believed in true love. He should have taken it down a long time ago, but that just hadn't happened. Jonny sneered a bit at the ecstatic turtle doves. *Tacky. Really should get rid of the thing.*

His phone rang. Jonny picked it up, grateful to be distracted from a train of thought threatening to lock him in a session of angry regrets. A woman's voice on the other end: "Oh, hi, this is Moa. Moa Malmberg. Maybe you remember me?"

Oh, yes. Jonny remembered her very well. Moa was a forensic lab tech, and their paths had crossed in quite remarkable circumstances a couple of years earlier, an apartment murder where the police had found a puppy with blood on its fur. Since the puppy was material evidence, Jonny had taken it to the lab, where he held the trembling creature with both hands as Moa carefully swabbed it for blood samples. The woman who owned the little dog was dead and her husband was behind bars, so Jonny felt he had no choice; he took the dog home and looked for a family to adopt it. Jonny remembered Moa's warm, approving look when he offered to foster the puppy for the interim.

"Sure," said Jonny into his phone. "Of course I do. How are you doing?"

"Okay, really. Okay. How did things turn out with the puppy?"

Jonny laughed at that. "A trustworthy colleague wanted it, so I thought it'd do just fine with him and his family."

"Aha. That's great."

Moa's end of the conversation felt a bit forced; maybe she was nervous. Jonny seemed to remember that Moa's husband had passed away a year before the incident with the dog, and Moa had worried about the poor little animal. She and Jonny were about the same age, but Moa was so slight and short that she looked considerably younger.

"I'm guessing," said Jonny, "that you're not calling just to inquire about . . . canine health?"

"Oh, right, sure," said Moa. "Exactly. Well, that is, I just wanted to hear about you. I mean . . . oh, God, am I fourteen years old again? So, listen. Would you like to have coffee or something? Sometime?"

Jonny's eyebrows rose. This was just about the last thing he'd expected, and his mind went blank. The comment about whether she was fourteen—was this some kind of invite? As far as he could remember, Jonny had never been . . . invited. He had no idea how to respond.

"But maybe you don't," Moa added quickly. "Maybe not interested, maybe not . . . perhaps it's not a good time at all, I mean . . ."

"Yeah, sure!" Jonny dug up his answer. "It's as good a time as any. A fine time. Prime time, outstanding as a penthouse overlooking Stureplan." He winced. People usually didn't understand his jokes.

It was a relief when Moa giggled and said, "Terrific. When can you? And where can you?"

They agreed to get together that same afternoon at the Fridhemsplan underground station, and then they'd improvise. Maybe a stroll followed by a coffee, or the other way around. After their goodbyes, Jonny sat motionless for a long time, staring at his mobile phone. Then his eyes turned to the poster on the wall. *Well, then. Might as well leave it up there for the time being.*

Jonny had just saved Moa's name and number in his contact list when he heard voices in the corridor outside his office. He got up and went to see what was going on.

A short, odd-looking, half-balding overweight man stood flailing at Christof Adler, who was holding up his hands and urging calm. The man, in his forties, wore a pair of rimless glasses that had slipped a bit awry.

"Excuse me," said Jonny Munther. "What's going on here?"

"Who's this gentleman?" asked the man self-righteously. Instead of losing his calm, Jonny simply answered, "Jonny Munther, detective superintendent. And you, sir?"

"Aha," said the pudgy man. "*Superintendent.* That's something quite different than this . . . this here . . . *assistant* fellow."

"His title is the entry-level rank, not a description of his duties."

"Whatever," the man said. "In any case, this assistant has adamantly refused to take this case seriously."

Christof Adler threw up his hands and tried to explain, but the DS stopped him with a gesture. "The gentleman's name, please? And what is this about a *case?*"

"My name is Wilmer Syd, and I telephoned this *assistant* a couple of days ago to report that my friend and colleague Martin Rudbeck has disappeared. Later this fellow came back to me with the most unbelievable explanations, but not one of them is true." Wilmer Syd started to get excited again. "First, I was told that Martin was supposedly in *Thailand*, which was absolutely mad, and when I succeeded in calling his phone, a different person answered, a man who simply found the phone in his carry-on bag."

"And how had it gotten there?" asked the detective superintendent.

"That is *your* job to investigate," snarled Wilmer Syd. "But when I called the *assistant* to inform him, it wasn't long before I was informed that Martin had been confirmed to be at Danderyd Hospital instead, and he is *not* there, so I've come up here myself, because if I telephone again, I'll probably be told it was all a misunderstanding and Martin is in fact on the moon!"

Wilmer Syd huffed and puffed and wiped his sweaty forehead on his sleeve, readying himself for another salvo. Carmen Sánchez stepped up to the group. To protect Christof, she declared, "*I* was the one who called the hospital, and they confirmed he should be in the isolation ward of the infectious diseases unit."

"Right!" cried Wilmer Syd. "Admitted for *Ebola*! Have you ever heard of such a thing?"

"They wouldn't give me his diagnosis," said Carmen. "But they did confirm he'd been admitted."

"Uh-huh, right!" said Wilmer Syd. "I don't know what fantastic sources you use, but I have my own contacts at Danderyd. It wasn't easy, but my colleague was eventually able to gain access to the infectious diseases section, dressed head to toe in protective equipment, to see with his own eyes. Yes, Martin is registered, *but he isn't there.*"

"Might he have been moved?" asked Jonny Munther.

Wilmer Syd shook his head so emphatically that two sweat drops flew from his brow and hit the floor. "No! There's no medical record of a transfer. He's registered in the isolation ward and he simply is not there."

"All this is really strange," said Christof Adler in his first involvement in the conversation other than being targeted for his ignorance. "I spoke with a neighbor in Täby, across from Rudbeck's villa, and she reported that Martin Rudbeck had been taken away in an ambulance. Maybe he's at some other hospital?"

"Then why would he be registered at Danderyd?" asked Wilmer Syd. "No, this is a conspiracy to hide the fact he was abducted."

"Abducted?" said Jonny Munther.

"Yes. Kidnapped, deprived of his liberty, I don't know your technical term. Carried off against his will. Maybe in an ambulance."

"Has there been any sort of . . . demand?" asked Carmen Sánchez.

"Don't ask me!" Wilmer Syd exclaimed. "It's not as if I'm a spider in a web, sitting by my phone and waiting for a kidnapper to call!"

"Does he have any relatives who might have received a ransom demand?" asked Jonny Munther. "If, hypothetically speaking, we suppose that this is in fact a kidnapping?"

"Martin has no family," said Wilmer Syd, adding with a touch of reverence, "he lives for his work."

"Have you visited his residence?" asked Jonny Munther.

"I don't have a key," Wilmer Syd told him. "But I've gone there several times and rung the bell. Why?"

Jonny Munther cleared his throat. "It could be that he's at home, so to speak, but is unable to come to the door."

"He might be ill, you mean?"

"Yes. Or . . . the other possibility."

"No, no, no. Martin was as healthy as could be, and if you're suggesting he might have taken his own life, you can just forget that. Not a chance. And if so, what's the meaning of this whole story about an ambulance and admission to Danderyd? And the fact his phone flew off to Thailand all by itself? No, no. Some cunning devil must have planned all this."

"Mm-hmm," replied Jonny Munther. "But if you'll excuse me, first I'll phone my colleagues in Täby and ask them to enter his residence before we undertake any further action in the matter."

"But I'm telling you that—"

"It's standard procedure," interrupted Jonny Munther, who'd gotten tired of this Wilmer Syd. The man had something stubbornly intrusive about him, as if he couldn't tolerate the fact that the police weren't investing all their resources when *his friend* might have disappeared. "Would you like to wait here?" invited Jonny Munther. "Or should I . . . ?"

"I will wait here," declared Wilmer Syd, straightening up. With a side glance at Christof Adler, he added, "Now that I finally have your attention. If I go home, you'll probably take a couple of days to come up with some new wild tale."

"Allow me to assure you that we do not make up wild tales here," said Jonny Munther. He gestured to a doorway. "Be so kind as to wait in the conference room."

After Wilmer Syd departed, Christof Adler said, "Sorry, but you need to understand that the reports I received—"

"I understand exactly," said Jonny Munther. "You've done nothing wrong. Now I must go phone Täby."

About an hour later Jonny Munther invited Wilmer Syd into his office to report a missing person. The Täby police had gone into the villa and found no trace of the doctor. Nor any note from him.

Jonny Munther brought up the current form on his computer and asked, "When was the last time you saw or spoke to Martin Rudbeck?"

As he tapped in the answer, he glanced at the Chagall poster, but he returned to the form when busybody Wilmer Syd asked why he was smiling. Did he find this situation comic?

30

July 10, daytime

Kim almost couldn't believe it, but Astrid went through the villa collecting tools and other items that might be useful in carving up Martin Rudbeck.

She was functioning better than she had for a long time. She had a mission, a problem to take care of. All her agonies and self-hatred were forgotten; she focused with tunnel vision on the problem of the corpse. Astrid felt she'd been liberated. That was absurd, of course, but nevertheless she embraced the sensation.

She and Kim had lined up a saw, an axe, knives, and pliers on the workbench. Kim took out two coveralls of thin plastic. He held out one to Astrid. "Here. Looks like this is going to be messy."

Astrid nodded. The coverall rustled as she pulled it on. She looked down at her hands. They seemed disconnected from the rest of her body as if remote controlled. They were numb. A slight trembling was the only sign they were living flesh. Would she really be able to manage cutting up a human being? How traumatic would that be? Something told her it'd be no worse than what had happened on Midsummer Eve.

"Kim?" she said. Her voice was *almost* steady.

"Mm-hmm?"

"What's it like? Can a traumatic experience get worse? Is it like a bag that just gets fuller and fuller, or if someone's experienced an awful trauma, is that it—finished, all done—and nothing worse can happen?"

"Not so sure, but I think it's like that bag."

"Ah. I see."

Astrid looked at Martin Rudbeck's dead body on the cot, that tongue still protruding. The old guy was disgusting, but what she was about to do to him was even more horrid. Not *him,* she corrected herself. *It. The body.*

The plan was for Astrid to cut the body open to expose the bones, and then Kim would cut it into pieces with a saw. Astrid raised the scalpel in her hand and stepped toward the cot. Where should she begin? At the shoulder? The elbow? The wrists? She turned to look at Kim and almost fainted. She had to step to one side to keep from collapsing.

"How . . . how little should the pieces be?" she asked.

Kim shrugged. "The smaller the better, I guess."

Astrid felt her stomach heave. "Mm-hmm. And then?"

"Then you bury it. Or sink it. Maybe both, in locations far from one another. I don't know. I guess that's how it's done if you're conscientious."

"Conscientious, right," said Astrid. "Sounds good."

"Can you manage?" asked Kim. He held up the saw. "If not, I'll just—"

"No, I'm okay," said Astrid, waving the scalpel and almost slicing her own hand. "It was my fault, I must . . . it's just, well, you know, so, so . . . *now.*"

Astrid took a deep breath and turned back to the job. She peered at the laid-out corpse, clenched her jaws, stepped forward, and pushed the scalpel into the crook of Martin Rudbeck's—*its*—arm. It slid smoothly into the soft flesh but then met resistance from a sinew or maybe a bone. Astrid gasped and let loose. The embedded scalpel sagged, then slipped out of the body and fell to the floor with a clatter. Since the heart wasn't beating, blood oozed in a slow, thick flow from the cut, drawn by gravity. Astrid covered her face with her hands. "Damn, damn!"

"We'll have to come up with something else," Kim said.

"No, no!" Astrid replied in a choked voice from behind her hands. "This is the best way. It's . . . conscientious. I need to do it, that's all. Damn!"

Astrid sought to take a deep breath but instead started to hyperventilate. Bright points of light danced before her eyes. She leaned forward, putting her hands on her thighs. Once her breathing steadied and her vision began to clear, she straightened up. "I'm completely opposed to killing and slaughtering animals, you know that."

"Right. That did come to my attention."

"Mm, but *purely theoretically* I'd thought that killing a human being and, like, cutting the person up . . . you could defend it if the person kind of *deserved* it. Evil deeds, I mean. You understand? You can't say that about animals, since they can't make moral decisions. That's what I thought. Theoretically."

"But as to applying it in practice . . ." said Kim, waving the saw. "Does this mean you're in favor of capital punishment?"

"No. No, I certainly am not. But in this case"—Astrid didn't look at the corpse but waved a hand in its direction—"it's already happened. How about you? Are you for the death penalty?"

Kim rubbed his chin with his free hand. "Let's say that I accept the proposition that certain persons deserve to die. But I don't think the government should execute people. So, no."

"Okay," said Astrid and finally succeeded in drawing the deep breath she'd been struggling for. She squatted and picked up the scalpel. She used it to point to Martin Rudbeck. "And that guy? Did he deserve to die?"

"You could probably say that."

"Why? Tell me, and maybe this will be easier."

Kim came forward and stood beside Astrid to get a better view of Martin Rudbeck's convulsed face and agonized expression. Kim grimaced. "He tortured children. He liked watching while others tortured children. The suffering of children pleased him, gave him release. He was the worst sort of human being."

"Okay," whispered Astrid and lifted the scalpel. "Okay, then." Her hand trembled slightly as she put the blade to the incision she'd started.

Just as the point entered the slit, Kim put a hand on her arm. "Astrid. Stop."

Astrid raised the scalpel, sighed, and said, "I can't."

"No, you can't. I know."

"You knew all along, didn't you?"

"I guessed."

"Why did you let me try, then?"

"So you'd know that you'd done all you could."

"I'm only fourteen, Kim."

"I know that."

"If you had kids, I wonder what they'd be like. After the way you grew up."

"I'm not planning to have children. That's one of the reasons."

Kim and Astrid stood there in their white plastic coveralls, staring down at the stretched-out corpse, holding their unused tools. It wasn't just a corpse; it was a *threat* far greater than its diminished presence. The pale, loose skin positively reeked of interrogations, trials, and long-term imprisonment. All of which constituted Martin Rudbeck's legacy, last will, and testament.

At that very moment a deafening rumble was heard. The heavy sliding door was pulled aside, and Julia Malmros appeared. She took a single step into the room but froze at the sight. She stood gasping for breath for a couple of seconds and her teeth began to chatter. At last she managed to exclaim, "Good God, what do you two think you're *doing*?"

31

July 10, daytime

Julia had gotten off the number 69 bus to Djurgårdsbrunnsvägen at the corner with Lidovägen ten minutes earlier. After it departed, she turned and saw the Kaknäs tower stretching impressively toward the heavens. The tower had been closed to the public because of an "elevated threat level" and now was no more than an unnecessarily elaborate telecommunications mast.

An elevated threat level.

That same general warning obliged people to present IDs to gain access to any broadcasting studio. TV4, for example. That thought reminded her of the awful Åsa Fors series, which in turn brought to mind the "heightened reality" label.

"Heightened reality," Julia Malmros said under her breath. "Elevated threat level, elevated goddamned . . . heightening."

She shook her shoulders and tried to redirect her thoughts as she walked along Lidovägen. The summer was at its zenith. Everything was green and fragrant under the cascading sunlight. She tried to get herself in tune with her surroundings. No luck. The notion of elevated threats had fixed itself in her mind. If anything was causing an elevated threat level, it was her relationship with Kim.

When Julia was in the mood to torment herself, as it seemed she currently was, she would recall how she'd forced herself on Kim at the summer cabin. It had seemed like a good idea at the time, but she'd been deeply ashamed afterward. Kim had mentioned the incident only once, but for Julia it persisted, an invisible brand of shame across her abdomen.

Julia left the street and entered a grove, where she cast herself on a bed of last year's leaves and stared up into the treetops. This just wouldn't do. She couldn't turn up at Kim's place in a fret, as sour as a dirty dishrag; she had to gain control of her thoughts. Julia closed her eyes and inhaled the scent of greenery. What was happening within her, really? She was probably scared. When she got frightened, she became angry, and that made her sad.

So? Stop being scared.

Easier said than done. But okay, what was she scared of? That Kim didn't want to have her around. Okay. And why did that frighten her? Because he was so unpredictable and she didn't know how she was supposed to talk to him or interpret his answers. Okay again. But even if Kim had his problems because of his background, he was still a fully sensible, rational person. He didn't have to share everything. Only a child or a crazy person does that.

Julia gathered a handful of dry leaves. They crackled when she clenched her fist around them. The bloodstorm had turned her into an irrational person unable to control her own impulses. Just look at her! Not so long ago, she'd been an esteemed writer of detective fiction, confident of herself on lecture panels and in salons, and now she was lying in a heap of leaves, her heart pulsing with panic.

Goddamned Kim Ribbing!

Julia flapped both hands, sending leaves flying, and sat up. *Basta ya.* She'd read enough about mythology to understand what she'd just done, even though unintentionally. She'd died and buried herself. A different Julia now arose and brushed leaves from her clothing, born anew. A woman not afraid to walk right up to Kim Ribbing and demand a straight answer, whatever it might be.

Okay, then. Julia wasn't one of those tree huggers whose belief in transition rites was so strong that she thought she'd truly been transformed, but she walked with a steadier step as she set off down the street toward the villa. She got to the gate and fished out the key she'd gotten from Kim. The lock was rusty, and as she wrestled to get the key to turn, she noticed that a couple of the vertical bars were slightly bent. She wasn't sure if that was new, so thought nothing more of it. The gate opened.

Still fortified in the "new" Julia's body, she went up the gravel drive and saw Kim's Honda chained to the stair railing, evidence he was at home. Her pulse accelerated, but what had she been expecting? To do something as cowardly as leaving a voicemail message? Telephone from the front yard and run away? No, sir, face-to-face was the new Julia's tune.

Her mind was so intent on how best to explain her mission that she was almost unaware she'd unlocked the front door. Only when she stepped into the abandoned office space did she pause, gather herself, and command her thundering heart to slow down. As she stood there with her arms across her chest, she noticed a door that had escaped her attention before. It was evident now because it was standing open. Julia went to it and found a stairway leading down to darkness.

"Ho, ho . . ." she said under her breath, as if afraid to awaken something in the dark that might come tearing up the stairs. No answer came, so she took a first tentative step downward. Then another. Julia's pupils widened in reaction to the dimness as she descended, holding her arms out so her fingertips brushed along the rough cement walls. At last she stepped onto a cement floor. Odors of earth and iron floated in the humid air, and the basement was considerably cooler than upstairs. A glint of light came through a gap along a metal sliding door, and Julia heard faint voices inside. She thought about repeating her "ho, ho," but instead allowed the *former*

Julia, the one who'd been a police officer, to take over. She went to the door and pulled it open.

For a moment she was deafened by the rumble of the door and blinded by the bright light inside. She stepped into the room, then halted. She saw what lay there, and all her reassuring thoughts about Kim Ribbing as a rational person were blown away.

32

July 10, daytime

"Good God, what do you two think you're *doing*?"

Astrid looked at the scalpel in her hand and the thin white plastic covering her arm, as if the answer to Julia Malmros's question might be written there. She came up with nothing. Her gaze turned to Martin Rudbeck's gaping mouth. No answer from it either.

Something happened in Astrid's mind. For some time now she'd been imagining herself in a tunnel, her eyes on a single goal, and that had been reassuring, almost comfortable. Now it was as if the tunnel had been enclosed by black plastic sheeting that Julia Malmros's question had torn open to let in the harsh light of reality. Yes, what *did* Astrid think she was doing?

Julia took another step, her gaze riveted on Martin Rudbeck's body, her lips quivering and her face distorted in a grimace. She stabbed one trembling finger toward the corpse. "Is he . . . dead?"

"Yep," said Kim, taking the scalpel from Astrid's hand, then depositing it and the saw on the table.

"Who . . . who?" asked Julia, pressing her hands to her stomach.

"Martin Rudbeck."

"The man who . . . who . . . ?"

"Yes," said Kim. "The man who."

Julia seemed to have run out of questions. She stood with hands to her belly, rigid as a statue. *Press and release, press and release.* She was breathing as if practicing CPR on herself. Her lips twitched but not a sound came out.

Astrid swallowed and inhaled, about to explain what she'd done, but Kim cut her off. "I killed him. It was an accident. But I killed him."

Julia's eyes went from Kim to Astrid to Martin Rudbeck before she released her hold on her gut and said, "But how . . . how can you involve Astrid in this? How could you?"

"It was a mistake."

Astrid wanted so much to protest and confess her own lethal involvement, and if she'd still been in the tunnel, she probably would have, but now the light burned away all certainty. Julia's question hit the nail on the head: Astrid *literally* did not understand what she was doing, and her head began to spin. She saw herself standing on the roof of a skyscraper, staring down at crowds urging her to jump.

Julia shook her head. "Accident? Mistake? That doesn't sound like you, Kim."

"Guess not, but that's how it is."

"Astrid!" snapped Julia.

"Mm-hmm?" said Astrid, mentally holding herself by the collar to keep away from the edge.

Julia pointed sternly to the door. "Leave here, Astrid. Now. Wait for me outside the house. I won't be long."

Astrid looked at Kim. He nodded. Julia was still pointing toward the door, and Astrid willingly took that direction out of the pathless, collapsing landscape around her. When she was about to pass Julia, the older woman snapped, "Coverall!"

A terribly creepy feeling lodged in Astrid's chest as she pulled off the thin plastic. Now that the corpse was behind her and she could no longer see it, she was convinced the dead body was staring at *her* instead. Accusing. Threatening her.

I'll track you down.

Astrid couldn't pull off the rustling plastic fast enough. She left it on the floor. She didn't dare look around as she raced up the stairs, because her irrational mind warned her that she'd see Martin Rudbeck stand up and pursue her. Possessed by panic, she took the stairs two at a time.

She had trouble breathing when she got outside. She pounded her chest with a fist. Then she took out her mobile and stabbed her rubbery thumbs against the screen to call Walter, her psychologist.

33

July 10, daytime

Julia and Kim stood staring at one another across the corpse of Martin Rudbeck. So it had come to this. During her years in the field, Julia had seen her share of dead bodies, and she was only slightly disturbed by the sight. No, it was the combination of the corpse, Kim, and, above all, Astrid that had plunged her into such a state of shock.

Julia became calm, frighteningly calm, after Astrid vanished up the stairs. The former Julia had stepped into her shoes, and that Julia was surveying a crime scene with a perpetrator and a victim. Simple as that.

"Kim," said Julia with steely calm. "What were you planning?"

"As I said," replied Kim, "it was an accident. I hadn't planned it."

"No. What *had* you planned?"

"To release him."

"How did he get here?"

Kim shrugged. "I brought him."

Julia assumed a much more complicated chain of events was hidden behind that brief reply, but that was immaterial for the moment. She stepped forward, stared Kim in the eyes, and said, "And how . . . what in *hell* were you thinking when you got Astrid involved in this?"

Kim didn't look away. His gaze was calm. "She wanted to help."

Julia could hardly believe her ears. "Now you've made her an accomplice. You understand that?"

Kim nodded. A faint smile played over his lips. "But not if no one finds out."

Julia squeezed her eyes shut in pain. Thinking was hard enough, and just a few minutes ago, she'd lain in a heap of leaves and decided to appeal to Kim Ribbing's rational mind. Now here she was, in front of a person whose aim was to get away with murder. Julia's eyes were still closed as she heard, first, a rustling and then Kim's voice. "Are you planning to report this?"

Julia opened her eyes to find Kim close to her. His black hair, earlier held back with a hairband, now fell across the shoulders of his white coverall. Something about his pale face in that frame made Julia think *Angel of Death.*

Julia studied Kim's large, light-blue eyes. "If I say yes, will you kill me too?"

From the moment Julia had entered the underground room, Kim had manifested a stoic, almost apathetic calm that nothing could disturb. But now his eyes blazed, he straightened up, and he clutched his head. "What kind of a thing is that to say? Of course I won't. What can you be *thinking* of me? I just want to know . . . what I must deal with. Good God, Julia, you shouldn't say things like that."

Julia's voice became ice cold. "That's hard to know. What I can or can't say. Since I don't know who you are. I never have."

Kim made an annoyed gesture, as if Julia was quibbling about trivialities. "All that's for later. I just want to know if you're planning to report it."

"And my answer is that I don't know. I'm not interested in getting involved. And there's probably not going to be any . . . *later.* This is mad, Kim, and I want no part of it."

"But you're going to tell on me?"

Julia snorted. With a change of words, Kim had moved her from "reporting" him to snitching on him. She refused to be moved by his implied suggestion she might be a *squealer.* Instead, she said, "I don't know, Kim. I do not know. You'll have to be satisfied with that. Now I must take care of Astrid."

Julia turned on her heel and went to the door. Kim's voice came just as she reached it.

"Julia?"

She stopped but didn't turn around. "Yes?"

"Why did you come here?"

The true reason for Julia's visit had disappeared without a trace. When she thought back, she couldn't help heaving a shuddering sigh. "That was in another life." Then she went up the stairs.

Julia found Astrid sitting on a bench outside. Her head was down and she was clutching her mobile phone in both hands. Julia sat next to her and patted her back. "Are you all right?"

"Not so good," said Astrid in a choked voice. "Called my shrink. He said to come over. He's on vacation. He's a nice man."

"I met him, didn't I? Walter?"

"Mmm."

"Seemed to be a good person."

"He is."

They sat together in silence, and Julia felt that, for the moment, they were sharing a terrible fate, dragged into the same situation through no fault of their own. After a while, Astrid looked up to Julia and spoke directly to her for the first time ever. "Julia?"

"Yes?"

"A psychologist is sworn to silence, right? Can I tell him? About this?"

Even though it was probably discouraging news for Astrid, Julia felt obliged to tell the truth. "If a serious crime has been committed, a psychologist can break confidentiality. He's not *obliged* to do so. But it's allowed."

Astrid nodded and slumped further into herself. "It's not that important. If I don't tell him."

"That's up to you."

No matter how unfortunate it was to put that responsibility on Astrid's shoulders, Julia felt a bit of relief the decision wasn't her own to make. If Astrid told her Walter fellow, he'd probably go to the police. He had no reason not to do so, considering that Kim had dragged Astrid into his own mad mess.

Julia suddenly wanted to burst into tears over how everything had gone to hell so suddenly, but she straightened her back and asked Astrid, "How will you get there? To Walter?"

Astrid made a vague gesture toward the street. "Bus, I suppose. And underground."

Julia took out her mobile. "Not on your life. I'm calling a taxi, and I'll go with you, okay? To make sure you get there."

Julia tapped in the number for Stockholm Taxi and was put on hold. She felt the weight of Astrid's head on her shoulder and heard the girl whisper, "Thank you, Julia."

34

July 10, daytime

The underground room was extremely quiet after the door at the top of the stairs shut. The faint buzzing of the fluorescent tube overhead was the only sound as Kim contemplated Martin Rudbeck's stark white body. He felt no anger or regret, but rather a profound *irritation* at the fact that this man who had plagued his youth was, with his death, continuing to do so and casting a shadow over his adult life.

Just before his fourteenth birthday, Kim had murdered his mother, father, and grandfather with a homemade, remote-controlled bomb aboard their boat. Holding his Nokia mobile phone, he'd experienced an unearthly feeling of peace when the heat wave from the explosion washed over him as he stood on the lawn of his grandfather's estate. The heavy burden of his crown of thorns broke away, and the fist clutching his heart relaxed its grip. That was then. And there.

It wasn't long before the implications came creeping in. During the years of research and experimenting required to assemble his bomb, Kim had fixated only on that goal, a huge blast to clean house and liberate him. It did, too, but at a price. Deep regrets began to hound him and deprive him of sleep, and there was nothing he could do about them. Nightmares came for him when he did doze off. He became more and more apathetic. He lay there stiff as a board, his body no more than the container of a silent howl. He started methodically carving slits in his skin for the howl to vent.

He was eventually institutionalized at Vamlinge, turned over to Martin Rudbeck's care. The next steps in his destruction took place. At first, the electroconvulsive shocks had a certain positive effect. The howling did disappear, but as the strength and frequency of the shock treatments increased, the howl was replaced by an enveloping black cloud under which Kim lay face down, scarcely able to breathe, unable to think coherently. The last session would probably have killed him outright if Rudbeck's assistant hadn't defied the doctor's orders.

Anyhow, he hadn't intended to kill Rudbeck. If that had been the idea, he could have simply let the tetrodotoxin take full effect, leaving Martin Rudbeck to die in his hallway. In his current frame of mind, he wouldn't have killed his parents either. His grandfather, maybe, but not his parents. Not that he missed them, but he now understood they'd been a couple of disgusting people who'd allowed his grandfather to have his fun in exchange for lavish financial support. He now understood his fourteen-year-old self, and none of that could be changed.

Only fragments of his parents had been recovered, while his grandfather had disappeared entirely. Probably sucked straight down to hell. Kim put one index finger to his lips and lightly tapped Martin Rudbeck's shoulder with the other.

"How about an explosion, Martin? Would that suit you?"

There was something alluring about that idea, but Kim had no interest in undertaking everything necessary to blast the corpse into manageable bits. It had been heartless of him to let Astrid try her approach, but the truth was that he'd been furious at her. Enough. Forget all that.

A properly placed explosive charge would do the job far more effectively and in a fraction of a second. Kim had good contacts via the internet, so it wouldn't be a problem to acquire the necessary material; no, the problem was in determining time and place. When and where do you blow a corpse to bits without someone hearing and dogs coming along later to sniff out DNA traces in the dust? Add to that the problem of transporting the body to the selected location.

Kim sank onto the chair, pressed his palms to his temples, and racked his brain, imagining drone views of deserted locations, in several of which he'd fought during his time with SSF, Stockholm Street Fighting. He grinned a little when his inner eye lingered over the place where he'd had his last battle. Kymlinge underground station had never been placed in service. That would be a thing—blow Martin Rudbeck sky high on the platform where the Silver Arrow, the underground train with its cargo of the dead, was rumored to stand. Wouldn't do, though; the explosion would be heard throughout the surrounding area.

While much of Kim's mind continued to hover above Stockholm spread out like a Google map, another part began to formulate an alternative. No matter how attractive the notion of a blast might be, to Kim it still seemed all too . . . barbaric. His snatching of Martin Rudbeck had been elegant, and an idea began to form, suggesting how to get rid of him with a certain finesse.

Kim got up, went to his computer, and called up the phony Pac-Man game that served as the port to the HackPack, a community of the like-minded who were experts in navigating the dark side of the web. As usual, Kim sighed in annoyance as he saw the little yellow figure moving along his path without managing to devour even a single dot. Experts, okay, but nerds as well. Kim checked the log and double-clicked a dot five down and two to the right. He was in.

Kim spent a short time saying hello and making caustic remarks. HackPack members weren't generally too given to small talk, and the only new item Kim snapped up was that the mysterious "Ces" was thought to have infiltrated the Riksbank, Sweden's central bank. The management had succeeded in hiding from the public the fact that, for a few minutes on July 8, interest rates had shot up to 3,000 percent. Although the problem had quickly been detected and dealt with, it had caused serious disruption in the money markets.

Someone claiming to have insider information wrote that the only reason they were able to fix the bug at all was that Ces had *let* them. This had been nothing but a warning shot. If Ces had intended it, the stock market would be in the sewer by now.

Kim admitted that this was interesting, and he'd be happy to hear more news about this Ces person, but right now he had a much more concrete problem. Could someone advise him how to create a person? Kim thought for a moment and added that he was not interested in any wisecracks about the birds and the bees.

35

July 10, afternoon

"You can take this case, Christof."

Jonny Munther was wearing a lightweight beige jacket Christof had never seen before, and the DS had slicked his graying hair back along the temples. Unless Christof was mistaken, Jonny Munther even had a whiff of some eau de cologne that might very well be Old Spice. Christof wasn't about to tell the DS he looked like a farmer on a holiday visit to Stockholm.

"Me?" said Christof Adler. "I've never, well, how to say it . . . led an investigation."

Jonny Munther grinned and slapped him on the back. "I don't think we need to stretch it that far. A person may be missing, true, but there's no *investigation* going on yet. Not even close. Gather the loose ends and then we'll see."

"Okay," said Christof, rubbing his neck. "Don't really know how to begin, that's all . . ."

Jonny nodded toward Carmen Sánchez's office. "Get Carmen to give you a hand, if she has time. She knows the ropes. Got to go now."

"May someone ask where?"

"No, someone may not."

Jonny Munther walked down the corridor, leaving after him a fragrant trail of the scent that Dad—or, better, Granddad—used to wear.

Christof hadn't needed to ask. The detective superintendent might just as well have been wearing a neon sign on his forehead flashing *Date! Date!* Christof very much doubted it had anything whatsoever to do with Tinder.

Christof stood there for a while, chewing on his thumbnail. He was confident he was acquainted with a fair number of the ropes, but even so, he didn't feel entirely prepared. He walked to Carmen's office. The door was open, but he rapped on the doorframe. Carmen looked up from her computer and gave him a quizzical look.

"Hello," said Christof. "Just wondering if maybe you might have time to take a quick ride? If you want?"

"Aha," said Carmen. "Looking for another one-night stand?"

Carmen enjoyed teasing Christof and pretending he was attracted to her. It never failed: Christof felt a warm blush climbing his cheeks. The reason Carmen's taunts worked so well was that Christof *was* attracted to her. Only, not like that. Okay, maybe a little, but he was happy with his Cecilia and would never think of putting his settled existence in danger the way some men did.

Christof refused to take the bait. "It's about this Martin Rudbeck guy."

"The one in the hospital? Infectious diseases ward?"

"Right, that's him. He's *registered,* but he's not there. It seems an ambulance picked him up at his residence in Täby and then . . . poof! Gone. I checked all the hospitals. He's not anywhere."

Carmen pulled at her lower lip. "An *ambulance?*"

"Mmm. A neighbor saw it."

"And where is that ambulance now?"

"No idea."

Carmen's lip got another pull, then she rose and put on the uniform jacket she'd hung over the back of her chair. "We'll go talk to the neighbor."

"Do you have time for that?" asked Christof.

Carmen nodded toward her computer. "Complaints of burglaries in a summer cabin area. Lists of stolen items. Any idea of the percentage of those we're likely to clear up?"

"Lower than the percentage for parliamentary representation?"

"Mm-hmm. More like equal to the Donald Duck party percentage."

They stepped out into the hall where the scent of Jonny Munther's aftershave lingered in the air. Christof sniffed loudly. "Recognize that?"

"Yes, thanks very much," said Carmen. "Smelled it all the way back in my office. Saw his . . . *outfit*, as well."

Christof assumed from Carmen's response that she'd drawn the same conclusions as he had about Jonny Munther's lunch excursion, so he simply asked, "Well, what do you think about it?"

Carmen Sánchez pressed the elevator call button and sighed. "I wish our dear detective superintendent all the luck in the world, but unless I'm mistaken, it's been more than thirty years since Jonny went out on a date."

The elevator door opened. Christof nodded up the corridor. "Wasn't that . . . Old Spice?"

Carmen stepped in. "Right. Old Spice. God help us all."

36

July 10, afternoon

Julia and Astrid sat silent in the back of the taxi during most of the trip to Östermalm. They had lots to discuss, but little of that could be done sitting behind the stranger in the driver's seat. When they passed Berwaldhallen, Julia took Astrid's hand and pressed it. "Will you be all right now?"

Astrid neither nodded nor shook her head, but her eyes started to glisten with tears. She whispered, "That was going to be, like . . . my refuge."

Julia knew Astrid was referring to the room in Kim's villa, now forbidden territory. She wished she could offer the girl alternative shelter, but her own flat had no extra room; her office didn't count. Maybe it made Julia a bad person, but she didn't intend to give that room up. It was *her* refuge.

Julia released Astrid's hand, reproached herself, and said, "If you need . . . I have a sofa that's okay to sleep on."

"It's all right," said Astrid. "There's nothing wrong with my uncle, he's just . . ."

Astrid's voice faded away, so Julia didn't learn what Astrid's Uncle Lasse just was. She glanced at the girl staring blankly over the waters of Nybroviken. Astrid could have been her daughter, if Jonny had had his way. Just a few years after they'd graduated from the police academy,

Jonny had started talking about a family. He'd wanted them to have three children.

The time had never been right. Something always got in the way, according to Julia, and the amazing thing was that she herself had believed it. In retrospect she understood she'd simply never wanted to have a child with Jonny, hadn't wanted to fix them together permanently with the epoxy of a new life. Throughout the many years with Jonny, she clung to that self-deception and invented the next difficult situation, the next thing that had to be accomplished *before* they had a child.

As the years passed, Jonny brought up the matter less frequently, finally dropping it completely and withdrawing into himself. Julia thought it wasn't unlikely she herself was responsible for making him the sad, embittered man she finally divorced. She'd destroyed Jonny Munther's dreams and then turned away from the wreckage in disdain. That hadn't been intentional, but when she sometimes faced up to brutal reality, she knew she was to blame. She tried not to think about it.

Only after they'd driven halfway down Strandvägen and turned to the right into Grevgatan did Julia come back to the here and now. The taxi pulled up before a door so elaborately ornamented that it was almost a *portal*. Child psychology, it certainly seemed, wasn't a poor man's game. Astrid probably had a similar thought, for she looked through the taxi window and couldn't help exclaiming, "Huh!"

"You haven't been here before?" asked Julia.

"Nope," said Astrid. "Only to the office."

"You think you can manage it on your own from here?"

Astrid gave a miserable little sniff. "That's just about all I can manage. For now." She opened the door, got out, and turned back. "Thanks for the ride."

"Hold on," said Julia. "Would you like to have my number? Just in case?"

They exchanged addresses and phone numbers. Astrid closed the taxi door and walked to the building entrance. Julia felt strong sympathy for the thin, hunched-over creature who mounted the stairs and pressed a button. New lives aren't the only ones that link us together; extinguished lives can do the same.

"Where to now?" asked the driver, turning halfway around.

"Old Town," said Julia. "Järntorget."

Julia asked to be let off at Skeppsbron, then stood for quite a while with her hands in her pockets as she stared out over the water.

Are you planning to report this?

Every moment that passed without reporting what she'd seen in Kim Ribbing's basement made her that much more responsible, because it gave him time to get rid of the evidence. *Failure to report a crime* was the charge for which Julia was making herself liable as she stood looking out toward Skeppsholmen.

No. That wasn't possible. No matter what Kim had done, Julia couldn't shun him that way, couldn't reduce him to a *perpetrator* whose crime would become a public scandal. All she had to do was imagine lifting her phone, tapping the number, and saying, "Hello, I want to report a murder," to realize that was impossible.

So . . . what was she thinking, then? With a touch of shame, Julia realized she was hoping more than anything that Kim would somehow come up with a clever way to do away with the body and erase all the traces. She was hoping he would *get away with it.* That's how far former Detective Superintendent Julia Malmros had come. *Aiding and abetting a criminal* was another charge that could be added.

Julia rubbed the dazzling sunshine from her eyes, turned her back to Skeppsholmen, and began striding along Södra Bankogränd. The deep shadowed streets between the medieval buildings felt more in tune with her mood than the cool, open expanses of water. When she got to Järntorget, somebody veered around her on an electric bike, the wheel juddering along the cobblestones. Julia stepped aside and almost collided with someone squatting on the pavement and fiddling with a motorcycle. She murmured an apology and continued toward her building. She wondered how long it would be before her awareness returned to normal. For the moment, she was somewhere far away.

Julia tapped in her code and pushed the door open. She didn't notice that the door failed to make the usual click when it settled back into the frame. She was about to start up the staircase when she heard the creak of leather and a hand smelling of grease clamped over her mouth. Hot breath filled her ear as someone behind her murmured, "Now we're going to take things *damned* easy, understand?"

Julia had no choice and nodded as well as she could. She inhaled noisily through her nostrils and mentally searched her own body for anything to use as a weapon. All that occurred to her was that her little keychain could serve as brass knuckles, if only she could extract it from her snug pocket. A violent backward movement, stamp on his foot, elbow across the Adam's apple. She no longer had the moves. For now, there was only a hand over her mouth, so she held herself still to keep this from escalating. She assumed this was the guy who'd been fiddling with his motorcycle in the street. He hadn't been a small man. Anything but.

The pressure over Julia's mouth increased. "You've been snooping around. You need to cut that out."

Julia remembered Jocke Bäckman's words in the Brunkeberg tunnel: *Go digging into all that, and you'll be the one who winds up buried.* She guessed that this was a first step toward that burial. Her heartbeat accelerated, but at the same time she had an ice-cold center that evaluated the situation and concluded that her life was probably not immediately in danger.

Julia said, "Mmpf," and the palm across her mouth loosened its grip; its owner warned her, "Don't do something stupid now."

How many times had she said the same thing during her police career? What constituted "something stupid" was different every time, but the recipient of the warning generally understood unless he was as high as a kite. *Something stupid* in this case probably meant screaming.

Julia's exhalation pushed against greasy skin and returned to her own face as she inquired calmly, "What exactly are you referring to?"

The hand clamped so hard over her mouth that her lower lip was pressed against her teeth and she tasted blood. "I'm *referring*," came the sarcastic, hissed answer, "to the fact you're talking to people you shouldn't be talking to. Lay off all that. Otherwise, you're done. Got it?"

Julia nodded. There was no ambiguity in the situation; she'd known that much the instant the hand had covered her mouth. She'd been aware of the danger, and the only thing that vexed her was that she hadn't been alert enough to be security conscious. Okay, right, on a day like this, maybe that was excusable.

"Good. Just so we're on the same page," the voice said. The hand moved away from Julia's mouth but then pinched her cheek with its thumb and index finger. There was strength in it, no doubt about it. Julia had been considering kicking him in the crotch if she got just a little room, but she now abandoned the idea. Things would turn bad fast if she missed the target. The hand relaxed its grip and the voice gave instructions. "And so you're going to keep standing here just like this. No sneaking a peek, you understand?"

Julia nodded. She hadn't the slightest intention of obeying, but for the moment she wanted only to put an end to this. Steps retreated toward the entrance, and she again heard the creaking of leather. Julia glanced around and saw the Apostates motorcycle club insignia on the back of the biker's jacket. A movement of his shoulder warned her that he was about to turn. She quickly looked forward as before.

A low grunt, followed by the opening and closing of the door. Julia stayed where she was. Half a minute later came the sound of a motorcycle engine starting. Julia stared up into the dark stairwell. That fleeting glance of the man wouldn't be enough to identify him among the club members she'd studied on the internet. But that hardly mattered.

She had no doubt at all that the True Swedes and the Apostates were closely linked. The question was the exact nature of that link, how it functioned, and which points they agreed on.

Julia put her hand to her throat, trying to count her pulse. At least eighty beats per minute. Not so bad, considering that she'd just been assaulted. Even so, she felt fear and adrenaline flooding her body, seeping into her knees and coaxing them to give way. She leaned against the wall and took deep, regular breaths.

What a hell of a day.

Julia couldn't stand the idea of sitting in her apartment and staring at the floor while her mildly traumatized consciousness ran amok. She took another couple of breaths and pushed off from the wall. Then she turned and went to the front door. She couldn't help peering toward the spot where her attacker had been squatting by his bike. Nothing there, of course. But that reassured her a little bit anyway.

On unsteady legs she took herself down Västerlånggatan, maneuvering her way through the streams of tourists, toward Irma Ryding's flat.

37

July 10, afternoon

Astrid Helander made her way up the grand circular stairway that led to the fifth, uppermost floor. There was an elevator, but Astrid wanted to use the slow climb to shake off some of what had happened to her at street level. Or, rather, well below street level.

She thought it was weird, but the memory that haunted her wasn't that of Martin Rudbeck's body arching in agony when she pressed the button, then collapsing onto the cot with that grotesque grimace on his rigid face.

Nor was it pressing the scalpel against the inside of his arm until it came up against resistance. The worst had been when she'd inserted the blade into that open slit and Kim had told her to stop. Just as she'd committed herself to the unthinkable and had decided to carry out the task. Yet she'd gratefully accepted Kim's *Astrid, stop.* She'd told him she couldn't do it. But she was lying. She didn't *want* to, but she would have persisted, all the way to the end. That was the horror of it.

Clinging to the railing, Astrid made her way to the top floor and stood before the door where dingy plastic letters formed the name *Berzelius* on a dark-blue velvet background. It looked as if her psychologist had lived here forever. She really knew almost nothing about Walter—except that she trusted him.

Astrid shut her eyes, consciously sought to relax. Then she pressed the doorbell. An old-fashioned *ding-dong* sounded inside just once. Astrid tried to regulate the rhythm of her breathing without knowing what that rhythm should be. Her ability to manipulate people emotionally felt weakened. It didn't work with Walter anyhow, as experience had shown. If there was really some meaning to "just be yourself," that's what she could be with him.

The door opened and Astrid couldn't help breaking into a smile. Walter was always properly dressed for their appointments in some patterned sweater over an ordinary light-blue shirt. He was wearing a collared shirt now, but it was a colorful short-sleeved Hawaiian number. Walter seemed to understand her reaction, for he gestured at his chest. "Like I said: on vacation."

"Like a charter flight, then," said Astrid.

Walter's gray hair was tousled around his head, and he had a dewlap under his chin even though he wasn't overweight. His eyes were light brown but with deep, dark wrinkles underneath, as if he was someone who'd seen too much. Astrid had never asked his age, but she guessed he was maybe seventy.

"Come in, come in," Walter said, and Astrid stepped into a hall with a ten-foot ceiling with crown molding.

"Not such a shabby address."

"Ah, family inheritance," said Walter. "In fact, I grew up here."

Astrid continued into the apartment, walking past a kitchen with a pass-through window and installations that had to date from the 1950s. An ancient rustic kitchen table stood under a wide window. Maybe little Walter had sat there to drink his morning hot chocolate before setting off to school. The very thought made her dizzy.

Astrid went into a living room that had that faint *old folks* smell. She didn't mind it, maybe because she was an old soul in a young body. The room was simply furnished. A sofa, a coffee table, a couple of Lamino armchairs. The television in the corner was so small that she suspected it was turned on only for the evening news. Walter gestured toward the chairs. "Shall we sit?"

"Which is mine?"

"You can sit where you like." Walter pointed to one of the Lamino chairs, the one that was a good deal more worn than the other. "That one's pretty much *my* chair, but I'm not terribly particular about it. If it appeals to you, sit there."

Astrid knew how to behave properly, so she chose the less used chair with fluffier sheepskin, while Walter dropped into his usual place. He folded his hands together and put them on his knees. The room became very quiet. Astrid heard the faint ticking of a pendulum clock in the next room.

"I don't know where to start," Astrid said.

"Wherever you like," said Walter. "We have plenty of time."

"Do we?"

Walter cleared his throat. "It's not my custom to receive my clients this way. This is the first time. So we can take as much time as necessary."

"Why are you making an exception for me?"

"Astrid. Both your parents were murdered two weeks ago. Right at your side. The fact that you can even stand up is remarkable. I understand that you have things to talk about."

"Mm," replied Astrid. "But this isn't about all that. Not at all."

"So, what is it about?"

Astrid crossed her arms to hug herself and leaned back to look up at the ceiling with its elegantly simple crystal chandelier. "Someone told me . . . that if a person admits committing a serious crime, you aren't *obliged* to report it, but you *can*. Is that right?"

"The professional standard is that a crime that could result in at least a year's imprisonment is sufficient justification for breaking confidentiality, so yes. But that's up to the practitioner's judgment."

"Okay. And if . . . the *culprit* is a minor and couldn't be sentenced to prison, then what?"

"Then the person's guardian is advised."

Uncle Lasse would be drawn into all this? That was the last thing Astrid wanted. If she was going to open her heart in here, she'd have to do it in more abstract terms.

"Walter," she said, "do you see me as capable of making my own choices?"

"Yes. I do."

"And that means . . . taking responsibility for my own actions?"

Walter's eyebrows rose and he frowned slightly in concern. "Astrid? What, exactly, has happened?"

Astrid knew that what she'd done couldn't be considered murder but rather manslaughter at worst. The problem was that Kim Ribbing had put in place the setup where the homicide occurred. No matter how open-minded Walter might be, Astrid knew there was very little chance he would bless her association with a former mental patient turned kidnapper. And Kim would probably be reported to the police.

Astrid took a baby step nearer to the crux of the matter. "I pressed a button. One I shouldn't have touched."

"Oh?"

Astrid glanced at the old man, who was now leaning forward in his armchair, though still with both hands folded before him. "Walter? Can you promise me you won't tell my uncle or say anything to him? If I describe it?"

Walter gave a puff of air and leaned back in his chair. "Unfortunately, I can't, Astrid. But I can, let us say, make a mental note that's what you prefer. What kind of . . . button . . . was it that you mentioned?"

Astrid thought of those tiny moments when people make enormous decisions. One step out from the platform of an underground station. A drill against someone's temple. Knives and jugulars. She was on the brink of revealing how pressing a button had caused a person's death, but her mouth refused to open. She felt Martin Rudbeck's accusing stare behind her, remembered how his lips had twisted into a rictus; now Rudbeck was expecting her humiliating confession. Astrid's throat went dry. She looked over her shoulder, but of course nothing was there. Except a couple of potted plants.

"Things went . . . bad," was all she managed to come up with.

Walter lifted his hand to his face and his middle finger brushed along his cheekbone as if in a futile attempt to smooth out his deep wrinkles. In a still voice he said, "Is this in some way linked to . . . what happened with your parents?"

"No, definitely not."

"It's completely . . . unrelated?"

"Right."

Astrid was feeling just a little calmer. Partly because she appreciated that Walter always spoke to her as he would to an adult, partly because it was a relief to talk about what she'd done, even in deliberately obscure terms. If only those invisible eyes would stop glaring and sending cold shivers up her spine. She told herself not to look over her shoulder again.

"I can't force you to tell me," Walter said, "but you sounded very distressed when you called."

"Yes. I really was. But then . . ."

"Then?"

Astrid didn't want to say that entering Walter's everyday home setting had helped her contain something that perhaps shouldn't have been kept secret. She gave him a stiff smile. "There was something that happened. I pressed a button. It caused consequences I couldn't have foreseen. I can't say any more than that."

Walter sat without speaking for a long while, tapping his nose with an index finger. At last he said, "I don't mean to sound sharp with you, but . . . it doesn't sound like we can discuss this in any meaningful fashion. You're holding back. You may be shielding someone; I don't know. But I wonder . . . is there someone else? Somebody you'd be willing to talk to?"

"Yes. Maybe."

"Then I think you should do that. I hear and see that something is seriously oppressing you. I don't think I need to explain how damaging it can be to deal with such a heavy burden all alone."

"I know," said Astrid and sneaked a look at Walter. "Do you intend to report me?"

Walter sniffed. "For what? You said you pressed a button. I find it difficult to imagine that as a call for help. But I really do wish that you'd be willing to describe whatever happened."

"I did want to," said Astrid, feeling another chill up her spine. "But not anymore. I'm sorry, Walter."

Walter held up his hands. "Nothing to be sorry about. I want to help you, Astrid, but you must reciprocate. Let me help."

"I know. Maybe next time."

Nothing more was said. Walter followed Astrid out to the hall. Before she opened the door, he said, "You're welcome back, anytime you need. And try to talk with someone. If you can."

Astrid nodded and hurried down the stairs. The cold eyes hovered a few feet behind her, never letting her out of sight. Astrid put one hand over the back of her neck as if expecting to ward off a blow.

38

July 10, afternoon

Jonny Munther wasn't at all comfortable in the beige summer jacket he'd found in a drawer in his office. He couldn't even remember when or why he'd bought it. It felt too tight, so maybe it was someone else's. It pulled and flapped around him in an unseemly fashion. Perspiration was beginning to trickle from his scalp as he approached the Fridhemsplan underground station. He should have just worn his uniform, clothing more appropriate for him.

Right, Jonny thought, *and how about a riot helmet and matching shield while you're at it?*

He'd have liked to have something in his hands. Maybe a bouquet of flowers, a box of chocolate, a bottle of wine . . .

Or a police baton.

Jonny stopped outside Commerce Bank and rubbed his face with his hands. He found a crumpled tissue in a jacket pocket and used it to wipe his brow. Why did it have to be so damned *warm?* As part of his recent self-education project, Jonny had read Camus's *The Stranger,* and so he knew to what ends undue heat could drive a person. Not that Jonny found high temperatures an excuse for murder, but there was something to the notion anyway. They could drive a man mad.

Take it easy, Jonny admonished himself. *We're meeting up, taking a little stroll. We talk about work. Then we separate and everything returns to normal. No big deal.*

Right, that would have been fine if it hadn't been for the damn jacket that made Jonny feel like a mental patient in a straitjacket on the way to a padded cell. *Stop it! This is do or die.* Jonny shrugged the jacket off and knotted it around his waist. His short-sleeved white shirt underneath was less annoying, since he'd worn it before. He continued toward the underground station.

He didn't recognize Moa at first. Partly because her hair had been cut short but also because she herself was so short. Moa had been in her element when they'd met in the forensic lab, her movements and attitudes projecting an authority that made her seem taller than she really was. But she turned out to be more than a head shorter than Jonny and had an almost waiflike build.

As for Moa, she recognized Jonny at first glance. As far as he knew, he hadn't made any significant changes to his appearance . . . ever. Sure, in the 1980s he'd worn his hair a little longer, but that was all. Moa gave Jonny a huge smile as he walked up and held out her hand. Jonny took it as gently as he would a baby bird, but Moa's grip was surprisingly firm, even though her hand almost disappeared into his.

"Hi!" she said.

"Yeah, hi," said Jonny, releasing her hand so he could pull at his shirtfront. "It's, uh, hot today."

"It is," said Moa. "And it'll probably stay that way for a while."

"Uh-huh, yes. Yep, it will."

They stood next to one another watching the traffic rush along Drottningholmsvägen. Finally, Jonny sighed, rubbed his sweaty neck, and said, "I'd better say it right up front. I'm not used to this sort of thing. At all."

"And when you say *this sort of thing,* you mean . . . ?"

Jonny turned to Moa. "It's just, you know"—he pointed his finger back and forth between them a couple of times, then finished the thought—"this *here.*"

"Then I can either reassure you or scare you to death, because neither am I used to"—Moa imitated Jonny's back-and-forth gesture and concluded the same way—"this *here.*"

"We're set up for disaster, I guess."

Moa laughed at that, and Jonny perked up. She'd liked his little joke, and that was something he wasn't used to, since he knew that his colleagues regarded him as something of a bore. Oh well, maybe she was just nervous and ready to laugh at anything.

"What do you say?" asked Moa. "Café? Or a stroll first?"

"Probably a walk," said Jonny. "So a person can, like, get used to it."

"My thought exactly."

"To City Hall?"

"Perfect."

They took the crossing to the opposite side of Drottningholmsvägen. Jonny felt this seemed to be going well, at least so far. He'd need to pay attention to his use of the word "like." That word tended to creep into his vocabulary when he was feeling uncertain. Like, he wasn't a teenager, after all. Even though he was feeling like one.

Once on the other side, Jonny stole a glance at Moa. Despite the difference in their strides, she was having no difficulty keeping up. No, in fact, something told Jonny she was holding back as she turned with a bouncy step toward Hantverkargatan.

"You seem really fit," Jonny said.

"I jog," said Moa. "And swim. And ski in the winter when I get the chance."

This would be the perfect opportunity for Jonny to discuss the physical activities he practiced. Six months earlier a colleague on the vice squad whose regular partner was ill had invited Jonny to try out pickleball. Jonny had played some tennis in his youth and was curious about the new sport that had spread like wildfire across the country.

He'd given it a go, and it had just about killed him. That was Jonny's most recent sporting venture, and he didn't think the anecdote was worth recounting. He knew he was in terrible shape, and that's all there was to it.

As if to compensate, Jonny set off at a good clip, swinging his arms, down Hantverkargatan straight toward City Hall, but Moa grabbed his shirttail and pointed to the right toward St. Eriksgatan. "Shouldn't we take North Mälarstrand instead? On a day like this?"

Jonny nodded and reminded himself it wasn't a question of getting to City Hall as fast as possible, but *strolling*, something he really didn't do. He'd wanted merely to move his frail carcass from point A to point B as efficiently as possible.

Time to take it down a notch, he told himself. *Stroll, you big lunk.* Jonny slowed and said, "You seem pretty familiar with Stockholm."

"I grew up here. Moved to Linköping only when I got my first job at the National Forensic Center. It was called the Swedish Forensic Laboratory back then."

"And how is it that you're back now?"

Moa was an only child, and her mother had lived out her last years as a widow. Her mother had passed away, and Moa had spent the past month cleaning out the apartment on Kocksgatan she'd inherited. She'd kept only enough to camp out there while thinking about what to do next. As she told him this, Jonny realized he'd unthinkingly accelerated his pace to get to North Mälarstrand, their next waypoint.

Stroll, you jerk. Promenade!

When they emerged into the glittering brilliance of the docks, Jonny chided himself. He put his hands behind his back and held his right wrist with his left hand. That might be a position more apt for *sauntering* than for strolling, but it worked. No rational human being would attempt to sprint in that posture.

"And what happens at your Linköping lab, then?" asked Jonny.

"They send us things from all across the country, as you know." Moa snapped her fingers. "A couple of weeks ago you presented us an entire boat, didn't you?"

"True. We didn't know what else to do. Sorry about that."

"Didn't land on my desk," Moa said with a laugh. "Anyway, a boat wouldn't be delivered directly to someone's *desk*, if you know what I mean."

"Yeah."

"Other than that, Linköping . . ." Moa looked out over the water where single sailboats were silhouetted, bobbing on the shimmering surface. "I assume you're familiar with our beloved Skäggetorp neighborhood?"

"Sure. It's a vulnerable area. In transition. Right up at the top of the list."

"*Especially* vulnerable area, if you please. So, there's always something going on, as they say. This week . . ." Moa peered up at Jonny. "You know about the True Swedes?"

"They're hard to miss."

"Mm. And they've got a man down there . . . I suppose I should call him a *politician*, really. A True Swede. He just barely missed being elected to the municipal council, but that didn't stop him. He has other platforms and he . . . incites people. Especially against Skäggetorp residents. I'm sure you can imagine."

"Pretty much, yeah."

City Hall's imposing tower was looming up with alarming speed, and Jonny held himself back a bit more, adjusted from sauntering to *ambling*. He enjoyed going along the docks while listening to Moa's low, slightly guttural voice, which contrasted with her insubstantial appearance. The discrepancy was sort of attractive.

"Okay," resumed Moa. "But that guy has a special interest, or more like an obsession. And it's children."

"Children?"

"Yes. The foreign-born—the *inferior folk*, as he calls them—who have so many children. He has graphs and lists and statistics and God knows what all that predict a total catastrophe for the gene pool in Linköping. Again, his words."

"Isn't that standard? In that kind of rhetoric?"

"Sure, but he's so extreme. Like I said: obsessed. As if every newborn with a different skin color is a direct threat to Swedish society, especially in Linköping."

"I'm beginning to get a notion where this is headed," said Jonny.

"Right. A couple of weeks ago, someone up and plants a bomb at the childcare clinic in Skäggetorp. Blows up half of the place. It was a miracle no one was killed. Shrapnel injured a nurse and a midwife. There were three newborns there when it happened."

"I read about that," said Jonny. "Thought it was strange there wasn't more of an uproar; I mean . . . a bomb attack against a clinic, it's just so . . . just something that should never happen."

"Right? But it happened in Skäggetorp and no one seems to care."

They turned off North Mälarstrand into the shady walk that led to City Hall. Jonny wished he'd turned their conversation toward more personal matters, but Moa's grim descriptions left no room for that, so he just said, "We're living in a strange time."

"Right," said Moa. "And how about you? What are you up to?"

"Me? I usually say I'm doing my part. What I can. What I can manage."

"But other than that? When you're not doing your part?"

Moa had unexpectedly turned their conversation to personal matters. Jonny didn't find that particularly to his advantage. He undid the top button of his shirt, rubbed his neck, and replied, "Yeah, what am I doing after hours? I read some."

"Really. I wouldn't have expected that. I read a lot too. What are you reading now?"

"Umm . . . the classics."

Jonny's personal education project consisted of plowing through the great writers of world literature to amend his essentially illiterate life. He'd just gotten started, and he wasn't confident enough to discuss it. After studying various lists on the internet, he'd realized that he'd just skimmed the surface. If anything, he'd barely *touched* the surface. He was saved from embarrassment by a little stand on the street outside City Hall. Jonny pointed. "Ice cream. Want some?"

"Sure!"

Moa chose a plain cone with a single scoop of vanilla. Jonny's stomach growled. He hadn't had lunch, so he allowed himself a waffle cone with scoops of strawberry and chocolate. He didn't dare order a third scoop, since that would risk making a mess. He felt clumsy, and besides, he didn't want to appear greedy.

They sat on a bench beside City Hall in the sunshine, consuming their ice cream in silence. The situation felt a bit uncomfortable, yet not uncomfortable at all. Something in Moa's attitude told Jonny it was okay to keep quiet. After a while, though, he nodded toward City Hall. "Do you know how many bricks that took to build?"

"Hmm," Moa responded. "I seem to remember from school it was about the same number as the population of the country, so . . . about eight million?"

"*You hit the skull in the casket,* as one of my colleagues would say. Exactly right."

"The skull in the casket?"

"Right. Ulrika Boberg. She's, well . . . special."

"Sounds like it."

Ulrika Boberg had gone back to the financial crimes unit after the Knektholmen investigation team was disbanded. Because of her special knowledge, she was given the principal responsibility for picking apart Frode Moe's financial transactions, which were tangled, to say the least. If she and Jonny happened to pass one another in the hallway, they nodded, nothing more. Jonny smiled a bit as he recalled some of Ulrika's more cryptic expressions. *A person doesn't set up a business like this to sell bed sheets to children.* No, indeed.

Jonny came back to the present. Moa. City Hall, where the sun was shining and casting shadows. Before him stood a man who seemed vaguely familiar, hands on his hips. The man was about his own age and looked like a bureaucrat. Maybe someone from the Department of Justice or the municipal office?

"Jonny!" exclaimed the man. "Jonny Munther! It's been such a long, long time!"

"It has," said Jonny truthfully. If he'd seen this guy anytime recently, he'd probably have recognized him.

"How's life treating you, then?" the man asked.

"Fine, thanks," said Jonny. "Not six feet under, yet."

The man chuckled as if Jonny had said something really witty. Now, it wasn't that Jonny *deplored* such interactions, since he understood that they reinforced social solidarity, but he still found them tedious. Engage in meaningless small talk, then say *we should get together and have a beer sometime.* Oh, sure, see you later.

The stranger nodded at Moa. "And who do we have here? Your little boy?"

Jonny was struck dumb. If he'd been physically capable of blushing bright red, this would have turned him tomato faced. He didn't blush, but his gut lurched, and he wanted nothing more than to hide himself, even though he didn't understand why. Oh, yeah, because without meaning to, he'd put Moa into a painful situation he didn't know how to resolve. Before Jonny could find the words, Moa sat up, shook the man's hand, and said, "Yessir. Bobby. Bobby Munther. Glad to meet ya."

"It's a pleasure, Bobby. Great. Sorry, got to scurry. But Jonny, how about if we get together for a beer sometime?"

Jonny nodded halfheartedly. Fortunately, the guy made no move to exchange phone numbers, which would have made his threat a reality. He went on toward City Hall with the stride of someone signaling, *Here comes somebody with important things to do, and he has no time to lose.*

"I apologize," said Jonny. "No idea who the hell that was."

"No problem," said Moa. "It's not the first time."

"That someone thought . . . you're my son?"

"Pooh!" Moa elbowed him. "No, you dummy. That I'm a boy. I just take it as a compliment that I look so much younger than I really am."

Jonny averted his eyes, wanting not to try to see her through the man's eyes. He mentally reviewed his impressions from the past half hour. It was true Moa had a relatively androgynous appearance that had become more evident with her bobbed hair. Maybe that face with almost no wrinkles, the broad shoulders, and the lack of womanly curves. Jonny understood she might pass for a boy with somewhat feminine traits. Was it even conceivable Jonny Munther could have had such a son? That thought in relation to Moa disturbed him, so he pushed it away.

Moa tapped the screen of the fitness monitor on her wrist. A clock face appeared. She got up, nodded south, toward the water, and said, "Well, I have to *scurry* too. I've got some paperwork to deal with."

"Okay," said Jonny, tossing the last of his cone into a trash basket so he could shake her hand. "It was lovely to see you. Really."

"Mm," said Moa. "Want to do it again?"

"Uh . . . *see* one another?"

Moa's eyes darted back and forth. She leaned a bit forward and spoke as if addressing a small child. "Yesss."

"Sure. Yeah. Happy to, really."

"Good. Then we can phone sometime."

Only when Moa had turned and taken a couple of steps did Jonny realize how unaware he'd been in the heat of the day of how much he'd enjoyed their encounter. He called, "Oh, hey!"

Moa turned. "Yes?"

Jonny grimaced in pretend displeasure and said, "Bobby Munther?"

"For sure!" said Moa and pushed back her hair, exaggerating a swagger. "Pleased, pleased to meet ya."

She turned on her heel and walked off with a spring in her step. Jonny stood there watching her go. There was something in the way she'd elbowed him in the side and said, "No, you dummy!" that had made the ice cream in Jonny's belly start to bubble. It didn't even occur to him that they'd forgotten to visit a café. An ice cream stand was more than enough.

39

July 10, afternoon

Kim hung a wicker basket on one arm. In it he deposited all the torture instruments he'd never had the slightest intention of using. They'd been there to frighten his involuntary guest. Their presumptive uses weren't hard to guess when they were assembled, but Kim was going to put them through the dishwasher and redistribute them about the house, each in its proper place. Some of the tools would remain together. A hammer, an awl, and pliers meant different things in different contexts. On a stainless-steel tray: screams and torture. In a tool chest: DIY.

Kim thought Martin Rudbeck's corpse behind him had begun to smell, but he was probably imagining it. Or maybe those were the doctor's "natural" body odors after being bound to a cot for three days unable to clean himself. Kim tossed two different scalpels into the basket and tried to ignore the smell. He was bone tired, hardly able to stand up straight.

Despite the sophistication of his capture of Martin Rudbeck, Kim hadn't ever had a clear idea of what he really wanted to accomplish. Some sort of spiritual peace, yes, but *how* he would achieve that peace had remained unclear. Nor had he achieved it, unless *mindless fatigue* counted as a sort of peace. He was tired of the whole mess and just wanted to be done.

He'd gotten several replies from HackPack members on how to go about constructing an identity. It certainly appeared possible but would probably take a couple of days. Kim had assigned various tasks and paid for them in advance before turning off his computer with an almost disgusted expression. Yes, he was tired, but above all, he was tired of himself. This lonely juggling and fiddling never stopped.

He'd been isolated at school. No friends. He'd sat in the corner minding his own business. He'd been alone in high school, too, concentrating on mastering and shaping his own body, pushing it beyond its natural limits to hold pain and anxiety at bay. No friends then either.

Paradoxically enough, the only time he'd felt himself to be truly included was the several months he'd participated in bouts with Stockholm Street Fighting. There was a remarkable, stressful *intimacy* with the man whose face you pounded and whose fists marked your body with dark bruises, a duet of pain, blended blood, groans, and panting as two combatants almost melded into one.

Add to that the escapes from the police when they were discovered. The flock of men who'd pounded each other that night would flee across abandoned industrial sites and empty schoolyards with blinking blue lights in pursuit, fueled by adrenaline and wild laughter, only to reconvene at another location at another time. Yes, that was probably the only time in Kim Ribbing's life he'd felt himself *close* to others.

And then along came that Julia Malmros woman. Kim dropped the last tool, an immersion heater, into the basket, then stood staring angrily at the dark-gray cement wall. What, really, had happened with Julia Malmros?

He remembered the first time they'd met, her many clueless questions about data security that had made Kim feel more *capable* than in ordinary life. How he'd suggested sex, how they'd gone to bed together, and how Julia had pouted as he was leaving her apartment after it was finished.

Nothing unusual about that. Kim had had similar hookups before. Not many, but some. Do what you both want, then *adios*. A strange thing had happened after his encounter with Julia. It came upon Kim as he made his way through the slush on Järntorget and turned into Västerlånggatan to go to the underground station.

He couldn't help it; he just stopped. Kim found himself standing outside the window of Bröd & Salt. His legs refused to move, a shiver ran through him, something warm and sticky oozed across his heart, and his throat constricted. He coughed at that and felt tears well up. He tried to will his legs to continue, but they went on strike, as if saying, *Nah, feels like we've walked all we want to.*

Only when he turned completely around to face Järntorget did they respond. His legs then took command and hauled him along until he stood outside Julia Malmros's door. Her name was posted on the intercom panel, but when his hand lifted itself to press the button, Kim regained control and lowered it, and he sagged down onto the granite step before the vaulted entryway. He sat there unmoving for several hours. He lost count of the number of times he tried to get up and leave, but his entire body was staging a sympathy strike. So he stayed there until Julia discovered him in the early afternoon, and all he managed to say was, "Damn it. Damn it to hell."

That's how it had started, and now it was over. Kim carried the basket across the room, intending to go up to the main level of the villa, but the corpse had an eerie attraction. He found himself standing by the body, the basket dangling in his hand. Had its skin taken on a slightly yellow tinge, or was he just imagining that?

Kim snorted. The truth of the matter was that he felt so damned lonely, he almost wished Martin Rudbeck would come back to life to continue their discussion. Anything but this damned silence.

Kim had made the fatal mistake of letting people into his life. For most of his nearly thirty years, he'd reinforced a tremendous ability to withstand isolation. Weeks might go by without a word to a single human being, and that had posed no problem for him. What he was now experiencing was a sensation he thought he'd exorcised from his system for good. He was experiencing *loss.*

Julia had reacted with disgust at Kim's crime and Astrid's involvement, and then she'd left. The two individuals he'd actually been concerned about were gone for good, he assumed, and there was nothing he could do. The game was over. His demons had conquered him at last.

"I don't give a shit what happens," Kim told Martin Rudbeck's lifeless body. "I do what I can and as much as I can. If that's not enough, then they can lock me up. Doesn't matter. I can rot in a cell just as easily as here." Kim's lips twisted in a tormented smile as he patted Martin Rudbeck's head. "Was that fun to hear?"

40

July 10, afternoon

"And you have no idea who he was?"

Irma Ryding placed a glass of white wine on the kitchen table before Julia, who'd gotten increasingly shaky as she walked the length of Västerlånggatan. Clearly, she'd managed to keep a cool head in a situation that would have thrown most people into a panic, but once it was over, the *implications* came crowding into her mind. Someone was watching her and was ready to turn to violence if necessary.

In contrast to Irma, Julia was no fan of taking stuff to blur her consciousness this early in the day, but she took the glass with both hands and downed the wine in one go like medicine. Irma held out the box, but Julia waved it away. "Thanks, that's enough. Got to watch myself, avoid excesses. Did I make a *total* fool of myself last night?"

"No," said Irma. "Some fun and games, that's all. Forget about it."

"Okay." Julia exhaled and went back to Irma's question. "No, I don't know who he was, but that hardly matters. A messenger."

Irma lowered herself into the chair on the other side of the table and gestured toward the boxed wine to indicate it was freely available if the spirit moved Julia. Then she asked, "And what exactly did he want?"

"That's what bothers me. They know somehow that I talked to Jocke Bäckman, and they didn't like it."

"And who are *they*?"

"The True Swedes. I suspect those Apostates are just a sort of tool for them, but I'm not sure."

"Hm. You planning to continue anyway?"

"I really have no idea, Irma. Maybe I should just cling to my . . . heightened reality."

"Perhaps. And that implies you're probably not interested in what I've found out?"

Julia knew Irma well enough to see that her indifference was fake. Her friend was bursting and eager to report, so Julia dutifully asked, "What did you find out?"

"Had to do with that Odin's eye, the symbol, remember?"

"Yes. Of course."

"I could deliver a long lecture, and maybe I will someday. There are links to the Gothic League and others, but we won't go into that now. Have you heard the expression *ecofascism*?"

"I've heard the word a couple of times, but that's all."

Irma nodded, glanced surreptitiously at the wine box, checked the kitchen clock, which showed it was just before two in the afternoon, then looked at the wine box again. Julia said nothing, letting Irma deal with her own inner struggle, knowing full well it wouldn't matter what anyone else said. Irma smacked her lips and shrugged slightly. The angel and the demon whispering in opposite ears had to consider it a tie, since Irma served herself only *half* a glass of wine. She took a swallow and gestured toward her hip. "An anti-misery potion."

"Do what you need to do," said Julia. "What was it you were going to say?"

"Ah, yes, that," said Irma and pushed the glass away. "Odin's eye is one of several symbols linked to the ideology of ecofascism. In short, it's all about a basic contention that humanity is on its way to destroying the planet because there are too many of us. *Far* too many."

"Not so earthshakingly original."

"No, but in contrast, the proposed solutions are detailed and very clear. For example, let contagious diseases run their course in poor countries. No assistance, no medicine. Let people die. Pandemics? Best thing in the world. War, too, if it's conducted in a high-tech way that doesn't destroy the environment. But what it comes down to is *let 'em all perish.*"

"And who's supposed to survive all this?"

"Aha! Guess. The elite, of course. The best of the best. The whole system is based on some form of autocracy. A ruling class that issues decrees and authorizations designed primarily to reduce the population. Abortion of all fetuses with birth defects, and the death penalty for a long list of crimes, since only inferior individuals engage in criminal activities. Mandatory permitting for all those desiring children, permission limited to a select few. Ecofascism claims not to aim at eliminating humanity, but its program comes close. All this to give nature a chance to recover."

"So you're saying that the True Swedes movement is actually a bunch of . . . environmental activists?"

"I doubt it. They're probably just picking the juiciest raisins out of that particular cake. The program resembles the thoughts of a Finnish philosopher. Wolf something, not the big bad wolf, but something like that. Imagine: A ship sinks and several people manage to get themselves into a lifeboat. Those who hate life will let the whole lot climb on board, to the point that the lifeboat sinks too. Those who *love* life, on the other hand . . ." Irma's ironic stress on the word "love" was accompanied by a sip of wine to fortify herself for the conclusion. "Those who love life will grab their axes and chop off the hands of others trying to climb aboard, so the lifeboat can sail off into the sunset with its worthy cargo. That's mine, by the way, the bit about the sunset."

"But axes? Are there axes aboard lifeboats?"

"According to Big Bad Wolf, or whatever his name is, yes, there are. Or maybe there's just *one* axe. That's just a quibble. The image is clear either way."

"And you think, then, that the True Swedes have embraced that ideology?"

"Don't ask me. They use the symbol. But it's common for symbols to be used in different connections, so they can always get away with it."

If Irma's speculations were correct, Jocke Bäckman's warning wasn't just an empty threat. If this really involved fascism, it mattered not at all if they'd stuck a little "eco" on the front end. The inferior members of society were marked for liquidation, and fascists tended to classify anyone not embracing their views as inferior. Such people deserved the chop. If Julia did anything to oppose them, it wouldn't help that she herself hadn't produced any children.

Julia sighed and slumped. "Right, I see. No choice for me other than to return to heightened reality, then."

"Do you have any ideas?"

"Not a one. Just play the role. After that damned television series, the good ship Åsa Fors is bound to be torpedoed. No possibility of a lifeboat for *that*."

"Don't forget that people are stupid."

Julia laughed bitterly. "And that's supposed to make me feel better? That the hellish series might succeed because people are idiots?"

"I was thinking mostly about provisions for your future. By the way, have you thought about what I suggested?"

"About what?"

"About the rights to my novels. Accepting them?" As Julia took in a breath to reply, Irma held up a hand like a traffic cop. "I haven't gotten around to doing the research, but since I have no living relatives, I believe that any income is forfeited to the state's unclaimed inheritance fund and probably winds up, God forbid, going to the Writers Guild. Is that something you'd wish on me?"

Julia had never really understood Irma's aversion to the Writers Guild. Irma didn't despise it quite as much as the Swedish Academy, but even so, she always responded with a dismissive sniff when it came up in conversation. There was something about the banding together of creatives that made her bristle. And you had to be careful about using the expression "creatives" around Irma Ryding, since she found it precious, pretentious, or—using her favorite expression—a pain in the butt.

"I don't want to think about that now, Irma."

"About what? My books? That much I can certainly understand, but—"

"No. About you. Dying, I mean."

"But dear, *sweet* little friend. That's going to happen in the not-too-distant future. Believe me, I can feel death sniffing at my backside. It's okay. I'm looking forward to being reunited with Sture, it's been all too long."

"You don't really believe that."

"No, I don't, but I damn well want to be where he is."

"But you have me," Julia said in a plaintive little voice.

Irma's face beamed with an expression that would accompany an *awww* when a child has just said something adorable. She reached across the table and took Julia's hand. "Yes, I do, and I'm grateful for that, but I'm sorry, sweetie. That's just not enough."

Julia looked down and stared at their two hands joined on the table. If only she could sit here forever, holding Irma's hand, maybe nothing terrible would ever come to pass. She finally released her grip despite that thought and said, "Okay. Check to see what happens with your royalties if you do nothing. If they go to someone or something you don't like, then . . . then I'll accept them. No matter how complicated *that* paperwork seems."

Irma gleefully clapped her hands. "That's that, then! Wasn't so hard, was it? You've just made a dying old woman very happy."

"Please, Irma . . ."

"Yes, yes, enough of that. I'll do the research. Shall we toast?"

"Sorry. Seems to me it's not something to celebrate."

"Oh, no? Okay, sure. When you want something done, you must do it yourself." This time Irma filled her glass to the brim. She hoisted it, toasted Julia, then toasted herself.

Julia gave her a dark look. "You really seem determined to accelerate the process."

"Nonsense. Wine's good for you. Don't you read the newspapers?"

"Probably not the right ones. The ones I read say that alcohol shortens lives."

"Exactly. Those are the crappy ones."

Irma had once commented that Julia's greatest wish was that she, Irma, should subsist on roots and bean sprouts, hike around with her cane, and wear colorful summer clothing by Gudrun Sjödén. Julia didn't understand how clothing came into the mix, but otherwise the analysis was correct. She wanted Irma to live, to live long, and preferably to outlive her, so Irma could inherit the royalties from *her* novels.

"What are you pondering there?" Irma asked over the lip of her wineglass.

Julia wasn't eager to share, so instead she raised another subject she wanted to discuss. "Irma? If you needed to get rid of a body, how would you go about it?"

"Aha!" Irma exclaimed and seemed to perk up. "Aha . . . so maybe you've got a little notion of a plot after all?"

"Let's suppose I do."

Julia had absolutely no intention of telling Irma what she'd seen in Kim's basement, no matter how close their friendship was. Aside from the fact that would be squealing, it would affect Irma's future opinion of Kim, to say the least.

Future? What future? There is no future.

No matter how much Julia turned it up and down or over and over in her mind, she couldn't share with Irma the image of Kim standing over a corpse, holding a saw and wearing a protective coverall. That was unthinkable. Not to mention Astrid standing at his side. No and no. Impossible.

Irma didn't notice Julia's uneasiness because she was fully absorbed in contemplating the problem at hand. She frowned. "I've had to do away with several bodies in my time, so to speak. Thirty-two novels, if I remember correctly. Amounts to quite a body count. Let's see . . ."

Julia had read about half of Irma's novels. They hovered somewhere between Sjöwall and Walöö's Martin Beck series and Agatha Christie's Poirot stories. Murder mysteries with puzzles to solve, though rawer than those of her British predecessor. Less tea and tweed, more alcohol and dirty shirts. Not as graphic as Julia's own creations, but still not as politely polished as Christie's *Oh, blimey, is that a corpse I spy?*

"What *isn't* so easy," said Irma, waving a finger as if scolding the clumsiness of a fictional murderer, "is cutting it up. You must be so *incredibly* precise, and in these days of DNA identification, there's very little chance that would work. Same's true of incineration. Hellishly high temperatures would be required to make certain the crime techs couldn't recover anything. In one of my first novels, there was a murderer who built a funeral pyre but got caught because they identified the victim from a dental chart. And these days, it's even more difficult, as I mentioned."

Irma was going full speed. Without noticing it, she reached out for the box wine to *fortify herself* but stopped and pulled her hand back.

"Okay," said Julia. "And what *would* work, in your opinion?"

"Hmm, yes. In two of my novels, I let the murderer get away, simply to avoid *always* fulfilling expectations. In one, he—no, she—put the corpse into a barrel filled with aqua regia, an acid bath. You know, nitric acid and hydrochloric acid. Dissolves practically *anything.* The disadvantage is that it takes a while. In the other novel, I had him run the body through a meat grinder and feed it to the pigs."

"Oh, my. Didn't read that one."

"No, it's out of print. I went a little too far that time. Or let's just say that I was ahead of my time. That sounds right, I think."

"But where did he get that kind of meat grinder?"

"They have 'em on pig farms. Bit of a challenge to get a corpse to one, but once you do, you're off to the races." Irma chuckled and nodded with a shiver of satisfaction. "That scene was a lot of fun to write, really. Yes, yes, I've had my moments."

"So you think the meat grinder and the pig farm would be the best choice?"

"Yes, I might well say so. Though it's already been done by *the one and only* Irma Ryding. But anyhow, as I said, almost no one's read the novel. I seem to recall it was titled *Swine*, a fine double entendre, and that was almost fifty years ago now, so you're welcome to use my inspiration. It'll be a little foretaste of life as the rights holder enjoying royalties from my incomparable life's work."

Julia didn't want to go down that rabbit hole again, so she tried to close the subject by saying, "Okay, then, great. Thanks."

Irma wasn't about to be distracted. She intertwined her fingers, put her elbows on the table, and placed her chin on her hands. Her eyes sparkled. "And what kind of story is this for which you need the assistance of the former queen of detective fiction?"

"Not clear," said Julia. "It's still vague."

"Are we talking Åsa Fors?"

"I don't think so." Julia had a sudden inspiration and knew how to get around this subject. "Maybe we could write it together?"

"Together? You and me?"

"Right? That's really popular these days. Just think: Ryding-Malmros. That would be worth something, don't you think?"

Irma grimaced. "Hmm. If so, Malmros-Ryding would be better." There was no missing the glint in Irma's eyes as she added, "But still a better joint pseudonym than that Lars Kepler guy."

Julia got up. "You'll think about it?"

"What? Your project or the name?"

"Both."

"I want to be called Swedenborg. Uh . . . Ronny Swendenborg. No! August Strindlund! Or wait . . . Horace . . . Horace *Jonnson*!"

Irma was so engaged in creating an alternate identity that she hardly noticed as Julia backed out of the kitchen and went to the hall to put on her shoes. When she opened the apartment door, Irma called from the kitchen. "I've got it! Pernilla Bläckfärg! Or, no! Eva-Britt Wattström! That'll do it!"

Julia shook her head and shut the door behind her, pleased despite everything that she'd stirred up Irma's creative juices. Don't they say you live longer or at least ward off dementia if you make sure your brain stays active, for example, with crossword puzzles? Julia was sure Irma would have a long list of names the next time she came to visit.

As she went down the stairs, Julia began seriously considering the possibility she and Irma might write something together. Other than the plot idea based on the True Swedes, her imagination really had almost nothing to work with. Trading ideas and writing something with Irma might kickstart some inspiration. In addition to exercising Irma's brain, it would give her friend a reason to stay alive. Not such a bad idea, really.

41

July 10, afternoon

Carmen Sánchez and Christof Adler had chatted mostly about their police colleagues and various television series as he drove along the highway, but when he took the exit to Täby, she turned to look at him. "Just out of curiosity: How is it that you don't want to *commit* to Cecilia? Isn't that how you put it? You two have been together now for . . . how long has it been?"

"Four years this August. Well, it depends on how you calculate it, but . . ."

"Four years. And you're happy with her and her daughter, Matilda, aren't you?"

Christof squirmed. Honest to God, this wasn't his favorite subject. As recently as two days before, Matilda had asked, "When are you and Mama going to get married?" Christof had then asked if that was something Matilda wanted, and she'd said yes, she wanted to wear a tiara and be a flower girl. Christof believed that he'd also get a yes from Cecilia if he ever got himself together to propose.

"Sure," said Christof. "Very. But, well, you know, I'm still young."

"You're not *that* young. How old are you anyway? Twenty-six?"

Christof cleared his throat. "Twenty-seven. And, you know, Cecilia is thirty-three; after all, she belongs to a different, you know—"

Carmen yelped with laughter. "*Generation*? Get a hold of yourself! What's the difference? Didn't they have *Bolibompa* on kids' TV when she was little too? Is there anything at all that makes it impossible to bridge the gap between the generations?"

Christof checked the vehicle's navigation system and saw that, luckily, they were only a few minutes from Lievägen. Instead of making any more excuses, he decided attack was the best defense. "How about you, then? You're not in a relationship, are you?"

"Nope. Never have been. Not for a long time anyway."

"And why's that?"

Carmen shrugged her broad shoulders. "No idea. I suspect men are a little scared of me for some reason."

"How about women, then?"

"Mm. Thought about trying that out, but I don't think it's the thing for me. I have my Bruno, and that's just fine."

Bruno was Carmen Sánchez's German shepherd, the one with which she'd started training years earlier to become a police dog handler. Bruno was a keen tracker but had been eliminated from the program because he was constantly getting distracted. Carmen insisted that he had ADHD and was disappointed no one had bothered to develop cognitive behavioral therapy for dogs.

Christof stopped before the low hedge around Elisabeth Svanström's house. She was the neighbor who'd spoken with him by phone, and he saw that, indeed, there was an excellent line of sight between her kitchen window and Martin Rudbeck's driveway.

Christof reached for the door handle, but Carmen Sánchez turned to him to ask, "Christof? Do *you* think I'm scary?"

Christof's eyebrows shot up. He looked Carmen up and down. He himself was five foot nine, and Carmen was a little taller, with so long a torso that her head almost touched the car ceiling. Her face was angular and a bit mannish without really being unattractive. When he got to her small brown eyes, she suddenly opened them wide as if to spook an intruder.

"Just a little," said Christof. "Looking like that, at least. And, any-way, *Bolibompa* was already on TV when Cecilia was a kid."

"Is that so?" commented Carmen and opened her door. "When I was small, it was called the kiddie channel, buddy. That's something we can discuss when it comes to generational differences."

Elisabeth Svanström's front door displayed a wooden plaque with her last name inscribed in blue and surrounded by flower garlands. Christof pushed the old-fashioned doorbell, which pealed so loudly that it startled him.

Inside there came a slightly quavering voice that called, "I'm com-ing, I'm coming," as it approached. The bolt turned and the door slowly opened. Elisabeth Svanström was a short, somewhat hunchbacked older woman with a bouffant halo of white hair. She peered at Christof and Carmen. "Oh dear. Have the forces of public order come to visit me?"

"Christof Adler," said Christof. "I spoke with you by phone yester-day. And this is Carmen Sánchez."

"Sánchez," Elisabeth Svanström echoed him. "Maybe that has something to do with Mexico?"

"Chile," said Carmen. "My parents came from there."

"Ah, *Chile*," Elisabeth said and clapped her hands. "I visited there when I was just a girl. Before that awful Pinochet, mind you. Valparaíso, just like in the song. With those . . . electric buses." Elisabeth fluttered her hands. "But here I stand just going on. Come in, come in! Can I serve you something? Coffee? Tea?"

"That's okay, thanks," said Christof, stepping into the hall. "We won't bother you for long."

"Oh, you're no bother," said Elisabeth and headed toward the kitchen. "It's quite nice to have a bit of a change. I suspect this has something to do with Rudbeck?"

"Yes, exactly," said Carmen, following her. "I hear you had some observations to share with us."

"Oh, I wouldn't exactly call them that."

Carmen and Christof came into a somewhat overdecorated kitchen with ornate shelves, knickknacks, and a kitchen table covered with a large crocheted doily. Elisabeth went to the window and pointed outside. "In any case, I was standing here when they came to get him."

Carmen stood beside her, looked out at Martin Rudbeck's house, and nodded. "And that was with an ambulance, was it?"

"Yes, and I was watching when they transferred him from the house. He looked completely done in, poor man."

"The people who came to fetch him, how were they—"

"Oh! Excuse me," said Elisabeth Svanström, straightening up to put a hand on Carmen Sánchez's shoulder. "That's just an expression; there was only *one* person."

"And you're sure of that?"

"Absolutely. Well, I can't swear that there wasn't somebody *inside* the ambulance, but there was only one who got out and then came back with Rudbeck. And if I may say so, I thought it was a little strange . . ."

Christof knew that interviewing witnesses was something of a Carmen Sánchez specialty, but he felt he should remind them he was there, so he quickly asked, "What seemed strange about it?"

Elisabeth took her hand from Carmen's shoulder and rubbed her own face. "Yes, well, I couldn't tell if it was a man or a woman. But he, or she . . . *they*, maybe people say these days, that's right, isn't it? So, *they* had a cap on *their* head and a kind of mask covering their mouth. One of those blue ones, you know? That was why there was no way to tell, how do you say, their gender identification."

"That cap," said Carmen. "Can you tell us something about it?"

"It was black. Completely black. Didn't look especially official . . . you know, from the municipality. Or am I wrong? Is it still the city councils that run the hospitals? Maybe they've all been privatized now?"

"These days we say *regional*," said Carmen. "But I understand what you mean."

"Yes, oh dear," said Elisabeth Svanström. "Nothing but changes, every time you turn around. Ah, yes, so it's the *region* that'll take care of me when I can't manage anymore. Doesn't sound too reassuring, but there's nothing to be done about it, I suppose. Are you sure you wouldn't like something to drink?"

They talked for a while longer, and the only new morsel that came out was that the person had worn a white coverall and plastic gloves. Carmen Sánchez praised Elisabeth for her observation skills, and after a long-drawn-out farewell ceremony including several additional recollections of Valparaíso, they left her and went out on the street.

The first thing Carmen Sánchez said was, "*One* person. Ambulances *always* carry two medical technicians. Never would a single person be sent out for a pickup."

"No," responded Christof. "And what was that about a mask? Okay, if Rudbeck really had Ebola, but then wouldn't it probably have involved one of those protective outfits that looks like a space suit?"

"Mm," said Carmen. "And I've never seen an ambulance tech wearing a black cap."

Christof Adler pushed his hands into his pockets, looked toward Martin Rudbeck's house, and sighed. "I hate to admit it, but it's looking more and more like that Wilmer Syd guy is right. This was a kidnapping and a damned clever one too."

42

July 10, afternoon

Julia Malmros was feeling a little paranoid when she stepped out of Irma Ryding's building. The assault on the stairs was still alarming, and she looked around to see if anyone was following. It was impossible to tell, with all those tourists in bright summer colors moving in both directions along Västerlånggatan.

Nearing Järntorget, she glanced through the portal that led to Mårten Trotzig Alley, Stockholm's narrowest street, and thought the person leaning against a wall and smoking was watching her all too closely. She walked faster and got to her building. She looked behind her before tapping in the code. The person from the alley had come out and now stood leaning against the corner of a building. The face was hidden by one of those straw sun visors some tourists wear.

Is there really someone following me?

That sun visor reassured Julia a little. She didn't think a member of the Apostates would be caught dead wearing such a thing. And besides, the individual was in a short-sleeved checkered shirt hardly appropriate for motorcycles and engine grease. She must be imagining things.

Nevertheless, Julia couldn't help paying extra close attention before ascending the staircase. She paused before the step where the hand had clamped across her mouth. She listened. Water was running in a pipe somewhere, but that was all. She continued up.

Once she got inside her apartment, Julia prepared a couple of slices of bread with cheese and ate them while looking out over Järntorget. If she'd seen the person from Mårten Trotzig Alley now standing there studying her window, she'd have gotten truly paranoid, but both he and his unbecoming sun visor had vanished. Julia slowed the frantic chewing of her cheese snack.

Once she'd consumed both slices, Julia wandered around in her apartment, arms across her chest, head down, thinking about aqua regia, funeral pyres, and voracious pigs. God help her, she had no plans to allow herself to sink into Kim Ribbing's madness, but even so, her thoughts couldn't tear themselves away from the problem: *How do you get rid of a corpse?* She tried to persuade herself this was a purely theoretical problem with which she, as a detective-story novelist, was occupied. Merely a thought experiment.

Goddamned Kim Ribbing.

The only reasonable thing to do was to distance herself from him and avoid him forever. In just a couple of seconds, everything she'd so carefully tried to construct had collapsed with a devastating crash, and that hurt. It hurt so much. Only now did she understand what the mere *possibility* of Kim Ribbing had meant to her. And now it was gone. Too late.

Julia knew she was starting to work herself up, so to distract herself, she sat down to her computer and did exactly what she shouldn't: She opened Flashback to see what was being written about her. There were some threads about her novels, but she picked a far more general one titled "Rumors about Julia Malmros?"

Is there that much to say about me?

Julia flicked through it, up and down, and found speculations about her divorce from Jonny, about the young man she was said to be meeting, and about who'd been hitting on her at the book fairs. If the list of known and less well-known writers Julia had supposedly bedded had been correct, she'd hardly have had time for any of the panels.

Quite a few posts about her disastrous Millennium project, and they were fairly evenly divided between those who thought what had happened was a shame and those who considered the outcome damned lucky. "What a scandal! This franchise keeps digging Stieg Larsson up out of his grave, and worse, this Malmros woman's a bungler even at that!" was a condemnation Julia committed to memory.

In one post so full of misspellings that it was hard to decipher, an imaginative illiterate claimed that Julia's depression at the refusal—*resfulal*—had been so great that she'd taken a boat to Knektholmen and mowed down everyone there. The fact that Julia wasn't under lock and key was because of a *kospiracy* that involved everyone of Jewish origins in the world of publishing. Julia shook her head but started feeling a little better. It was unbelievable how many nutjobs were out there.

And finally, all the posts inevitable for any woman in the public eye. On one hand, fantasies about how and where Julia should be screwed and, on the other, detailed descriptions of how completely unfuckable she was. Someone who wrote appreciatively about Julia's body got a comment that he might as well do his business with the bunghole of a barrel. Julia couldn't help glancing down at her own belly. Okay, she wasn't in tip-top form, but was it fair to call her a *barrel?* She got over it by dismissing him as an incel and didn't take it personally. *Good for you, girl,* she told herself.

There was one commenter whose name came up frequently as she scrolled. He—she assumed the writer had to be male—called himself JustForFun and used a headshot of Jack Nicholson as his profile picture. Julia felt growing unease as she went through his posts. He seemed to be watching her.

He knew where she lived and the places she frequented and shopped. That she would hang out at the Angel Pub, that she regularly visited Irma Ryding, and that recently she'd been taking the number 69 bus. JustForFun didn't know *where* she took the bus but said it was only a matter of time before he found out.

Tsk-tsk, someone commented. Sounds like you're hoping to have some hard dicky dipping.

LOL, wrote JustForFun. If the opportunity comes up . . .

Uh-oh! was the answer. Sounds like Malmros should watch out in dark streets, and there's plenty of them in Old Town.

Julia blinked a couple of times, not believing it. These two men—they had to be men—were *joking* about how she should be raped?

This was almost certainly empty bro talk, but even so, she got a cold lump in her belly realizing those two sat imagining and even *writing* about such things. Julia turned off the computer and fiercely rubbed her eyes.

Okay, right, let those famished men have their nasty fantasies. But the really scary thing was that she seemed to have a *stalker.* There was no other explanation for the fact that the individual in question had such detailed knowledge of her daily routine. Someone was following her. As if she didn't have enough problems already.

Despite herself, Julia went back to the kitchen window to survey Järntorget. What if the person with the sunshade was JustForFun? He was nowhere in sight, and Julia hadn't seen his face. What does a stalker look like, anyway? Anything at all, but probably with an air of failure hanging about him. What person with a meaningful life would devote himself to stalking a half-known celebrity? *A loser.*

Julia stepped away from the window and took another couple of turns around the apartment. She felt completely shattered and knew she couldn't possibly manage to get started with something productive. Maybe she should just sit down and drink herself senseless? That was always a possibility. Not a *good* solution, but at least it'd be something to do. She took a mental inventory of what she had on hand and found that not only was tipsiness achievable but so was total inebriation, if she so chose. Once she got started, that was generally what she was looking for. Working on blacking out.

Julia squatted in front of the liquor cabinet with the idea of starting carefully by sipping a single malt, then switching to vodka and cola once she began to get serious about it. Her fingers were just about to close around the bottle of Macallan, twelve years old, when the intercom buzzed. Julia started so violently that she lost her balance, fell over backward, and slammed down on her tailbone.

"Goddamn it to holy hell!" growled Julia as the pain shot up her spine. The intercom buzzed again. She thought about ignoring it. It was probably just some journalist wanting to know if she'd gone to bed with Frode Moe, maybe at the book fair? She staggered out to the hall, pressed the Talk button, and said, "Yes? Who is it?"

The stalker, Julia told herself, but then she heard Astrid Helander's voice. "Hey, this is Astrid. Can I come up? There's something I need to tell you."

43

July 10, afternoon

"I'll be there in half an hour, max," the Täby police locksmith had told them. Carmen and Christof had agreed it would be best to rely on the man's expertise, since he'd already unlocked and locked the doors in question once before. They walked around the house and discovered a small, agreeably shaded garden. A hammock stood in one corner. It creaked and squeaked when Carmen sat down in it.

A glassed-in veranda looked out on the garden. Christof went to one of the windows, cupped his hands around his eyes, and peered inside. Lots of potted plants lined the windowsills. A couple were wilting, apparently because they hadn't been watered. Christof caught sight of a trail of dirt on the floor that led to a broken flowerpot.

"Hey," he called Carmen. "I see a pot that fell on the floor."

"What kind of plant?"

"Some kind of cactus, I think."

"It's probably dead."

"What do you mean?"

"I mean it's no big deal. We'll look when the locksmith gets here. Come sit down. That is, unless you think I'm too *scary*."

Christof did as he was told. The hammock was narrow, and he had to move his rear toward one end as best he could so their arms wouldn't brush against one another. He was *almost* comfortable enough with

Carmen not to mind slight physical contact but not entirely. And of course Carmen noticed his squirming; she spread out her arms so that one was behind Christof's back. Then she planted her legs in a proper *manspread.*

"Hah! Oh, yeah," said Carmen. "We need to stop meeting like this."

"Like what?"

"Oh, you know. Driving around together, searching villas and apartments and coming back empty-handed. Seems like it's getting to be our thing."

"What are you talking about? We found an iPad."

"Astrid found it. Wasn't us."

"And that emerald ring."

"Mm. Wasn't really a breakthrough in the investigation."

Christof frowned at her. "What's with you? Are you feeling sad?"

Carmen wrinkled her nose and seemed about to reply with a wisecrack but instead withdrew her arms and put her hands in her lap. "I really should be a dog handler. That's why I wanted to join the police. Then Bruno turned out the way he did, and that was the end of that. And now . . . I don't know. Here I am, sitting with you, roasting in the summer heat and waiting for the privilege of going through another house where we won't find a thing."

"Maybe you could imagine me as a dog . . . ?"

Carmen smiled. "There's nothing wrong with you, I'm just a little *fed up.* Is it going to go on like this until I retire at last?"

"What's going on? Are you thinking about quitting?"

"Yeah. I really am."

"Please stay."

"But why?"

Christof raised both hands and gestured toward Martin Rudbeck's villa. "If you don't, who will I have to search houses and apartments with?"

The locksmith took his time. Almost an hour went by, and Christof and Carmen got so bored that they started rocking the hammock back and forth, higher and higher, just to have something to do. And, natu-rally, that was when the locksmith came around the corner of the house. There was a tearing sound from the hammock, and the guy said, "Ah! Here you are, sitting and having a good time." He jabbed a thumb back over his shoulder. "I've been waiting out front for fifteen minutes."

Christof and Carmen put their feet on the ground. The hammock didn't collapse. "Sorry," said Carmen. "It was so hot out there."

The locksmith wiped his forehead with his sleeve. "Yeah, right. I noticed."

"Will the lock take a long time?" asked Christof.

"Already done. All that's left is for present company to come inside. I'm getting to know that door."

They went around the house to find the front door slightly open. The locksmith asked what it was all about.

"Missing person," said Carmen. "Possible kidnapping."

"Ah, right, I see. I thought it looked a little strange when I was in there last time."

"You didn't touch anything, did you?"

"Nope. But we weren't wearing coveralls and that kind of gear, so . . . might be some contamination. I just noticed there's an extra key on a hook by the door. You can use it to lock up. Can't stay, got things to do."

"Okay, thanks," said Carmen. "And maybe you won't tell *everybody* we were rocking in the hammock?"

He grinned. "It's going straight out on the radio."

Technically speaking, this wasn't yet an investigation, since there'd been no formal decision to start an inquiry. Even so, Carmen and Christof put on single-use plastic shoe covers before going inside. It was probably a useless precaution, since the Täby police had already been tramping around in there, but they wanted to demonstrate their professionalism, show they weren't the types who'd rock a hammock to pieces.

The rag rug in the hall seemed more in disarray than normal. It looked as if someone had *thrown* it down. Carmen pulled out her mobile and snapped a photo, after which Christof put the rug back in its proper place and they slowly approached the kitchen. They scanned the walls, door trim, and floor molding. Nothing seemed out of place.

But in the kitchen—a vase of cut flowers lay turned over on the table. Water had run across it and down to the floor. Several drawers and counter doors stood open, and the rug here also had been disturbed. Christof went around the table, stopped, then pointed. "Look."

A large carving knife lay on the parquet floor in front of the refrigerator. Christof squatted to study it. No signs of blood on the blade. It could have been wiped clean, of course, but then why would a presumptive criminal have left it on the floor?

"Move back a bit," Carmen said. She used her mobile phone to take a closeup and then various other views showing the knife's position.

"What do you think?" asked Christof.

"Nothing at all," said Carmen. "Except maybe that *something* definitely happened here." She pursed up her mouth. "And that it's a lot more in order than Olof Helander's summer cabin."

Christof continued into the living room, which was dominated by a big sofa and a television almost as large. There was no sign of a fight or a search, but he noticed something white between two sofa cushions. He took it delicately between his thumb and forefinger, extracted it, and saw a slip of paper with text scribbled on it. He read it, set it down, and pulled on a plastic glove. He picked it up and went back to the kitchen to show Carmen.

"Look at this," he said. "If this isn't a clue, I don't know what is."

Carmen leaned over to read what was written in blue ink: *You have 48 hours to give it back or you'll get grabbed yourself.* She looked wide-eyed at Christof. "Okay," she said. "Looks like it might be time to talk to the prosecutor and get her call on this."

44

July 10, late afternoon

Kim Ribbing's clattering keyboard echoed through the desolate abandoned office space downstairs. He quickly reread a description of decomposition and how it varied according to the surrounding earth, temperature, and humidity. He chewed a bite from a kebab pizza delivered by Foodora and leaned back in the wobbly desk chair.

The sunshine through the dirty windows lit up the desks left hither and thither across the wall-to-wall carpet. The dust that lay heavy over every surface had so infiltrated the carpet that anyone walking across it sent up small clouds of motes that swirled and danced in the sunbeams. It was, in short, a terribly dismal locale, isolated and abandoned.

How did I come to buy this place?

Kim knew the answer, of course. He'd needed a space where he could complete his Martin Rudbeck project. The former Haitian embassy's most important feature had undoubtedly been the underground room, and the rest was gravy. Now, where Kim was seated, the whole affair seemed totally insane. He'd have put the villa up for sale instantly and gone back to living in hotel rooms if it hadn't been for the *problem.*

Kim was becoming despondent. If everything had gone according to plan, Martin Rudbeck would have been returned to his nasty existence by now with the knowledge that a sword of Damocles in the form of an incriminating video hung over his head. Now, though, Kim was the one looking up at the sword. He knew the police had begun inquiries. Very little time was left.

Despite that, his brain was refusing to cooperate. Kim was usually good at quickly assessing a situation and determining how to solve or elude problems, but that just wasn't happening. He had neither desire nor inspiration. He'd lost all interest, and he felt as decrepit as the room where he was sitting. Kim was about to stuff a bit of cold kebab meat in his mouth when the doorbell rang.

He glanced at the basement door where the open padlock hung on its hasp. He rose and reluctantly started to go shut it, but then stopped and shrugged. If the police had come to search the villa, a padlock wouldn't impede them. He left it open and went to the front door. Maybe this was the end.

Julia Malmros stood on the porch with Astrid Helander one step behind her. Kim looked from one to the other, and yet again his brain refused to evaluate the situation. Until Astrid stepped in front of Julia and said, "I confessed."

Unable to rouse his brain, Kim asked, "Confessed . . . what?"

"That it was me. I did it."

Then Kim understood. Granted, in a purely technical sense, Astrid had pressed the button, but it was Kim who had set up all the arrangements that made that lethal act possible. As Kim sought to come up with a reply, Julia said, "That changes things. A lot. May we come in?"

Kim stepped back and gestured that they were welcome. They were, weren't they? Yes, something roused in the abandoned room of Kim's innermost being and told him they were indeed welcome. And he'd been waiting for them without daring to hope they would come.

Astrid had no more stepped inside before indignantly pointing to the desk where he'd been sitting. "What the hell! I leave you alone for a couple of hours, and the first thing you do is rush out and buy yourself *kebab pizza?*"

"A deliveryman brought it," said Kim, picking up his laptop to go upstairs.

"So what?" said Astrid. "As if that would make it any better! Do you know what their working conditions are?"

"No," said Kim. "But I suspect I'm about to be informed."

As they went up the stairs, Astrid launched into an explanation of the gig economy and its effect on human beings and the environment, but Julia intervened, saying, "Astrid, can we take this up another time?"

"Sure. I'm just sad to see that you two *also* must be idiots."

Kim understood from Astrid's "also" that, despite everything, her expectations of him and Julia were somewhat higher than those she had of other people, which in his present condition still felt a little encouraging. They settled around the kitchen table. Kim was about to break character and say he was glad they'd come, but Julia stopped him.

"Okay, Kim," she said, wagging her index finger to show she intended to deliver her piece and wasn't going to accept any interruptions. "First of all, I find it was terribly irresponsible of you to drag Astrid into all this—"

"He didn't drag me in," said Astrid. "I was the one who—"

Julia menaced Astrid with that index finger, warning her to shut her mouth. "Yes, that's what you said. But no matter, it's atrocious that Kim had that . . . person here while you were in the house. And when I was here too, isn't that right, Kim?"

"Yes."

"Yes. And I do *not* like to think that he was lying down there while you and I"—Julia glanced at Astrid and changed her choice of words—"did what we did."

"Hey, I'm not five years old," said Astrid. "You can—"

"I know I can!" said Julia and glared at Astrid. "But I don't *choose* to. Can you accept that? Or do you want details?"

"Oh, God, no."

"Thought so. Well, when you carried out this . . . I don't even know what I can call it . . . this *operation* . . . doing what you did down there in the basement while Astrid and I came and went . . . What were you thinking, Kim?"

The series of careful plans Kim had designed and carried out had now come to seem a bit absurd, even to him, since everything had been blown apart, so he said, "I wasn't thinking very much."

Julia's tone became a little more aggrieved. "That is *no excuse*. I remember when we were on Tärnö and you were looking for a house to purchase. You said you had *special needs*, and I assume those were directly connected with this escapade of yours. So don't you try to pretend that the whole thing wasn't thoroughly planned."

"Yes. It was. But now I don't know. Not anymore."

"What don't you know?"

"Why I did it. Really. I just did it. I was convinced that it would . . . help."

"May I ask something?" said Astrid.

Frustrated, Julia made a sweeping gesture inviting Astrid to take the stage. She accepted. "Trauma's a weird thing. That's what I'm learning. Sometimes it's like you're reliving it over and over again and . . . a person can feel like doing really extreme things to suppress it."

Julia's voice was much milder when she replied. "Are you speaking about yourself now?"

"No, I'm really not. That's weird, I guess. But I thought that maybe Kim . . ."

Julia turned to Kim, who sat staring at his hands. "Is that true?"

Kim slowly shook his head. "I have no idea, Julia. None. But is that all you came here for? To blame me? I'm very aware of what I've done."

A silence descended around the table. Julia regarded Kim for a long time before taking a deep breath and slowly releasing it through her nostrils. "No. We came to help you. And, eventually, Astrid. If we can."

Kim nodded and looked from Julia to Astrid, then back to Julia. He opened his laptop, called up a video, and tapped the space bar. Julia frowned as she leaned closer to the screen, pointed, and said, "But isn't that Carmen Sánchez and what's his name . . . Christof?"

The screen image showed Carmen looking around the glassed-in veranda as Christof came into the frame and approached the sofa. He leaned forward and pulled out a slip of paper.

"Where's this?" asked Julia. "What are they doing? And how was this captured?"

For the first time since the two women arrived, a trace of a smile played across Kim's lips. "Which question should I answer first?"

"Doesn't matter. You choose."

Kim pointed to the screen where Christof Adler was now reading the paper he'd discovered. "Okay, this is Martin Rudbeck's living room, about an hour ago, and—"

"Hold on!" said Astrid, with an expression of childish glee despite the situation. "Can I guess?"

"Sure," said Kim.

"It's his television, right? Is this from inside his TV?"

"It is."

Astrid seemed to have completely forgotten the business at hand as she clapped and cried in delight, "Wow! Oh, gosh, how clever!" Julia's hard look made Astrid lower her hands and assume a contrite expression.

"I planted a few clues," said Kim. "That's one. To make it look like a more . . . conventional kidnapping. But I don't think those'll buy much time." Carmen had left the veranda, and when Christof stepped out of the frame, the screen went dark. "It records only when it detects motion," Kim explained.

He turned off the laptop, and Julia drummed her fingers on the tabletop. She asked, "When you say they won't 'buy much time,' what exactly do you mean?"

"They'll start looking for other clues. Real ones. And they may find some."

"Okay," said Julia. "Now I want something from you. I want you to tell us exactly, in every detail, how you managed it when you . . ." Julia jerked her head toward the basement door. "When you picked him up and took him away."

"I don't see what use that would be," said Kim.

After an exasperated sniff she gave him a somewhat patronizing smile. "Kim, you have no idea how many investigations I've been a part of. I myself lost count a long time ago. So I don't think you'll find any better source to tell you how they think and why and what their next steps will be."

Kim nodded and gave Julia a look that held a great deal of tenderness. Then he started recounting the sequence of his actions. Astrid set her elbows on the table, put her hands around her face, and seemed more comfortable. Julia thought she understood why. From this point on, they were all in this together. Julia folded her hands in her lap and set her face in a neutral expression, unwilling to reveal that she basically felt the same way.

45

July 10, late afternoon

When Carmen and Christof got back to headquarters, they huddled in one of the smaller conference rooms to go over what they knew about the abduction and the evidence they'd found in Martin Rudbeck's villa. They connected Carmen's phone to a monitor and went through the pictures. When they got to the image of the note, Christof said, "It makes you wonder what *it* is. Something somebody wanted back?"

"We'll have to go through the house again," said Carmen. "Check more closely."

"Tell me you're joking! Didn't we get enough of that already when we . . ."

Carmen grinned. "The technicians do that job. That is, if we can get a warrant to search the place."

"Why wouldn't we? Isn't it clear as day this was an abduction?"

"Clear as day? That's saying a lot. I think we can just say that there are reasonable grounds for suspicion. What do you think happened in there?"

"Isn't that your thing?" asked Christof. "Hypothesizing?"

"Sure. But now I want to hear the police assistant's version."

Carmen didn't lose an opportunity to poke Christof for not getting down to business and applying for promotion to inspector. He'd been on board long enough and could have gotten it some time ago.

The truth was that Christof wasn't comfortable with the thought of increased supervisory responsibility and was also afraid they wouldn't promote him if he applied. It came down to the fact that he was simply scared of being rejected.

He rolled his eyes. "Okay. Clearly something happened, some sort of struggle. The rugs, the flowerpots, the knife on the floor . . ."

"Right. How do you explain that?"

"I'd guess that the victim tried to defend himself. Maybe the knife was knocked from his hand."

"And the open drawers and cupboards?"

"Someone must have been searching for *it*. Whatever they wanted back."

"Mmm. And why weren't *all* the cupboards and drawers open? Why weren't things thrown on the floor? How come the search was so haphazard?"

"Maybe the perpetrator found *it*."

"Possible. And then?"

Christof shook his head. "Huh? Why 'and then'?"

"Assume the intruder found *it*. Then what does he do, since we're supposing now that the perp's a man? He straps Rudbeck to a gurney, hauls him out to an ambulance, and drives off. Why doesn't Rudbeck resist?"

"Yeah, but the neighbor already told us that. Said he was obviously unconscious."

"Yes. And why was that?"

Christof almost said it was obvious that Rudbeck had been unconscious after being knocked on the head or something, but he stopped. He squinted at Carmen. "What are you trying to say? You have a different theory, maybe?"

"Not exactly. I'm just playing devil's advocate, so you don't jump to conclusions."

"I don't jump . . ." Christof began but then realized he'd begun to insist on his description of the events. Not good. Not coherent enough to merit a promotion. Even so, he pouted a little as he said, "Let us assume *hypothetically* that he was unconscious because of a blow to the head or something like that."

"Something like that," echoed Carmen in a tone that made Christof cringe a little. She continued, "It's not like what you see in the films. A pop on the head, the victim drops unconscious, wakes up a few hours later, says, 'What happened?' In real life . . ."

"I *know* it's not like in the movies," said Christof sourly. "I *know* that head trauma can cause—"

Before Christof managed to elaborate on his knowledge of the potentially fatal consequences of head trauma and swelling of the brain, Carmen waved toward the room's window to the hall and called, "Hello! Hey! Can you come in here a minute?"

Christof looked around and saw Jonny Munther lumbering through the door. Ever since returning from his lunch break, the DS had been distant, probably lost in dreams. It wasn't unusual for Jonny Munther to detach from his surroundings and sink into introspective musings, but something different was going on. Christof assumed it was related to the Old Spice–scented cloud, an assumption he would never be so reckless as to mention.

"Oh? Yes?" said Jonny Munther. "Something to discuss?"

"You remember that missing person in Täby?" asked Carmen.

Jonny flicked a hand impatiently. "Yeah, sure. What's up with him?"

"Got a minute?"

"I was about to go home, but—"

"Won't take long."

"Okay, okay," said Jonny and took a seat. As far as Christof was aware, the DS lived alone in a sublet and had no reason to be particularly eager to get back to it. Even so, Jonny twiddled his thumbs as Carmen briefed him on what they'd learned and showed him the pictures from the presumed scene of the crime. She suggested they'd probably want to seek a warrant to investigate.

Once she'd concluded, Jonny Munther sat for a while looking up at the fluorescent tube lighting the room, his lips slightly twitching as he mumbled under his breath. Then he lowered his gaze, leaned across the table, and said, "You two want my opinion?"

"Yeah," said Carmen. "That was, like, the idea."

"I think," said Jonny, demonstratively rubbing his chin, "someone's trying to get us to play Sherlock Holmes."

"Can you develop that for us?"

"All of this," said Jonny with a gesture that included Carmen's notebook and the wall monitor displaying the knife in front of the fridge. "It feels like a setup, practically theatrical, to send us off on a wild goose chase. It's too pat, if I can put it that way. I've seen this before. Trying to make it look like a crime different from the one actually committed."

"Mm," said Carmen. "I had some similar thoughts." Christof flung up his hands without a word. So *that* was what she was doing when she sat there claiming to be a devil's advocate! Carmen ignored him, pointed to the monitor, and said, "But why was this so sloppy, while the business with the ambulance was so . . . elaborate?"

"No idea," said Jonny with a shrug. "Maybe the criminal was in a hurry."

"Why?"

"Beats me. You can't expect me to sit here and solve the case for you with pure speculation. I'm not . . ." Jonny tried to recall the name of that Greek philosopher who applied deductive reasoning to discover truth, but it escaped him, and he had to resort to lame repetition: "Sherlock Holmes."

"You still called him a *criminal* and said it was a *case*," said Carmen Sánchez. "Does that imply that we're ready to make a call on this? Work it for real?"

"I'll take a look at it before I leave," said Jonny and got up. "If I were you two, I'd concentrate on the ambulance. Where it came from and where it went."

"Does this mean that I'm leading the investigation?" asked Carmen.

Jonny Munther smiled wearily. "Yes, Carmen. It does." He rapped the table a couple of times to signal that the session was adjourned and went toward the door with an energy that contrasted with his supposed desire to go home. Before he reached it, Carmen spoke up. "Hey, Jonny, by the way?"

Carmen didn't have a habit of using Jonny Munther's first name like that. Jonny stopped but didn't turn around. "Yes, *Carmen*?"

"How'd your date go?"

A slight shiver seemed to go up Jonny Munther's spine. He put out his hands in a limp gesture and looked about to reply but just shook his head and left the room.

"You're out of your mind!" Christof said. "Asking him like that!"

"What d'you mean?" said Carmen, opening her eyes wide. "Wanted to remind him he's human after all. Might be good to remember if he's looking for love."

"Still, you're crazy. Now what'll we do?"

"Now?" Carmen said, looking at the wall clock. "We've already put in some unpaid overtime, so we'll go home and take up the business with the ambulance first thing in the morning."

Christof had only just opened the front door when Matilda rushed into the hall with a red Switch control in her left hand and a blue one in her right. "Mario party!" she cried and held out her hands, then added with a burst of generosity, "You get to choose your color!"

"Red. Is it okay if I take off my shoes first?"

Matilda rolled her eyes dramatically and shrugged. "Yeah, *sure*. But I'm gonna have red, so you get blue."

"I thought I got to choose," Christof said as he untied his laces.

"You did, but you chose the *wrong* one."

In fact, the game platform was Christof's, and sometimes he took it to work with him. Lately, though, Matilda had gotten increasingly interested, and if Christof worked longer hours with the game device in his satchel, Matilda was furious by the time he came home. She claimed she'd almost *diiiieeed* of boredom that afternoon. She was limited to one hour of video games a day, but that didn't count when she played with a partner, and she knew how to turn that to her advantage.

After getting his shoes off, he went to the kitchen with Matilda trailing close behind. Cecilia stood stirring a stew with a strong smell of curry. "What's for dinner?" he asked.

"Fish stew," said Cecilia. "Can you see if we have chutney?"

Christof gave her a light kiss on the neck and, despite the fragrant curry, caught the faint scent of flowers on her skin and in her hair. Cecilia worked in a flower shop, and Christof was pleased she brought her job home with her, so to speak.

"Oohhh!" said Matilda. "Stop what you're doing. And we've got *scads* of chutney, a thousand jars at least. Come on!"

Before Christof followed Matilda to the living room, he checked the fridge and confirmed the girl was right. Certainly not a thousand jars, but there were two. He gave Cecilia a thumbs-up; she smiled and threw him a kiss.

When are you and Mama going to get married?

Every time that subject came to Christof's mind, it was as if someone had run a cold, wet dishrag down his back. He couldn't explain it. When he looked over his shoulder and saw the contours of Cecilia's slim back through her white T-shirt, heard her humming some Lady Gaga hit, he couldn't understand what frightened him about spending the rest of his life with this woman.

Maybe he should throw himself into it, go down on one knee and offer her a ring? Was that how you proposed? At least that would get Carmen Sánchez to shut her trap. Christof shook his head at himself. To him, shutting traps didn't sound like the best reason for a proposal, and besides, there was that icy dishrag up his back again as he settled next to Matilda on a cushion on the floor.

"What're you shaking your head for?" asked Matilda and called up the screen so they could choose their characters.

"'Cause I'm thinking how sad you'll be when I *crush* you," Christof said and chose Luigi, as usual.

"No way, you," said Matilda. "We're gonna play in *collaborative* mode."

That was probably the longest word Matilda knew, and she looked quite pleased she'd pronounced it correctly. She chose the character for whom she had an almost inexplicable attraction: Mario. Perhaps because he was the one who least resembled Princess Peach, who in Matilda's opinion was "super lame."

When they'd paddled their rubber raft down the current a bit and gotten through a couple of minor challenges, Matilda asked, unconcerned, "Hey, did you catch any bad guys today?"

"Not exactly, no," said Christof, his mind calling up the staged scene in Martin Rudbeck's residence. It bothered him that Jonny Munther had so quickly dismissed what Christof had considered a mesmerizing puzzle and told them it wasn't a puzzle at all, merely casually scattered pieces impossible to put together.

Tomorrow he would do his very best to track down that ambulance. He already had a couple of ideas, and as he went through them in his mind, Matilda began hopping on her cushion, frantically working the controller, and crying, "Paddle! Hey, get paddling!"

Christof didn't make it in time. The boat had already gone sideways in the current when he began working his own controller. They missed a landing with a clock that would have given them extra time, and the game was over. Matilda threw down her controller and cried, "Oooooh! Why are you so *out of it?*"

"Awfully sorry," said Christof. And then dinner was ready.

46

July 10, late afternoon

Once Kim Ribbing had finished his account of the abduction of Martin Rudbeck, Julia sat looking through the kitchen window for a long time. Astrid asked, "You think it'll work, all that stuff with the clues? The note and the rest of it?"

"Dunno," said Kim. "Wanted to draw things out, just in case."

"In case what?"

"In case he couldn't, for some reason or other . . . didn't come back."

Astrid fell silent and nervously scratched her thigh. Julia shook her head and said, "I don't think they'll go for it. I got the impression Sánchez is pretty smart. I don't think that *I* would have swallowed it. Too obvious."

"Like I told you, I was really in a hurry."

"Right, I know. Not criticizing, just evaluating. I assume the ambulance has been reported stolen and they'll start reviewing traffic cameras."

"I changed the license plate number."

"Okay, that's good," said Julia, startled to find herself sitting here praising a lawbreaker for adroit deception. *But that's what it's come to.* She continued, "But that won't hold them up very long. They'll be really keen on locating that ambulance. What did you do with it?"

Kim told them, and this time Astrid praised his ingenuity. Julia wasn't quite as impressed, commenting, "Clever, granted. But not watertight. They'll make a breakthrough sooner or later. The question is whether there's any risk they'll find traces of you in there."

"That's always a possibility, but I was extremely careful."

"And you didn't plant any . . . fake clues there?"

"No."

Julia leaned back in her chair, feeling like Irma Ryding resisting her boxed wine. Into her mind popped that hopelessly trite image of an angel on one shoulder and a devil on the other whispering conflicting advice.

Earlier, the angel had been adamantly warning her about the sins of omission and *aiding and abetting* without getting Julia's full attention. Now it had stepped up its campaign and was emphasizing *sheltering a felon*, while the devil was hopping merrily up and down on her collarbone. Julia wasn't certain whether there was a technical difference in the statutes, but it seemed likely, since she was actively involved now.

Julia looked at Kim, who sat frowning and twisting a long strand of black hair around a finger. How had it come to this? She'd posed several variations of that question to herself earlier, but the stakes were much higher now. She was plotting to help deceive her former colleagues, and why? For what purpose? *Why?* Was this like Irma Ryding and her alcohol? Had Julia become an addict or, at least, codependent?

She pushed away that unpleasant thought, which led her to raise a different, equally urgent matter. "I was assaulted earlier today. Threatened."

Kim let go of the strand of hair. "What? By who?"

"Couldn't tell. Someone from that biker club. The Apostates, remember?"

"Hey, hold on a minute!" exclaimed Astrid, holding up her hands. "Why would a biker club attack *you*?"

"I've been doing a little research into the True Swedes. And they're evidently not too pleased about it."

Kim peered at Julia's body and face, then asked, "Did they hurt you?"

"No. Scared me, more than anything. He said if I didn't quit what I was doing . . . I'd pay for it."

"So what are you planning to do?"

"I honestly have no idea," said Julia. "I must admit I was frightened. I'm not as tough as I thought I was."

"I think you're tough," said Astrid. "For your age, at least."

Julia raised an eyebrow at the backhanded compliment. "Thank you. So touching to hear."

"Thinking about giving up on it?" asked Kim.

Julia gave him a look, pointed to herself, and tapped her chest to remind him she wasn't exactly robust. Or young either. "What can I do?" The conversation had gotten a bit uncomfortable for her, so she tried to shut it down. "We don't need to discuss it anymore."

Kim got lost in thought, and Astrid's left hand started fumbling with her right. She yanked and twisted and pulled off a bejeweled ring and put it on the table. "I don't know, but maybe this might be useful somehow?"

Julia leaned forward and studied the ring that sparkled in the sunlight slanting through the kitchen window. It was hardly in keeping with Astrid's general appearance. Her hair was carelessly pulled back, her mascara had run a bit, and she was wearing a black T-shirt with the single word "Psycho" printed in white. Judging from the font, the reference was to the film rather than to the person in the T-shirt. Julia pointed to the ring. "What on earth is that?"

"An emerald," said Astrid. "It was Mama's. I think it's really valuable."

"What are you getting at?" asked Kim.

"Nothing yet," said Astrid. "But it's been my experience that valuable things can be useful when you want to con people."

"And you've got a lot of experience with . . . conning people?" asked Julia.

"Maybe we don't need to discuss that so much," said Astrid. "But yes, I do. Let's imagine that this ring, that's the *it*. The thing mentioned in the note."

Kim picked up the emerald solitaire and examined it from various angles before returning it to Astrid. "Impressive. But not valuable enough to make someone do . . . what I did."

"Come on! Are you some kind of expert or something?"

"No, but my mother had quite a few rings. And she was always happy to tell anyone how much they were worth."

Astrid put the ring back on her finger and gave Kim a sharp look. "How come you never talk about your parents?"

"I just mentioned my mother."

"Not exactly a case of information overload."

Kim gave Astrid a dark look. "My parents are of no interest at all. They're gone. End of subject."

Like Astrid, Julia knew nothing about Kim's parents except that they'd died along with his grandfather in a boat accident. But she knew Kim well enough to tell from his posture that the subject was extremely sensitive, so she hurried to say, "And now? What'll we do now?"

"I think I have an idea," said Kim. "Not so simple, but if it works, then . . . we kill two birds with one stone."

47

July 10, evening

Jonny Munther had intended to call Moa Malmberg as soon as he got back to his little sublet at Odenplan, but when he settled into his easy chair and brought up her number, he lost courage. He became conscious of his sweaty armpits, and after a thoroughly sticky day, he decided to take a long shower instead.

Afterward, when he'd finished vigorously toweling himself dry, he pulled on his bathrobe without thinking about it. But when he entered the living room again, he stopped to sniff the fabric. He found no trace of that Kim Ribbing guy because he'd washed the robe on the hottest cycle, but as a result, the scent of salt and sunshine had disappeared along with all the years he'd been on Tärnö with Julia.

Jonny sank into the armchair and let his arms hang limply between his knees. The bathrobe gaped open. He felt slightly pathetic, as he often did. At headquarters he got by, carrying out his job with reasonably bold creativity, but as soon as he returned to *life*, he felt he was missing out. There was just nothing to it, and his so-called personal life was no more than a route to trudge along to the next workday.

Jonny thought a bit about the disappearance of Martin Rudbeck and felt a bit uplifted that his many years of experience had brought him to conclude that the "clues" were mere fakes. Then he sank into unhappy musing. What if he were wrong? Really, it was unprofessional to wave away a possible solution, but it had seemed so obvious the clues were intended to mislead them. But what if the perpetrator was now sitting up on a branch somewhere and laughing his ass off at Jonny's stupidity?

Let it be. Tomorrow's another day.

Jonny snorted and got up from his armchair. He couldn't even think in anything but platitudes. He went to the kitchen and checked the freezer, where he found a meal so covered with frost that he couldn't see what it was. Didn't matter. He put it in the microwave and readied himself for an unpleasant surprise.

While waiting for the meal to heat, he turned on his computer, called up Spotify, and randomly chose a Shostakovich symphony. "Shostakovich"—one of those names it seemed a person should recognize. Part of Jonny's project of improving his general knowledge of literature and music.

The microwave oven hummed as horns bleated and percussion crashed at irregular intervals from the computer speakers. Jonny shook his head. Hey, what was wrong with creating a *melody*? He'd tried Shostakovich a couple of times before, and there was one time, somewhere in it, he'd actually come across a really beautiful tune. Why couldn't the guy just stick to that? Even that melody had dissolved into dissonant blaring and noise.

Jonny toughed it out for about a minute before giving up and calling up some Tchaikovsky. That was different—you could even hum along if you felt like it. Jonny wasn't in the mood just then, but he let the piano concerto continue until the microwave dinged. He took out the container and found it held a Thai chicken dish with rice.

Jonny sat at the kitchen table, lowered the volume of the Tchaikovsky playerman's diligent but melodious hammering, reached for a spoon and a can of light beer, and began to shovel the dry rice and curry sauce into his mouth. He stopped suddenly, the spoon halfway to his mouth.

Playerman? That can't be the right word, can it? Musician? Pianist?

With his mouth half open, Jonny stared down at the contents of the carton. They evoked queasy memories of a stabbing murder. He paid no attention to the odor that practically seared his nostrils. Then he snapped his fingers and scooped up more grub, pleased with himself.

Interpreter! Tchaikovsky interpreter. What a hell of a word.

Jonny scarcely noticed the taste of the chicken curry. Once that was done and his beer bottle was empty, he remained seated at the kitchen table looking out at a lonely, exhaust-stained alder with leaves limp in the summer heat. He listened to traffic and the distant voices of people in the street. *I probably should take a walk somewhere.*

Right. But where? Going to the local pub wasn't on Jonny Munther's list of things to do, but maybe he could take a stroll. The bathrobe had slid open during his frugal meal, revealing his curly gray chest hair. He pulled it tighter around him and knew he wasn't going out on any promenade, for he wasn't going to bother to get dressed. Things just were as they were.

Jonny tossed the food carton into the trash, rinsed the spoon and dried it with a dishcloth, dropped the beer bottle into the recycle bin. Three hours left until he could reasonably lie down and go to sleep. It was a hell of a thing, all this time for which each human being had to find something to do. Oh well, not too long ago he'd read Karin Boye's *Kallocain* and gotten a glimpse of how things might be if the government took control of everyone's free time. Pretty dismal, to say the least.

That thought sent him back to his easy chair, where he picked up *Oliver Twist* by Dickens and resumed from where he'd left off. After ten minutes he'd had enough. Jonny had stopped reading Swedish detective novels long before this, since they were marred by the same problem he had with Dickens: all that *irony*. Not a single description of an event or person that wasn't from some sort of distance. Maybe Jonny was too demanding, but he wasn't interested in mildly comic portrayals when everything seemed to conspire to disappoint him.

Jonny was on the way to having his morose thoughts drag him down into a morass of self-pity when his phone rang. He assumed it was job related, but when he picked up the phone, caller ID showed him *Moa Malmberg*. Jonny froze and dragged his fingers through his hair despite the fact this wasn't a video call.

Jonny was about to swipe right to answer, when he stopped, fingers still in the air. What should he say? Act like he would with a random number, or react to show he knew it was Moa on the line? The ringing continued as he pondered his dilemma, repeating the ringtone of the guitar intro to "Smoke on the Water," and Jonny started to panic.

He pulled himself together, fearing the ringing would stop, swiped, and said, "Yes, this is Jonny."

"Hey, this is Moa," she said. "Thought you had me in your contacts?"

"Yeah, right, I didn't check to see."

"Maybe you have me down as *Bobby*?"

Jonny groaned. He had just about managed to suppress the memory of that painful incident outside City Hall, but Moa obviously wasn't going to let him forget it. "I'm really sorry—"

"Skip it," said Moa. "Just joking. Like I said, it's happened before."

Jonny half closed his eyes, and when he called up a mental picture, he had difficulty understanding how anyone could mistake her for a young man. Above all, that smooth, slender neck was nothing like a man's. Nor was the shape of her lips. Jonny cleared his throat and asked in a choked voice, "Everything going okay otherwise?"

"Oh, sure. It's just fascinating how much paperwork a death creates and leaves behind."

"Anything I can do?"

"Nope—except come over for dinner tomorrow if you can. And want to."

Some substance welled up along Jonny's tongue and gums and stuck them together. When he'd mentioned that he wasn't used to this kind of thing, he hadn't exaggerated. Since Julia Malmros had left, he hadn't met a woman where there were *intentions* in play. And Julia had been his first.

Now, now, Jonny tried to calm himself. Maybe that wasn't the situation at all. Someone can invite a colleague over for dinner without hearing wedding bells ringing in the distance or expecting a great big hug. Besides, the prospect of a home-cooked meal was appealing just on its own.

"Yes, with pleasure," Jonny managed to reply. "I'd like that. Sure."

"Great," said Moa. "There's just one thing you need to know."

Without realizing it Jonny had been clutching one edge of his robe so hard that his knuckles were aching. He let go and said, "Oh, really?"

"Maybe I mentioned that my husband, Marcus, died just two years ago? Cancer. Long, drawn out. Horrible. I can't claim that I've gotten over it. Time heals all, et cetera, et cetera. But it leaves enormous scars, at least in my case. I'm not all there. It's like he's a shadow inside me, all the time, a shadow I don't even *want* to disappear, you understand?"

"I think so."

"Just want you to be aware that you're not going to be visiting a blank slate when you come to dinner. It's scribbled full of really dark nuances. I'm managing it, managing it fairly well, looking for patches of light and living in those. But just so you understand."

"And now I do," said Jonny. Moa's account left no doubt at all that there were intentions, which prompted Jonny to gather his courage and really take a chance. "Is it okay if I say something? On a different subject?"

"Please do."

"You have a really beautiful voice. I hear it even more clearly now on the phone. You could be an audiobook narrator."

Moa laughed, a light, pure burst of sound with no shadow at all. "You know what? No need to explain how it happened, but in fact I have recorded a couple of audiobooks. Detective novels. By nobody you've ever heard of, but thanks for the compliment."

"Excuse me if I sounded unfeeling," said Jonny. "I didn't mean that—"

"No problem," said Moa. "Like I said. I just wanted that out in the open."

"I understand," said Jonny. "But you know, I'm not a particularly sensitive sort of guy when it comes to such things."

"As for that," said Moa, "I'm completely convinced that you're wrong. Let's say seven o'clock tomorrow?"

48

July 10, evening

Astrid went to her room after Kim and Julia left the villa. She turned on her computer and logged into the Animal Action forum. The first thing she saw was a new post titled "Stop the Fur Industry—Skin a Mink Farmer Today." The post was illustrated with an impressively detailed color drawing of a wicked-looking peasant farmer who'd been stripped of his skin so that the muscles and nerves gleamed red. Astrid hit Like.

She'd been following the forum for a couple of years, and the posts had gotten increasingly threatening in tone. An attack on a poultry farm was planned in coded language; hunters would become the hunted if ever the anonymous poster managed to lay hands on a weapon. A pig farmer's machines had been torched by an arsonist. And so on.

Astrid had been following the discussions simply because she was interested in seeing which way the fringes of her own movement were moving, but she'd been satisfied to limit her own contribution to brutally honest video reports. But something had changed since her parents were killed. Astrid didn't understand it herself, but she was feeling a great deal more sympathy for those who wanted to take radical, hands-on action to stop slaughter, hunting, and exploitation of animals.

Nothing had made a difference! There was no meaning to "more humane" methods of raising animals or "ecologically" feeding pigs and poultry simply to assuage guilty consciences. You had to get down to the root of the evil: humanity's arrogant assumption that it had the right to exploit animals for profit and nourishment.

Nourishment, that's right. In that respect, summer was the worst time of year for Astrid. Through the open window before her she caught the faint scent of a grill where someone was searing a body part to enjoy with "a good glass of wine." Magazine inserts and even whole newspapers were devoted to tips for the perfect barbecue.

The lack of empathy left Astrid nauseated. Those people sat around glowing coals over which a murdered, chopped-up animal lay sizzling, and they toasted one another with their fine wines, having the time of their lives. They themselves should be trussed to a spit and rotated over open flames. That gave her an idea.

Using her alias, Murder Machine, Astrid began to draw up a recipe for "grilled barbecuer," the best way to go about preparing a whole barbecue enthusiast for a perfect cannibal evening. Start with a week of forcing a marinade down his gullet through a funnel, the way people did with geese to obtain foie gras, and then . . .

Astrid's phone rang. Caller ID showed *Larsa*. Astrid moaned. Her uncle had tried to call five times during the day, and she hadn't picked up. She knew that wasn't a long-term solution, so she put the phone to her ear. "Yes, hello. This is Astrid."

"Where are you?" asked her uncle. "I've been calling all day."

"Oh, yeah, oops!" said Astrid. "Didn't have my phone with me."

If her uncle had known her better, he wouldn't have believed that. Astrid *never* went anywhere without her phone. But now he merely said, "Aha, I see. When are you coming home?"

Astrid wrinkled her nose. Even though her description of him to Kim had painted her uncle in unjustifiably dismal terms, there was no way she could consider the room in his apartment to be her "home." It was merely a place with a bed where she could rest her head. And she didn't want to.

"I dunno," said Astrid. "I have some stuff to do."

"Astrid, you were out all last night too. I'm responsible for you, and . . . actually, where are you right now?"

"I told you already. A friend has a house down by Gärdet. I have a room here."

"And that friend . . . is no doubt that guy who brought you back from Vamlinge on his motorcycle?"

"Yes. Exactly."

Astrid found it ominous that her uncle referred to Kim as "that guy" even though Astrid had told him Kim's name. Her uncle's voice gave her the image of someone standing there glaring, arms across his chest. "Then I wish to meet that individual. And see how you're really living."

"No need for that."

"Oh, yes, Astrid, it's necessary. I can't simply let you run around willy-nilly. I want to see what conditions you're in. Otherwise, I'll put an end to this."

Astrid protested a couple more times without effect, then they negotiated. Her uncle would come visit the following afternoon at four o'clock to "check it out," as Uncle Lasse expressed it in his attempt to use teenager-speak. Astrid ended the call and said *willy-nilly* aloud to herself a couple of times. What did that even mean?

She went back to her recipe for marinated grill master but found she'd lost interest. When she thought about what to do *after* the marinade, images of Martin Rudbeck intruded. Astrid was alone in the house, and the guy was still lying in the basement.

Over the course of the afternoon, the eerie sensation of something hovering at her back, intent on giving her the evil eye and doing her harm, had diminished, but now dry terror filled Astrid's chest and clutched her throat. When she listened close, she thought she heard a *shuffling* somewhere downstairs, probably the corpse creeping slowly up the stairs to take its revenge.

Astrid placed her hands flat on the tabletop, closed her eyes, and practiced deep breathing. The sound she was hearing wasn't from downstairs at all; it was simply the wind rustling in the trees. Even so, it was somewhat unnerving, to say the least, to know that the cadaver of a human being she herself had killed was lying thirty feet beneath her. Even after pushing away the thought of a lurking corpse, she had the impression that a sort of angry, malicious gas was emanating from the basement.

She hugged herself and sat stock still, fearing anxiety would over-whelm her. It didn't, so she was able to retake control and devote herself to the assignment Kim had given her. She opened YouTube and began sampling screams from clips of horror films. After listening to more than two dozen panic-stricken women from, among others, *Friday the 13th*, *The Texas Chain Saw Massacre*, and, of course, *Scream*, she decided to go to the source.

Perhaps inspired by the T-shirt she was wearing, she took a clip of Janet Leigh's scream from the shower scene in *Psycho*. It was so wonderfully pure and clear. The problem was the jarring strings overlaid on the soundtrack. Astrid opened an equalizer and began the task of filtering them out.

49

Julia Malmros had a reputation as a troubled young girl when she entered ninth grade, one of those who sneak a cigarette at recess, hang out with bad boys, and never study. She was at risk of not being admitted by any reputable high school. Her father called her in for a heart-to-heart talk during Christmas holidays and laid down the law. He stopped her allowance and told her she was going to stay home after school and on weekends.

By then Julia had begun to tire of *la vida cabrón*. Classmates had stopped admiring her escapades as a pretend rebel, and most of them now saw her just as a delinquent. Julia therefore made the classic New Year's resolution: She was going to shape up. Go to classes, do homework, get her grades up to qualify for an arts and sciences track.

That was why her heart was in her throat one February day as she raced down the school corridor to her social studies class. She'd overslept. She opened the classroom door and found the room empty. Julia checked her schedule and realized she'd gotten the day wrong. She was tardy, but it was to math class.

She slumped against the doorframe and stood there, despondent, her eyes squeezed shut. *Damn it all.* She really was *trying*, so why was everything against her? Opening her eyes, about to turn and hurry to the math room, she caught sight of the social studies teacher's handbag hanging on the back of the chair behind the desk.

Julia glanced right and left along the deserted hall. In a flash her good intentions were blown away, and . . . *opportunity makes the thief.* She strode forward, opened the handbag, pulled out the teacher's wallet, and filched two ten-kronor notes. She stuffed the cash in her pocket, put everything else where it had been, and ran to class.

She vaguely recalled spending the money that same afternoon on candy, cigarettes, and the latest *OK!* magazine.

That coup went off without a hitch, but her conscience started bothering her. She'd *stolen* from her teacher, a person she really liked. That made her a thief, a delinquent. *A criminal,* her father would have said. What had she been thinking? She hadn't been thinking at all. She'd simply given in to temptation.

She'd wished more than anything she could undo it, and when she finally started receiving her allowance again, she would go around with two ten-kronor notes in her pocket so she could stuff them into the teacher's purse when the opportunity arose. But she never got the chance. Julia finished ninth grade with superior marks and a sense of guilt that never really went away.

That memory revisited Julia for at least the thousandth time when she unlocked her building's front door on her return from Kim Ribbing's villa. She'd often thought she should write a letter, explain what had happened, and pay the money back with interest. And interest upon the interest. She'd never brought herself to do it, and now her teacher had passed away. *Snip, snap, snout, that mark will never come out.*

If a mere twenty kronor had made her feel like that, what would her conscience do after she helped people conceal a corpse and get away with murder? She was already feeling terribly jittery. She foresaw unavoidable consequence: This wouldn't merely jam a crown of thorns on her head; a whole damned thorn patch would occupy her soul.

Despite that, she couldn't stop seeking possibilities and speculating about ways to solve the problem. Her latest thoughts had centered around the legend of the "Nybro Bay lounge." Put the corpse's feet into poured concrete and dump it overboard, maybe somewhere conveniently close along Djurgårdsbrunn bay. Of course, that was entirely unrealistic. No practical means of transporting it there, enormous risk of discovery. And drastic consequences.

Julia practiced the restraint she'd counseled to Irma, resisting the box of red wine and instead brewing herself a cup of tea to take to her desk. She checked her email. The first item she noticed was a message with the subject line Yeah yeah yeah! sent by someone unknown. After recent events, Julia was no fan of mail from anyone not on her contact list, but she opened it because the title sounded vaguely threatening.

Hi, the text read, Emma Berglund at Bluefish here. Wonderful that we got to meet you!

Bluefish was the production company with ultimate responsibility for the Åsa Fors series. Julia couldn't recall this Emma Berglund and certainly didn't remember any "wonderful" meeting. But there'd been so many faces and names, and so little wonderful about the experience. She kept reading.

Just wanted to tell you TV4 has moved us to Saturdays at 8 p.m. Imagine that! Prime time! Watch out, world, here comes Åsa Fors, just like *Idol* and *Let's Dance*! We broke out the champagne when we heard, so treat yourself to a glass too! Love and kisses! Emma

P.S. It would be super for the marketing campaign if you could write a little something to say what you think of the series!

Julia stared at the screen. The only thing that occurred to her was to wonder why Emma hadn't put an exclamation point after her signature too. Then the news sank in, and she understood the implications.

Idol, *Let's Dance*, and Åsa Fors. *Gentle Steel.*

The series had been scheduled for ten o'clock on Friday evenings, allowing Julia to console herself that it might run without attracting much attention. Not a chance of that now, and Julia really did find herself wanting a glass of bubbly. Or, better, a couple of bottles.

She was about to ring Irma Ryding to complain, but she stopped herself from initiating a conversation that would all too likely turn into a booze fest. Her pulse accelerated. She'd told Irma the series would sink Åsa Fors. This was worse: It would torpedo her creation and leave nothing but wreckage floating on a lead-gray sea. Julia clutched her desk and put her face down on it.

Calm down. This, too, will pass. Keep your perspective.

Julia looked up at the bookshelves with multiple editions of her novels. She seemed to recall something that a writer—was it Raymond Chandler?—once said when asked whether a series of mediocre film versions had destroyed his novels. Raymond, assuming that's who it was, had looked up at his row of novels on the shelf and said, "No. I think they look exactly the same as before."

Good response. Tough. That's how to punch back. That's the way to think. Julia resumed breathing and tried to put herself in that frame of mind. It wasn't as if the trite reimagining was going to ruin her life's work and spill her heart's blood; a few stories she'd made up had become a huge TV series, and she'd been well paid for them. Leave it at that.

Julia reread Emma Berglund's message and decided she could live with it. Sure, she could. The problem was the P.S., the suggestion it would be *super* if she could write something about her thoughts for the PR people. She thought the series was trash, but that was hardly what they wanted to hear. She'd be the Swedish opposite to all the "super excited" Americans in film and television industries. Hugely frantic? On fire? Festively hyped up? Could she stretch it to "intensely awaiting"? That much was true, though not in the way they wanted.

Julia's fingers hovered over the keyboard, but the only image that presented itself was that of floating wreckage abandoned in a vast ocean. Then her eyes flew open wide, and she sat bolt upright in her desk chair.

Tärnö!

Of course. The Djurgårdsbrunn bay wasn't deeper than twenty-five feet—yes, she'd checked—but the waters around Tärnö were two hundred, deeper in some places. No risk anyone would notice something on the bottom, no matter how clear the water.

Julia got up from her desk and paced a couple of times around the little room, running her fingertips across the spines of the books. You'd first have to cross the channel to the mainland in the motorboat, pull it ashore in some deserted place accessible by road. The body could be stored in the trunk of the car; her Prius had enough room. It would have to be wrapped in something, a net, maybe, and weighted down . . .

Hold your horses, girl.

Julia stopped, her fingertips brushing the thick cover of *Ulysses.* Was she getting serious about this and planning it as more than a thought experiment? Was she willing to get involved in something, say, a *thousand times* more criminal than swiping a couple of tens from a handbag, something that would hound her with guilt for the rest of her life?

No, she truly did not want that. But she wanted to protect Kim. Despite the ups and downs in the surges of their bloodstorm, he'd somehow become her responsibility that time she'd found him huddled in front of her building. True, he had power over her, and of course he was an adult able to fend for himself. On one level. On another, he was an extremely lonely, socially incapable person with a tenuous grip on reality. Someone who needed protection and care.

That thought galvanized Julia. She patted James Joyce as if he were a lapdog and told herself it was like that trashy pop music Kim listened to, reaching out beyond himself to be close to a beloved. Through fire and water, rain and snow, and so on. That's what it *really* was all about.

Julia was feeling almost inebriated by the thought of her possible transcendence. She picked up her mobile and called "Kim Cracker."

50

July 10, evening

The vibration from the phone in Kim's inside pocket was feeble as a fly walking across his heart because he'd put it on the lowest setting. He ignored it. For several hours he'd been lying concealed on a hill on the far edge of Lux Park on Lilla Essingen, which was no place for conversation.

The brick edifice down the hill had once been the factory that produced Barnängen's talcum powder, but it now was the Apostates clubhouse. The biker gang dealt in another type of powder. Talcum is often used to cut cocaine. Maybe they'd found some old stock, but the link to talcum was probably just a coincidence. The building simply fit the club's needs. At some distance from the much larger but also shuttered Electrolux factory, Barnängen's former factory was secure because it was so isolated. According to what Kim could make out through a long-distance nightscope, there weren't even any cameras mounted outside. The imposing wooden door had a cipher lock, of course, but that shouldn't pose a problem.

The building had two stories. Kim had gotten a look at part of the lower floor when a caravan of six motorcycles rolled in. The ground level looked almost empty, so it was probably used only as a garage. In contrast, the upstairs windows were barred and curtained, probably to hide a remote *man cave* for lounging, boozing, and conspiring.

Later, as Kim still lay in wait, quietly rumbling cycles filed out, leaving one behind. At least *one* person was in the building, which suited Kim just fine. Any more would be problematic but probably still doable.

After the bikers rolled away, accelerating toward the E4, and the sound faded, Kim descended the hill and walked casually toward the building, as if he were an evening stroller with a passing interest in buildings slated for demolition. The plan had been to tear down the old factory to make room for houses, but that proposal had gotten stuck at the building authority when the Apostates had moved in. Subtle threats might have been made.

With that same attitude of indifferent curiosity, Kim walked to one of the big windows on the ground level and peered inside. It was essentially empty, as he'd expected. He'd hoped that only *one* motorcycle would be there, and he scowled when he spotted three more. Groups were much more dangerous than individuals; unpredictability became a factor.

Kim saw spiral staircases at either end. A couple of blinking red diodes at ceiling level caught his attention, so although Apostates were at the top of the food chain after crushing the competition, they weren't entirely heedless. Those motion detectors were mounted high in the two visible corners, so the other two were probably similarly equipped. No one could simply go barreling in; the alarms would go off.

Studying the three additional motorcycles, Kim saw that one had no front wheel, and tools lay on the floor beside the others. They were probably parked for repair and might not indicate the presence of more bikers. *Might* not. Kim didn't care much for that word in situations like this.

Kim left the window and ambled along the building, hands in his pockets, to the main door. Through his binoculars he'd made out something worth closer inspection, if it was what he thought. And it was. As he walked by a couple of yards away in the fading evening light, he saw a rectangle about eight inches square. A cat door.

Kim continued toward Lux Park, a faint grin on his face. The Apostates were so cocksure, they didn't care about that minor breach in their stout defenses. Clearly, a person couldn't get in that way. Even if Kim had been a contortionist able to disjoint himself at will, he couldn't have gotten his head through. On the other hand, the cat door offered the opportunity to test the club's defenses.

Kim walked to the water's edge, sat on a rock, and looked out over Lake Mälaren to where the gleaming arches of the western bridge marked the entrance to Riddarfjärden bay. The quiet here was astonishing; this central location was so isolated from the rest of Stockholm. Traffic noises were audible in the distance, and he heard the low stutter of a two-stroke engine a hundred yards away. In the stillness, it was difficult to imagine the implements of violence and destruction stored in that building. Things that go bang in the night and firearms that sent people screaming . . . though not now. At present, nothing disturbed the peaceful evening but the sputtering of a motor hardly strong enough to power a two-person boat.

Kim shifted so his back was to the water. It might be good to go on the attack, but he doubted it. Could just as well wait and see what happened. If he'd been able to choose, he would have monitored the former talc factory for several days and nights, charting movements and patterns to get a full picture. He didn't have that freedom. He was forced by necessity and a certain amount of stress to do something. He didn't like that at all.

The hell squad of motorcycles out on a night cruise could return at any moment. Kim had no fallback plan to deal with that contingency. He was a good street fighter, but he wouldn't have a chance against that many, not when a group fired up with adrenaline and testosterone launched into him. Kim rested his elbows on his knees and contemplated the possibility this evening might be his last.

As a child and youth, Kim had often wanted to quit this life, and he'd even made some attempts to do so. The attempt to drown himself in the lake on his grandfather's estate had come the closest to succeeding.

He'd also tried a razorblade, a rope, and a couple of forks stuck into an electrical outlet, but life had stubbornly clung to him. Kim wasn't sure why; perhaps his will hadn't been strong enough. Maybe he even would have finally thrashed his way up out of the lake if the gardener hadn't come to save him. There was no way of telling.

Since he'd been discharged from treatment and set free from institutions, he hadn't cared whether he lived or died. He'd put himself into situations where his life hung from a thread but had never again made a deliberate attempt at suicide. To his own astonishment, he'd struggled as hard as he could to remain alive, even though it was meaningless. Maybe that very struggle was what intrigued him.

And now?

Kim peered at the former talc factory. The noise of the outboard motor behind him had faded, and the building was shrouded in silence. As he'd sat in the empty office space in his villa, chewing the slice of cold kebab pizza, he'd felt the indifference of his youth and the desperation of his childhood catching up to him. Then Julia and Astrid had rung the doorbell. And now here he was, about to take up the struggle again.

Sitting on the rock, examining his life from various perspectives, Kim had been so distracted that at first he didn't understand what was happening when something brushed against his leg with a timid "meow?" Although that's exactly what he'd been expecting and hoping.

An orange tabby rubbed its head against his shin as it waved—or, rather, wagged—a tail that appeared to have been cut short. Kim scratched the cat behind its ears and explored its neck. No collar; domesticated though probably formerly feral, no doubt a member of the clientele allowed to use the cat door.

"Shush, shush, Peter No Tail," said Kim, taking the cat onto his lap. "Wanna help me out with something?"

The cat tapped its head against Kim's stomach and purred. It seemed to have no objections.

51

July 10, evening

Jonny Munther's bedroom could be called *spartan*, even though soldiers of Sparta often campaigned in even starker circumstances, according to the condensed world history survey Jonny had read through about six months earlier.

A colleague had been assigned to Spain, and when Jonny took the sublet, it had been decorated with framed prints of the sort you buy at IKEA: construction workers on lunch break above the New York City skyline, van Gogh sunflowers, and Hokusai's wave. Jonny had found them distracting when it was time to go to sleep, especially the workers munching sandwiches over the abyss, and the first thing he did was take them down.

That had left stark white walls punctuated with screw holes, a narrow single bed and adjoining night table, a chair, and a wardrobe. It reminded him a lot of his boyhood room in Ersta outside Norrtälje, the difference being that there'd been at least *one* decorative touch there: an enlargement of a photo of a boy dragging a pig by its tail that his father had won in a crossword puzzle competition. He'd hung it over Jonny's bed because he thought it was funny.

Jonny pulled off his bathrobe and hung it on the chair back, then wormed his way under a duvet with a pattern of large, colorful lilies.

It had belonged to the owner, and Jonny was completely indifferent to it. Whose business was it if he slept under a gaudy display of flowers?

Jonny pulled the sheet up to his nose, shut out the distant street sounds, and pretended it was a morning in Ersta during summer break. On school mornings he didn't have to help in the garden, but in summer he had his chores. Back then Jonny had moaned and groaned at being a farm boy obliged to get up early to gather eggs and to milk the cows by hand because their teats were too sensitive for the milking machine.

Now, in retrospect, those were his fondest memories: The sun just peeking above the horizon, the clean air scented with the sweet smell of manure. Chickens clucking in their coop and a cow's warm belly against his forehead as he carefully squeezed and pulled. Papa's strong hand clapping his shoulder when he did a good job.

Jonny blinked a couple of times and looked up at the ceiling, intermittently illuminated through the venetian blinds by the headlights of passing vehicles. He could feel very lonely at times like these, but now there might be some consolation in sight. Jonny turned on his side to pick up his mobile from the bedside table. He opened the Storytel app and tapped *Moa Malmberg* into the search field.

Bingo! Moa was listed as the narrator of four books in a series called Stockholm by Night by a writer Jonny had never heard of. The first of them was titled *Conspiracy at the Top*. Jonny pressed the Listen icon. Moa's dark, agreeable voice immediately streamed from the phone speaker as she gave the novel's credits. Then the story began.

"Detective Superintendent Hardy Bengtsson hadn't yet had his morning coffee and was in a foul humor when he got to the station . . ."

Oh, yes, Jonny thought. *That's certainly familiar.*

Jonny Munther folded his hands across his stomach and closed his eyes, a little smile playing across his lips. Despite all expectation he became engaged in the story within ten minutes and would find it difficult to stop listening. Ah, well, what did that matter? He had Moa with him, in a way, and he could allow himself a sleepless night from time to time.

52

The striped cat hung limp as a dishrag under Kim's arm, still purring as he carried it to the door and lowered himself onto his haunches. He put the cat down; it turned and nosed Kim's knee. Kim turned it to face the cat door and gave it a little push. Its truncated tail stood straight up but relaxed as the cat slunk all the way through. Kim got up, took a few steps back, and waited.

A couple of minutes went by. Nothing happened. He looked around, then stretched out on his stomach and pushed the door up a bit to peer through the opening. The cat sat in the middle of the garage by the parked motorcycle. When it heard the quiet swish of the cat door, it looked around at him and said "meow?" as if to ask what Kim was expecting.

Nothing. It had already done its job. Kim got to his feet and examined the cipher lock. There was nothing robust about it; it was the sort you might encounter on any door in town. Kim had the tools to unscrew the cover and even electronic gear to short-circuit the lock, but he took a stab at the simplest method of all: He put on a head lamp, cupped his hands around the panel, and breathed heavily on it.

Kim shook his head in disbelief. The Apostates really should have a talk with their security guy. Six of the buttons showed condensation, while the oily film left by thumbs and index fingers on the three regularly used buttons made them brightly reflective. Those numbers were 1, 3, and 9.

Is it going to be as simple as this?

Kim punched in 1-9-3-3 and the door clicked. He rolled his eyes. Of course the Apostates would use the year of Hitler's rise to power in Germany for their door code. Maybe they just didn't care. Or weren't the sharpest knives in the drawer.

Kim checked behind himself one last time and listened for sounds of approaching bikes. Nothing. He took off his backpack and got down flat on his belly. He pushed the door open and wriggled his way inside. When he'd gotten all the way through without triggering an alarm, he carefully pushed the door shut behind him and crawled across the cement floor, dragging his pack with him.

Kim had had a bit of luck with the Apostates being cat lovers or at least not minding having cats around. He'd guessed that was why their motion sensors were aimed high enough that a stray cat waltzing through the door wouldn't set off the alarms. His assumption proved correct. He wasn't yet ready to celebrate that success as he dragged the backpack across the floor, for it might be bulky enough to set them off.

Kim pushed himself forward with his elbows, and he'd made it halfway to the staircase when the striped tabby came padding over. It started licking his cheek with its rough little tongue. Kim squinted up and saw its docked tail waving from side to side. A thought occurred to him. Someone in the Apostates could have clipped its tail to that length to keep it from setting off the alarm. Maybe Lilla Essingen was crawling with cats with docked tails. He'd better stay as low as possible. Kim pushed the cat away, whispered, "Thanks for the help, but that's enough now," and continued.

The space stank of dirty oil, gasoline, and engine grease. His windbreaker caught on irregularities in the cement floor. He advanced a yard or so, stopped, and listened. No sounds except the faint hum of the ventilation system and the purring of the cat stubbornly sticking to his side.

Kim neared the spiral staircase and again looked around the ground floor space. There was nothing in the garage but the bikes and a couple of packing cases. Those were pushed against the wall and didn't offer any cover. He'd have nowhere to hide if someone came in. He tightened his jaws. It was a real shame he hadn't had time to log their movements. He didn't like trusting himself to chance, but it was too late now to change his mind. He wriggled forward to the lowest step of the spiral staircase.

Kim looked up at the balefully gleaming red eye of the motion detector. He doubted the sensors were aimed at the stairs too, but it would be stupid to take risks after getting this far. Kim pushed the pack ahead of him as he squirmed his way up the spiral steps like a big, blindly exploring insect larva. The cat remained below, its head tilted as it watched him go.

The reek of grease and gasoline grew sharper with every successive stair, while from the open door at the top of the stairs emanated the smells of beer and cigarette smoke. Was that the sound of someone breathing? Kim turned his head, listening closely, and started when he heard rustling and a slap. He looked back over his shoulder and saw the cat's gleaming yellow gaze below. The escape route was clear. He could still abort this mad business.

He closed his eyes and listened intently. Someone cleared his throat, and then there was . . . a long snuffling sound. Someone up there was stretched out asleep. Kim pushed his pack up another couple of steps and was beginning to believe that his luck would hold, which wasn't the usual case. Still no sound from upstairs other than regular breathing, so Kim took a chance and pushed the backpack up onto the landing where it would be visible to anyone in the room.

He almost cried out when he felt a sudden movement across his back, but he realized what was happening before the cat nuzzled his neck. He put his brow against the top step and let the cat use the back of his head as a ramp. Kim raised his head and peered across the landing.

Fly-specked yellow lampshades hung from the ceiling and illuminated a room where a well-worn black leather sofa was positioned before a huge television screen. The sofa was flanked by a couple of armchairs. An assortment of empty beer cans stood on the coffee table beside an overflowing ashtray. On that sofa a man in a leather biker's outfit lay sleeping on his back. One arm hung over the edge. The cat went forward and sniffed his fingers.

If it were possible for a cat to wrinkle its nose, the cat's abrupt shake of its head showed that was just what it intended. It shivered and slunk beneath the sofa. Kim got to his feet and quietly ascended the remaining stairs.

He was inside the den of the damned, the headquarters of the Apostates. Nothing in the room indicated that the place was different from any other miserably shabby den. Dust bunnies on the floor reminded him of Moebius's apartment. Here, too, empty pizza boxes were scattered among candy wrappers and other trash. The only difference was that, in this place, the general mess included beer cans and booze bottles. Looked like nobody was willing to be a wuss and clean things up. The flooring was of heavy planking stained here and there with unidentifiable liquids.

Kim glided forward silently to a half-open door and pushed it to look inside. It didn't creak. The room on the other side was probably an office but looked more like a trash bin, a place where bikers tossed documents and papers they didn't know what to do with. Some papers lay in piles, and individual sheets were scattered across the desk and on the floor. There was an ancient laptop, but Kim wasn't interested in it. He returned to the main room.

The man on the sofa slept with his mouth open. From time to time he groaned, smacked his lips, or cleared his throat. A leather jacket with the club emblem hung on the back of the sofa. Their logo was an upside-down cross with a death's head jammed onto the top. Kim moved forward with extreme care, wary of creaking floorboards, till he reached the jacket and could search its pockets.

The inside pocket held a mobile phone he assumed to be the property of the sleeping man. A crumpled receipt was in an exterior pocket. Kim smoothed it out and read it. A six-pack of 3.2 beer and two packages of chocolate wafers, purchased at Circle-K a week earlier. Gangster life was evidently not too glamorous. Kim pocketed the receipt and turned on the phone. It required a code or fingerprint ID.

Kim stared down at the sleeper, who had begun to snore quietly. Nothing of particular interest here and not what he'd come looking for, but Kim squatted anyway and gently set the phone's print reader against the index finger of the man's dangling hand. Fortunately, it was the correct hand. The phone unlocked.

Kim quickly reviewed the contact list but found nothing of real interest, no names that meant anything to him. He happened to flick open the photo library, which consisted of only a couple dozen images, mostly of bikers partying and raising their cans or glasses to the camera, showing off their biceps, or pointing to their tattoos. Sloppy scenes of extreme squalor.

A better composed image made Kim stiffen. Without mentioning it to Julia, he'd done a deep search on Apostates chieftain Dennis Hamberg and Claes-Göran Schwarzkopf but had found no connections. And now he had an extraordinary one right here in his hand.

A photo showed the two men shaking hands before a banner depicting an eye with a cross through the pupil. The remarkable aspect was that the picture seemed to be an *official* pose, for both men were looking into the camera. It was reminiscent of world leaders shaking to celebrate an agreement of some kind or, why not, that picture of Elvis and Nixon shaking hands in front of the American flag.

The man on the sofa grimaced and took a quarter turn so that his sleeping face was turned toward the room. Kim backed out of his potential line of sight and decided he had no time for detail work. With his own mobile he took a photo of the image before returning the phone to the man's jacket. Now on to the important business.

Kim fished in the outer pocket of his pack and took out a small plastic container and a glass vial with an eyedropper. He ran his hands through his hair so it stood up around his head, pulled his jacket loosely over one shoulder, then slung his backpack crooked behind him. Finally, he unscrewed the dropper from the vial of glycerin, took up a bit of the liquid, looked up at the ceiling, and put one drop into each eye.

Kim blinked and his vision became blurry. He'd tried it out before, so he knew that now his eyes had a glassy, drugged appearance. He unscrewed the cap of the plastic container and leaned over the sleeping man's head. Through the blurry mist covering his corneas, Kim saw that the thinning hair of the man's scalp was pulled back into a ponytail.

A few strands had strayed from the ponytail. Kim took a sharp breath, seized them, and yanked. The man grunted sharply and put his hands to his head. Meanwhile, Kim quickly slipped the hairs into the plastic container, screwed it tight, and put it in his pocket. Then he let his features sag and started lurching from side to side where he stood.

The man sat bolt upright and looked wildly around him before catching sight of Kim, who'd started drooling, waving his hands and excitedly slurring his words. "Hey, heyah, jus' gotta getta fix, see, like they say. Lookin' fer horse but coke's okay too, got any stuff?"

The biker stood up and glared at Kim. Kim backed off, holding up his hands with an alarmed grin. "Cool, buddy, cool. Jus' came for my stuff, right. Don' get all riled."

"How the *hell* did you get in here?" the man said, taking a menacing step toward Kim.

Kim waved vaguely. "Huh? Wide open down there. So I jus' walked in, any prob' with that?"

"It's a *fucking big* problem, you goddamned junkie," the man said, grabbing Kim's shoulder.

"Bu' shit, buddy, ooww!" whined Kim. As the man frog-marched him toward the stairs, Kim lashed out with his right hand and scraped the biker's cheek, leaving red streaks as he bellowed, "Le' me alone, f' crissake!"

The biker released Kim long enough to check his cheek. His face turned mean when he saw blood on his fingertips. He clenched his fists. Kim set his jaw and relaxed his neck. When the right cross came hurtling toward him, he lowered his head slightly to avoid taking it on the chin.

Kim's body and head went with it, but the blow was hard and no playacting was required to tumble to the floor in a limp heap. He nearly passed out, whimpering, "Don' kill me, bud, no *neeeed* to fight, jus' wanna score some coke!"

"Filthy pile of shit," said the man, who then seized him by the collar and hauled him toward the stairs, muttering, "I oughta finish you off right here. You're damn lucky I'm in such a *fucking* good mood, see?"

Kim kept whining and sniveling as the biker hauled him downstairs, Kim's steel-toed boots banging on the metal steps. They got to the bottom and the alarm went off. The biker released Kim's jacket, groaned *"Fuck!"* and threw Kim to the cement floor before bounding back upstairs.

Kim rolled over onto his back and blinked several times, trying to squeeze the glycerin out of his eyes. His cheek throbbed and he tasted blood in his mouth. He squinted up at the motion detector. He had a can of silicone spray in his pocket he'd planned to use to neutralize the motion detectors without making it obvious. But they'd been installed too high in the corners.

A yellow flash came down the stairs, and he felt whiskers tickling his ear. Kim's face had started to swell, and his mouth was numb, so the "sweet kitty" he tried to whisper came out only as "swee' ki'y." No need now to remember to alter his speech to give the impression he was high as a kite.

The alarm stopped. Kim rolled back into the position where the biker had flung him. He resumed whimpering. That wasn't difficult, since his head was full of snot and he was feeling sorry for himself. The man came thundering down the stairs and declared, "Dammit, I should whip your sorry ass," but merely dragged Kim to the door, opened it, and threw him onto the gravel walk.

"If I see you here again," the guy said, putting his index finger on a point right between his eyes, "I'll put a slug right here on you, you got that?"

"Got it, man, got it, tha's cool, just need a fix, a little whatever you got, 'm on fire here, see?"

"Just be glad you're still alive!" The biker turned back into the downstairs space. The door started to close but halted. He growled, "You, too, you crappy cat." He was holding the ginger tabby by the scruff of the neck. He cast it violently out, sending it flying in a snarling, screeching arc. Far more acrobatic than Kim, it landed on its feet. The door slammed.

Kim lay sprawled on the gravel, looking at the cat, which calmly licked its paws as if to say, *So what? Doesn't bother me at all.* It lifted its head to look at Kim. *How 'bout you?* With one hand on his neck, Kim tried to massage away the painful aftereffects of the biker's blow. He groaned, "Okay, thanks. Not that bad."

Supporting himself with his hands, Kim managed to get to his feet with some difficulty and stagger to the back of the hill, where he'd parked his own bike. The cat trailed after him. Kim tottered, holding his hands out like a zombie, half stunned, his head throbbing and buzzing. He probed his mouth with his tongue for broken teeth but detected no damage.

He got as far as his bike but had to sit on the ground there for a while. The cat prowled around him, obviously wanting to be petted, but Kim was careful to hold his hands out of reach. Once he began to feel better, he used his teeth to open a side pocket of his pack and work a small ziplock bag free. He used his elbows to turn the pack over and shake it. Among the contents that spilled from it were his headlamp and a toothpick.

Using his left hand only, he managed to don the headlamp and turn it on. The cat peered with great interest as Kim used the toothpick to scrape beneath the nails of his right hand, the ones that had bloodied the biker's cheek. He fished beneath each nail, wiped the toothpick on the inside of the little bag, then went on to the next nail.

Once he'd lifted everything embedded beneath his nails, Kim zipped the bag shut and held it out for the cat to inspect. "Hard to believe that's worth anything, right?" The cat expressed no opinion but reached for the bag. Kim held it back and smiled, which made his mouth ache. He smiled anyway.

53

July 11, morning

Christof thought about Gandalf as he took the elevator at police head-quarters. Cecilia had gone to bed early the previous evening, tired from a long day preparing an unusually large number of wreaths. He'd kissed the top of her head and wished her sweet dreams and inhaled her floral fragrance. He'd gone to the living room to write a little fan fiction.

He wanted to write a tale about Gandalf as a young man. Long before Bilbo and the Ring, even before Gandalf came to Valinor, the Blessed Realm, where he changed his name to Olórin. Tolkien had written that Gandalf was an angelic being who'd assumed human form, so it wasn't clear he'd *ever* been young. Christof intended to ignore Tolkien and instead endow the grand wizard with elfin qualities, making him long-lived but not immortal.

Christof was quite pleased with the couple of pages describing Gandalf and Galadriel's first encounter. He knew that if anyone ever read it, he'd get shit for the way he'd structured it. He was basing it on Tolkien's universe but writing it for his own enjoyment. He liked thinking about Gandalf.

The elevator doors opened, and Christof put aside thoughts of Lothlórien and Glamdring to concentrate on the day's tasks. Entering the open office, he saw Markus Lind, one of the hockey jocks, grinning at him. "Let's Swing!" started playing on Markus's computer. Christof sighed and walked toward him. The music continued.

We can swing-swing-swing, you and me . . .
We can sing-sing-sing, lala-lala . . .

Markus tapped a key and the music stopped. He gave Christof a look of feigned innocence. "Yes? Something the matter?"

"Don't mess around with me," said Christof.

"What's wrong, can't a guy listen to Jimmy Jansson?" Markus sniffed. "And, anyway, who around here has the right to talk about *messing around?*"

"How did you find out?" Christof asked wearily.

Markus shrugged. "I used to work in Täby. Had a beer yesterday with some of the guys. Enjoyed it. Learned a lot."

"And you're going to spread it?"

Markus's expression softened. He shook his head. "No way. But shouldn't a guy be allowed to tease a little?"

"I suppose he should," said Christof. He turned his back to go to the conference room where Carmen Sánchez was already waiting. The music resumed behind him.

I'm a king-king-king,
But maybe for just a day . . .

Christof whirled around. Markus stopped the tune and held his hands up to signal, *That's it. No more.*

Carmen put down her mobile phone and shook her head as he entered the conference room. "The Danderyd ambulance was reported stolen a few days ago and hasn't turned up. Chatted with the transportation division just now, and they haven't caught it on any of their cameras."

"Wow, hard at work already!" said Christof, dropping into the chair next to her. "How is it possible the cameras haven't picked it up?"

"Might have hidden or altered the number."

"Switched plates, maybe?"

"Also possible."

Carmen got up and went to the coffee corner, pumped a mugful, and motioned to inquire if Christof wanted some. He'd drunk an energy drink on the way in, so he turned down the offer. Carmen sipped her coffee and leaned against the table. "Okay. Hasn't been spotted in traffic. For the time being we're assuming it hasn't been burned or anything like that. Otherwise, we'd have heard."

"Driven off a pier somewhere?" suggested Christof.

"Possible but unlikely. And I doubt it's outside the country. You wouldn't drive an ambulance onto a ferry just like that. We can assume for now that it's *parked* somewhere. Where would you ditch a stolen ambulance?"

Christof had in fact pondered that a bit before Middle Earth and Mordor had taken over his thoughts. "I'd put it inside, somewhere. A garage or a barn or someplace like that. If that wasn't possible, I'd park it with lots of other vehicles. *Hide it in plain sight*, like."

"So you're thinking a shopping center, a sports arena . . ."

"Right. Or, maybe better, one of those long-term airport parking lots. Arlanda or Bromma." That had seemed a good idea when Christof was contemplating the problem, but as the implications of the work involved sank their claws into him, he put his head in his hands. "Hold on, I take it back. Will we have to spend a whole day inspecting parked cars?"

"We'll do what we must do. Sounds like a good idea."

The door opened. Jonny Munther stuck his head through the doorway but didn't enter, showing he wasn't going to stay long. "Good morning," he said. "How's it going?"

Carmen and Christof exchanged a glance. The detective superintendent had dark rings under his eyes and looked as if he hadn't slept a wink. Despite that, he seemed uncharacteristically chipper. The tiniest trace of an encouraging smile was playing around his lips.

"Hi there," said Carmen. Jonny nodded. Before he could withdraw, she asked, "Boss? If you wanted to hide a stolen ambulance, where would you put it?"

"Assuming I didn't have a garage?"

"Right."

Jonny thought for a couple of seconds. "Long-term airport parking." He considered his own conclusion, nodded, closed the door.

Christof threw up his hands. "Yeah, yeah, yeah. There goes our day. And how about him? What do you think? An away game?"

Carmen came back to the table, sat, and put her coffee cup down. She stared at him. "What are you saying?"

Christof jabbed his thumb toward Jonny Munther, still visible as he crossed the open office. "The boss. An away game. Meaning he slept, or didn't sleep, somewhere other than at his place."

"Is that what they say in the guys' locker room? An away game?"

Christof stared at the desk. "It's a common expression," he mumbled. "Everyone uses it."

"First time I've heard it. Perhaps it's time to turn our attention to work?"

Christof nodded but kept his eyes on the grain of the wooden desktop, afraid his expression would show how uncomfortable he felt. It was true: "An away game" was an expression thrown around in the locker room. Christof didn't think Carmen would appreciate some of the other expressions used there. Especially not those describing women like herself.

Christof cleared his throat. He focused on the ambulance problem, and his spirits lifted a bit. "But you're saying we have to go through the parking lots? How many does Arlanda have? Five? Six?"

"More, probably," said Carmen. "Swedavia manages most of them, but some independent ones are farther out. Benstocken's just one of them; some have really bizarre names."

Christof's mood crashed. "But we don't have to get out of the car, do we?" he appealed. "I mean, an ambulance is going to stand out."

"Hmm," said Carmen. "Sounds like that could be your assignment. It's better done on foot, so you don't miss anything. Think of it as an *away game*. You'd enjoy that."

"Tell me you're joking!"

Carmen broke into a hearty, quite masculine laugh and slapped Christof on the shoulder. "Of course I am! Every parking business logs the vehicles in and out. I have some experience with this kind of thing. The operator gives us the digital files and we run the license plate number against them."

"Which might have been changed," Christof cautioned her.

"Right," said Carmen and checked the paper before her. "But what are we working from? FGH 371. There's only *so many* changes you could make. The *F* can become an *E*, the *3* can become an *8*, and a *1* can be changed to a *4* or maybe a *7*. There's maybe ten or so combinations, I can't do the math."

"Twelve, I think," said Christof.

"Okay," said Carmen. "I was probably out sick during that class. If I were a kidnapper, I'd change as many as possible."

"That would make EGH 877."

"Umm, or EGH 874. Wanna bet which one? I think one of those will be the winner."

"Let's wait till we find it."

"Just a sec," said Carmen. She pulled out her laptop, tapped a bit, then said, "Okay, EGH 874 is a 2012 white Golf, and there is no EGH 877. Maybe that one was junked." Carmen picked up her phone. "You take Swedavia, I'll call the independent lots. They might need to be persuaded."

Christof's assignment took only fifteen minutes. Swedavia was happy to cooperate and promptly emailed a digital copy of its logs. Christof wrote out the possible combinations and found he was right; there were indeed twelve. He ran them all against the Swedavia files and came up with nothing. Then he ran the correct license plate number. No hit.

While Carmen cajoled Benstocken and the others, Christof paced around the conference room. He suspected Carmen would get the same negative results, since the obvious tactic would have been to leave the ambulance in one of the largest lots where it'd stand out the least. And he'd just checked those.

Christof continued circling the table, thinking about parked ambulances. If it had been abandoned somewhere in the city, a traffic warden would have noticed it by now, so that was an unpromising alternative. He continued trudging and trying to visualize ambulances. All kinds of ambulances. Ambulances in rows, ambulances stacked on top of each other.

Carmen put down her phone at last and shook her head. Christof said, "I've got a different approach. In fact, if you think about it, it's probably the best way."

"Which is?"

"Where would nobody notice an ambulance? In a parking lot for ambulances!"

Carmen scratched her head. "Sure, but Danderyd must keep track of its own vehicles. They'd have found it by now."

"No," said Christof. "Not if it was left at a *different* hospital. Talk about *hiding in plain sight*!"

54

July 11, morning

Before Julia Malmros unlocked the door to her father's apartment, she took several deep breaths and made a conscious effort to relax her tensed shoulders. Partly to recover after climbing the stairs, partly to fill her lungs with fresh air before confronting an apartment in which the air was foul enough to *taste*. At least that was the sensation she always got.

Yep, she was right about that. After turning the key and opening the door, she'd been struck in the face by odors of dust, rotting food, urine, and old-man smell. She knew she'd no longer notice them after being in the apartment for a few minutes, but the first impression was that of stumbling into a predator's den. Her instinct shouted *flee, run, run away!* She didn't, of course. After all, he was her father.

The home health service's obligatory cleaning was superficial and never got down to the underlying sources of the horrible stink. Julia had offered several times to pay a service for a deep clean. Her father had refused, grumping that he didn't want to have strangers rooting around and touching his things.

"Hey, hello! It's just me," said Julia after closing the door and taking off her shoes, which practically stuck to the floor. If that deep clean was ever to be done, she, the good daughter, would have to do it. The good daughter had unhappily acknowledged as much to herself but also had weighed the time that would take against the time probably remaining for her father. It wasn't worth it. He almost never left his bed.

Julia shook away her shame at neglecting the dignity of her next of kin and went to the bedroom. As usual, she found her father under a blanket, leaning against a couple of pillows and glaring at a television screen. The TV was dark and layered with fine dust.

"Hi, Papa," she said, patting the knotty, veined hand that lay upon the blanket. She nodded at the television. "What happened with your snooker?"

Competitions featuring balls and cues had been just about all her father watched for several years now. An occasional nature program, if there wasn't too much action and movement, since those gave him a headache, but snooker was his usual choice.

"Ah," said Papa. "They're useless. Never get the ball in the hole."

Julia had sat with him a few times, watching. She had the opposite impression. The players had seemed unbelievably skillful at sinking the balls. A thought occurred to her. "Maybe you were watching carom billiards? That table has no holes."

"No holes?" Papa said. "What's the point of that?"

Julia had a vague notion of the rules of carom billiards but knew an explanation would tire her father, so she just said, "No, you're right. How are you doing?"

Papa looked down at his wasted body. "As you can see, ready to be composted."

"Don't say such things."

"I'll say whatever I want. Can't sleep, can't eat, can hardly take a piss by myself. I just lie here looking at nothing and waiting for the end. That'll be damn welcome, I tell you. Only problem is that I won't realize how fine it is."

"That's life."

"No, it's not. Should've drowned myself in the sea at Tärnö when I still could."

This sort of talk went on until Julia sternly told him to stop it. She was using his perhaps imminent death as her secret excuse not to clean, but that didn't mean she was looking forward to it. There'd be so much to *deal with*. Add to that Irma Ryding's nagging about the publishing rights, as well as, for God's sake, the corpse in Kim's basement. Death, death everywhere, death wherever she turned.

Her father got surly after Julia's rebuke and glared at the dark television screen as if it had intentionally offended him by featuring incompetent snooker players. Julia's thoughts went to Tärnö. Vanishing into the sea.

"Papa?" she asked after a long silence. "Can it ever be right to conceal a criminal?"

"What are you talking about?"

"Let's say a person has committed a crime and then you help that person cover it up. Are there circumstances when that can be the right thing to do?"

"Why are you asking? Has Jonny gotten himself into some kind of trouble? I *warned* you, don't you ever forget it."

Despite Julia's repeated efforts to explain, her father persisted in his delusion that she was still married to Jonny Munther. The divorce should have pleased him, since Papa had strongly opposed the marriage, calling Jonny a dim farm boy who'd never amount to anything. Incredibly, he was the only person in the world who didn't accept the divorce. Unless you counted Jonny himself.

"No," said Julia. "That's not it. But if someone you really like has done something illegal. Speaking purely *personally*, isn't it right to help that person? To shield them, to take care of them?"

Halfway through it, Julia saw her father's attention wane and his gaze drift away. That hardly mattered. In fact, she was just sitting here talking to herself before an audience. She was sure he'd forget what she said as soon as she left the room.

"Hmm, hmm," her father said and frowned. "I'm hungry now."

"Should I . . . ?"

"Yes, thanks."

Julia got up and went to the kitchen. For once, the sink was empty except for a couple of spoons. Some slightly more ambitious person from home health services must have had a couple of minutes to spare. Julia opened the refrigerator and found a pile of plastic trays with ready-made meals. Most had been opened and put back after her papa had eaten a bite or two. He refused to have them thrown away.

Julia made a quick inventory. Mold had appeared on three of them. She slipped those into the trash bag as quietly as she could. Another had no signs of mold but stank, so it joined the others. She took out an unopened container holding a slice of meatloaf with rice on the side. She put it into the microwave and looked through the little plastic containers of salad. She chose the one that looked least wilted.

She got a spoon and a napkin from a kitchen drawer. The microwave dinged. She took out the tray and pulled off the plastic covering. It actually smelled agreeable, certainly better than the rest of the apartment. She returned to the bedroom with tray in hand. "Okay, Papa. Time for lunch."

"Lunch?" her father said. He glanced at his wrist where he no longer wore his heavy watch because it chafed. "Isn't it a bit early?"

"Brunch, then," said Julia. "Linner, whatever you want to call it. Here's food."

She lowered the tray so Papa could see the contents. He leaned forward and studied the meat and sauce. "I'm not hungry."

"But you just told me . . ."

"Yeah, yeah, yeah. I say a lot of things. You remember the seagull?"

Julia pushed some of her father's notes off the bedside table so she could set the meal tray there. Papa scribbled lots of important things that came to mind, put the notes down, and immediately forgot about them.

"No. What seagull?"

Even though he had trouble remembering what had happened minutes earlier, some of his memories of bygone days were sharp. Certain hidden parts of his brain had managed to stay alive in the swamp of his dementia. As for Julia, she had no memory of any seagull.

"Was just thinking about what you said about shielding, taking care," Papa said. "And then up popped that seagull. In the shoebox."

Papa's short-term memory was remarkably selective. He didn't remember he'd asked for food, but he'd come up with an answer for Julia when she thought he'd stopped paying attention. His mention of a shoebox brought an image to mind: a ball of fluff, a little bird bill nipping at Julia's finger, and a bright blue sky.

"You remember?" her father asked.

"Vaguely," said Julia.

"Aha, see? I remember every detail. You came home with that tiny thing in your hands, said you'd found it abandoned. You were crying, I believe, but that's how you always were."

"What do you mean?"

"That was you, with your talent for dramatizing everything so you were the center of attention. Same with that little birdie, *oh, oh, oh,* you made such a hullabaloo, shrieking to heaven and earth about how you were going to help that nasty little thing."

Scattered memories had fallen into place, and Julia remembered now that she'd kept that shoebox in her bed so she could listen to the little seagull chick peeping inside. How heroic she'd felt for sheltering the weak and the helpless. But she didn't remember how it ended.

"Right. But how did it turn out?" asked Julia.

Papa chuckled. "Just like you'd expect. That little gull didn't get any rest, you hovered over it the whole time, petting and feeding and doing your big number so everyone would see how clever you were. It survived your attention for two days and then died. That was a big scene too, naturally. Big burial, pulled out all the stops. You pampered that gull to death. To show off."

The story had taken a turn Julia didn't care for at all, and it didn't correspond to her memories. What was Papa trying to tell her? That what she was doing for Kim now was just *showing off* to prove she was important?

"I did the best I could," Julia muttered. "It would have died on the spot otherwise."

"I don't know about that," her father said. "When you were done with your howling and feeling sorry for yourself, I asked you to show me where you'd found your birdie. Turned out it was in a gull nest out on the bluff. Mama gull was probably out looking for food but then along came the Good Samaritan and interfered, and things ended up as they did."

Julia had a sour taste in her mouth. It was terribly hurtful that Papa's memory was acute when it came to some things, and she *despised* that little self-righteous girl roaming the bluffs, her pigtails flying, the seagull chick in her hand. She hated the fact that the very same youngster still dwelled inside Julia herself. How pitiful that was, an image straight out of Mikael Wiehe's ballad "The Girl and the Crow."

Julia got to her feet. "I have to go now."

"Well, that was quick," her father said. "Didn't like that story? I've got some more that'll teach you about yourself if you care to listen."

"Thanks, that'll do for now," said Julia. "I was eight years old. It's not so relevant to who I am now."

"Ah," said Papa. "A zebra never loses its stripes, you know."

Julia felt rage building inside her, anger at a father sitting in his bed like a living corpse and holding court over her when she was doing the best she could. She wanted to hurt him in return and in her agitation saw the best way to do it was by confirming his comment about stripes.

"I'm sure you're right," she said. "You know, I swiped twenty kronor from my teacher's bag when I was in ninth grade. Grabbed the chance. Put my hand right down into the bag, took the money from her wallet, simple as that."

She hoped to provoke an expression of shock and dismay on her father's face but got no reaction. He looked at her, indifferent, so she upped the ante. "Did you hear me? I was a *thief.* I committed a *crime* when I was just fourteen."

Papa waved his hand in a lazy gesture. "Yeah, sure, I know all about that."

Julia was so astonished that she sank back into her chair. "What? You do?"

"Sure. Somebody saw you, the teacher telephoned me, and I paid her back. Told her I'd give you a real talking-to, so she shouldn't say anything about it."

Julia shook her head. "I remember getting yelled at for all sorts of things, but not for *that.*"

"No," Papa said. "I saw how hard you were working to raise your grades and all that, so I decided it probably wasn't necessary. But if you'd done it again . . . well. But you didn't, as far as I know."

"No," said Julia. "I didn't. My conscience haunted me about that one time."

"Sure," said Papa. "Thought so. Could see it on you. And now it's too late to cry over spilled milk."

Her father leaned back against the pillow and closed his eyes. Julia sat there crestfallen, staring at him. This was almost too much to comprehend. Too much about herself, too much about her father. He hadn't spoken to her this much or this coherently in years. Was it a good sign or a bad one? Julia was suddenly seized by the fear that he was about to die.

"Papa?"

Her father didn't open his eyes. "Hmm?"

"Thanks. Thank you. Tell me, you're not planning to die on me now, are you?"

"Not going anywhere. Not even to the other side, apparently."

Julia remained there, picking at her fingernails until Papa's mouth sagged open and he started snoring softly. She got up, went to the kitchen, opened the cabinet under the sink, located Ajax and a scrub brush. She took off her knit top and filled a bucket with warm water.

The bathroom, she said to herself. *I can do the bathroom at least. That'll do for now.*

55

Kim brought his motorcycle to a stop at the gates of North Cemetery, and Astrid dismounted. She returned his helmet and asked if she'd be allowed to keep the biking leathers. Kim looked up into the streaming sunlight and said, "It's getting warm."

"It'll probably be worth it anyhow," said Astrid and wiggled within the outfit to assure Kim she was comfortable in the all-too-large biker's outfit she'd last worn when he whisked her away from Vamlinge.

"Okay," said Kim and jabbed a thumb toward Karolinska Hospital across the street. "Just remember what to do. In case."

"In case," said Astrid and held up her Kånken backpack. "I remember."

"Great."

Astrid pointed to his chin. "You still look like hell."

Kim had borrowed some foundation from Astrid to try to hide the worst yellow and red discolorations on his swollen cheek. He was trying to avoid attracting attention, but his efforts hadn't disguised much. "Nothing to be done. See you later."

Kim nodded goodbye, rolled down the road, and turned off into the hospital grounds. He parked his bike in the lot by a van bearing the logo of Näslund Cleaners. Maybe he should hire them for his basement once this was all over. Although "cleaners" was one of the vaguest work titles he'd ever heard.

Kim had carefully collected his hair beneath his black baseball cap. He had stashed a pair of single-use plastic gloves in the outside pocket of his small backpack. It would be stupid to leave traces of himself *now*. There was nothing to be done about his clothing. Couldn't simply parade around the hospital grounds in full personal protective gear.

The hospital's ambulance fleet had its own garage. When Kim had scouted the place earlier, he'd found three vehicles parked in the back by a loading dock for some unknown reason. Maybe to be repaired or decommissioned. After accomplishing his mission of abducting Martin Rudbeck, he'd left "his" ambulance next to them.

Ambulance driver Kenneth Klint must have reported the vehicle as stolen as soon as he finished his breakfast at Espresso House in central Mörby, but it wasn't as if the hospital data system was connected to that of the police. Most people were innately too lazy to think of doing such a thing. Anyone noticing an ambulance that looked out of place would hardly be motivated to try to get to the bottom of the matter. The typical reaction would be a shrug, in the belief it was somebody else's problem.

This was no sure thing. Kim hadn't succeeded in figuring out the standard operating procedures for ambulances. If the hospital kept a sharp eye on all its fleet, they'd have located it days earlier. Or someone might have noticed his alterations on the license plate and gotten suspicious.

Probably not. But there was the additional, more worrisome risk that the police might have already found it. The camera in Rudbeck's television had shown Carmen and Christof going through the house, so they were investigating already. He didn't expect much from the false clues he'd planted, so no doubt their next focus would be the ambulance. The only question was how quick they'd be about it.

The area around the loading dock was screened by a hedge that ran the length of the rear of the hospital, so Kim couldn't lay eyes on the ambulances. He slowed his pace and inched forward until he got to a corner where he was still shielded by the bushes but could peer out to survey the ambulance lot. *Aha!* The ambulance hadn't budged from where he'd parked it, as far as he could make out, though now only two others were with it.

Okay. Here we go.

One principle applicable to taking suspicious action was that in no way should it *appear* suspicious. You march in and get on with it as if it were the most natural thing in the world. People are generally reluctant to intervene, and that was in his favor. *Should that guy really be in here? Huh, he looks like he knows what he's doing, so it's probably all right. Not my problem.*

It was never that simple in practice. Your brain concentrates on a task, but your body isn't always in sync. Kim's solution was simple. He persuaded himself that nothing fishy was going on until the last moment, when it became absolutely necessary to execute the trickery.

Accordingly, Kim sauntered in the direction of the ambulances without a thought in his head, for all the world as if it might be fun to check out what the rear of the hospital looked like. His actions and bearing were no different from those of the casual stroller who'd peeked into Barnängen's former factory. He looked unconcerned as he gazed around nonchalantly, making sure no surveillance cameras were monitoring the area.

Only when he came alongside the ambulance did he call his brain into the game. He pulled on plastic gloves and stepped swiftly aside to check the rear door. Unlocked, just as he'd left it. Kim glanced around one last time, slipped into the back compartment, and pulled the door shut behind him.

The narrow space was totally dark, which gave Kim an unpleasant flashback as he groped to extract the headlamp from his backpack. He'd spent summers at Roshult in the power of his grandfather. The old man wasn't satisfied merely with abuse and systematic torture; he found it amusing to lock Kim in an old firewood chest when he deemed that his grandson needed to be softened up a bit.

Kim had been only five years old the first time it happened, and he'd been terrified, thinking that rats, monsters, and ghosts surrounded him in the stifling darkness. He couldn't stop screaming. Grandfather was quite pleased when he opened the lid and found a quivering lump of humanity.

Kim gradually succeeded in taking control of his imaginings, to keep them from going wild. He lay huddled up in the firewood chest, pretending he'd been kidnapped by pirates, robbers, or elves, and he used those dark hours to visualize the fantastic, unknown places he'd find when he was released. That meant the return to reality was a disappointment, both for him and for Grandfather, who lost little time inventing new ways to try to break his spirit.

Kim pulled the headlamp on and adjusted it on his forehead, turned it on, and thought, *Kidnapped.* Even though he preferred the word *abducted* for his Martin Rudbeck operation, hadn't the doctor essentially been kidnapped? Wasn't that one of the Apostates' notorious fields of activity?

It was indeed. Only six months earlier a senior Ericsson telecom executive, entitled to an annual bonus of millions of kronor, had vanished for a week. When he eventually reappeared, disheveled and pale, he refused to discuss the matter. Everyone assumed the Apostates were behind it and a ransom had been paid, but that was never confirmed publicly. People didn't want to suggest that kidnapping was a lucrative business, even though it was.

The ambulance looked untouched. It appeared that no one had been inside. He took out the ziplock bag and the plastic container, the contents of which he'd paid for handsomely. He worked his jaws, opened and shut his mouth a couple of times. His face ached terribly. Both his tongue and chin were still swollen. It would be worth it, if everything went the way he hoped.

Kim looked around the interior and thought, *Okay. I'm a kidnapper. Where do I shed a couple of hairs?*

There was no obvious answer, and Kim made do by shaking the three strands from the container onto the gurney, where he assumed they'd be found. He used a plastic spatula to scrape up some of the substance in the bag, thought for a moment, then smeared it along the rails used to push or pull the gurney. The skin cells might have come from a hand, so a grip would be the place for them. Appropriate.

Finishing up, Kim pulled out the wrinkled Circle-K receipt for beer and chocolate wafers. He wadded it up and tossed it into a corner. Must have fallen out of a pocket while the kidnapper was wrestling the gurney in place. The receipt was linked to a credit card number, and the police should have no problem tracking down the user.

Still wearing gloves, Kim stuffed the container and plastic bag back into his pack and swept the beam of his headlamp around the space. Nothing appeared to have changed since he first got inside, while he *really* hoped that the results obtained by a CSI tech would be different. He'd done all he could.

Kim hefted the pack and was about to push open the door when he heard a vehicle approaching. A car? He stopped, doused the headlamp, froze in place, and listened. Kim sent telepathic commands as the engine sounds came closer. *Drive past, keep going.* But no. Gravel crunched and the vehicle halted behind the ambulance. A couple of doors opened, then closed. He heard muffled voices.

He had nowhere to conceal himself, nowhere to go, no way to hide his face. The voices came closer, and Kim thought he recognized them. The same officers who'd dealt with him during the Knektholmen investigation, Carmen Sánchez and Christof Adler. Nothing wrong with those two, other than that they were *right here, right now.*

Kim straightened his back, dropped his hands to his sides with a rustling sound, and stood motionless, waiting. Just as the door started to open, a bone-chilling scream rang out.

56

July 11, morning

If Christof Adler had had the ability to purr like a cat, that's what he'd have been doing as he and Carmen Sánchez drove toward Karolinska Hospital. His intuition had proven correct. They'd called the fleet superintendent there, who'd gone out to look at ambulances taken out of service. He'd told them initially that there was no vehicle with that plate on the premises, but when they asked him to take a closer look, he'd found that numbers had been altered with a black marker. They told him not to touch anything and immediately set out to inspect it.

As they rode along, Carmen asserted that she'd won the bet because the number had been changed to EGH 874, just as she'd guessed, but she magnanimously offered to overlook that, since it was Christof who'd solved the problem.

Hey, hey, Christof thought, clasping his hands across his stomach as Carmen took the ramp onto the E20. *Adler the master sleuth to the rescue.*

Carmen glanced at him. "Do you have to look so *enormously* pleased?"

"Hey, now, what are you talking about? We should decide to drive out to Arlanda airport instead?"

"That was a reasonable suggestion."

"It was. But mine was better."

"Arlanda was your idea too."

"Yeah, see? I'm a guy of many ideas, I am."

Carmen shook her head and said nothing more, concentrating on the highway. Not so Christof. He sat tranquilly leaning back and contemplating the office buildings as they slipped past beyond the window. Even though he quite liked police work, he usually had a constant uneasy feeling he really wasn't suited for it. But not today. Now he was a fully qualified colleague allowed to enjoy the fruits of his genius, and he let himself luxuriate in that feeling for now.

Carmen took the exit toward the hospital and soon swung into the parking lot, where she turned onto a wide footpath to drive around back.

"Nicely done," Christof said.

"Are you being sarcastic? Is that your approach from now on?"

"Nah," said Christof, pointing to the navigation panel, which displayed the expected approach to the ambulance lot. "I meant it. Clever."

"Hmm," said Carmen. She turned into a gravel lot where three ambulances were parked along a loading dock. Christof spotted the vehicle with the suspect plate, and Carmen pulled up a few feet away. They got out and shut the patrol car doors.

Christof stood there with his hands on his hips. "So it was here all the time."

"Yep," said Carmen. "But maybe not *all* the time."

"Don't be so negative," said Christof, grabbing the handle of the ambulance's rear door. "You've got to—"

Both he and Carmen were startled by a bloodcurdling scream from behind the hedge at the far end of the dock. Carmen glanced at Christof and rushed toward the hedge, unbuttoning her holster as she went. The scream kept going on and on.

Someone, a woman, was being brutally murdered. Christof followed Carmen. His fingers trembled—for the first time in his life, he got out his pistol. What the hell was happening?

They got to the hedge and the scream kept on and on, undiminished, and Christof thought there was something strange about the way it *sounded*, as if . . . He couldn't put his finger on it but followed Carmen as she plunged into the hedge and then bellowed in frustration, "Where the hell *is* she?"

A nanosecond before Christof caught sight of "her," it dawned on him what had sounded off. Faint *violin* sounds behind the screams. Muted but present. Shrieking, howling violins behind the terrified screaming. Both he and Carmen saw the little Bluetooth speaker on the grassy space behind the hedge.

Carmen bent over, snatched up the speaker, and glared at the source of the noise. She shook the device. It stopped. She screwed up her face. "What is this?"

"*Psycho*," said Christof miserably. "The shower scene in *Psycho*."

57

It was all Astrid's idea. If the police turned up while Kim was inside the ambulance, as soon as she'd distracted them with Janet Leigh's vocal performance and Kim had gotten away, they'd hop on the motorcycle and drive off. That suited her taste for action, and she imagined the *Mission: Impossible* theme playing in the background.

Kim had turned down her suggestion. Astrid's speaker was no more than a precaution of last resort to protect the operation, but if it was used, they would need to behave in as normal a fashion as possible. Starting a motorcycle would draw attention. Instead, they would simply walk around the hospital, take the main entrance, and meet in the cafeteria.

As Astrid jogged around the building, she jabbed her phone to stop the sound file streaming to the speaker. Kim had come up with a dongle that upgraded the phone to Bluetooth 5 with a reach of more than three hundred feet. Astrid had stationed herself at a safe distance to keep watch.

The leather biker's outfit creaked and snapped as Astrid ran. She grinned to herself. *Got a little action in, anyhow.* As she rounded the corner and continued toward the entrance, she mentally played the theme: *dum-dum-dumdum, dum-dum-dumdum, deedah, deedah!* Just for fun, she made a couple of broad swings of her arms à la Tom Cruise before she lowered the tempo, slowed to a walk, and went through the revolving doors.

No matter how normal and ordinary she tried to appear, people were sneaking looks at her as she walked in, her dark hair spread across the shoulders of the biker outfit. All thoughts of the difficulties she was struggling with in her life had vanished instantly. She was just so freaking *cool*.

Astrid's excitement had calmed a bit by the time she paid for a cup of brewed coffee, the only thing available. She didn't like coffee that much, but it seemed appropriate. *Cool chick, black coffee.* Astrid scowled at the box of skim milk and poured as much oat milk as would fit in the paper cup. It had to be *drinkable*. She slurped the teeniest bit of liquid and carried it to a table.

Astrid looked around and came back to earth. The cafeteria was half full, and most of the people looked miserable Two were in patient gowns, one of them connected to an IV drip. Astrid sipped her coffee and sighed. Adventure is so fleeting. Before you know it, you're back in the old *everyday*.

Still . . . there was something about the feeling of her body against the biker leathers; the costume kind of held her up and made her, if not invisible, practically invulnerable. Astrid put her elbows on the table and sat with her legs spread. Here she was, the girl who'd *fooled the cops.*

Kim came through the revolving doors a couple of minutes later. Astrid was impressed to see he looked completely unconcerned even though he'd been mere seconds from being arrested. He saw Astrid and nodded. She nodded back.

"Hey," said Kim when he slipped into the chair across from her.

"Hiya," Astrid said as casually as she could. Then she couldn't contain herself. She leaned over the table and whispered, "That was just terrific. Good grief, did we ever fool 'em!"

"Uh-huh, right," said Kim. "You did a good job."

"Is that all you have to say?"

"What more should I say? Thanks for the help. Really. I'm lucky you were with me. Okay?"

Astrid crossed her arms and pouted. She herself didn't know what she was seeking or what she wanted Kim to say. She just didn't want the adventure to be over, and it could continue if they *talked* about it. But she restrained herself and tried to take a more adult tone. "Did you get done what you wanted?"

"Sure did," said Kim and got to his feet. "But I don't think we should sit here together. *In case* they come in. I have no idea how much they know. We can meet at the bike an hour from now."

"Okay," said Astrid. "Just one thing."

"Uh-huh?"

"You should buy me a new speaker."

"Just tell me which one you want. I'll take care of it."

"Great," said Astrid. "*And . . .*" Kim's posture showed he was on his way out, but he paused to listen. Astrid didn't let herself be rushed; she took a sip of her coffee, then she pinched the biker leather at the level of her collarbone. "And I want to have this."

"You know that it's leather, right? From an animal?"

Astrid rolled her eyes. "It's not as if I'm asking to *buy* it. I just want to *get* it from you. All right?"

Kim stared darkly at her for a moment but then nodded. "At the bike. In an hour."

"Yep," said Astrid. "It's a date."

58

July 11, morning

Kim left an apparently very pleased Astrid Helander behind in the cafeteria. He hadn't shared her childish enthusiasm, but she'd carried out her role perfectly, and he was granting her his biker outfit even though he couldn't see what use she'd have for it. Maybe just to have it ready as a tougher, sheltering skin she could crawl into if things started feeling bad. He was well acquainted with that kind of thinking. Or maybe she merely wanted it as a sort of crutch. Okay, never mind, she'd earned it.

With nothing in mind but putting a little distance between himself and Astrid, Kim strode to the elevators and studied the titles for each floor. Karolinska Hospital offered an immense number of specializations, a couple of which Kim had never heard of. For example, what was involved in "Psycho-oncology"? Curing cancer by telepathy? When Kim stepped into the elevator, he chose the seventh floor, which housed several departments, including Pediatric Neurology. That, at least, was a subject with which he was familiar.

The corridors on the seventh floor had that special *sterility* typical of hospitals. The nurses moved silently, almost religiously, gliding on their thick rubber soles. Kim found a small waiting area with six empty chairs. A rack held magazines and newspapers. A painting of the Little Mermaid hung on the wall. He doubted there was any risk the police would search the hospital, but after the near disaster in the ambulance, it seemed a good idea to withdraw from circulation for a while and evaluate the situation.

When Kim had gotten back from Lilla Essingen the previous night, he'd found five missed calls from Julia Malmros but no text messages. He assumed she wanted to talk about something too sensitive or complicated to summarize in a text. With his painful joints and aching jaw, he hadn't been in the mood.

He'd found a bag of frozen vegetarian "meatballs" Astrid had purchased, sat at the kitchen table, and applied the cold package to his chin, hoping to reduce the swelling. Astrid had decided it would be okay to spend the night in her room in her uncle's Svarvargatan apartment. She'd texted Kim that Uncle Lasse would come calling at four o'clock the next afternoon to "check things out." Kim had no idea what that meant and didn't know what he could do to make the place "checkable." Avoiding an inspection of the basement was certainly a given.

He'd had exchanges with a couple of HackPackers who were building the profile of a fictitious person for him, paid the bill in Bitcoin, and finally gone to bed, his chin seeming to have diminished from the size of a handball to that of a tennis ball. He hadn't known if it was advisable to refreeze Astrid's meatballs, so he'd stuck the bag in the fridge. He'd probably find a use for it.

That morning Kim had called Julia. He hadn't described the events of the previous evening or the scheme for Karolinska Hospital later in the morning. Didn't want her to get any more involved than absolutely necessary. He believed she'd approve of that decision. If she knew.

So Kim was astounded and shocked when Julia related her thoughts concerning the depths around Tärnö, which could easily swallow a corpse and never disgorge it. For once in his life, Kim found himself speechless. That she was willing to go to such lengths for him was so unexpected that it spooked him. He'd finally found the words to tell her he was working on another solution, but admitted it would probably be good to have a plan B. Their conversation had ended uncomfortably without further discussion of the problem. Then Kim had gone to pick up Astrid, they'd done their number with the ambulance, and here he was on the seventh floor, sitting in a hospital waiting room like any of a thousand other people.

Kim thought he could understand Astrid and her youthful enthusiasm for adventure, but Julia Malmros astounded him. She'd reacted like a law-abiding citizen at first, appalled by Kim's doings in the basement. Then the pendulum had swung the other way, passing through acceptance and arriving at willingness to become an *accessory*. Kim was a bit leery of her flexible ethics and thought it best to keep her as far out of it as possible.

He leaned back in the uncomfortable chair and closed his eyes. His mind started to flash back to the events at the ambulance. He opened his eyes and looked around for something to distract him. The rack held newspapers, one with a headline about Hitler, another about the Swedish royal family, and a third with an article about the Swedish singer and accordionist Kikki Danielsson. None of those interested him. Seemed like a weird assortment to offer neurologically impaired youngsters.

Aha.

The other wall had shelves full of magazines. Kim got up, went through them, and found a couple of Bamse children's comics. Those were much more interesting than Hitler and the king of Sweden. He took them back to his seat and began reading.

Bamse the bear had been Kim's favorite; what he liked was the *world* in which Bamse frolicked. Throughout his tortured childhood and youth, Kim had found a bit of consolation in the simple, pure reality among The Three Hills, Grandmother on High Mountain, and L'il Hop's tree stump. And Skalman, Skalman most of all, who always came up with a solution to save the day.

Kim preferred tales in which the characters stayed home and dealt with everyday problems. Unfortunately, Bamse the bear was always setting out for adventure, and Kim found him a bit of a bully when he pushed timid Li'l Hop to go along. "Aren't you a real friend?" That was emotional blackmail, an approach Skalman never used.

Kim preferred the older publications that depicted the times before both Bamse and Li'l Hop had families and when Skalman was featured more prominently. Fortunately, one of the old series had been reprinted in the magazine Kim picked up; equally fortunately, it wasn't about some bold adventure with trolls and giants but instead about Li'l Hop's problems with his carrot garden. That was exactly the tonic Kim needed, and he read it several times. Naturally, Skalman was the one who fixed things in the end.

Out of the corner of his eye, Kim saw a nurse with short blond hair who'd passed along the corridor several times. Kim had memorized every detail of the carrot garden story by the time she appeared in the doorway and asked, "Excuse me, are you waiting for someone?"

"I am," said Kim, putting down the comic. "My grandfather. They're doing an amputation."

"Oh dear. You're in the wrong place. This is a pediatric ward."

"I see," said Kim, rising and nodding toward the picture of the Little Mermaid. "Actually, I did think that was a little strange."

He checked his phone as he stepped into the corridor and saw he had ten minutes left before meeting Astrid. He wouldn't be able to do much more than go home to change his clothes. He had a funeral to attend.

He left through the main doors and took a lengthy detour around the hospital to get to the parking lot. He saw lots of activity in the ambulance yard. Another police car had arrived, along with a van Kim assumed belonged to the CSI team. He was curious how they'd interpret the role the shower scene from *Psycho* had played in the events.

Astrid was waiting beside the Honda with the leather outfit zipped up to her chin and the helmet under her arm. "Hey," she said. "What did you do?"

"Improved my mind," said Kim, getting into the saddle. "Hop aboard."

59

July 11, afternoon

When Julia Malmros had finished thoroughly cleaning her father's bathroom, she experienced a sort of Diderot effect. The French philosopher's problem arose when he realized that his elegant new dressing gown made everything else in his residence look shabby, so he bought new things for his home to match the new garment. Papa's bathroom was the same. Tile, toilet, and porcelain sink smelled clean and sparkled white, making the rest of the apartment seem even more disgusting than before. The gleaming bathroom shined a harsh light that revealed the squalor of the rest of the flat in sharp relief.

Julia resigned herself to the inevitable and started on the kitchen. Two hours and five pails of water later, the kitchen couldn't quite rival the bathroom's porcelain shine, but at least it no longer looked rat infested. Her backache was the signal that she needed to stop there for now. She kissed her father's cheek and left.

She took the underground and the bus to Gärdet because she'd been struck by Kim's evasiveness during their phone conversation that morning. Granted, Julia's suggestions about Tärnö might have sounded extreme, but shouldn't he have appreciated the fact that, in order to assist him, she was willing to step so far across her own moral boundaries? *Hardly.* Kim had mostly sounded . . . distant, if not downright dismissive. Julia sniffed in annoyance as she sat on the bus. She'd just wanted to help.

You pampered that little gull to death just to show off.

Yeah, okay, but this was entirely different! She wasn't putting Kim's life in danger by trying to spare him from a long prison sentence. She just wanted to show him that . . . Julia slumped in her seat. *That she wanted his admiration.* Yes. Oh yes. But it *was* immoral to do things purely for selfish reasons, for that would automatically make them wrong. *So there. Take that.*

Julia stood at the foot of the porch stairs. Hearing faint music, she cocked her head and listened closely. A low, crooning lullaby set to a tinkling piano seemed to come from behind the villa. Julia walked around the building and into the backyard. She'd glimpsed it through the upstairs window but had never been there.

The area was in a disarray similar to that of her father's apartment. At least it was natural, not disgusting, merely the result of neglect. Thorn bushes were half choked by knee-high grass and immense numbers of stinging nettles. Lengthy new branches of unpruned fruit trees rose toward the sky in search of water. Fluff from thousands of withering dandelions swirled in the air before a dense forest patch mostly of fir trees.

A simple garden table with matching chairs stood in the high grass a few yards behind the villa. Astrid Helander sat there, reading a book in the shade of a striped parasol as torn and full of holes as the sails of a pirate ship. The lullaby came from a mobile phone on the table. A can of Trocadero soda sat next to it. A choir of angelic voices replaced the lullaby as Julia approached. Astrid saw Julia, picked up the phone, and silenced the choir.

"Hi," said Julia, nodding at the phone. "Beautiful. What is it?"

"Music from *Pan's Labyrinth*," said Astrid. "My favorite film. Gonna ask what I'm reading too?"

"Yes, I certainly should," Julia said as she got to the table. Astrid raised the book to show the cover. *Crime and Punishment* by Dostoevsky.

"Appropriate," said Julia. She pulled out a chair in such bad shape that she tested it with one hand first. She seated herself.

"Pure coincidence," said Astrid with a wry smile. "Picked it up from home before . . . before all this happened."

"Hmm," said Julia. "How are you feeling about this?"

"What do you mean?"

Julia looked at the wildflowers blooming randomly around them and the dark wall of firs at the far end of the property. Good question: What, exactly, did she mean? She certainly wanted to make sure that Astrid was in one piece after everything the girl had gone through in recent weeks.

"I don't know," said Julia. "Just wanted to see if you were okay."

"I am," Astrid said. She put her phone back on the table and took a swig of Trocadero.

Julia pointed to the phone. "Wouldn't it be better to use some sort of . . . speaker to stream music?"

"Don't have one," said Astrid and made a strange face.

"I can buy you one if you want."

"Thanks. I'd like that."

Julia nodded, remembering the one Irma Ryding had in her book-case and referred to as "Bossy" instead of the trademarked name that sounded something like that. Julia had forgotten to hydrate while clean-ing, and her tongue felt stuck to the roof of her mouth. She gestured at the soft drink can. "Okay if I take a sip?"

"Why wouldn't it be?"

"It's just, maybe you're worried about . . ."

"Retiree cooties?"

Julia didn't bother to point out that she was nowhere near retire-ment age. She took a couple of swigs of the lukewarm liquid. Astrid watched her closely. There was always something watchful about Astrid's gaze. She seemed to be continuously evaluating things around her.

Astrid leaned forward. "Can you do me a favor?"

"Depends on what it is, but you can certainly ask."

Astrid waved toward the villa. "My uncle's coming this afternoon at four o'clock. To check out the place, as he put it. Could you be here then?"

"Sure . . . but why?"

"Good heavens, you know." Astrid shrugged. "So it seems a little closer to normal around here."

Julia snorted at that. "You think this is *normal?* Me and Kim?"

"More normal than just Kim, anyhow."

Julia understood her reasoning. She nodded. "Sure, I can be here to meet him. Four o'clock, right? Where is he, anyway? Kim?"

Astrid yawned. "Had to go to some funeral."

"Funeral?"

"Yeah?"

"For . . . who?"

"No idea. Just said he had to go to Skogs church."

Julia glanced at Astrid. The girl had been sitting in Hope Chapel at the same location just a few days earlier, accepting condolences after her parents' funeral ceremony. She showed not a flicker of emotion when she mentioned that church.

Julia didn't understand what funeral Kim wanted to attend or why. As far as she knew, he had no interest in any relatives living or dead. A friend maybe? Julia wasn't aware he had any. Maybe she should try to find out. She wanted to speak to Kim face-to-face anyway.

Julia got up. "Well, okay, I'll be back by four." She plucked at her thin blue knit top with the bright yellow zipper. "And this? Is it normal enough for you? Or too much like an old *retiree?*"

Astrid peered at Julia over the top of her sunglasses. "Maybe not quite enough. But I get it, you're doing your best, it'll be fine. But it won't do for a funeral."

60

July 11, afternoon

Carmen Sánchez and Christof Adler had returned to headquarters after their expedition to Karolinska Hospital. They'd stayed long enough after the arrival of the technicians to learn that—well, well!—a few biological traces had been located. Since this was by no means a high-priority case, the analyses would take quite a while. In addition, they'd found a receipt. Carmen photographed it before handing it over for testing.

Back in the office, Carmen had phoned the Circle-K shop indicated on the receipt, but they'd required more than just a phone call to share information from their records. Carmen had an inspiration. She contacted the tax fraud office and gave them the credit card number, which provided immediate results. They had the owner's name because some scammer had tried to charge something on it. Patrik Hedemyr, registered in Solna.

A quick check had confirmed that Patrik "Petey" Hedemyr, born in 1994, was one of several known members of the Apostates bikers club. Both his fingerprints and DNA profile were on record because he'd served time from 2015 to 2017 for assault and battery. Carmen finished off by calling the National Forensic Center with Petey's name and national ID number and asked if the results could be fast-tracked since she had grounds to suspect a crime. They could be, but that wouldn't happen overnight, so she'd just have to wait and see.

Carmen and Christof prepared to huddle in the conference room to brief Jonny Munther. When he arrived, it took Carmen a couple of seconds to figure out what about him had changed. Then the penny dropped. She ran a hand through her own hair. "Been to the hairdresser lately, have we?"

Jonny's graying hair usually covered the top of his ears and tended to hang in untidy curls in the back, but this time he was all sharp lines, nothing out of place, his neck carefully shaved. Jonny's mouth turned down. "What d'you mean? Just chopped at it a bit with scissors, like always. Okay, *yes*, I had it done, so what? What's on your mind?"

Carmen let Christof summarize and take credit for finding the ambulance that had almost certainly been used to abduct Martin Rudbeck, their summoning of the crime techs, the discoveries in the ambulance. He finished by describing the horrific screams and the loudspeaker. Jonny raised both hands to halt the narrative. "Hold on there, what did you say? *Psycho*?"

"Right," said Christof. "You know, the shower scene. When Norman Bates comes in disguised as his mother, holding a big knife—"

"Thanks. Already saw the movie," said Jonny. "But what do you make of that?"

Christof glanced at Carmen, whose face was expressionless. "We don't know," he said. "But that's what happened. The techs took the speaker in case . . . it could give them a clue."

"Hmm," said Jonny. "This smells like a rat in a bag, as Ulrika Boberg would have said."

"You miss her?" asked Carmen. "You quote her a lot."

"Nope," said Jonny. "But she was certainly quotable. Well, then. *Psycho*, my, my! The ambulance, those red herrings at Rudbeck's place. Feels like someone's pulling our leg, playing tricks like you see in the movies. Doesn't happen often in the real world."

"And what do we do to avoid being fooled?" asked Carmen.

"That's up to you two. Or, rather, up to *you*. I think we can make do with a single investigator for this case, since—"

"What?" cried Christof. "It was *me* who—"

"Who what? Who took the phone call from that Wilmer Syd guy? You think that gives you some sort of exemption from other assignments?"

"Now, now, boss," said Carmen. "Don't be mean to Christof. He made his contribution."

"I don't doubt it," said Jonny Munther. "But there's plenty of officers on vacation now, and tomorrow they're going to need a lot of boots on the ground to keep watch on a—what should I call it?—a demonstration, a political rally? Whatever you call it, it's likely to get rowdy, and we need the manpower."

Christof had crossed his arms and his lips were pressed tight in displeasure, so Carmen spoke for him. "What exactly is going on?"

Jonny shook his head as if he couldn't believe it. "It's that guy Schwarzkopf. The True Swedes. He's got a permit to—yeah, talk about misuse of police resources!—to organize a demonstration at the Roslagstull traffic circle."

"That's a little weird," said Carmen. "Why there? And why should we—"

"Because . . ." Jonny put his face in his hands and heaved a sigh. "Because he's planning to bring along a dog dressed up as the prophet Mohammed. You understand? A 'roundabout dog,' like those art installations they used to put up. But this one's going to be live and on a leash."

"Oh, my God," said Carmen.

"*My God*, indeed. He's told the newspapers. This may get really ugly, and *that's* why," Jonny said, gesturing at Christof, "we need people on the scene. I do hope you have no objections."

Christof refused to look at Jonny. "I do as I'm told."

"Fine. And with that, we can declare this meeting adjourned. Carmen, you keep me briefed, and Christof, you talk with the riot squad leader about tomorrow and find out what he needs." He got to his feet.

"Just one thing," said Carmen.

Another deep sigh. "Do I get to guess? Something about my haircut? If you really must know, I'm invited to dinner tonight, and I don't want to turn up looking like a bum. Going to poke me anymore now?"

"Not at all," said Carmen, leaning over and rooting around in her bag. "Nothing but tender thoughts. Here." She'd taken out a small dark-blue bottle. She put it on the table before Jonny. "This is for you."

Jonny picked it up and peered at the label. "Boss. Bottled Night. What is this?"

Carmen mimed splashing on aftershave. "Something that's not Old Spice. Something . . . more alluring. In my opinion."

Jonny hefted the bottle in one hand, then uncapped it and sniffed the pump sprayer. He seemed to like what he smelled. It took him a moment, but he said, "Ah. Yes, okay. Thanks, then. But maybe we can avoid being so horribly *familiar* in the future?"

"No promises," said Carmen.

Christof sat there fuming after Jonny left while Carmen jotted a couple of notes concerning ideas for further investigation. They seemed to have neglected the phone and passport that had magically taken themselves off to Thailand; also, there was the question of how Rudbeck had been registered at Danderyd Hospital as an Ebola patient. *One step forward, two steps back.*

"Cologne, good Lord," Christof commented finally. "Some folks around here know how to get in good with the boss."

"Yep, that's right," said Carmen. "That's how to stay in charge of an investigation. Listen and learn."

61

July 11, afternoon

Not only was the black blouse Julia borrowed from Astrid made of polyester, it was too tight, and it stuck to her skin as she hurried across the churchyard in the summer heat. She'd checked the obituaries, and the only ceremony that seemed likely was at Skogs church's Hope Chapel at 2:00 p.m. Emil Andersson, born in 1952. Donations in his memory may be made to Save the Children.

Julia had never heard Kim mention an Emil Andersson, and maybe that was just an excuse he made to Astrid to forestall questions about where he was going. Besides, it seemed unlikely that a *funeral service* would be held on such a splendid summer day. As she toiled her way up the hill to Hope Chapel, doing her best to keep the blouse from gapping across her belly, Julia was feeling stupid. Stupid and thirsty.

You're doing your best. That must be a good thing.

Even though Julia's expression hadn't betrayed her reaction, Astrid's comment on her clothing choice had hit her hard. She knew that the blue knit shirt with the zipper was simply the first thing that had appeared when she opened her wardrobe that morning. Yes, okay, it had spent quite a long time in the laundry basket, and she hadn't worn it regularly for maybe fifteen years, but things like that happened. It's a sin and an affront to your clothes to leave them in the back of the closet.

You're trying too hard.

Uh-huh, right. So what? Somewhere in an *Amelia* magazine, Julia had read that a relationship with someone younger could make a person feel and act younger. Upon reflection, she seemed to recall that the article applied mostly to men. Women, on the other hand, seem to have the self-destructive tendency to feel just that much older.

Julia heard organ music beyond the chapel's closed doors. She leaned over to catch her breath, hands on her knees. Perspiration trickled down her forehead, and a couple of long strands of gray hair straggled before her face.

Shut up about my appearance, Julia snarled at her own thoughts. She found a hair clip in her pocket and fashioned her hair into a bun on her neck more appropriate for mourning. Those thoughts refused to stop. They mocked her hairstyle, throwing up a picture of Julius Caesar's shrewish wife. Crossed arms, hair in a bun, saying, *Aha! So it pleases the gentleman to come home at last?*

Casting aside her misgivings, Julia stood up and did her best to wipe her brow on her sleeve, but the polyester fabric merely spread the moisture. She flapped the bottom of the blouse one last time, stepped forward, opened the door slightly, and put her head through.

The organ music resounded, and Julia recognized the hymn "Far Beyond Spaces Wide." A white coffin with a pathetic flower arrangement stood before the choir, and perhaps twenty people sat in the front pews. Julia caught sight of a man's head with shoulder-length black hair far in the back. No mistaking him. Julia entered and slipped as quietly as she could into the pew to sit beside him. He looked at her in surprise. "Hi," she whispered.

"Hi," Kim said in a whisper as the organ music continued. "How did you know I was here?"

"Astrid said." Julia nodded toward the coffin. "Who's that?"

"Emil Andersson," said Kim and turned his attention back to the front.

"Oh," said Julia and looked at the single red rose Kim held in his right hand. "But who is—who *was* he to you?"

"It's a long story."

That was one of Kim's standard replies, even though he almost never told long stories. Julia gave him a sidelong look and saw his jaws tighten. She assumed this Emil Andersson had something to do with Kim's boyhood. For once, Kim looked grieved and attentive as he sat upright, his eyes on the coffin, like a child caught in the wrong place but doing his best to maintain his dignity.

Julia hesitated. She clenched her sweaty hands a couple of times and wiped them on her jeans before taking Kim's left hand into her own. She leaned close. "I'm here for you. You know that, don't you?"

Kim's fingers quivered slightly as he turned his head and looked into Julia's eyes. "No. I didn't. Thanks."

The organ fell silent and they said nothing more to one another. Kim didn't release her hand. A priest delivered some final words and then people began standing in the pews to file past the coffin. Kim squeezed Julia's hand. "Just a minute." He left his place and went forward toward the choir. Julia remained and watched him. He hadn't changed; he still looked like a child lost in an incomprehensible world. Julia put her hand, now icy, over her heart.

When Kim's turn came to approach the coffin, he deposited his rose, made a slight bow, and pulled out his mobile phone to take a couple of photos. A framed portrait stood on the coffin lid; Julia assumed that's what he was capturing. When he'd finished, he nodded at the few remaining mourners in the queue behind him. They nodded back.

"Come," Kim said when he got to where Julia was sitting. "We can go now."

Some of the mourners were lingering outside. When Kim and Julia left the chapel, an elderly man with gray, slicked-back hair and an impeccable black suit came up to Kim. "I don't believe we've met. How did you happen to know Emil, if I may ask?"

"I didn't," said Kim. "He was an acquaintance of my father."

"Ah, I see. And what is your father's name?"

"Was. His name was Oskar Karlsson. He was in construction. You'll excuse me, I hope, I'm in a bit of a hurry."

Kim and Julia walked down the slope side by side, and when they were out of earshot of the chapel, Julia asked, "Your father's name was Oskar Karlsson? And he was in *construction*?"

"Like I told you," said Kim, "it's a long story. You want a ride?"

62

July 11, afternoon

It was almost half past three when Astrid Helander put *Crime and Punishment* down on the garden table. She stood for a moment and stretched, so hard that her joints quietly popped. She'd sat essentially motionless for the past half hour, the turning of pages her only physical activity.

Fyodor Dostoevsky. The mere sound of his name had suggested a dense, difficult, ancient text. But not at all. Astrid had been riveted, following the murder of the pawnbroker and his sister, then Raskolnikov's subsequent doubts, guilt, and hallucinations. At times Astrid was so transfixed by the described events that she completely forgot she was reading a novel, not *participating* in the story. Top marks, Fyodor.

Of course, the tale somewhat resembled her own current plight, and perhaps a good deal of the story's power came from that. Astrid was a murderer too, or at least a killer. But though she fully identified with Raskolnikov, she didn't feel the same way about what she'd done.

Astrid had been tormented by the knowledge that only the day before she'd been ready to cut up a human being and she'd have done so, even though she found the idea repugnant. Now, with a bit more distance, she saw it in a different light. She'd been ready to atone for her mistake, no matter how disgusting the act of contrition. She clearly had a strength of character that Raskolnikov lacked, and that consoled her.

Or maybe she really was a psycho.

There was a decisive difference, however. Raskolnikov was obsessed with the fantastic belief he was superhuman. He devoted feverish days and weeks to planning his murder, so it was as premeditated as you could possibly imagine. Her own act had been a momentary impulse, and all she'd done was press a button. It wasn't something she'd *wanted* to do, and so there was no need for her to berate herself to the very edge of self-destruction as Raskolnikov had done. But what she couldn't shed was the feeling she was being watched. Haunted and constantly looking back over her shoulder to keep the corpse from creeping up on her.

She got up from the garden chair, taking the novel and the empty soda can. There was a door at the rear of the house, but it was reinforced and couldn't be opened, so Astrid went around to enter from the front. As she approached the porch stairs, she heard a motorcycle.

It sounded like Kim's Honda. Astrid listened, seated herself on the bottom step, and smiled to herself. Ever since Kim had rescued her from Vamlinge, she'd loved the thrill of riding behind him on the bike. The closeness to him, the speed, and the mere knowledge she was safe in someone else's hands. Not much *girl power* to it, but it was terrific to be *swept away* like that.

The motor slowed and the Honda came into sight beyond the gate. Astrid went rigid. Julia Malmros was straddling the bike behind Kim. Astrid normally wouldn't have recognized her because of the helmet and visor, but she was wearing Astrid's black blouse.

My blouse. My place.

Astrid knew she was being absurd, but she couldn't shake the feeling Julia Malmros was interfering with something that belonged to Astrid herself. Or was she simply jealous? Entirely possible, but no matter; the sight of her made Astrid feel awful.

Kim climbed off the bike and Julia put her feet down to balance it while Kim went to unlock the gate. He saw Astrid and raised a hand in greeting. She nodded shortly in reply. Julia Malmros took off the helmet and shook out her long gray hair. Astrid wrinkled her nose.

Old lady pensioner!

Well, at least Julia wasn't wearing the biker outfit that was currently draped on a hanger on the wall of Astrid's room. That was something at least. Kim got back on, the Honda sputtered forward, then took the gravel drive to the villa with a low growl. Julia's hair billowed around her shoulders, and Astrid reluctantly had to admit that even if she was an old lady pensioner, she made for a pretty cool one. Even though she wasn't actually retired.

Kim braked before the porch and killed the engine. Julia got off. Kim put down the kickstand and said, "Hello."

"Hello, hello," said Astrid. "So you're both gonna stay here?"

"Yes," said Julia. "We're going to be normal, after all. For your uncle."

Astrid slapped a palm to her forehead. Her involvement in Raskolnikov's misdeeds had made her forget Uncle Lasse's intention to check things out. She looked at her phone and it was a quarter to four. No chance to try to take measures to normalize the house, whatever they might be.

"Can I use this?" asked Julia, pointing to herself and Astrid's black blouse.

"It's too tight," said Astrid resentfully.

"Nothing I can do about that for the moment," said Julia. "Do you have something else?"

"Don't think so," Astrid said. "We have quite different physiques."

Julia's eyebrows shot up. She stared at Astrid a couple of seconds too long, so she'd obviously caught the implied criticism. Astrid looked away, knowing she'd sounded petty. Julia wanted to help, after all. Astrid was about to say something to make up for it, when Kim commented, "I'm sure I have a T-shirt you can use."

Julia went up the stairs without looking at Astrid. Something was bothering Astrid, a *closeness* between those two she hadn't observed earlier. Or maybe it was her jealous heart distorting things. She needed to shape up. Astrid reminded herself to slap her own face a couple of times when she got the chance. She rose.

She'd made it halfway up the stairs when she heard Julia burst into laughter. Astrid's mood sank. *Now* what was so wonderfully funny? Getting to the landing, she saw Julia holding a T-shirt to her chest. It was big enough to fit her, but it featured the printed image of a marijuana leaf.

"What do you think?" Julia asked when she saw Astrid. "Won't this be just *perfect*?"

Kim smiled crookedly. "Bought it at Schiphol. Lot of 'em there."

"Mm-hm," said Julia. "Don't really think so. And not the one with Santa Sangre or whatever her name is."

"Santa Muerte," said Kim. "No, that one's not exactly you."

"I may have something," said Astrid and went to her room. Most of her clothes were still at the Strandvägen place. Some were at her uncle's, and only a few were in the bureau next to her bed in Kim's house. Astrid pulled out a drawer and found a white blouse with frills, a lace collar, and mother-of-pearl buttons.

"Here," she said, handing Julia the blouse. "Looks like this one's a little larger."

Julia examined the blouse with an amused smile. "You really do want me to look like a little old lady, don't you?"

Astrid crossed her arms. "That's my style. Period. Take it or leave it."

Astrid looked away as Julia, not in the least shy, took off the black blouse with some difficulty. In her peripheral vision Astrid glimpsed a racy red bra. Old lady wanted to show herself off in all her glory. Astrid clenched her fists and reminded herself again to shape up. She took the black blouse back. Although she was holding it only waist high, she caught a distinct odor of perspiration. She was certainly *not* going to wear it before putting it through the wash.

The white blouse fit Julia better. *Yes,* thought Astrid with a touch of bitterness, *it really does suit her,* and Kim's approving nod testified as much. Something really *had* changed between these two. Maybe something at that funeral ceremony? No way was Astrid going to ask.

"We might as well brew some coffee," Julia said. "You always offer a visitor coffee. Nothing's more normal than that."

Astrid was starting to regret what she'd said about being normal. It was all too easy to joke about it, but she did want her uncle to have a positive, *everyday* impression of her in Kim's villa so he'd let her spend more time there. That was crucial.

The coffee was ready and the cups were on the table when the doorbell rang ten minutes later. There was no coffee cake, but Julia had located a Marabou chocolate bar, divided it into squares, and put it on a plate.

"Sit," said Astrid as if commanding a couple of dogs. "I'll go down and let him in."

Astrid wanted to avoid assailing her uncle with information overload. She descended the steps two at a time and opened the front door. Uncle Lasse was wearing a lightweight summer jacket over a pale blue shirt. He held out a box of Aladdin chocolates. "See, I wasn't sure, but I thought I should probably bring something." Astrid thanked him even though she suspected his chocolates were just as nonvegan as those on the kitchen table upstairs. She wouldn't eat either type.

"Hey, let me say right away," her uncle said, "what a place! Not often you get to see something like this."

"That's true," said Astrid. "Come in."

Her uncle came inside and took a couple of steps, then stopped and looked around. "Is this an office building?"

"Used to be," said Astrid. "We live upstairs. Come this way."

She pointed to the staircase, but he stopped at the bottom and peered at a photo hanging on the wall. A black man in a uniform, saluting, his face stern. Uncle Lasse pointed at him. "And what kind of guy is that?"

"Not a clue," Astrid said. "It was here already. Come on, there's coffee upstairs."

Both Julia and Kim got up when she brought her uncle into the kitchen. Kim held out his hand. "Hi there. I'm Kim. We already met.

And I think that's Papa Doc, or maybe Baby Doc, in the photo downstairs. This used to be the Haitian embassy. A long time ago."

"Oh, okay, I see," her uncle said, shaking Julia's hand as well. "Seems a little unusual, doesn't it? They were dictators, those two, weren't they?"

"Yep," said Kim. "It's a pretty strange place, that's a fact."

Bothered, Astrid cleared her throat. This encounter was no more than a couple of minutes old, and already the words "unusual" and "strange" were being bandied about. And who the heck was *Baby Doc*—what kind of a name was that? Astrid pushed her uncle to take a chair and poured coffee for him. He drank a sip. "Well, imagine that. Haiti's embassy. That sure is . . . an original touch."

Kim and Julia had seated themselves side by side across the table from him, quite close to one another. They usually sat facing one another, and Astrid couldn't tell if this change meant something or was simply because they wanted to appear conventionally respectable. Kim with his bright blue eyes and cascade of black hair, and Julia with gray hair just as long and her buttoned-up lace collar—to Astrid they looked like a couple of space aliens cosplaying ordinary life.

Astrid got up and turned on the kitchen faucet. "And we have running water here." She went to the fridge, opened it, and declared, "And there's food." She shut the fridge before her uncle could notice it was almost empty after Astrid's severe edit of the contents. Her uncle gave Julia a funny look but got only a resigned gesture in return.

"Okay," her uncle said. "So, I guess you've got various . . . facilities you wanted to demonstrate?"

Astrid knew she was acting a bit odd, but she was nervous and didn't know what to do, so she said, "My room. You can see my room."

"That's okay," her uncle said. "For now, let's sit here in peace and quiet and drink our coffee."

Astrid sat back down, but *peace and quiet* was a state of being that was beyond her reach. She poured herself coffee, didn't add oat milk, drank it so quickly that it burned her mouth.

Uncle Lasse noticed the platter with the chocolate squares. "Shouldn't you add some from the box?"

Astrid felt so upset and annoyed that the truth popped out of her mouth. "No. There's animals in them."

"Oh? There are *animals* in the box?"

"Augh!" said Astrid. "This is too much for me!"

"She meant dairy products," Julia said. "After all, cream and milk are ingredients in most chocolate."

Astrid crossed her arms and stared at a table leg. Somehow everything had started to go wrong as soon as she saw Julia riding on the bike behind Kim, and now these *grown-ups* were talking about her in the third person as if she didn't exist. Worse, part of her was aware that she was acting like a stubborn teenager. *So what?* She happened to *be* a stubborn teenager!

After more small talk, her uncle came to the purpose of his visit. "Yes, well, I'm not so pleased that Astrid's spending so much time away from home."

Astrid sniffed at that but said nothing. How could you be *away from home* when the place you were away from wasn't even home?

"No," said Kim. "I understand. But I believe she's doing much better here."

"And she's no trouble at all," added Julia. "The opposite, in fact. We enjoy hosting her."

Astrid was astounded. Appalled, in fact, but still said nothing. *She* was the one who had a room here, Kim had invited *her*, while Julia was an occasional drop-in sitting there and talking as if she was co-owner of the place.

"Uh-huh, that's good to hear," her uncle said. "But I think it'd be enough for her to stay here only once a week."

Astrid felt a lump in her throat. Was she going to be forced to spend *six days a week* in that deadly dull apartment on Svarvargatan? She felt a deep chill and couldn't find a word to say as her whole life fell to pieces around her.

"I really think that she'd like to be here more often," said Kim.

"I do too," said Julia.

"Hmm," the uncle grunted. He finished his coffee, then put the cup down on the saucer with a clatter. He seemed a bit nervous as well. "I don't mean to pry, but might I ask . . . about the relationship between you two?"

Despite the numbness she felt, Astrid couldn't resist peering up at them, because she wanted to see how Julia and Kim would respond. She could scarcely have been more astounded. In reply, Kim put his hand over Julia's there on the table and said, "We have opted to join in festive connubial bliss."

Astrid thought her ears were playing tricks on her. *Festive connubial bliss?* Why would Kim say that? And how was it that her uncle seemed reassured to hear Julia and Kim were party animals? And what was that tender, surprised expression on Julia's face as she regarded Kim?

Astrid didn't understand. She hated not understanding, and she couldn't endure this situation any longer, so she got up and left to go sit on the landing and figure out what to do. Nothing came to her. Her uncle emerged from the kitchen a couple of minutes later and said, "Well, okay, now come along home with me."

Astrid despaired and tried to come up with objections. Then it occurred to her. She humbly lowered her head and said, "Okay, I'm coming," then started down the stairs in front of her uncle.

Halfway down, Astrid stumbled and fell headfirst down the last eight or ten steps. She bent forward and made an apparently uncontrolled somersault, landing on her back at the bottom. She strained one shoulder but moaned and groaned and rubbed it as if she'd shattered it.

"My God, Astrid," Uncle Lasse cried and leaped down the stairs to kneel beside her. "How did that happen? Are you injured?"

"I huuuurt myself!" wailed Astrid, pressing tears from her eyes. Probably just as well she didn't have her fake blood; that would have *terrified* Uncle Lasse.

"I saw, I saw," her uncle said. "But how was that even possible?"

"Got dizzy," Astrid said in a low voice. "Didn't want to say anything, but all those stone steps down from your apartment . . . I fell twice. Knocked myself all *black and blue.*"

Rapid footsteps descended the stairs as Julia rushed to the accident scene. She knelt at Astrid's side. "Should I call an ambulance?"

"Nooo!" Astrid gasped. "It's all right. But I should stay here and rest a little."

Astrid turned her head as if in pain and peered up the stairs. Kim was leaning against the rail, watching with a neutral expression that showed he understood exactly what she was doing. He might even be having difficulty holding back a grin.

63

Jonny Munther had asked the assistant at the flower shop at St. Eriks Square to put together a bouquet appropriate for a hospitality gift. Asked what sort of event this was, Jonny had muttered that it was a dinner for two. She'd asked, "A date, then?" and Jonny had replied, "Something like that, yes," without knowing if it was or not.

Once that difficulty was dealt with, another arose. The florist wanted to know how much he intended to spend. Jonny hadn't the least idea what would be appropriate and had to ask her for advice. She wanted to know if this was a *first* date, and well, he supposed you could say it was. Jonny was grateful she didn't offer him a range of prices but just declared, "Three hundred," and so it was.

Despite his lack of experience Jonny thought the bouquet she put together was lovely and somewhat imposing, so he thanked her for the help. She wrapped the flowers in paper and handed them over, then tilted her head. "Excuse me, aren't you Jonny Munther?"

Jonny was a bit taken aback but had no choice but to confirm that he was indeed Jonny Munther. The clerk pointed to herself. "Cecilia. I live with Christof. Christof Adler."

"Oh, really!" said Jonny and extended his hand. "Pleased to meet you. I've heard a lot about you." He hadn't, not at all, but that was just what you were supposed to say.

"And so have I, about you," said Cecilia in a tone that showed she *had* in fact heard a lot and maybe not all of it was positive. Jonny didn't know what else to say, so he lifted the bouquet in a farewell salute, thanked her again, and went to the door. Behind him he heard her call, "Good luck!"

Jonny stopped, turned back, and said, "Maybe you don't need to let Christof hear *all* the details about this?"

"What's to tell? You came in, bought flowers, then you left."

"Right. But still . . ."

"Okay, sure," said Cecilia. She shrugged and mimed zipping her mouth shut. "But you have to promise to buy your flowers from me from now on."

"I don't know if that'll be a thing."

"Flowers are always a thing," Cecilia said. Jonny left the shop. He didn't know if he'd made his blunder worse by asking for Cecilia's silence. She and Christof might have a good laugh that evening, but he really didn't think so. The woman seemed sincere, and Christof could probably count himself lucky. Jonny decided that nothing could be done about it and went into the underground station to get the train to Medborgarplatsen.

Kocksgatan ran straight as an arrow, so it was easy to find Moa's building, and she'd texted him the door code that afternoon. Jonny entered a cool, dark vaulted entryway and stood there for a moment appreciating it after his walk the length of Folkungagatan in bright sunlight. Should he remove the wrapping paper before offering her the bouquet? He could have asked Cecilia if that was customary, but it was too late now, and the wrapping would just have to stay in place.

Jonny had wanted to make sure not to be late, and it was now twenty to seven. It wouldn't be good to arrive too early, that much etiquette he knew. He walked through the archway and emerged into a small courtyard with a table and chair beside a well-used grill. Jonny sat down with the bouquet in his lap.

He couldn't identify the scent at first, and he looked around for flower beds. He saw none, so he sniffed the bouquet. Then he remembered: Bottled Night, the scent Carmen Sánchez had given him. Had he used too much? Jonny sighed. He was a total neophyte when it came to these things. Moa had said she was inexperienced too, of course, but how could anyone take seriously someone as totally naive as Jonny Munther?

Take sex, for example. Jonny's throat closed up just at the thought of it. Not at sex as *sex*, but at the preliminaries, what would be expected or not expected of him. And, well, yes, sex as *sex*. Julia Malmros was the only woman he'd ever gone to bed with and that was so long ago now. Would he even be up to it? *It's just like riding a bike,* Jonny Munther told himself, trying to work up some enthusiasm. But it wasn't. In fact, the two activities were *entirely* different.

Jonny had always been the designated driver for his high school classmates. Partly because of his vehicle, a slow-moving jerry-rigged motorized buggy called an EPA tractor, and partly because he didn't care much for alcohol. Many a night Jonny had sat alone at the wheel, driving with a pile of boys and girls drunkenly messing around in the back. In fact, a whole crew of them had once joined their voices in an old song by Siw Malmkvist.

Jonny hummed it to himself as he sat in the courtyard holding his bouquet. He had an intense desire to leave and go home. Too much ambiguity, too much potential pain. But he stayed there, tormenting himself until it got to seven o'clock, when he went up two flights of stairs and rang the doorbell labeled "Marklund."

Moa was pleased by the bouquet. Praising it, she found a vase and put it in water. Jonny admitted that he wasn't responsible for the arrangement; if he'd had to choose, he'd probably have turned up with ten red roses or something equally unimaginative.

Moa put the vase in the center of the dining table, which along with its matching chairs was among the very few furnishings in the apartment. Then she looked at Jonny. "You tend to underestimate your-self, don't you?"

"Guess so," said Jonny. "I dunno, it's just that I feel, like, clumsy in certain circumstances."

Like, thought Jonny. *Whatever that means.*

Moa held up her right hand. "Then that's my cue to reveal that I also can be very awkward. Look."

Jonny studied the hand that she held out toward him and saw it trembling. Moa closed it into a fist and lay it over her heart, then said, "So can we agree just to forget about that? You're here, I'm here, and now we'll have our meal together and not worry about it. Okay?"

"Okay," said Jonny, and his nerves did calm down. Moa squatted to peer through the oven window where a gratin was bubbling, and Jonny was impressed by the soft grace of her movements. He liked watching her. So far, so good, and besides . . . Jonny cleared his throat. "I've been listening to you."

Moa looked up and frowned. "You've been *listening* to me? How so? Is the place bugged?"

"No, I mean, the book!" said Jonny. "The audiobook."

"Oh, Lord," said Moa, putting her face into her hands. "Hardy Bengtsson?"

"The very same," said Jonny.

"Deepest apologies," said Moa. "A friend of mine has a studio where they do those recordings, and he asked me to . . ."

"No need to apologize," said Jonny. "It was thrilling. I never sus-pected that the minister of justice was behind it all. And your reading is really good."

"Thanks," said Moa and pulled on an oven mitt. "But it's so improbable, all of it, don't you think? Nothing like real police work."

"I have enough of that every day," said Jonny. "It was really nice to get away from it for a while." The ease of their conversation encouraged him, and he added, "In your company, at least."

Moa gave Jonny a fleeting smile and opened the oven door. She muttered, "Stockholm by Night, oh my goodness," and took out the potato gratin. The smell of it made Jonny's mouth water. Foil-wrapped lumps he'd noticed on the chopping block turned out to contain grilled chicken, and from the fridge Moa took out a bowl of salad mixed with avocado and mango pieces. "Will you set the table for us?"

Jonny opened a cupboard that was barer than any he'd ever seen. Two plates and two glasses. Even his sublet was better equipped, and that wasn't saying much. He put out what he'd found and asked, "What are you planning to do? With the apartment, I mean."

"Why?" asked Moa. "Are you in the market for something?"

That thought hadn't even occurred to Jonny. "Nah, this place must be over my budget. Just wondering if you plan on staying in the city."

Their places were laid. Moa gestured to him to take a seat. She opened a bottle of wine. Then she wrinkled her nose with a sniff, shook her head, and said, "Typical Stockholmer. *The city*. As if there weren't any others. And no, I haven't decided. It all depends."

"I'm really a country boy," said Jonny, settling into his chair. "Just another Stockholm immigrant."

"Those are the worst," said Moa. "Cheers!"

The chicken was both crisp and juicy, and the creamy potato gratin was so good Jonny involuntarily groaned with pleasure. He glanced at Moa, abashed. She tapped her fork on the dish and said, "My blend of Västerbotten cheese and Parmesan. A country lad, you said? How did you wind up with the police?"

Jonny had been asked that before, and he had both an answer and a story. When he was eight years old, the toolshed in the garden had been burgled. The chainsaw and the lawn mower were stolen, among other things. Jonny's father had telephoned the police, mostly to substantiate an insurance claim, but a few hours later a police cruiser pulled up to the farm and out climbed a man who'd made a lasting impression on Jonny.

Jonny had sat wide-eyed on the rickety old two-seater bench in the kitchen, listening attentively as the uniformed policeman interviewed his parents about the thefts. The officer had a deliberate, friendly manner and occasionally gave a sympathetic *aha* or *mm-hmm*. With that uniform, his tall and impressive physique, and his thick, well-groomed hair, he'd seemed to Jonny like a visitor from another planet. From a finer, safer, more secure world.

He'd never forgotten that impression. Graduating from high school with reasonably good marks, he'd come across a brochure describing the police academy. He was eager to leave farm life, and what could possibly be better than the profession he'd had a glimpse of when he was eight years old? He applied and was accepted. The plan had been to return to Norrtälje once he'd finished his training, but . . .

"But then I met Julia," Jonny said with a sigh. "And she had no intention of becoming a 'barefoot peasant wife,' as she expressed it. That's what happened."

"Okay," said Moa, scraping up the last of the gratin from her plate. "And what happened with the lawn mower and the rest of it?"

"Probably went to eastern Europe on the ferry from Kapellskär," said Jonny. "That was typical in those days. Probably still is."

Jonny tried to change the subject to Moa and her work, but she wasn't very forthcoming. She took two bowls of lemon sherbet from the freezer, not only homemade but also the best Jonny had eaten in years.

Moa asked what was keeping Jonny busy currently, and he told her about the disappearance of Martin Rudbeck, even though it wasn't his own case—the clues in the residence Jonny had dismissed as planted, along with that day's dramatic discovery of the ambulance with traces inside. And the hope of useful results from the DNA analysis once Moa's colleagues completed their work.

"Ha ha," said Moa. "That'll take some time, and anyway . . ." She sipped her wine and gave Jonny a thoughtful look. "Anyway, I don't think you should stake your hopes on them."

"Why's that?"

"It's just, see, I think this is sounding like that TV show *Murder Squad.* Or Hardy Bengtsson, even."

"What do you mean?"

Moa counted on her fingers. "A receipt that's easy to trace. *Visible* biological material on the gurney. And some strands of hair *with the roots intact.* From a professional forensic perspective, I think those clues are the same as the ones in the residence: simply too good to be true."

"But isn't it good to have the roots?" said Jonny. "DNA segmentation can be carried out by . . ." His voice died away when he caught Moa's expression asking, *Are you going to mansplain my own job to me?*

"Of course, hair strands with intact roots might be found at the scene of a crime," said Moa patiently. "But that's generally when there's been a struggle. There wasn't one here, was there?"

"No, not as far as I know."

"No, then. And those hairs with intact roots were tidily waiting on the gurney, a little present especially for the crime techs? No, I don't buy it."

"So what did happen, in your opinion?"

"Exactly what I said. The real perpetrator got into that ambulance and left those traces to mislead you."

"Hmm," said Jonny. "Seems to me it does sound a bit like Hardy Bengtsson."

"That's just my reaction. Take it for what it's worth. Are you planning to listen to more of the audiobooks?"

"Any of those you read, yes."

Moa filled Jonny's empty wineglass. A silence descended. Jonny wondered if he'd gone too far. Even if there was nothing criminal in seeking out a publicly available audiobook, there was still an element of *eavesdropping* when Jonny listened for the reason he did, and with what you might call a *yearning.*

Each drank wine in a silence that didn't feel as comfortable as the one they'd experienced eating ice cream on the bench by City Hall.

Bobby Munther, Jonny thought and grimaced, which made Moa ask, "What's on your mind?"

"Aw, nothing," said Jonny. "How easy it is to be deceived just because you really *want* to be."

"Mm," said Moa and put down her glass. She straightened up as if about to deliver a speech and said, "So, it's like this."

"It? What's that?"

"With me. The fact is that I've got that dark shadow in me I mentioned. Marcus's shadow."

"Right," said Jonny. "I understand, and I have no intention at all of—"

"But," said Moa, holding up an index finger to silence him, "I also see the world around me as it is, maybe better than most people. I *concentrate* on being present in the moment. The shadow's there, but I refuse to *sink into it.* I'm here now, and I want to live, you understand? Maybe I'll even be able to love again. You never know."

Jonny didn't dare say anything. He simply nodded and took a gulp—too big a gulp—of his wine. He didn't know if to Moa "love" meant psychological or physical, but he found that made little difference; her comment was reassuring.

"So, be patient with me, Jonny Munther," said Moa. "It *may* be that we have something good going on here."

"I concur," said Jonny.

"I concur?" echoed Moa. "Where do you come up with your pillow talk? From the Swedish Legal Code? Whatever. I was all set to sell this apartment, but now . . . now I'm not so sure anymore."

"Because . . . because of me?" Jonny stammered.

"No, because of the interest rates and the real estate market. *Yes,* because of you, dummy. I have a job in Stockholm if I want it."

There it was again. *Dummy.* Jonny couldn't understand why that mild reproach made him flush with warmth. It didn't matter; Moa sat there opening her heart to him. Told him that he, Jonny Munther, could make a woman like her, Moa, contemplate sweeping changes in her life simply to remain in his vicinity. Jonny had drunk only two glasses of wine but felt thoroughly inebriated.

Nothing more was said on the subject. As far as Jonny was concerned, it was as if a bomb had exploded. Anything afterward would amount to no more than pops from a cap gun. They remained at the kitchen table and talked until they'd finished the bottle. It was extremely pleasant, and Jonny's insides wouldn't stop quivering after that initial explosion.

At half past nine, Jonny thought it would be advisable to wind things up. *Thanks for the fine meal and the wonderful company,* and so on. As he stood in her front hall about to open the door, Moa went up on tiptoes in front of him, but her brow didn't even reach his chin.

"Come here, you dummy," she said, and Jonny leaned over. Moa planted a gentle kiss on his cheek and whispered, "You're a good man, Jonny Munther." She sniffed deeply and added, "You smell good too."

Jonny wasn't aware of Kocksgatan and turned on autopilot into Folkungagatan. The touch of Moa's lips remained vivid on his cheek and radiated numbing waves through his brain. Only when he got close to the underground station did he come back to his senses. He halted and shook his head in dismay.

There he'd sat speculating and worrying about sex, and then he'd been so deeply satisfied by a simple kiss and a few whispered words. *You're a good man, Jonny Munther.* When was the last time someone had said that to him? Had anyone *ever* said it? Not as far as he could recall. Maybe it was odd, but for the moment it made him feel exalted.

Jonny leaned against a building front and took deep breaths. People and vehicles passed by. He tried to recapture the sight of Moa and be *there.* He looked across the street at the lit windows of the McDonald's, where people were nibbling French fries and drinking milkshakes. The world was beautiful.

Standing absolutely still, he retained the feeling that everything was precisely as it should be.

Then he remembered. The *Murder Squad* TV show. The detective Hardy Bengtsson. Jonny hadn't told Moa about the speaker playing the scream from *Psycho*. Add that to Moa's opinions about planted evidence, and suspicion raised its ugly head.

The intensity of the high that Moa had inspired began to fade. Jonny took out his phone and called Carmen Sánchez. She answered on the second ring. Jonny heard a television playing in the background.

"Hi, boss," said Carmen. "Ringing up *now*?"

For one dizzy moment Jonny thought he'd called Carmen to tell her what had happened with Moa. He *hadn't*, naturally, so he squeezed his eyes tight, opened them again, and said, "Yeah, sorry. But I was just thinking. The patrol car you and Christof used today for the stuff about the ambulance. Did it have one of those cameras on the instrument panel?"

"A *dashcam*, you mean?"

"Yeah, that's it. Did it? Pointing ahead?"

"Sure. Those are standard these days."

"So, there's a video?" asked Jonny. "From the time you arrived until you got into the ambulance?"

"Should be, on the hard disk. Why?"

"Had a thought. Maybe you could call up that recording in the morning."

"Sure, no problem, but what are you looking for?"

"Like I said, just a thought. See you tomorrow."

"Hup, hup, hup!" said Carmen to hold him back. "How was your date? Did Bottled Night deliver for you?"

Jonny's throat tightened, and tears threatened to flow, so all he said was, "Delivered fine. Good night."

64

July 11, evening

Astrid's aches miraculously mended—mostly—once her uncle left the villa. She got to her feet as soon as the front door shut and went up the stairs, rubbing a shoulder. Julia stood astonished on the ground floor, while Kim, still leaning against the railing, nodded at Astrid's massaging hand. "Hurt yourself?"

"A little bit, yeah."

"Not skilled enough, then."

Astrid opened her eyes wide. "What? Didn't you *see* what I did? I fell halfway down—"

"Sure," Kim interrupted. "But you took it with the tip of your shoulder instead of the shoulder blade. That interrupted the movement."

For once, Astrid was speechless. Julia got up to the landing and said, "Well, *I* thought it was really impressive. I'd have broken my neck."

Astrid paid no attention to Julia; she didn't want her approval. The girl pointed down the stairs and told Kim, "So why don't you show me how it's done, huh?"

"Don't need to," said Kim. "Besides, I'm out of practice."

"Then don't go around criticizing others!"

Astrid was in a truly bad mood for hours, but she did lighten up considerably after her uncle phoned. He inquired about her health, said it was "acceptable" for Astrid to spend a bit more time at Kim's place, at least during summer vacation. And she had to *promise* she'd always keep a hand on the railing when she went downstairs at Svarvargatan. She promised. Crossed her heart and hoped to die.

They sat chatting for a while, playing a few hands of crazy eights. Kim told them he was "working it out," but nothing more was said about the corpse in the underground room. From Astrid's attitude, sneaky looks, and small sighs it was clear to Julia that the girl was impatient for her to depart.

Kim showed no such inclination, so Julia had no intention of leaving. As the ten o'clock hour approached, it appeared that Astrid had resigned herself to that fact. She put down her cards in the middle of a round, muttered "good night," and went to her room. She made sure they heard her lock the door behind her.

Julia gathered the cards. "I don't think Astrid likes me."

"I think she does," said Kim. "She just doesn't want you to stay here. One's different from the other."

"Maybe. Did you think about what I suggested? About Tärnö?"

"I did, in fact. Ready for bed?"

"And . . . Astrid?"

"What about Astrid?"

"Oh, never mind."

Julia didn't know whether *go to bed* included making love, but if it did, she thought Kim should understand her hesitation concerning Astrid. Julia was *not* so liberal, call it reckless, as to engage in intercourse in a room next to that of a fourteen-year-old girl.

They went to the bedroom, but Kim gave no sign of his intentions, if indeed he had any, and Julia's fingers were clumsy as she unbuttoned the blouse Astrid had lent her. Only when she was about to put it down in the usual place did she notice that something was missing from the room.

"Where's the trunk?" Julia asked, gesturing toward the space beside the futuristic floor lamp. "The seaman's chest?"

"Oh, yeah, that," said Kim as he pulled off his T-shirt. "It . . . it's in use."

"And is it in the basement?"

"Yeah," said Kim, pulling off his jeans. "That's where it is."

"What are you planning to do with it?"

Kim tossed his socks onto the big round chair. "Can we stop talking now?"

Julia saw he had the beginnings of an erection. "Yes, we can," she said, shed the rest of her clothing, and slipped under the blanket to Kim.

Julia quickly became aware both of Kim's intentions and of his unconcern about their possible effect on Astrid. Julia had never sought to keep lovemaking so *silent* that it became a sort of game. They lay facing one another, their gazes meeting as Kim carefully penetrated her and withdrew. The bed was brand new and didn't creak. The only sound was a faint, sticky swishing and a quiet rasp as Julia ran her hands over Kim's scarred back. She clamped a hand over her mouth when she felt like crying out. And then it was finished.

They lay close together for a long time, and when they finally drew apart, Julia was awed by how much satisfaction could be achieved with so little effort. She gently ran the back of her hand across Kim's uninjured cheek. "Lovely."

"Mm," said Kim.

"I don't mean to break the mood," whispered Julia, "but, seriously, what are you planning to do? With the body?"

One side of Kim's mouth twitched, and he whispered, "Can you think of a more mood-breaking subject?"

"No, I really can't."

"And?"

"And . . . good night. Sleep tight."

Kim folded his hands over his stomach and closed his eyes. Julia remained lying on her side, looking at him. In the earliest days of their bloodstorm, they'd made love more ardently and intensely, even desperately, but never as *intimately* as this. Maybe they really hadn't made love before; they'd just fucked.

Was this somehow connected to what Julia had said in the chapel? Assuring him she was there for him? It didn't matter. She was glad she'd told him, and never had it felt truer than right now. She shook her head, looked up, put her arms behind her pillow, and closed her eyes. She was exactly where she should be, and she hadn't felt this peaceful in a very long time.

III

July 12–14

65

July 12, morning

There were birds that morning.

Jonny Munther was usually so intent on the business of the day that he was oblivious to any movement or sound; they blurred together in the background. Not so that morning. Even though mating season was past, the birds were twittering in the trees. And he saw people going about their everyday business, some even walking fine-looking dogs. The morning was warm, and traffic flowed smoothly along St. Eriksgatan. Stockholm was a fine place for a morning stroll.

Jonny had gotten a text message from Moa just as he was leaving his apartment. Mentioning the previous evening, she wrote that she hoped they'd soon be able to continue their *lovely thing*, and Jonny had responded that he was looking forward to that.

He cut across Kronoberg Park, where headstones in the ancient Jewish cemetery stood as a memento mori. Jonny admonished himself not to get overexcited, not to have such high hopes. Everything was still delicate and tentative. It could slip out of their hands and shatter. But still . . . on a morning such as this, surely he could be permitted to loosen the constraints on his desires, couldn't he? The birds were out there, even in the trees of central Stockholm.

Jonny got more serious as he approached the entrance to police headquarters. After all, he couldn't come waltzing into the office with his head full of twittering birds; Carmen Sánchez would be on him in a flash, and Jonny had no desire to describe his recent amorous escapades. He appreciated the scent he'd received from her, thanks, but after that it was *cease and desist.*

He exited the elevator and rapidly crossed the open space to his private office. He closed the door behind him and hung his summer-weight jacket on a coat hook, safely out of the way for the moment. He wanted to hold on to his good mood as long as possible and not have to bother with trivialities. Jonny windmilled his arms a couple of times to expand his chest enough to accommodate his swelling heart but then noticed a small white envelope on his desk. Someone had written what looked like a license plate number on the outside of the envelope with a fountain pen.

Jonny opened the envelope, and a flash drive fell out. It wasn't labeled. Mystified, Jonny turned the little plastic object over and around, still not understanding. Then he remembered. What was the thing called? *Dashcam.* This should be the video Jonny had asked for, so the registration number would be the license plate on the patrol car. He inserted the drive into the USB port of his computer and a file with the plate number and yesterday's date popped up on the screen.

It was a shot in the dark, an idea that had come to Jonny when he'd thought more about the scream from *Psycho.* That scream could have been a way to distract attention from the ambulance. It could have been unrelated, but still that notion was worth verifying. Jonny started the video and got a firsthand perspective of the departure from the police garage.

He knew the route by heart, so he fast-forwarded the recording. He immediately seemed to be racing at high speed along the E20. He whizzed down the off-ramp for Karolinska Hospital, then slowed the recording to normal speed. The cruiser drove the length of the loading dock and pulled up behind an ambulance. The image shook slightly when the doors were slammed, and shortly afterward Carmen and

Christof were visible through the windshield walking toward the rear door of the ambulance. Christof reached for the handle.

The video had no soundtrack, but Jonny knew what was happening when his colleagues stopped in their tracks and then ran toward a thick hedge at the far end of the loading dock.

But—what the hell?!?

Jonny gasped and leaned into the screen as he saw the ambulance door open. And it was *exactly* as he'd suspected: Someone had been in there the whole time!

Jonny squinted at the screen as a slim figure emerged and carefully shut the door.

The figure turned to jog away, and Jonny Munther couldn't believe his eyes. He rewound the video to make sure. He rubbed his eyes and scratched his head. Again! Jonny sank back into his office chair. Not for his life could he understand how all this hung together, but there wasn't the least doubt: The man who emerged from the ambulance was *that Kim Ribbing guy.*

66

July 12, morning

Kim Ribbing was awakened by a rumbling he couldn't identify. It vibrated the bedframe, shook the bed linens, and tickled his earlobe. His eyes opened, and he realized his mobile phone was vibrating violently against the bedside table. He hadn't set an alarm and had no idea why the phone was acting so weird. It was certainly insisting on his attention.

Kim groped for the frantic phone, which writhed and jerked like a kitten trying to escape. He heard Julia Malmros get out of bed behind him. The room was stifling, and the phone almost slipped away from his sweaty palm as he jabbed it, trying to figure out what was going on.

What is happening here?

The bedroom door opened, but Kim paid no attention. A green WhatsApp icon pulsated and flashed on his screen. Kim had never downloaded WhatsApp. That worried him but he couldn't stop himself from pressing the icon.

The text message was from a bizarre, probably auto-generated sender. Good morning. Possibly important information: Detective Superintendent Jonny Munther is at this moment sitting in front of a screen and viewing the attached video clip. Best wishes, Ces.

Kim scrolled down and found a still image of an ambulance. *The* ambulance. He hit Play and was rewarded with the sight of Carmen

Sánchez and Christof Adler racing out of view. The back of the ambulance opened. Kim saw himself get out and jog away toward the parking lot. His face was clearly visible when he passed in front of the patrol car.

Kim Ribbing was rarely overwhelmed, but this sight almost struck him dead. He dropped the phone, which landed upside down on the bed. He pressed his sweaty hands to his face.

Idiot, idiot, idiot. I checked for cameras, but I didn't think of the police car.

You could have a plan that was as detailed and sophisticated as you liked, but overlook *just one detail*, one staring artificial eye, and that single flaw was enough to send everything flying. Kim watched the video again. Not a speck of doubt. Jonny Munther knew very well what Kim looked like and would like nothing better than to get at him. In short, Kim was *cooked*.

Ces?

What possible interest would the hacker of the Mossad and infiltrator of Sweden's central bank have in warning Kim he was up to his neck in shit? No time to wonder about that. How could he get out of this? No way at all, as far as Kim could see. A proper, detailed escape plan hadn't been part of his preparations, since he'd been confident he wouldn't get caught.

Kim's mind was almost never silent and empty, but now he was at a total loss. He saw no possible outcome other than letting the inescapable system of so-called justice have its way with him.

The bedroom door swung open. Julia Malmros had wrapped Kim's bathrobe about her and had a mischievous little smile on her lips. "Listen, Kim, I was wondering, *really*—"

"Not now," said Kim and waved her away, dismissing her from the room. "Not now, Julia."

67

July 12, morning

Julia was startled awake by a noise that sounded like a wasp on steroids. The loud, angry buzzing came from Kim's side of the bed. She felt thoroughly rested and physically relaxed, drifting in the lovely memory of a beautiful evening. Only after climbing out of bed and pulling Kim's bathrobe around her did she realize how hot the room was. She left the stuffy bedroom and went to the kitchen.

Perspiration trickled between her breasts as she opened the refrigerator and took out a box of juice. She pressed the carton to her cheeks and brow without finding much relief, then squatted to open the freezer compartment, hoping to find a couple of ice cubes. She shut her eyes, enjoying the chill that billowed across her feverish skin. She peered inside and pulled out a drawer to see whether there was any ice.

Whether there was any!

All three drawers were chock full of bagged ice. It wasn't hard to guess what it was for, even though Julia didn't know the details. Less obvious was the dark-blue object she saw through the glass front of the topmost drawer. She wasn't much wiser when she pulled out the drawer. A brand-new skipper's cap lay on top of the ice, one like those worn by the grubby old sailors on Tärnö. She touched the cap and found it ice cold as well. Julia puffed in exasperation. Huh? This was a nut she couldn't crack.

Forgetting her desire for a cold drink, Julia closed the freezer and took three swallows of juice directly from the carton. She put it back in the fridge, wiped her mouth with the back of one hand, and thought, *Hurray for* la vida cabrón. The enigma of the sailor's cap didn't bother her or disturb her happy mood.

Wasn't it Harry Brandelius who liked to wear a skipper's cap? That old cap and his pipe. Julia hummed "The Old North Sea" on her way back to the bedroom. The door to Astrid's room was open and the girl was nowhere to be seen. Julia hoped that she hadn't left the villa in disgust because she'd overheard them the night before. Julia and Kim had kept very quiet and done their best to be considerate. At least to a *certain* degree.

She opened the bedroom door. Kim sat in bed with an expression she'd never seen before. Absolutely astounded or . . . horrified? Julia felt no qualms at this. Instead, she smiled a little and said, "Listen, Kim, I was wondering, *really*—"

"Not now," said Kim with an angry wave as if he just wanted her to disappear. "Not now, Julia."

Julia backed through the doorway and shut the door but stood there glaring, her arms at her sides. *So that's how it is,* she thought. *It was nice while it lasted. And now we're back to square one.*

Goddamned Kim Ribbing.

68

July 12, morning

Christof Adler had gotten his marching orders for Claes-Göran Schwarzkopf's Roslagstull demonstration. He'd collected his riot gear, which he didn't like at all, and before setting out, he went in to see Carmen Sánchez for a little moral support. She whistled when she saw Christof holding his helmet and dressed in the heavy, black official armor. "Wow! You almost look like a real policeman."

"Don't feel like one," Christof said. "I *hate* this kind of thing. Why couldn't they just call people back from leave?"

Carmen shook her head and picked up her phone. "But seriously, you look damn yummy. Should I take a photo? So you can show Cecilia?"

"No way," said Christof and looked down at the gleaming body armor and leather straps across his chest. "Or . . . yeah, sure. If you really want to, that is."

Christof set his helmet in the crook of his arm, straightened up, and pretended to look off into the distance. Carmen snapped the picture and showed him. "Here you go. Send that one to her and there'll be a mattress waiting for you in the hall when you get home. Guaranteed!"

"Mm, sure," said Christof and slumped back into his usual posture. "And what'll we do with Matilda if it is? Any ideas? Can we have a serious discussion now?"

"Of course," Carmen said. "But let me tell you anyhow, you look thoroughly . . . authentic. No need to worry about that."

"Okay, thanks. But I'm wondering . . . if it really becomes, you know, a *riot*. People pushing and shoving, throwing things. How's a guy supposed to . . . I'm not used to confrontation, I can't just—"

"Listen," Carmen said. "You're there to uphold the law, okay? You'll use just enough force to see that people don't get more injured than they would otherwise."

"Yeah, but how do I decide—"

The door to Carmen's room slammed open, interrupting him, and Jonny Munther rushed in with a laptop. "Get this! All hell has broken loose now!"

"What hell are you talking about?" Carmen asked.

"That Kim Ribbing guy. He's a demon, that one. Look here!" Jonny put the laptop onto the table and clicked a video file. Carmen and Christof both recognized the ambulance they'd searched the day before and saw themselves racing out of the picture.

Christof pointed at the screen. "Is that our dashcam? From the patrol car?"

"Yes," said Carmen. "Recorded from inside the cruiser."

"Quiet now," said Jonny Munther. "Watch!"

The back door of the ambulance opened and out came a man maybe in his forties with blond, curly hair. He looked after Carmen and Christof before shutting the ambulance door, jogging past the camera, and disappearing from the frame. The screen went dark.

"That's a hell of a thing," said Christof. "So there *was* somebody inside the ambulance. I thought—"

"But what the hell?" muttered Jonny Munther, resetting the video. The curly-haired man leaped backward into the screen, and Jonny Munther froze the image at the exact moment the guy passed before the patrol car. The face was as clearly visible as it could be. The detective superintendent leaned closer to the laptop, and Carmen Sánchez said, "Sorry, but . . . that's not Kim Ribbing. No resemblance at all."

Jonny threw up his hands, staring at the screen. "It *was* Kim Ribbing! Just now!"

"Ah . . ." said Christof, "that sounds weird."

Jonny waved a clenched fist at the curly-haired stranger, infuriated by the guy's pleased expression, then slammed it on the table-top. "Somebody's *done* something to this! It's been altered. I saw Kim Ribbing!"

"Okay," said Carmen. "But now it's obviously *not* him, so . . ."

Christof glanced at his watch. "I gotta go. But how about that? There really was somebody inside that ambulance."

"It was Ribbing," growled Jonny Munther and clenched his jaws. "I know what I saw and I'm not about to forget it."

69

July 12, morning

Kim Ribbing had been lying spread-eagled on the bed, his mind a complete blank. He was waiting for the police, probably with Julia Malmros's ex-husband leading the charge. It was all over now. The worst possible outcome was on its way, with nothing he could do about it. He'd be deprived of his liberty and locked up in an institution again. That was his greatest fear. The mere thought paralyzed him.

When his phone started buzzing again, he scarcely had the strength to reach out for it. His life was at its end.

Hello again, the text read. The video you saw doesn't exist anymore. Here's the replacement.

It was the same still image of the ambulance, so Kim didn't understand. He extended a limp index finger and hit the Play icon. He watched with half-closed eyes. Then he watched again. His paralysis drained away, and Kim sat up in bed, staring at his phone, frowning, his lips pressed together. If what he'd just seen was a deep fake, it had been done in world-record time. Someone had digitally swapped out his face. Kim grasped the phone and tapped furiously with both thumbs. What do you mean, the other video doesn't exist?

The answer appeared instantly. It's not in any system or storage medium. It's gone. Nice curls, right? Don't worry. He's purely imaginary.

Kim replied, I don't understand. How can you pop up here like some deus ex machina? Why are you doing this?

Don't flatter. I'm no god. Not yet. Call me your guardian angel. You're welcome. Ces.

70

July 12, morning

The digital rallying call from Animal Action had reached Astrid when she got up that morning and started her laptop: an assembly at Roslagstull at the same time as the True Swedes' demonstration. Clearly it wasn't an invitation to a party but rather to a counterdemonstration, and the message provided details about the plans and what participants should bring.

Astrid didn't really see the point in turning up as characters in a flash mob but decided to go anyway. Though Kim and Julia had done their best to be quiet last night, Astrid had heard what they were up to. Maybe it was childish of her, but she couldn't face spending the morning seeing them act nonchalant when she knew what they'd been doing to one another's bodies. Astrid found it disgusting. She guessed she was probably asexual.

If not, wouldn't she have felt some sort of excitement hearing the faint sounds of their intercourse? The thought of how Kim . . . but even if she was still a bit attracted to him, it wasn't like *that*. Not at all. The thought of sex, all that physical grappling, gave Astrid no feeling other than nausea. She was practically certain she would never think of engaging in such loathsome activity.

Astrid dressed quickly and in silence, left the villa, took the bus to the underground station, and caught the train to Odenplan. She went into the Office Depot next to the National Library and bought a big sheet of paper, rubber bands, tape, and the cheapest scissors she could find. Then she sat on a bench in Observatory Park and put together something vaguely resembling the cone hat that a Star Boy wears when accompanying Saint Lucia at the traditional December ceremony. Her cone hat wasn't decorated with stars, but it did have a long rubber band to secure it under the chin. She tried it on and found that it fit very well.

It was quite a bizarre concept for a flash mob, prompting Astrid to spend some time reading about Hugo Ball, who was mentioned in the instructions. Once she'd done that, she had a somewhat better understanding of the aim but found it entirely too exaggerated and "artistic" for her taste. Oh well, she was in the mood for a little mischief, and something like this would probably do the trick. She stowed her things in her bag, carried the cone under one arm, and walked northward up Sveavägen. She'd exchanged texts with other participants, and they were meeting in Bellevue Park.

This was the first time since Midsummer Eve and the death of her parents that Astrid would meet up with people of her own age. Most activists were at least a couple of years older, and some were a *great deal* older, but all those with whom she stayed in contact were girls her age. She assumed they knew what had happened, and she dreaded another round of condolences like the one she'd toughed out at Skogs church. Walking along Sveavägen, she decided to forestall anybody who tried to express weepy sympathy.

Approaching Roslagstull, Astrid saw that a lot of people had already gathered in the traffic circle. It was half an hour before the True Swedes' carnival show. Police officers were stationed around the center of the roundabout, which was marked off with blue-and-white police tape. Conserving a space, like in a zoo. Though come to think of it, "show" was probably the wrong word; this was more like a circus. Astrid turned off to the left at the sign for the Carl Eldh Museum. Four girls were sitting a little way up the grassy slope below the Bellevue Café. Four girls and . . .

"Algot?" said Astrid. "What are you doing here?"

Algot Mörner was in her class. He was the person Astrid was FaceTiming with when hell broke loose on Midsummer Eve. She knew he was infatuated with her. What she *didn't* know was whether she was willing to forgive him for videoing their FaceTime chat without her knowledge, God only knows why. Okay, God wasn't the only one who could guess his motivation, which was completely . . . disgusting.

"What d'you mean?" said Algot, sitting at a distance from the girls and already starting to blush. "It's a demonstration, right?"

Astrid stood staring at him. "You don't care about animal rights, as far as I know. Right?"

"But I really do," Algot said. "For example, I liked every one of your posts."

Astrid rolled her eyes. "Okay, for what *that's* worth."

That's when Astrid realized that the four girls on the lawn were staring at her, speechless. Astrid took the offensive as planned, held up her hands, and said, "I'm sure you all know what happened. To me. I've got no need to talk about it and no need for anybody to *say* anything, okay? One word from anyone, and that person gets her face slapped. Understood?"

That last threat was an exaggeration. Astrid didn't intend to slap anyone who simply tried to be friendly, but she wanted to make herself clear. Threats of violence usually did the trick. She settled beside them on the grass and nobody said a word.

Algot sneaked a look at Astrid. "And besides," he muttered, "I don't like the True Swedes."

"No," said Astrid. "But that's not why we're here. You got your cone?"

Algot lit up and held out a real Star Boy cone hat, gold stars and all. "Found it in the basement. From our Saint Lucia in fifth grade. Remember?"

"I thought you were a troll," Astrid said. "Or a gingerbread boy."

Algot frowned, disappointed. "That was third grade, actually. Anyhow, I remember *you* from fifth grade. Hard to forget."

Astrid had despised the Saint Lucia ceremony. Without telling anyone, she'd made herself a devil costume for that evening, pitchfork and all. That had led to grim discussions both with the school principal and with her parents. Saint Lucia and school were subjects Astrid didn't care to discuss, so she turned to the girls. "Can anybody explain to me exactly why we're doing this?"

Sixteen-year-old Karolin, a poetry lover, said, "It's, like, dada. You know, surrealism, but . . . weirder. It's a poem about elephants. And now with climate change drying everything up, the elephants dying, and . . . yeah, that's how I understood it."

"I didn't understand it at all," said Vilda, who was fourteen, like Astrid. "But I like the cone hats. People will notice us."

"And he was wearing a cone," Algot put in. "The guy who read it."

"Hugo Ball," said Astrid. "His name is Hugo Ball, and I still think it's all damn . . . lame. Cones, a nonsense poem, and dried-up elephants. Like, who the hell's going to make the connection?"

"Probably one of the older people came up with the idea," Karolin said. "Seems like it, anyhow."

Astrid nodded and looked around at the circle of girls on the slope. Algot, obviously an outsider, was the only boy. Many of Astrid's followers on social media made themselves look desperately dreary and identified with the torments of animals, which resonated with their own. The group before her looked . . . healthier. Maybe active engagement gave vitality to their lives.

Astrid considered herself somewhere between those extremes. On one hand, she didn't feel any particular solidarity with these girls, whose parents were often engaged in environmental campaigns and had inspired their daughters with their keen moral indignation. On the other hand, she felt sympathy for morose teens merely seeking ways to torment themselves. If she had to choose, she'd probably go for the second group. She thought the girls on the slope shared all too *healthy* a vibe.

Shouts reached them from the traffic circle. Everyone turned in that direction. "Looks like something's happening," Algot said.

They rose and walked together toward Roslagstull, where the crowd had grown considerably. Astrid trailed a couple of yards behind the others, and Algot slowed to match her pace. He carefully patted her shoulder. "Hey? How're you doing?"

Astrid didn't answer. She held up a fist to remind Algot of her threat.

71

July 12, morning

Christof Adler couldn't understand how the True Swedes had managed to get a permit to demonstrate at the traffic circle. Maybe because most people were on vacation, some inattentive rookie must have let it slip through. Probably an outright idiot. The lawn was already crowded fifteen minutes before the scheduled start time, and people were spilling out into the street, blocking traffic.

Advocates and opponents of the True Swedes, with or without signs, chanted slogans, blew whistles, or just yelled and shrieked. Cars caught in the roundabout honked, and several motorcycle riders whose bikes had been allowed onto the grassy center space revved their engines. The sun blazed, and Christof was dripping with perspiration inside the heavy riot gear as he and a dozen other officers stood in a tight cordon to keep people out of the blocked-off central area.

A fellow officer on Christof's left squinted angrily at the crowd, a sour look on his face. Christof said, "What a waste of resources, right?"

His colleague gave him a curt nod. "This is the price of democracy." Christof was a bit embarrassed by his own tepid support for freedom of speech until the officer added, "That's what some people claim."

It was an open secret that quite a few police officers sympathized with the True Swedes' demands for tougher measures, especially against the foreign-born. Maybe this guy was one. Christof wiped the sweat from his brow and said nothing more.

He yearned to return to his desk, his laptop, his files, and the calm, air-conditioned open office space. It was almost unbelievable that both his office environment and the place where he was now posted were included in a police officer's job description. This was the so-called *real world*, no doubt about it, and Christof was extremely uncomfortable in it.

By a couple of minutes before eleven, the traffic circle was jammed. The line of vehicles trying to transit Roslagsvägen stretched as far as the eye could see. A police van with lights flashing arrived from the city center and pulled up in front of the international school. Its side door slid open and Claes-Göran Schwarzkopf got out, escorted by four officers in riot gear. Schwarzkopf wore a shoulder bag and held a black rottweiler on a leash.

The dog evidently had the same attitude toward the event as Christof did. The animal trembled, intimidated, its ears flat against its head as it peered about.

The sight of the True Swedes' party leader riled the crowd, and the noise level immediately rose several decibels. Signs waved and fists raised. Press photographers jockeyed for position.

Claes-Göran Schwarzkopf seemed the only person untroubled by the chaos. With a smirk, he pushed his hair off his forehead and nodded to let the police escort know he was ready. One of them offered him a helmet, but Schwarzkopf just shook his head. He did seem to be wearing a bulletproof vest under his shirt. The group set off in lockstep toward the blocked-off center of the traffic circle.

The bikers had left their motorcycles and blended in with the crowd. Now they came together and helped the forces of public order open the way for the man and his dog. Schwarzkopf walked tall and smiled with satisfaction at the tumult, while the dog almost crawled along the ground, its tail literally between its legs. An egg came flying and smashed against a police helmet. The yolk that ran down the visor shimmered light green, suggesting that the *best-by* date was long past.

The escort had to push back the scuffling crowd with its shields, but surprisingly enough, they managed, with the bikers' help, to part the sea of bodies and get to where Christof was stationed. The officer who had spoken to Christof nodded at Schwarzkopf and lifted the blue-and-white tape to give him access to the center of the traffic circle.

At this range, Christof saw that Claes-Göran Schwarzkopf wasn't quite as serene as he might appear. He didn't seem worried or frightened, but a mad light burned in his eyes. He blazed with determination, projecting a kind of superhuman harshness. As if he weren't merely a man but instead an embodied *cause* to be advanced at any price. The sight was impressive and a bit frightening.

Schwarzkopf ducked under the tape and dragged the dog along. For a moment he stood in the eye of the storm looking around. When he was satisfied that all eyes were on him, he raised an index finger high—*and now, for my next trick!*—and from his shoulder bag pulled out a false beard and a turban.

Angry shouts in several languages rang out, and a shock ran through the crowd as people shoved and surged forward. Christof took a strong stance, planting both feet to keep people out of the cordoned center. Sweat ran into his eyes. Like Sisyphus rolling his huge stone, he lowered his head and used both arms. People lost their balance, fell over, screamed. A firecracker flew past Christof's head and landed behind him. It burst, and the dog howled.

Christof glanced back and saw Schwarzkopf had put the turban on the trembling dog's head. The crowd erupted. Something smashed into Christof's helmet and nearly deafened him. A muscular man with a long beard stood in front of him yelling, *"Allahu akbar!"* The man's eyes burned with a fury equal to Schwarzkopf's.

Things were getting seriously out of hand. Christof knew the real boiling point was coming. That would be when Schwarzkopf put the beard on the dog and fully insulted the prophet. This was all extremely, stupidly comic and yet in deadly, bloody earnest.

Christof's ears rang as he shook the sweat from his eyes and looked out over the roiling human mass. He thought of the battle at Helm's Deep, and he desperately wanted Gandalf to ride up and take charge. That wasn't possible in the real world. Unfortunately. Christof hated the real world at that moment.

Then something happened. Lots of white cones popped up in the crowd and a choir of voices chanted, *"Jolifanto bambla ô falli bambla, jolifanto bambla ô falli bambla!"* Among the waving True Swedes signs an enormous new banner unfurled, depicting elephant babies lying dead on barren savanna plains.

People turned to see what was going on, and the pressure let up a bit. Cameras turned toward the cone hats moving randomly through the crowd to loud chants of *"jolifanto bambla ô falli bambla."* Christof thought he saw Astrid Helander wearing a cone hat. His head reeled.

A new howl erupted from the mass, and when Christof looked back, he saw that the dog in the center was now fully kitted out with the beard and turban. It huddled flat on the ground even though Claes-Göran Schwarzkopf was yanking the leash. The animal couldn't have expressed its opinion more clearly even if it had put its paws over its turbaned head. Just like Christof, it wanted to be anywhere but here.

The rottweiler's reluctance to participate did nothing to dampen the effect on the spectators. Enraged people screamed and pressed forward in a many-headed wave. Christof thought smoke must be rising as his organs cooked in the steamy heat. He staggered under the pressure of thrusting arms and shoulders, and the white cone hats swayed and danced before his sweat-blurred gaze as "jolifanto bambla" echoed in his mind. This was real life, and it was as close to hell as Christof Adler had ever been.

When something smashed into his helmet, a deep, vibrant sound filled Christof's head and blunted his consciousness. His legs gave way, his vision dimmed, and he fell backward into a pool of blessed darkness and silence.

72

July 12, morning

Kim heaved the crate full of bags of ice off his shoulder, placed it on the basement floor, and opened the seaman's chest. The ice previously inside had melted, and a faint odor of putrefaction rose from the interior. Kim spent a couple of minutes clearing out the sopping wet blue plastic bags to expose Martin Rudbeck's shrouded shape. The white sheet in which he'd wrapped the corpse was sodden and somewhat stained, unfortunately. Kim readied himself and undid one end of the makeshift shroud to reveal the doctor's face.

Kim was no expert, but as far as he could judge, nothing in Martin Rudbeck's expression suggested he'd died by violent means and had been iced down for not quite twenty-four hours. He was presentable. Kim leaned close, held his breath, groped behind Rudbeck's neck, and tilted the head forward. He took the skipper's cap from his own head and placed it on the doctor's, then settled the corpse's head back against the edge of the chest. Attention to the tiniest details guarantees a convincing presentation.

Kim thought about Ces as he covered the body with fresh ice. Kim had spent quite a while going through his own phone's operating system and contents in search of smuggled code that could explain the phone's remarkable behavior. He'd found nothing. He must be dealing with a *magical being* clever enough to wipe out all traces of intrusion.

This was equally frustrating and thrilling. Ces was a worthy adversary, if *adversary* was even the correct word. Ces had rescued him from an impossible fix, and Kim would readily express his gratitude if only he could understand *why.*

Kim's hands were numb by the time he placed the last bag on the corpse, covering it completely. At no time in the process had he considered that he was working on a real, dead human being. The doctor had been no more than a practical problem for some time. Kim shut and padlocked the chest, left the underground room, and went up the stairs two at a time.

Kim suspected time was short. If Ces's report was true and Jonny Munther had really been watching the video of the ambulance, the detective superintendent was hardly likely to drop the inquiry because the video had been altered. Jonny had taken a dislike to Kim at their first encounter on Tärnö, and Kim's effort to send the forces of public order on a wild goose chase wouldn't have improved that attitude.

Kim turned on his laptop and opened an encrypted email with a message signed *Beelzebub.* It had several attachments. Kim's eyebrows rose when he saw Beelzebub wanted a hundred thousand kronor in Bitcoin for organizing the creation of a human being.

The reason for that hefty charge became clear when Kim opened the attachments. Beelzebub's work had been *meticulous.* A registered identity and corresponding death certificate from the tax authorities would have sufficed, but here was documentation for the entire fictitious life of Johan Andersson, born 1953 and died July 7, 2019, five days ago.

Tax returns from the past three years confirmed that Johan Andersson had received a generous pension and income from investments. Paperwork showed he'd insured both his villa and his automobile. An employment contract. The deed to the villa, purchased in 2002 with his wife Lillian, who'd died five years ago. And to top it off, a photocopy of his passport with a computer-generated photo that resembled Martin Rudbeck.

Beelzebub and his collaborators must have worked around the clock since receiving the assignment. It was as if Kim had asked a handyman to fix a dripping faucet and had come back to find a completely renovated kitchen. It was a thorough, solid job, and Kim transferred the requested sum. Then he devoted himself to cleaning up traces of the assignment and altering QR codes.

Kim had an almost pathological ability to concentrate, and it was only a couple of hours later, when he shut down his laptop, that he happened to think of Julia Malmros. Kim mentally reviewed the events of the morning and saw himself waving her off and saying, "Not now, Julia." Then she'd left.

Kim sighed. If he was right, his gesture and curt comment would *not* be interpreted to mean that he didn't have time to talk just then. She'd assumed something else. Something completely different.

73

July 12, afternoon

"I simply don't know if it's worth it," said Julia, stirring the coffee in which she had, exceptionally, put two sugar cubes, because she knew she needed some perking up.

"Worth what?" asked Irma, squinting through the smoke of her cigarillo. That, also, was unusual. Previously, Irma had been smoking only at the pub, claiming that it was mostly "for appearance's sake."

"Our conflict," said Julia. "Our disappointments. First, he invites me in, then he pushes me out. I can't put up with these swings. I'm too old for this. All I want is . . ."

Julia couldn't finish that sentence. Irma tilted her head, studying her. "Yes? What is it you want, Julia Malmros?"

The fact that Irma had said her whole name was at least as ominous as when she called her "girl," for it was a clear sign Irma thought she was getting herself needlessly spun up. Quite possible, but Julia was miserable not knowing where she stood with Kim and tired of constantly speculating on the lay of the land. She couldn't think straight any longer, hadn't written a coherent sentence in ages.

What is it I want?

Julia looked around the kitchen as if the answer to Irma's question lay somewhere in Irma's bookcases. Only then did she notice that something had changed. Many books had disappeared, and those that remained looked lonely, leaning against one another as if seeking warmth and consolation.

"What did you do with your books?"

"Ah," said Irma with a discreet little cough. "A bit of death cleaning."

"Irma, you're not going to die. You're going to write a book with me, that's what you're going to do."

"You think the world needs more novels? Besides, you didn't answer my question. What is it you really want?"

Julia stared into her coffee cup and saw her own eyes reflected in the liquid. That made her think of days on Tärnö when the vast, calm expanse of the deep sea lay like a mirror reflecting the lazy clouds floating above. "Peace and quiet," she said. "I want peace and quiet."

Irma barked out something between a laugh and a cough and pointed her cigarillo at herself. "Look at me. Here you have someone with lots of peace and quiet. Look festive to you? Be content that you still have the capacity to get yourself into trouble."

"*Definitely* a capacity I think you still have."

"Referring to my weed, are you? Uh-uh, it wasn't *me* who let down her hair and wiggled her bottom."

Julia lowered her head. It was almost fascinating how she was always the one in the wrong, no matter what the subject was. Irma had hardly said a word about the evening Julia cut loose in a haze of marijuana smoke. It wasn't something Julia was tempted to take up as therapy, so she tried to change the subject. "Hear anything more about those True Swedes, then?"

Luckily, Irma took the bait, grinned, and said, "You heard about the demonstration?"

"No. What demonstration?"

Irma erupted in one of her hacking laughs, stubbed out her cigarillo, and said, "That guy Schwarzkopf. Forget about doggy artwork in traffic circles; he presented a living roundabout dog at Roslagstull. Total chaos. Here, watch."

Irma picked up her phone and peered at the screen. She brought up a clip from YouTube, started it, and handed Julia the phone. Julia's hand clenched involuntarily as a cacophony of shouts, yells, screams, and cries burst from the speaker.

At first only shoulders and backs were visible in the waving, jerky image; the videographer was being jostled this way and that. Then he or she must have raised the phone high overhead to capture a better picture of what was happening. A sea of surging heads, raised fists and mobile phones, signs, and . . . Julia put her face close to the screen to make sure she was seeing right. Yes. All across the crowd, swaying here and there, were white cone hats. A rhythmic chanting was part of the general uproar, but Julia couldn't make out a single word, unless "joli-fanto" counted as a word.

A line of policemen with riot shields had established a corridor through the crowd along which a hunched-over Claes-Göran Schwarzkopf was dragging a leashed rottweiler wearing a turban. The animal was resisting, and Schwarzkopf was dragging it across the grass. Eggs, rocks, and clumps of dirt hurtled through the air. One man managed to reach through the protective cordon, snatched the turban from the dog's head, and held it up in triumph before trying to set it on fire with a lighter. He failed. Then the screen went dark.

"Good Lord!" said Julia, handing back the phone. "What was the reason for all that?"

"Clear as day," said Irma. "To show that Muslims can be riled up by the sight of a dog, if it's decked out in a certain way. That Swedes can be riled by the sight of excited Muslims. General polarization. Us versus them. It's just getting worse. I'm glad I won't have to live through it."

Julia moaned at that and said, "Irma, can you stop using every single subject for an excuse to discuss your rapidly approaching demise? I'm really fed up with it."

For once, Irma was the one to admit fault. She held up both hands. "Point taken. I'll restrain myself. But then *you* must tell me what you're planning to do about your bloodstorm guy."

"Irma, I don't know. The fact is . . ." Julia shut her eyes for a moment, again seeing Tärnö in her mind's eye. "I don't want a bloodstorm or a total standstill. I just want . . . a gentle breeze. Maybe a moderate wind."

74

July 12, daytime

Jonny Munther was in a rotten mood when he got back to headquarters after his discussion with the prosecutor. He hadn't gotten permission to investigate Kim Ribbing, let alone a search warrant for the man's residence. Jonny's earnest assertion of what he'd seen in the dashcam video was insufficient, since he couldn't present any such video. Or, at least, not one with Kim Ribbing in it.

"I hear you," Liselott Ahrnander said, "and I believe what you're saying. But you must understand that's not enough. Would you expect to appear at some future trial and tell the judge you had evidence that *no longer exists?*"

"It's not a matter of evidence," Jonny had said. "It's a matter of what I *know.* I looked up this Ribbing guy, and he has every reason in the world to go after the victim. He was a witness in a trial where—"

"Jonny," Liselott interrupted, "someone having a *reason* to commit a crime isn't the same thing as actually committing it."

"I know that. But it's a matter of taking action to rescue a kidnapped citizen before something worse can happen."

"Yes. And it's a shame there's not a single piece of *existing* evidence. What do you think happened with that video?"

"No idea. But that Ribbing guy knows his way around computers. He fiddled with it somehow."

Liselott sighed. "Hear how vague and speculative all this is? Come back when you have something solid to go on, and I'll make sure to address your concerns. And now, unless there's something else . . ."

Jonny's mood wasn't improved when he got to the office and found Christof Adler sprawled in a chair, his uniform unbuttoned and his hair plastered to his skull. Carmen Sánchez was fanning him with a newspaper. What was wrong with today's youth? As soon as things got a little hot, all sorts of therapists and psychologists came running to put them back on their feet. Things were different when Jonny was in the field. In the old days, you just clenched your jaws and plowed ahead. At least that's how he remembered it.

"What's this?" said Jonny and gave Christof a displeased look. "What happened with our Queen of Sheba? Should I go fetch some wine and grapes too?"

"We should be nice to Christof," said Carmen. "It was obviously total chaos out there."

"In fact, I passed out," said Christof in a weak voice.

"Yeah, but here you are in one piece," said Jonny. "Maybe you're suffering from PTSD too?"

The stunned look disappeared from Christof's face. "Say what you want," he snapped. "You weren't there. It was beyond hellish."

Jonny realized he was voicing his own bad humor, so he dropped the sarcasm. In a friendly tone he said, "Oh well, whatever. But you might be pleased to hear you can be of use in the Rudbeck case again."

"Do we even have a *case*?" asked Carmen. "How'd it go with Liselott?"

"Not great," was all Jonny said. "But I'm in charge, and now I want to keep an eye on that Ribbing guy. Christof, I want you to do it. Watch his residence, find out what he's up to."

"That's better than this," said Christof, who seemed to perk up a little. "Anything's better than what I just went through."

"Sorry, hold the phone," said Carmen Sánchez. "If Kim Ribbing is really mixed up in this business, isn't there a possibility Julia Malmros knows about it? After all, they seem to have—" Seeing Jonny's sour expression, Carmen hesitantly concluded, ". . . something going on."

"Correct," said Jonny. "But I'm not ready to yank them in for an official interrogation as long as we don't have a *case.*"

"Maybe unofficially. Just, you know . . . a little conversation?"

"I'll think about it," said Jonny.

In fact, that was one of the first things that had crossed Jonny's mind when he saw the video of the ambulance. His ex-wife might know something, might even be involved. The passionate kiss Jonny had witnessed in that helicopter over the North Sea suggested they had more than merely *something going on.*

But he was reluctant to discuss it with Julia. His initial desire to know more about her relationship with that much younger man had reversed itself, and now he actively *didn't* want to know. Didn't want to think about it or root around in it. *Let it be.* At the same time, he knew that was an unprofessional attitude. Julia could very well know something. Jonny needed to get himself together.

"While you're thinking it over," said Carmen, "I may have some good news to deliver."

"And that is?"

"I talked with Wilmer Syd. Remember him? The one who set this whole circus going. He says Martin Rudbeck's passport and phone are on their way home. The man with the bag where they ended up lands at Arlanda late tonight. I'm thinking, maybe, fingerprints or some such."

"Hardly likely," said Jonny. "The fellow who has 'em probably contaminated them by handling them."

"Maybe, maybe not," said Carmen. "Wilmer Syd specifically told him not to touch the things any more than necessary. There's still a chance."

Christof Adler seemed to have recovered from the worst of his heat exhaustion. He straightened up in his chair. "But we don't have Ribbing's prints for comparison, do we?"

Carmen Sánchez's face lit up in satisfaction. "In fact, we do. He's in the system because he was convicted of disorderly conduct and disturbing the peace."

"What?" said Jonny. "That shrimp?"

Carmen Sánchez's expression was anything but sympathetic. "Well, after what he did in Shanghai and then in Norway, seems to me that 'shrimp' is hardly an appropriate description, no matter how you feel about him."

Jonny pressed his lips together and his mouth turned down as he realized he had unintentionally revealed his personal attitude toward a suspect. Another reminder that he really needed to shape up.

"He was in some kind of fight club," Carmen continued. "And one time some of the members got arrested. So, yes, we do have his prints."

"That's all well and good," said Jonny, making sure he was speaking in a more authoritative tone. "But this isn't a high-priority case. For God's sake, it isn't a case at all, formally speaking. We won't get results for weeks or months."

"Mm-hmm," said Carmen and gave Jonny a hopeful look. "It would be just great if someone happened to be personally acquainted with a forensic specialist, wouldn't it?"

75

July 12, daytime

"What a crappy demonstration," said Astrid Helander as she crammed her cone hat into a trash basket outside the Circle-K on Birger Jarlsgatan. She stared expectantly at the star-spangled cone hat Algot held, and he tucked it under his arm as if to protect it. Astrid shook her head. "What's this? Planning to show it off again sometime?"

"No, but, you know, Mama's a bit . . ." Algot thought of a better explanation for his mother's possible ire and suddenly looked relieved. "My little brother might need it."

"You have siblings?"

"Mm. I have a big sister and little brother."

"Ha, imagine that. Always thought you were an only child."

"Why?"

"Just did, that's all."

They continued toward Odengatan. Astrid didn't want to explain that her assumption about Algot as an only child was because he seemed terribly spoiled, even goofy. Oh well, Astrid was an only child. While her parents were still alive, she'd considered herself bratty, not spoiled. And definitely not goofy.

"Now what'll we do?" asked Algot.

"Butterick's."

"Butt . . . the novelty shop with disguises and stuff?"

"Mm-hmm. But I'm not sure. Haven't decided yet."

"About what?"

Astrid couldn't tell him why a visit to Butterick's was urgent, so she simply said, "I'm supposed to help a person. But I don't know if I really want to."

"What kind of person?"

"You met him. He wanted to watch your clever little video."

That reminder that Algot had covertly recorded their FaceTime call made him blush furiously, and he said nothing more as they walked down Odengatan to Sveavägen. Only as they passed the School of Economics did Algot gather the courage to ask, "Are you a . . . thing? You and him, that death metal guy, what's he to you?"

"No, definitely not. We are not a thing, and he's not a death metal guy."

"What is he, then?"

That question made Astrid frown. What *was* Kim Ribbing, actually? A hacker, rich, psychologically disturbed, a kidnapper, a genius, a shitty damn meat eater? Hard to define an umbrella under which all those epithets could fit. Astrid didn't know what to say, so she countered by tossing the question right back at him. "And how about you? What would you say *you* are? Anything?"

Algot brightened, as if pleased to hear that Astrid wanted to know about his own self-image. "Gamer. Yesterday I was the *last man standing* in PUBG."

Astrid hadn't the slightest idea what that meant but figured it would be appropriate to say "congratulations," so she did.

"Thanks," said Algot. "I picked off a nasty thug almost as soon as I landed. Got really lucky and found a DMR that was hidden in a . . ."

Algot went on and on as they walked along Sveavägen. Astrid stopped listening, fully preoccupied with the question of whether she was going to help Kim or not. She knew it was childish to feel so spited by the sounds of lovemaking the previous night, but hey, she was a child, after all. She decided to leave it to chance. Or to fate.

By the time they got to Hötorget, Algot's lecture about imaginary geography and different weapons was finally finished. Astrid sat on a step outside Stockholm's orchestra hall, not far from the statue of Orpheus. Algot settled three feet away from her and looked around. "What'll we do?"

"Don't know, exactly," said Astrid. "But I thought I'd get myself some cash. For Butterick's."

"Okay. How?"

Right, that was the question. Astrid's gaze glided along the street, taking in merchants selling fruit and flowers, the Sergel Cinema, people sitting on the steps eating ice cream, the taxi stand, and the Hötorg food hall. She was trying to put together a believable story. She took a sneaky glance at the cone hat under Algot's arm. You had to use whatever was at hand, but *that* particular item didn't inspire her.

She'd decided that the success or failure of her con would determine her subsequent course of action. If it worked, she'd support Kim; otherwise, forget it. Astrid pondered for a few minutes more, then turned to Algot. "You have to help."

"Me? How?"

"Listen carefully . . ."

Algot got very jittery when he received his instructions but promised to do his best. Astrid left him on the steps and set out into the square. She didn't miss a beat as she passed a flower stall, reached out, and swiped a single white rose. She continued toward the taxi stand.

Toward the front of the queue of waiting taxis, Astrid took a deep breath, plunged into autosuggestion mode, and started patting her pockets, whimpering and pushing out the tears. A well-dressed woman in her sixties came by. Perfect. Astrid stepped into her way, pressed the white rose to her heart, and said, "Excuse me, I'm so sorry, but I'm on my way to my grandmother's funeral and I've lost my phone!"

The woman was skeptical as she inspected Astrid, who fortunately was wearing a black blouse with frills. "Oh, really?"

Astrid sniveled, rubbed her eyes, and said, "Mama gave me five hundred for the taxi, and it was in the case, and . . . ooooh, I loved Granny *so much*."

"You have my sympathy," the woman said. "But what does that have to do with me?"

The woman's attitude made it clear she was about to walk away, but just then Algot ran up holding Astrid's phone. He held it out. "Heya, hi! This is yours, isn't it? You dropped it."

"Oh!" said Astrid. "Gosh, thanks!"

Astrid took the phone and thought about kissing Algot's cheek but decided that might be going too far. Besides, she didn't want to.

"Well! Now that's nice. Everything's all right again," the well-dressed woman said after casting a puzzled glance at the Star Boy cone Algot had under his arm. "Now I must—"

Astrid opened the phone case and gasped. "What?! My money's gone!" She turned to Algot and cried, "Was it *you* that took it?"

It was only a game, but Algot was so frightened by Astrid's voice and frantic attitude that he quickly backed away. "No! What d'you mean? I wouldn't have returned your phone then, would I? But I did see a boy pick it up and put it back down."

"Nooo! So he took my money! I needed it to go to Granny's funeral! Now I can't!"

The well-dressed woman shifted from one foot to the other. As Astrid had hoped, Algot's sudden appearance had given her sob story some credibility. Or maybe the woman, like so many people, was simply intrigued to have been lured into this little drama and wanted to see how it turned out.

"Well, listen," said Algot, taking out his own phone, "the thing is, I can send you some with Swish. I've only got about a hundred, but . . . you can have it."

"Really?" said Astrid. "That's super cool of you, but . . ."

Astrid went to the taxi queue and was careful to choose a private cab, since they were almost always more expensive than metered taxis.

She tapped on the window. When it lowered, she asked in a trembling voice, "Hi, 'scuse me, but how much does it cost to get to Skogs church from here? And I'm *really in a hurry.*"

She couldn't make out the driver's face, but a palm with outstretched fingers came through the window, and a voice said, "Five hundred. Top speed."

Astrid clutched her face in her hands and wailed. Peering through her fingers, she saw the woman's hand hovering reluctantly at her pocket, but altruism won out at last, and her hand completed its motion. She patted Astrid's shoulder. "I can't be stingier than this young man. Four hundred, all right? What's your phone number?"

The woman received both Astrid's number and an effusive stream of thanks. Throughout it all, Algot stood there like a post, staring at Astrid with his mouth hanging open. She didn't know whether he was impressed or frightened, but it didn't matter to her. The main thing was that he'd done his bit. With a last tearful thank-you, Astrid slipped into the back seat of the taxi and shut the door.

The taxi rolled away. Astrid twisted and looked through the back window, saw the woman say something to Algot and put a hand on his shoulder before continuing on her way toward Kungsgatan. When the taxi stopped for the red light at Sveavägen, Astrid pretended she was about to throw up and cried, "I can't stand it! Granny was an old *witch*! *No way* am I going to her funeral!"

Before the driver could object, she leaped out of the taxi and jogged back toward the Orpheus statue. She huddled behind its base long enough to see whether the driver was going to come after her. He obviously decided it wouldn't be worth the effort for a drive of only fifty yards. When the light changed, he signaled a right turn and disappeared behind the orchestra hall.

Algot hadn't managed to close his mouth by the time Astrid got to him. She put her finger under his chin and smartly snapped it shut. Algot's teeth clicked, then he opened his mouth and blurted, "You are a damn *phenomenon*!"

Astrid couldn't tell if that was admiration or a condemnation of her emotional manipulation of the donor, but she didn't care. She wiped her wet cheeks and examined the mascara on her fingers. "Four hundred. Lots of screaming, not much of a yield."

"Huh?"

"It's like the song about the farmer who tried to shear a pig. A lot of pain for not much gain. The heck with it. It worked anyhow."

"Yeah," said Algot and held up his phone. "And how about my hundred?"

"What? Did you actually send it?"

"Uh, yeah?"

"You've got a lot to learn. Let's go to Butterick's."

76

July 12, afternoon

Julia Malmros had started to get the shakes of caffeine overdose, the feeling there's some other person quivering inside you, even if it's not obvious to others. Irma Ryding's little flat felt like a refuge, a hiding place from all the difficulties of the wider world. Julia had remained seated at Irma's kitchen table, chatting and downing cup after cup of coffee without paying attention to her consumption. When she got up from her chair, she discovered her legs were unsteady. She had to hold the edge of the table.

"Oopsie," said Irma. "You going to start getting old-lady cramps now too?"

"No, it's just . . . too much caffeine."

"I'll say. That's better than cramps. Those'll get you."

Inevitably, Irma had brought out her boxed wine after a few hours of talk. Julia had declined, so Irma hadn't poured any for herself. She'd kept the coffee party going instead, though she'd had far less than Julia.

"No," Julia said. "I really should . . ."

Julia had no idea what she really should do. She had no time to invent something, because the doorbell rang. She glanced at Irma. "Are you expecting a visitor?"

"Not really."

"Maybe somebody selling something?"

Irma made a dismissive sound. "It's not like December, when they come knocking and trying to sell Christmas magazines, you know. Can you go to the door?"

Julia's attitude toward security had changed since she was assaulted and also discovered she had a *stalker*. She'd taken to avoiding dark corners and unpopulated streets; she was always listening for steps behind her. She wasn't about to open a door simply because someone had rung the bell. She put an eye to the peephole, started in surprise, and felt an unpleasant surge of sour coffee in her throat. She opened the door.

She couldn't believe it. "Kim? What are you doing here? How'd you even know I was here?"

Kim shrugged. "Just guessed. And Irma Ryding wasn't too hard to find."

"Who is it?" called Irma from the kitchen. "If they're selling Parmesan, I want some."

Julia had told Kim about Irma's "puffing" and even about their shared marijuana evening that one time, though without going into the more painful details. It was quite likely that's why Kim was wearing his marijuana leaf T-shirt from Amsterdam over his thin long-sleeved jersey. Kim's black hair was clean and combed back so it fell to his shoulders and created an additional frame for the bright green leaf.

"No," Julia called back. "It's not Parmesan!"

"Saffron, then? I *don't* want that!"

Julia beckoned to Kim. The quivering person inside her skin got even more shaky. She couldn't decide whether to be glad Kim had made the effort to track her down or fear the impending collision of her two worlds. She'd have preferred a one-on-one conversation with Kim to get to a basic understanding of their relationship, but they couldn't stand whispering in the hall like a couple of burglars. No choice: It was make or break time.

"Irma," said Julia as they entered the kitchen, "this is Kim. Kim, Irma."

Julia expected Kim to step forward and hold out his hand, but something in Irma's stare made him stop at Julia's side. Time stood still, at least for a few seconds. Then Irma slapped her hands on the table, threw back her head, and laughed gleefully. She pointed to Kim's T-shirt. "I gather you've been briefed?"

"Yep," said Kim. "It's always good to fit in when you come visiting."

Irma waved Kim forward. "Come here and let me get a closer look at you."

Kim did as requested and stood next to the table, where Irma calmly inspected him from top to toe. "Aha. So that's how you look."

"Yes," said Kim. "And that's how *you* look."

"Yep," said Irma. "This is how we look."

"Nothing to be done."

"Not a single thing."

Kim looked around the kitchen and jerked his thumb over his shoulder toward the hall. "Julia said you had an *incredible* number of books, but I can't say that I agree. A lot, yes, but—"

"I've been death cleaning."

"Ah," said Kim. "I see. I've been doing that all my life."

Julia leaned against the kitchen counter, looking back and forth between the two of them as if following a tennis match. They didn't seem to need a referee or ball boys; they calmly volleyed as if they'd done this forever. She relaxed and let herself take a little satisfaction from the fact that Kim had actually looked for her. That was something.

"My other books are in the living room," Irma said. "In cartons. Piles of them. Take whatever you wish. Take 'em all if you want."

"Nope," said Kim. "Like I said, I try to avoid . . . accumulating things. But I will take Julia's last two, if you've got them. Already read the first two."

Irma wagged her finger. "No way, José. *Those* pearls I'm keeping. Anything else, fine."

The conversation had taken a turn that pleased and astonished Julia. She hadn't known Kim wanted to read her novels or that Irma valued them that much. Her trembling became an inner quaking of delight as she volunteered in a slightly choked voice, "You can get them from me. I have loads."

Kim nodded without taking his eyes off Irma. Some of Julia's pleasure waned. Hello? She was the one who'd *written* the novels they were talking about. Kim and Irma went on to another subject, and Julia lost interest. Their tennis match continued smoothly without her intervention. She felt excluded, as usual, and, typically, she was angry that she felt sorry for herself.

They fell silent for a moment. Irma rested her chin on her hand, regarded Kim thoughtfully, and asked, "So then, Kim. If *you* had a dead body you needed to make disappear, how would you go about it?"

That made Kim look around at Julia. His questioning expression was filled with alarm. Julia let go of the counter, raised her hands, and cried out merrily, "Ah, ha ha ha! Irma and I were discussing the plot of a thriller we might be writing together."

"About someone who needed to get rid of a corpse?" Kim asked with a dangerous edge to his voice.

"Don't remember if we said that was in the plot," Irma chimed in. "But anyhow, it's a thought."

Irma's face squinched as she looked at Kim and noticed the sudden shift of mood. Julia was quick to change the subject. "But we're having trouble agreeing on a pseudonym. You have any ideas?"

"Pseudonym?" said Kim, staring at Julia as if he didn't understand the word. His thoughts were obviously elsewhere.

She pretended not to notice the fire in his gaze and tried to sound nonchalant. "Yes, you know—an assumed name to stand for the two of us."

Irma had clearly decided to try to defuse the tension, because she chuckled and said, "I suggested—"

"Jack Wall," Kim interrupted.

"Huh?" Irma said. "Jack Wall. Whatever for?"

Kim shrugged. "Sounds like an author of detective stories. Great meeting you, Irma, but I have to be getting along."

Kim strode out of the kitchen, and Julia gave Irma an apologetic look before hurrying after. Behind them she heard Irma murmuring, "Jack Wall . . . Jack Wall?"

Julia plunged down the stairs after Kim, who was descending rapidly, his hair streaming behind him. Only when they'd reached the street could she put a hand on his arm and gasp, "Sorry. But I. Raised it. Only as. A purely. Theoretical problem. Didn't say. Anything."

"And then you came up with that business about Tärnö?"

"That was. About the. Same time."

Julia was lightheaded from caffeine, adrenaline, and simple breathlessness. She grabbed a drainpipe with both hands, leaned over, and took several deep breaths. "So. What are you planning to do? With *that thing?*"

A couple of seconds passed. No answer. She looked up to see Kim contemplating her, his arms across his chest. He gave a short shake of his head. "I think it's best not to tell you."

Then he left.

Julia remained behind, leaning against the drainpipe, head down as she stared at a crust of dried dogshit between two cobblestones. Kim had come looking for her and now he'd gone off alone. Doors open, then they shut. Would this never end?

77

July 12, afternoon

"What do you think?"

Moa opened and then closed one of the three drawers in a white lacquered plywood desk. A label identified the model as "Malm." Pushing the drawer back in took some doing, and it protested with a hollow sound. Jonny tapped his knuckle on the desktop and decided that the material was decidedly flimsy.

"Nah," said Jonny. "Seems kind of small."

Almost all the furnishings in his parents' home were heavy, dark wooden pieces, many of them passed down through generations. He hadn't been strong enough to pull out the big desk's drawers until he was twelve years old. Malm was the complete opposite. Bright, light, and rickety.

"Check the price," said Moa.

Jonny did. It was 490 kronor. What kind of a desk could you get for that amount? The answer was obvious; it was right in front of him. You got Malm. Jonny assumed that the name, meaning "mineral ore," was supposed to evoke solidity and stability—in other words, the very qualities the desk did not possess. Jonny was no fan of IKEA.

He'd phoned Moa to say he needed a little help, and she'd said that was a lucky coincidence, for so did she. Accordingly, Jonny had set out to Kungens Kurva, fifteen miles south of Stockholm, under the pretext of "meeting with an external consultant," which was certainly no falsehood, even though giving advice on furniture wouldn't normally be part of it.

To the extent Jonny had provided advice, it had fallen on deaf ears. Moa almost always chose the least expensive version. The Ivar bookcase for 489 kronor had filled Jonny with dismay. It seemed to teeter on the verge of collapse, even before anything was placed on its flimsy shelves.

The only thing that kept Jonny's spirits up was the *implication* of their circular wanderings. Moa had decided to stay in Stockholm, and she needed furniture for the empty flat on Kocksgatan. She'd indicated, not just hinted, that her move was somehow connected with DS Jonny Munther. Was he going to sulk over her furniture choices? No, ma'am. But he couldn't keep himself from saying, "Maybe you could think *just a little bit* about a more solid version?"

Moa ran a fingertip along Malm's smooth surface. "I told you already. It'll be this one. Will you write it down for me?"

Jonny nodded and noted the price and the corresponding section of the pickup area. IKEA's little pencil was hard to grasp in his big fingers, and the purchase form looked as if a seven-year-old with poor motor skills had filled it out.

Yes, indeed, Moa had made things clear. With her move to Stockholm she intended to commence a new phase in her life, one of radical simplification. She'd been tempted by the idea for some time but hadn't pursued it while in her old digs in Linköping. Uncertain what she meant by "simplification," Jonny had asked her to explain.

In all aspects of her life, Moa intended to limit herself only to what was absolutely necessary. No frivolous or expensive purchases, whether of food, clothing, or anything else. Forget restaurant meals; no cinema visits. She would make an exception for theater productions but would limit those. In this way she could get along on half her salary, and the other half she'd donate to SOS Children's Villages.

"Of course, that's noble of you," Jonny had said, "but might I be so impolite as to ask . . . why?"

"I'm just fed up with it all. The whole circus. I want to be one, simple individual in this world. To contribute. And I believe it'll do me good. So, basically, it's selfish."

"Doesn't sound selfish to my ears."

"Then maybe your ears are tuned to the wrong channel. Anyway, what were you saying about a passport?"

Jonny told her about the passport and telephone that had flown off to Thailand all by themselves. How there was a chance that whoever had orchestrated this had left prints on the items now back in Stockholm. How urgent it was, how it couldn't wait.

"Okay," said Moa. "I can handle that. I really should take them to Linköping, but the Stockholm lab will do, if I can get in."

"That's something *I* can arrange," said Jonny. "And it'd be a good chance to look at the place. If you're thinking of working there, I mean."

"My idea was to work more remotely, but we'll see. If there's anything to be found on the passport, I'll probably detect it. And now, let's do the living room."

A simple table, a woven polyester rug, and that atrocious Ivar bookcase. And to top it all off, a rickety bamboo pedestal to hold a potted plant. Jonny thought of his own sublet and the only large piece of furniture he'd bought for himself. "Chairs, then? Armchairs, a sofa?"

Moa grinned. "Actually, that's the only splurge I'm going to allow myself. Decided to buy two Fatboy chairs. Clever, huh?"

"Fatboy?"

"Sure, you know. Beanbag chairs, we used to call them. Sacks full of plastic beads."

It was at that moment that Jonny had an insight: Moa didn't just want to simplify and start a new phase in life, she really wanted to *start over*, like a teenager about to move into her first apartment. Visiting IKEA, buying beanbag chairs, oh my goodness. And then what? Mac and cheese and hot dogs?

When they'd finished their tour and were on their way to the warehouse to find the items on Jonny's smudgy list, Moa paused in the section with frames and posters. "Do you think you *know* who could have handled the passport?"

"No," said Jonny. "I'm *certain.*"

"Because of the video you mentioned? That was weird. Let's hear it again."

Jonny gave her a fuller description of how he'd received the flash drive with recordings from the vehicle's dashcam, how he'd seen Kim Ribbing with his own eyes, and how the video had shown a different person only minutes later.

"But the file on the flash drive was just a copy," Moa said. "Did you check the original? On the server?"

"I did, and it was identical. Not a trace of him. And the individual in the film isn't in our system."

"And you're *absolutely* sure it was that fellow Ribbing?"

"As sure as I'm standing here next to you."

Moa started wending her way through the maze of corridors again, shaking her head. "If so, that's incredible. In fact, impossible. I've never heard of anyone who could mount a convincing deep fake that quickly. It should have taken hours."

"Right," said Jonny, involuntarily grinding his teeth. "He's a clever son of a bitch."

"Oh my," said Moa, surprised. "You've had to deal with him before?"

Jonny hemmed and hawed. "In a manner of speaking. But that's a different story."

"Okay," said Moa. "But 'clever' doesn't sound quite right. I think it's more like 'supernatural.'"

"That," said Jonny, "is a possibility I'm *not* going to consider."

The pickup area was as vast as an airplane hangar. Jonny had to help Moa decipher his scrawls as they went down the corridors. He pushed a metal cart they quickly filled with flat-packed items.

When they finally located Malm and squatted down next to each other to make sure the numbers were correct, Jonny pointed to the sketch on the carton. "Knobs. You need to get knobs."

"Knobs?" said Moa, amused, as if it were funny to hear her big companion using such a word.

"Yeah, you know. Knobs. To pull out the drawers. I saw they're not included."

"Knobs?"

"Right. Knobs."

"Come here."

Moa put a hand behind Jonny's neck, pulled him to her, and kissed him. Jonny almost fell as he swayed toward her; as his lips met hers, he put a hand on the Malm carton to steady himself and keep from falling over. Her warm breath filled his mouth. Her tongue sought and found his.

So it had come to this. Adult human beings, sitting and smooching in the IKEA warehouse in the middle of the afternoon—it was a new start for Jonny Munther too. For a moment his chest tensed as he worried that someone might see. Then he forgot his reluctance and went all in. It was just so damn wonderful to kiss. To be kissed. After all this time.

Jonny gasped when their faces parted at last, for he'd forgotten to breathe. He looked into Moa's shining eyes and felt like an awkward teenager, not knowing what to say. Maybe something about IKEA. That maybe it wasn't so dull here after all. But his newly kissed lips felt almost numb, so he just murmured "mm-hmm," then grabbed the Malm carton and heaved it onto the cart before straightening up, his knees audibly popping.

"Okay," Jonny managed to croak, "so we're finished, right?"

"Oh, no!" said Moa, getting up with far more grace and ease than he had.

Jonny was a bit intimidated by her tone and responded with only, "No? You're sure?"

"No," said Moa. "Now we have to go home and screw it all together."

78

July 12, afternoon

The thin plastic bags on Astrid Helander's wrist rattled as she and Algot left Butterick's and plunged into the crowd along Drottninggatan. She deftly folded the receipt into a tiny paper airplane and tossed it toward a trash basket. The plane veered, dove, and then, astonishingly, disappeared into the basket.

"Wow," Algot said. "High five!"

Astrid showed no surprise at her remarkable feat and nonchalantly held up her free hand for Algot to slap. Algot looked around excitedly; he was obviously having a grand time and expecting Astrid to guide him. Demonstrations, a successful con, and the art of paper airplanes! What next?

"And now?" he asked. "What'll we do now?"

Astrid was getting tired of enriching Algot's dreary little existence. He was polite and had played his role in her hustle very well, but he was awfully doglike, the way he followed her around, obeyed her commands, and marveled at her. She'd put him through his paces and they both deserved a rest, so Astrid said, "Nothing else. Fun's over."

Algot was as dismayed as if his own personal rain cloud had dumped on his head. He fidgeted, shifted from one foot to the other, and looked uncertainly at Astrid. Something told her he was trying to gather the courage to say something she didn't want to hear. Algot was just a big baby, so it was entirely possible he was going to beg, *Do I have a chance with you?*

To avoid that kind of embarrassment, Astrid pointed at the entrance to the central underground station. "Off you go!" She jerked a thumb over her own shoulder. "And I'm going this way. Thanks. See you later, alligator."

Before Algot could come up with the obvious response, Astrid turned on her heel and merged with the crowd, continuing and not looking back until she figured she was out of sight. Then she stopped and leaned against one of the new, heavier stone lions the city had installed after a truck mowed down a crowd of people two years earlier. She remembered that every time she walked Drottninggatan.

She needed some quiet time to think after the cacophony of that useless demonstration and Algot's blah-blah-blah. She held the shopping bags to her chest and tried to think how to assist Kim the following day. She'd objected to today's demonstrations, but a flash mob actually might be a good alternative. She needed to think about it. But first . . .

Astrid tapped her phone. Julia Malmros's number rang and rang. Astrid was about to give up when Julia answered in a muted voice. "Yes, hello. Astrid?"

"Hey. Just wanted to see if you planned on sleeping over tonight. 'Cause if so . . ."

Astrid didn't want to endure a repeat performance of the previous night's frolics. It would be better to stay with her uncle, try to allay his concern about her frequent absences.

Julia sighed. "'Fraid not. You don't have to worry. I won't be going back."

"What do you mean? Why?"

"I think it's all over between me and Kim. So . . . no need for you to worry. But it was great getting to know you a little better. Take care, Astrid. Have a wonderful life."

"Hold on," said Astrid. "Just a minute . . . What for? Why's it all over?"

"Because I'm an idiot."

"Okay, got that, but that's not what I was asking. You may be an idiot, but Kim's a total pain in the ass sometimes. And?"

"What do you mean, 'and'?"

Irritated, Astrid waved her hand. "Where are you, anyway?"

"Old Town. Why?"

"Okay. I'm on Drottninggatan. If you walk toward me and I walk toward you, we should meet somewhere around the parliament building. Okay?"

"But why?"

"Just hang up and do as I say, that's all. See you soon."

Astrid stuffed her phone back in her pocket, shaking her head. What was *with* these people, really? She'd really like to talk to Walter, who seemed to be the only grown-up around. But she had no time for that.

When Astrid was ten, the same year Julia Malmros had given her the thousand-piece puzzle, her parents were at each other's throats out on Tärnö. Maybe because Mama had discovered something to do with her papa's shady business affairs, Astrid didn't know. They'd quarreled and shouted and she'd threatened to divorce him.

That was the summer Astrid discovered her talent for emotional manipulation to get people to do what she wanted. She'd subtly guilt-tripped them to start reconciling little by little. When things got really bad, she used her newfound talent to hold her breath until she passed out. By the time they all returned to Stockholm, the crisis was over.

Astrid started walking toward Old Town, the Butterick's bags swinging back and forth on her wrist. She was perplexed by her own behavior. Shouldn't she be glad to be rid of Julia Malmros? Maybe, but since her parents had died, she didn't want anyone else to disappear. Especially not anyone she'd gotten used to.

And people were acting like such fools—wasn't it about time for somebody to take charge and stir things up? Someone certainly had to be the adult in the room, even if she was only fourteen years old.

79

July 12, afternoon

Christof Adler had never experienced a day so starkly divided. In the morning: chaos, catastrophe, shouts, and panic. In the afternoon: sitting on a tree stump in a silent forest, peering through binoculars to keep watch on a villa. No points for guessing which assignment he preferred.

Christof had sat for about half an hour without seeing any movement, but then Kim Ribbing rode up on his motorcycle. He opened the gate, went up the gravel drive, parked, then vanished into the villa. Christof jotted down the time in his notebook. He didn't know exactly what he was supposed to look for, but Jonny Munther had told him to keep watch, and watch was exactly what he was keeping.

Christof sat for a while studying the windows but couldn't see a thing. He lowered the binoculars, and his thoughts turned to Gandalf, as they so often did. He'd been weighing something really daring for his fan fiction piece: a love story between Gandalf and Galadriel.

Quite elvish, of course. Very chaste and noble. Christof sometimes overheard comments that he was a bit of a prude, probably because he didn't join in rowdy locker-room talk after bandy matches. Okay, maybe he *was* prudish, but he preferred to think of himself as romantic. Or inhibited. Or both.

With that thought, he texted Cecilia. Hi, darling. Sitting in a forest, missing you. Smelling the scent of your hair in my nostrils, tasting your lovely neck on my lips. Your very own Christof. He hesitated at that "tasting your neck" but thought he'd be a bit bold anyway. He added heart emojis and sent it.

The answer came half a minute later. I got mamas phne yuk cringe kissykissykissy.

Christof groaned. Obviously, Matilda had gone to the florist shop after school and Cecilia had given her the phone to keep her occupied. Talk about bad timing! So much for romance. He hoped he'd be more successful with Gandalf and Galadriel; they didn't have such problems.

Christof looked up from the screen and glimpsed movement down at the villa. He looked through the binoculars and gasped.

What the hell?

Kim Ribbing emerged from the front door holding a shovel. He put it over his shoulder as he strode down the porch steps, walked to the corner of the house, and disappeared from sight. An excavation was imminent in the back garden, and it was hard *not* to see the implications.

Christof noted the time and wrote *KR comes out with shovel, walks to garden.* He weighed his alternatives. The fence and trees in the back made it impossible to see what Ribbing was up to, and Christof wasn't authorized to enter the property, was he? He chewed his nails and decided to wait.

Not half an hour later some individuals came down the sidewalk only about ten yards from Christof. He thought the bushes and low-lying trees hid him sufficiently but slipped off his stump and crouched behind it anyway. When they passed an opening in the foliage, Christof recognized Julia Malmros and Astrid Helander. As they approached the entry to the villa, their backs were to him. He carefully recorded their arrival.

Ribbing had reappeared in the meantime and was sitting on the front stairs. He said something Christof couldn't catch, and they responded. Astrid seemed upset. Christof swore under his breath. If he'd just been smart enough to bring a parabolic microphone, he could have monitored their discussion. Now he was baffled, and the only thing he could do was try to decipher the pantomime. What could they be talking about? He couldn't even guess.

80

July 12, afternoon

Kim Ribbing brushed the dirt from his hands and sank down on the sun-warmed steps as he watched Julia and Astrid walking up the drive. The dynamic between them had altered, and Astrid, in the lead, was obviously in charge. It couldn't have been clearer if she'd had Julia on a leash.

"Hi," Kim called tentatively. "It's you two, is it?"

"Shut up," said Astrid with a cross expression. Then she pointed to the steps next to Kim. "Julia, sit down."

Julia gave Kim a timid look. He leaned over and brushed dust from the step to invite her. She advanced, sat down hunched over, and gave Astrid a plaintive look. The girl crossed her arms and stared at them. "Can you two please tell me what you're doing to one another?"

"As far as I know, nothing," said Kim.

Astrid blew out an exasperated sigh before continuing. "Oh, no? You're not doing a damn thing other than tormenting each other. How old are you? Don't you see that you're terrible role models?"

"I have no intention of being any kind of role model," said Kim.

"Clearly, but you are, whether you like it or not. That's not something *you* can decide, you know."

"I know that I'm a terrible example," said Julia. "That's why I never—"

"Arrgh!" Astrid rolled her eyes. "Don't you start feeling sorry for yourself and playing the martyr again! And sit up straight, for God's sake!"

"Astrid," said Kim, "can you try to calm down a little?"

That request made her even more furious. She waved a menacing finger at Kim. "I'll calm down if and when the two of you shape up!"

"And how, exactly, is that shaping up supposed to take place?"

Astrid glared at Kim as if she couldn't believe her ears. She shook her head and held up one hand, a quarter of an inch separating her thumb and index finger. "Listen, I'm just *this close* to walking off and leaving you to your . . . idiotic squabbling!"

Kim and Julia exchanged a glance. A timid smile flickered across Julia's lips. She cleared her throat. "Astrid's referring to the way we handle our relationship."

"That's *one* way of putting it," said Astrid. "Or you might say that you two blockheads have got to get your act together. That's what *I'd* say."

"And what do you think we should do?" asked Kim.

Astrid jerked her chin toward Julia. "Yeah, for instance, you can start by putting your arm around Julia. Can't you see she's miserable as hell?"

Kim did as Astrid demanded and felt Julia's entire body quiver when he cupped her shoulder with his hand. He pressed it carefully.

Julia leaned into him. "I'm sorry about what happened at Irma's. It was thoughtless of me to say what I did."

"Yeah," said Kim. "But really, I didn't need to . . . I overreacted. Everything's a bit . . . messy, to put it mildly."

"Yes. I understand that."

"So there, right?" Astrid threw up her hands. "That wasn't so damn hard, was it?" She made a disgusted gesture. "Okay. Now you can kiss each other."

Julia sniffled. "I think that you just reached the limits of your . . . authority, Astrid."

"Forget it, then. But don't you get started again tonight."

"I'm sorry, Astrid," said Kim. "But actually, *you're* not the one to decide that."

Astrid looked up to the skies as if appealing for strength. "What kind of thanks is that? I get you back together even though I don't want to, and now you're . . . oh, yes, right. Go ahead, get down and dirty. Don't pay any attention to me!"

"And now who's being the martyr?" asked Kim.

Astrid seemed about to renew her attack but groaned to show she'd given up. She dropped her hands and sank down to the bottom step at their feet. Julia ran a hand over the girl's shoulder. "We'll try to hold ourselves back, but shouldn't you be at your uncle's this evening anyway?"

"Dream on, lady," said Astrid. "I'll go there tomorrow. Kim said things are going to be happening."

"Mm," said Kim, leaning forward to put his head between Astrid's and Julia's. He murmured, "Don't look now, but we're being watched. Just as I expected. And that changes things a bit. I'm going to need your help. Can I count on you?"

Julia looked at Astrid. They exchanged quick nods. Julia asked, "What should we do?"

Kim glanced quickly along the drive and caught yet another glint of sun off a camera or binocular lens. He got up and said, "I think it's best we take this inside."

81

July 12–13, nighttime

It was almost half past ten when Jonny Munther put the last screw into the Ivar bookcase. Malm was already set up; so was the coffee table he'd forgotten the name of, and Moa Malmberg's living room was a waste heap of plastic and cardboard. The little IKEA wrench clinked as Jonny dropped it. With a groan, he stretched out full length on the floor.

"Probably should have bought an armchair," said Jonny when Moa came into the room.

"Already ordered the Fatboys," she said. "They'll be here the day after tomorrow. And oh, look, here's a place to sit."

She set her feet on either side of his rib cage, lowered her rear, and sat on his stomach. She patted his cheek and let her index finger wander through his curly gray chest hair. She leaned over, put her lips to his ear, and whispered, "At least I've got a bed, and maybe that's the most important thing right now. Or what does the detective superintendent think?"

Jonny's voice was choked. "The detective superintendent agrees."

At 11:14 p.m. Julia Malmros wrung out the mop for the nth time; she'd lost count. The underground room reeked of Ajax and bleach. She, Kim, and Astrid had scrubbed every surface Martin Rudbeck could have touched, every nook and cranny where he might have left any biological traces.

She knew it was virtually impossible to eliminate *everything*. With modern technology, a flake of skin or an eyebrow hair could prove that a certain person had been at a given place, but she doubted that such a thorough search would take place once the body was no longer in the vicinity.

The seaman's chest had stood in a corner as they worked, a mute reminder of what was at stake. Water from melted ice seeped from its bottom corners. That would have to wait until the morning when the chest was gone, assuming everything went according to plan.

"Hey, listen, guys," said Julia, leaning the mop against the wall. "What do you say? Shall we call it a day?"

At 12:21 a.m. Algot Mörner turned off his computer after totally blowing a PUBG game. He'd found it hard to maintain the necessary awareness and concentration, since his thoughts kept returning to Astrid Helander. He'd analyzed the events of the day, what Astrid had said and done, and what he'd said and done, down to the tiniest detail.

The results were disheartening. Algot couldn't for his life figure out what to do to get Astrid to want to be with him or even fall for him. He wanted so terribly much to be with her, and a shudder of pleasure went through him at the recollection of her fingers under his chin.

That was when, *bam*, he'd got a bullet through the head and the game was over.

At 2:23 a.m. Astrid awoke from a nightmare. She'd found herself locked in a seaman's chest slowly sinking to the bottom of the sea. She lay huddled and cramped, kicking the lid and the walls of the chest as water rose around her, but they wouldn't yield. Finally, there was only a dwindling bubble of air in one corner from which Astrid sucked in her last terrified breath.

Then she awoke. Her heart was hammering so hard it roared in her ears. She looked at the wall separating her room from Kim's bedroom. Quiet snoring was the only sound. Probably Julia. Astrid couldn't understand why she'd put so much energy into reuniting Julia and Kim, but what was done, was done.

Oh well, chalk it up as a good deed. Astrid pulled her knees up to her chest, rolled onto her side, and tried to go back to sleep.

At 4:21 a.m. a plane landed at Arlanda five hours late. Electrician Sören Bolinder was back from Thailand. In his carry-on was a plastic bag containing the passport and the telephone of a certain Martin Rudbeck, completely unknown to him.

A female police officer met him at the gate. She introduced herself as Carmen Sánchez. She accepted the plastic bag and carefully sealed it inside a larger ziplock bag.

"Okay, then," Sören said. "It was that important, then."

"Yep," said Carmen. "It was indeed."

82

July 13, morning

The first thing Jonny Munther did when he awoke just after eight o'clock was check his mobile phone. Yes! At 4:32 he'd received a text from Carmen Sánchez informing him that Martin Rudbeck's fugitive belongings were now secured, so all they needed was for him to provide headquarters with the appropriate expertise if he so pleased.

Jonny smiled at the "appropriate expertise," who lay sleeping with her back to him, her mouth slightly open. Lovemaking that night had started with some awkward fumbling, but gradually it had become marvelous. Jonny hadn't been sure he still had it in him, but once he'd overcome his initial doubts, his body had done what it was designed to do.

He had no idea what lay ahead, but leaving that aside, at least this *one* night he and Moa had melted together, and those memories would light his life for a long time. Jonny leaned over and brushed his lips across her brow before cautiously getting out of the sheets. Hers was a single bed, and Jonny had spent a couple of uncomfortable hours seeking a reasonable sleeping position, then drifted off at last, fully exhausted.

He got to his feet, and his joints felt as if they needed oiling. He staggered a bit on his way to collect his clothes from the living room. The previous night had exercised untrained muscles, and the detective superintendent's stiff and aching body felt like a creaky machine. But his mind was serene and clear, despite the lack of sleep.

Jonny had to hunt through the mess of plastic and cardboard to locate his clothes. He gathered Moa's at the same time, folded them nicely, and placed them upon Ivar. Yep, things had gotten a bit wild there at first, and once they were naked, a certain shyness had overcome them. But even so, undressing one another in the midst of all that packing material—that was something new. Despite his aches, Jonny felt younger than he had in a long time. Or, anyway, less old.

After dressing, he had to search the kitchen for equipment to brew coffee. As water ran through the filter, he texted Carmen Sánchez to tell her to leave the parcel at the reception desk. He figured that would mean Moa wouldn't have to pass through their section to go down to the lab.

Carmen obviously hadn't gone to bed after her trip to Arlanda, for her reply was almost instantaneous: *No way. Come up and say hi.* Jonny grunted at that. No matter how much he appreciated Carmen, he couldn't stand her interest in his private life.

Okay, it was true that before the excursion to IKEA, Jonny had made sure to spray himself with Bottled Night, so Carmen had earned a point there. And it wasn't as if Jonny was ashamed of Moa—quite the opposite—but he wasn't ready to expose her to Carmen's teasing. Oh well, if Jonny had a motto, it had to be "What will be, will be."

When the coffee was ready, Jonny poured a mugful for himself and another for Moa, then returned to the bedroom. Moa was awake now and rolled onto her side when he entered. She propped her head on one hand and looked at him. Jonny was uncertain how to address her in this new situation. Both "darling" and "dearest" seemed exaggerated, "my lovely" sounded stupid, and there was no way he could force himself to call her "sweetheart."

Jonny found refuge in a Danish expression and held up one mug. "Coffee, my precious."

Moa raised an eyebrow as if to say *not bad* and took the mug in both hands, blew on the hot brew, and had a little sip. Jonny sat next to her on the bed and said, "The things have arrived, so we can simply go in when you feel up to it."

Moa nodded. "Is it urgent?"

"Not exactly . . . I guess urgent is a relative term, but it'll be good if we can get it done."

As Jonny sat on the edge of the bed looking at Moa sipping the hot coffee—her hair tousled, her lips somewhat swollen from Jonny's kisses—his desire to put Kim Ribbing behind bars suddenly seemed far, far away. Not to say Jonny was going to let him get off, not at all. A crime had been committed, and Jonny's job was to solve crimes, but his personal zeal for doing so had ebbed after his night with Moa.

They drank their coffee and said nothing, merely glancing at one another from time to time and smiling. There was little to add to what their bodies had communicated several hours earlier. Moa finished her coffee, put her mug on the floor, and said, "Okay, let's get going. Just got to throw on some clothes."

If Jonny's getting out of bed had resembled a creaky, squeaky machine, Moa's resembled that of a newly awakened feline. She slipped smoothly out of the sheets and padded toward the living room. Jonny said, "I took the liberty of gathering your clothes. They were a little . . . spread out."

Moa looked back and favored him with a big smile. "I can imagine."

Jonny looked down, suddenly abashed by her nudity. He put down his mug, laced his fingers together, and lowered his head as if in prayer.

Let this work. I want this.

83

Christof Adler was back at his post by half past eight. He was better prepared today, having brought a parabolic microphone and a thermos of coffee as well as a cushion for the tree stump.

He'd sat half an hour slowly drinking coffee when he heard a rustling in the dry leaves. A hedgehog waddled out from the bushes, softly snuffling. Christof watched it pass only a couple of feet from him and vanish behind the tangled roots of a fallen tree. The high point of his day so far.

He was extremely bored, he couldn't deny it. Christof enjoyed the scenes in cop films and TV shows with investigators on a stakeout. Sitting in a car, eating lousy food, chatting about this and that while they kept watch on some building. Yeah, it was the *company* that Christof missed. He was a social creature at heart, happiest with other people around. A hedgehog wasn't much of a substitute.

This meant he wasn't used to entertaining himself with his own thoughts. For fun, he started going through the characters of *The Lord of the Rings* to see how many he could name. He kept his eyes on the villa and got to forty-seven before giving up. Still nothing moving over there.

A blue tit chirped somewhere in the branches overhead. Christof put on the earphones and aimed the parabolic mic in its direction. Birdsong filled his ears. He nodded to its rhythm, trying to predict the next warbling phrase. Then he took off the headphones and poured some more coffee. He took a swig and sighed. This felt a bit silly. It was about time for something to happen. Anything at all.

It was nearly ten when the villa's front door opened. Christof picked up the binoculars and watched Kim come out and descend the front stairs. A blue baseball cap sat atop his head, and his black hair whipped across a long-sleeved T-shirt with some kind of Mexican motif. Then Christof remembered: Santa Muerte. Ribbing had been wearing that shirt when making his statement for the Frode Moe case.

Christof assumed Ribbing would take the motorcycle, but this time he came down the gravel drive, opened the gate, and walked along the road toward Gärdet and the city. Christof hesitated. Jonny Munther had told him to keep an eye on Kim Ribbing, not on the villa.

Christof quickly collected his things, stuffed them into his backpack, and cached it behind the stump. He made his way through the underbrush, hunched over and careful about where he set his feet so as not to step on the hedgehog. He followed Kim Ribbing at a discreet distance.

84

July 13, morning

"Moa, Carmen. Carmen, Moa," said Jonny Munther and raised his hands as a sign he was taking no responsibility for what happened next.

Carmen Sánchez took Moa Malmberg's outstretched hand and held it as she frankly examined the older woman. Moa examined Carmen right back. Then they both smiled as if their mutual inspection had satisfied them both. They ended their shake.

"Wish I could say I'd heard a lot about you," said Carmen. "But I'd be lying."

"Same here," said Moa.

"Mm-hmm," said Carmen and nodded at Jonny. "He's not exactly a source of information overload."

"I am standing right here," said Jonny.

"See?" said Carmen. "Nothing but the most obvious."

"Can we get to work, maybe?" said Jonny, who had no patience for joking social chat.

"Absolutely," said Carmen. She turned to her desk, picked up the ziplock bag from Arlanda, and handed it to Moa along with a sheet of paper. "I called up the prints you're looking for, okay?"

"Sure," said Moa. "I like to drive stick shift." She held the bag close to her eyes and turned it, inspecting the contents. "Shouldn't be a problem. If there's anything, I'll be able to find it."

"Excellent," said Jonny. "And the quicker, the better. We informed the people at the NFC, so we can get right to work."

Moa looked at Jonny and seemed about to say something, but she glanced at Carmen, tightened her lips, and walked toward the elevator with the bag in one hand.

Carmen waited until Moa was out of earshot. "*The quicker, the better?* Is that what a man says to a woman he just spent the night with?"

Jonny was taken aback. "What do you know about it?"

"It's obvious," said Carmen. "You can sense it. And a man doesn't say things like *hop to it, kiddo.*"

"That's *not* what I said!"

"No," said Carmen, nodding toward the elevator Moa had just entered. "But that's what she heard. Pay attention, Jonny Munther. You'd better watch what you say to that one."

Jonny pouted a bit. "I do the best I can."

"Mm-hmm. So, do better."

The discussion had taken a turn Jonny Munther didn't like at all. Personal matters, relationship counseling. His ringing phone saved him. The screen showed *Christof Adler.* He could have taken the call standing next to Carmen, but he used it as an excuse. "Gotta take this." He fled into his office.

85

July 13, morning

Christof had been expecting to spend the whole day sitting in the shadowy underbrush, so he'd worn a hoodie over a long-sleeved knit shirt. He started sweating as Kim followed the street through Gärdet and the sun blazed down from a clear blue sky. There was no likelihood of losing sight of Ribbing in the open expanse, so Christof stopped, took off the hoodie, and knotted it around his waist. He peered at the lean figure with black hair billowing down his back a hundred yards ahead.

Where is he going?

Ribbing got to Berwaldhallen ten minutes later and turned right toward the radio and television studios. Christof took out his phone and called Jonny Munther, who was unusually slow to pick up. "Hey," said Christof. "Ribbing's out walking. Right now he's on the street leading to Swedish Radio."

"Oh, really," said the detective superintendent. "What's he going to do there?"

"No, I mean, I don't think he's going to the radio studios, but he's headed in that direction."

"Um-hmm? And?"

Christof rubbed his sweaty neck, feeling stupid. "It's just, I wanted to tell you. Give you an update. How's it going on your end?"

"Just fine, thanks for asking. Keep your eyes on Ribbing. If there's a match with his prints, I'll want to know exactly where he is."

"Roger that."

Christof put away his phone and saw that Kim Ribbing wasn't planning to visit Swedish Radio. Or Swedish Television either. He turned left at the traffic circle at the end of Oxenstiernsgatan and started up Valhallavägen. Christof closed to within fifty yards since there were many people on the sidewalks.

Was he the one who'd get the order to arrest Ribbing if the fingerprints matched? Christof wasn't carrying cuffs. If an arrest was required, he could only hope Ribbing would agree to follow him peaceably.

Ribbing walked along the sidewalk on the south side of Valhallavägen, while Christof followed on the strollers' path in the median where trees offered some shade. They'd been walking for more than half an hour, seemingly with no goal in sight. Christof's back pocket vibrated as his phone rang. He took it out and glanced at Ribbing before accepting the call. He almost lost his man because just then Ribbing disappeared through the doors of Fältöversten shopping center. Christof jammed his phone back in his pocket and raced across the street to follow his quarry, his phone buzzing in his back pocket the whole time.

86

July 13, morning

Moa came through the elevator doors only twenty-five minutes later. Catching sight of Jonny, she gave him a sign that consoled the detective superintendent and delighted his heart: thumbs-up. Partly because her attitude showed she wasn't angry at him for his brusque behavior, partly because . . .

"Is it true?" asked Jonny when Moa came into the section. "You got a hit?"

"Practically certain," said Moa. "It's rare to find one that's a hundred percent sure, but for a partial print, this one's as close as they get."

"Just so we're entirely clear here," said Jonny, "you're confirming that Kim Ribbing's fingerprint is on the passport?"

"On the phone too," said Moa. "With, let's call it, ninety-eight percent certainty."

Jonny slapped a hand to his forehead, and only now was the revelation clear. He felt obliged to say it out loud. "Good God, so it *was* that Ribbing guy who abducted Rudbeck with the ambulance!"

"Meh," said Moa. "That would require a different chain of evidence, but . . . a lot points in that direction."

"Now we're damn sure to get a search warrant. But first . . ."

Jonny Munther was so excited that he almost dropped his phone as he pressed the quick-dial number for Christof Adler to order him to bring Ribbing in. The phone rang for a long time, but Christof didn't answer. Gritting his teeth, Jonny muttered, "Come on, come on, we've *got* him."

87

July 13, morning

Christof entered the air-conditioned shopping center and found the temperature noticeably cooler and quite agreeable. His hammering heart slowed when he saw Ribbing in front of the window of a clothing store about a hundred feet away. Christof's phone had continued buzzing insistently the whole time, and he could finally take it out to respond.

"Yes, hello?" said Christof just as loud electronic music erupted in the shopping center, making it difficult to hear his boss. Christof squeezed his eyes shut and covered his other ear with a hand to hear better.

"Sorry, what was that?" shouted Christof over the music now thumping so loudly it made his chest vibrate.

"Take him!" yelled Jonny Munther on the other end. "Bring Ribbing in now!"

"Okay, okay!" said Christof just as the music got louder.

Christof lowered his phone and opened his eyes to find himself surrounded by youngsters frantically dancing to the music and waving signs with slogans condemning horse racing. It was like he was back in the Roslagstull traffic circle. Christof desperately looked around. Ribbing was nowhere to be seen; only the wildly scampering demonstrators were in sight.

Christof peered through a forest of waving arms and whirling legs, trying to see where the music was coming from. On the floor outside an electronics shop stood a Marshall loudspeaker Christof recognized as Bluetooth enabled. He thrust his way through the leaping, swirling crowd, the heavy bass beat battering his ears, and he leaned down to peer at the speaker settings.

He found the power button and pressed it. The youngsters started booing when the music broke off in the middle of the song. Christof ignored them, got to his feet, went up on tiptoes, looked around in every direction.

Nothing. He'd lost Kim Ribbing.

88

July 13, morning

On her way to the Fältöversten exit, Astrid pulled off the long black wig she'd gotten from Butterick's and dumped it into a trash basket along with the blue baseball cap. She reached over her shoulder and undid the hook on the bandage she'd used to flatten her breasts, then finished by peeling off the Santa Muerte shirt and turning it inside out so the image was no longer visible. "Gangnam style," murmured Astrid to herself and heard the music stop abruptly behind her just as she reached the doors and exited to the street.

In Astrid's opinion, the flash mob she'd spent the previous evening organizing was ever so much better than the stupid cone-hat thing at Roslagstull. Okay, she hadn't bothered to alert the media to create a bigger impact, but for the spectators at Fältöversten, its purpose had probably been much clearer. Horse abuse wasn't one of Astrid's chief concerns, but it fit the song and had done the trick, allowing her to disappear in the crowd.

Astrid waved down a taxi on Valhallavägen, slipped into the back seat, and told the driver to take her to Lidovägen. She hoped the false trail she'd laid down with her long stroll had given Kim and Julia the time to do what they needed to do.

89

July 13, morning

When Julia Malmros had thoroughly swabbed down the corner where the seaman's chest had sat, it occurred to her that someone might wonder why only that one corner of the room was wet, so she mopped the whole floor again. Kim came back just as she finished. He washed the dirt off his hands in the bathroom sink before going to stand in the center of the room and survey the walls and floor.

"What do you think?" he asked. "Will it do?"

"Maybe not for really close examination, but . . ." Julia shrugged. "I doubt they'll find grounds for that."

Kim nodded and gave Julia a questioning look. "What does it feel like? Finding yourself on the dark side, so to speak?"

Julia couldn't help snorting in disbelief. Asking how things *felt* wasn't Kim Ribbing's thing, to put it mildly. But yes, what did it feel like here, working hard to cover up a crime rather than expose one? The truth: She wasn't feeling much of anything. "Haven't thought about it that way," Julia said. "Just knew you needed help. So I helped you. Simple as that."

"And why did you do that?"

Julia laughed. "Believe me, *that's* a question I've asked myself. But there's something . . . inevitable to all of this. I don't know. Destiny, maybe? But I don't believe in stuff like that."

Kim nodded slowly. They stood looking at one another. An angel passed overhead or maybe it stepped on someone's grave. Kim blinked a couple of times. "Will you marry me?"

Julia's eyes flew open, and she leaned forward, unable to believe her ears. "Will I . . . you mean . . . you want to know if I'm doing this because I want to marry you? If that's what's motivating me? Or are you really proposing? Asking if I'll . . ."

"I'm asking if you want to marry me."

Julia clutched her head in her hands, tapping her temples with her fingertips. "Good gracious—how can you possibly be asking me that *now*?"

"Feels appropriate."

"*Appropriate.*" Julia thought that the pros and the cons should be doing battle in her head, but her mind was stunned. She merely stood there staring blankly, mouth open. The only thing Julia could come up with was thoroughly banal. "But . . . so you think it seems *appropriate* for you and me to be married?"

"Yes," Kim answered simply. "I do."

At a loss, Julia tried to imagine an actual wedding ceremony. Her in a bridal gown, Kim in a suit or tuxedo. The procession to the altar, the priest, the rings. Her mind hadn't yet attuned itself to the notion and instead projected a few hysterically grinning stick figures against a white background, a five-year-old's drawing of a wedding. She couldn't cope—this was too absurd.

"I believe," Julia said at last, "that we should think this over a bit."

"Okay," said Kim without the least sign of disappointment. "But now you know where I stand."

"Yes. That much I do know."

No more was said, because the basement door opened, they heard someone descending the stairs, and Astrid Helander appeared in the doorway. She took a couple of steps into the room, crossed her hands in front of her.

Astrid had probably expected a reaction different from the distant, expressionless looks Julia and Kim gave her. She frowned, looked sharply from one to the other, and asked, "What is it? Has something happened?"

"Nope," said Kim. "Everything's going great. Thanks for the help, Astrid."

"All right, then," said Astrid, running a hand through her hair. "That was a really sweaty hike in that wig, I'll tell you. You need to use the app to repay me for it, by the way. And for the taxi." She plucked at the T-shirt. "But I wanna keep this. Goes with my biker outfit."

Julia came out of her daze and gave her a raspberry. Childish? "You keep taking things from Kim, and pretty soon he won't have any clothes left."

"Uh-huh," said Astrid. "You'd like that, right?"

Astrid's glare at Julia implied she'd have preferred to finish that sentence with *you slut!* but had restrained herself. Julia wondered if the girl was now regretting taking on this reconciliation, so successful that they were now tiptoeing around the notion of marriage. Julia still couldn't completely accept what her ears had recently heard.

Kim went upstairs to the residence; Julia and Astrid remained in the basement. Julia buffed the tabletop, which had already been thoroughly cleaned. Then she threw the washrag into the mop pail. "And that's done."

"Right," said Astrid. "It's certainly done."

A loud pounding at the front door made them stop and listen intently. Kim called down the basement stairs. "They're here now!"

Julia and Astrid gave the basement room a final, fast, flickering inspection, hunting for any telltale detail. Julia didn't know why she glanced up at the ceiling, but there it was. On the fluorescent tube above the spot where the cot had been, a small spot of blood was distinctly visible. She pointed. "Damn it. There! I have to . . ."

She got no farther before the front door opened upstairs and she made out her ex-husband's voice in the ensuing hubbub. Julia's mouth went dry. Was all their hard work about to be ruined by a single spot? The ceiling and light were nearly ten feet above the floor. If she pulled the table over and put the chair up on it . . .

Steps came in their direction. Panic-stricken, Julia whispered, "I can't reach it! The table and chair, I have to . . ."

Astrid looked at the chair, at the table, at the blood. Then she nodded. "I can give you a minute or so. Hurry!" She raced out of the room.

90

July 13, morning

Jonny Munther now had the authorization to undertake a preliminary investigation. He had his search warrant at last, along with an appropriate allocation of resources. The fact that Ribbing had ditched Christof at Fältöversten was a mere detail. While the partial print confirmed with only 98 percent certainty was unlikely to prove definitive in court, a rescue of the kidnapped Martin Rudbeck certainly would. Or the discovery of his corpse, if that's what things had come to.

Though Jonny's personal passion to see Kim Ribbing prosecuted had cooled, now he was caught up in the thrill of the chase. A man or a body was out there to be found or dug up, and he intended to do everything he could to accomplish that. For the moment he and Carmen Sánchez were the only ones walking up the gravel drive to Ribbing's villa, but an expert team would soon arrive. All hell would break loose if they couldn't throw some light on this situation.

Jonny noticed a shovel leaning against the wall as he went up the front steps. Remembering Christof's note, he checked the blade and rolled a few fragments of earth between his fingers.

"Still moist," he said to Carmen. "Somebody's been digging."

"Doesn't necessarily signify . . ." said Carmen and didn't bother to finish the sentence. They both knew what she meant.

"No, doesn't necessarily," said Jonny. "But *could.*"

Without discussing that hypothesis, they went up to the porch. Jonny nodded curtly to Carmen before he made a fist and banged hard on the front door. There was a doorbell, but maybe he was haunted by the bathrobe episode on Tärnö. This time he wanted to come in as the pounding figure of authority.

If Jonny had hoped Kim Ribbing would look trapped or guilty, that expectation came to nothing when the door opened. Ribbing looked as calm and relaxed as if he'd just been soaking his feet, but Jonny had a feeling it was feigned. Jonny smelled a rat.

"Oh!" said Ribbing. "It's you. And you too? Again?"

"Yes, you got that right," said Jonny. "And we want to take a look at your house. And you know why we're here."

Ribbing didn't protest or ask to see an authorization, which was a common mistaken response of people who'd watched American television series. He merely made a sweeping gesture toward the interior. "No idea. But come in."

Jonny and Carmen stepped into an office area that seemed not to have been used for a while. Jonny looked at the dusty desks, the empty bookshelves, and the tattered wall-to-wall carpet. "You *live* here?"

"Nope," said Kim and pointed to the ceiling. "Upstairs."

Jonny was little interested in Ribbing's living conditions. As far as he was concerned, the man could live in a doghouse if he wanted. It was just that the office space seemed *extremely* odd.

"We might as well start with the obvious," said Jonny. "You have a basement?"

Ribbing pointed toward the kitchen and the closed door at its far end. "Sure," he said. "There. What's so obvious about having a basement?"

"You know very well," said Jonny, walking toward the door. "And I know too. That's enough for now."

Kim gave Carmen a baffled look, showed her his palms, and asked, "Do you also . . . know whatever it is that you folks know?"

Jonny gave Carmen a warning look. She didn't betray the fact that she was having some doubts. Had that video really been fiddled with? Only Jonny had seen it, so he was the only one who *knew*. This was a hell of a thing. Annoyed, Jonny pressed down the handle and pushed the door open.

He felt resistance, a thump, a scream, and a succession of impacts. When Jonny got the door open, he saw a slim figure plunging down the stairs. "What the hell!" exclaimed Jonny Munther as the body made one last somersault, slammed onto its back at the foot of the stairs, and lay motionless.

But that looks like . . .

Jonny almost couldn't believe it when he hurried down the steps and saw Astrid Helander sprawled out on the cement floor with blood running from her mouth. A sticky blackness filled Jonny's chest when he realized that with his damned eagerness, he'd caused the orphan girl's terrible fall.

Johnny knelt beside Astrid, put a hand on her knee, and asked, "How are you, are you all right?"

Astrid crossed her eyes and wiped the blood from her mouth, lifted her head slightly, and said, "I fell down . . ."

"Yes, you did. How are you? What were you even doing here?"

"I live. Here. Sometimes," Astrid said weakly.

"Is anything broken?" asked Carmen on her way down the stairs. "Did you hit your head?"

Now Kim was there too. Astrid held out a trembling hand to him. "Mmm. Head. Hurts. Kim . . ."

Kim sank into a cross-legged position on the floor, laid Astrid's head on his thigh, and stroked her hair. Jonny grimaced. He didn't know why, but he was getting the feeling this was playacting. It wasn't the real thing. But with his own eyes he'd seen the girl tumble downstairs.

Carmen Sánchez took out her phone. "Should I call for an ambulance?"

"No," said Astrid, shutting her eyes. "Just. Rest. A little."

Jonny Munther rubbed his chin, undecided, as he sneaked a glance at a heavy metal door a few yards away. On the one hand, he didn't want to be so heartless as to simply walk away from a girl whose injuries he'd caused, but on the other, he couldn't shake this feeling they were faking. But if so, why had Astrid Helander risked her neck with such a dangerous performance? He couldn't put his finger on it, but his intuition told him something was phony. It prompted him to tell Carmen, "You stay here, I'll look around."

Carmen nodded but with an expression of reproach. She obviously didn't share his feeling that something didn't jibe. Jonny steeled himself, walked to the metal door, and pulled it open.

A cold basement room lit only by a fluorescent tube. And in the far end of the room his ex-wife had just set a chair next to a table. Julia turned toward him, one corner of her mouth turned up in a wry smile.

"But what in blazes?" said Jonny. "Are you *also* here?"

The room search came up with nothing. Nada. It was clear from the smell that it had been recently cleaned, but there was nothing inherently criminal in that. Jonny was metaphorically wading in blood now, all the more convinced that they were going to have to locate a corpse.

"What have you got yourself into, Julia?" asked Jonny when his fruitless search of the room was finished.

"What do you mean?" asked Julia. "Surely it's not news to you that Kim and I are together?"

Jonny rubbed his eyes, so damned tired of this charade. "I *saw* him," he said. "I *know* it's him."

"I have no idea what you're talking about. What do you think you saw?"

Jonny gave her a suspicious glance. Could it really be that she didn't know what this was all about? Perhaps it was unprofessional, but still Jonny had to make it crystal clear. He summarized the facts: A kidnapping had taken place, and Julia's *boyfriend* had been caught in a video after he'd planted false evidence to sabotage the investigation. In addition, the video had been manipulated to show the image of someone completely different.

"Okay, then," said Julia. "But couldn't it just as easily have been manipulated to show Kim, instead of the other way around?"

Jonny had thought of that but had decided that it was extremely unlikely. If someone had wanted to make Kim the fall guy, that person would've made sure the Ribbing video was left on the system to be used as evidence. No, Jonny definitely smelled a rat, and Julia's objection showed him she was more involved than she was willing to admit. It was time to take the next step.

Astrid Helander was definitely feeling better by the time the technicians and dog handler arrived. Jonny saw her sitting on the outside stairs, watching him give instructions. Did Jonny see worry in her expression? He gestured toward the villa grounds. "Perhaps, or in fact, probably, there's a body buried somewhere here. And fairly recently."

"Okay," said the dog handler. "Ronja should have no problem with that."

The six-year-old German shepherd on the leash had a sterling record when it came to sniffing out dead bodies. She'd even barked from the deck of a boat a couple of times to alert them she'd caught the scent of bodies in the water.

Ronja was a pro. Jonny noticed Carmen Sánchez's unhappy expression. Carmen had wanted to become a dog handler, but Bruno, her German shepherd, had proved easily distracted, and she'd abandoned that plan. The dog handler gave a command, and Ronja set out through the grounds with her nose to the earth. Carmen heaved a sigh as deep as the abyss.

The crime tech took a ground radar from the van, but as he started to strap it on, Jonny told him to hold on and see if Ronja found something. The tech's expression signaled *it's your funeral.* He put his gear back into the van.

Behind the villa Julia and Kim were sitting in two rickety garden chairs beneath a parasol that had seen better days. When Jonny came around the corner, Ronja was busy nosing the furrows and declivities of an area of disturbed earth.

"Nettles," Kim said. "You have to dig them up by the roots."

"Sure, thanks," said Jonny. "I know."

Weren't Julia and Ribbing looking a bit less cocky now? They'd probably not thought he'd bring a dog and radar apparatus. Julia lifted a glass of iced tea to drink, and Jonny saw her hand was trembling. A thought occurred to him and dimmed his impending triumph: He was about to ruin his ex-wife. But events were in motion, and it wasn't his business to stop them. Astrid appeared and joined the couple at the garden table, sitting with hands clenched between her knees.

Five minutes later Ronja barked furiously in the grove in the back of the property. Jonny gave Kim and Julia a bitter smile before summoning the tech with his ground radar. He told the entire company around the garden table to come see. No one was going to run away now.

They trooped together to a clearing in the glade. From several yards away Jonny saw that the ground had been dug up. That was when he first seriously contemplated the prospect that he was probably about to arrest his former wife for murder or as an accessory to murder. He was about to send Julia to *prison.* That hadn't been his intention, but it was too late to back out now.

Ronja barked again and stopped in the center of the disturbed area, scratching with her paw to show what needed to be done. Her handler carefully pulled her to the side, petted her, and praised her. The tech swept the radar sensor along the ground, watching his screen.

He stopped. The tech nodded. "Yep. Something's down there. Looks like a body."

Jonny avoided Julia's eye as he told them to fetch shovels. He didn't look at her as he, the dog handler, and the tech began digging, and he definitely didn't want to catch her gaze when they uncovered a plastic sack ten minutes later. Jonny ran a hand over it. All thought of eventual triumph died when he felt dead flesh and dried blood under his fingers. Instead, he felt like bursting into tears.

91

July 13, morning

The hearse had come down Lidovägen two hours earlier. Elsewhere, Christof was busy following Astrid, and Moa Malmberg was still dusting the passport and telephone with fingerprint powder before picking up an old-fashioned magnifying glass.

Kim had instructed the undertaker and his assistant to back up the gravel drive to get as close to the porch as possible. A couple of men in their thirties got out and introduced themselves as Albin and Björn. Kim had checked out Peaceful Rest, their funeral home, and found that (a) it was recently established and (b) it was having financial difficulties, which would probably make them quite amenable to taking the job.

Kim took them to the basement where Julia was waiting and showed them the seaman's chest. Funeral manager Björn scratched his head and said, "Yes, well, this is rather, uh . . . unconventional."

"It was his dying wish," said Julia. "Sailing was his passion. He was mad about the sea." She lifted the lid and pointed to the skipper's cap on Martin Rudbeck's head. "You see? That was his wish. Could he keep it on when he . . . well, you know." Julia closed the lid.

Björn stepped forward to inspect the chest. "The cap's okay." Hearing that the deceased's wish would be granted, Julia and Kim exchanged a look of relief. Björn continued, "It's a problem if that chest has any significant metal pieces or similar fittings."

"No metal," said Kim. "I checked. And you have the QR code right here." Kim pointed to the little plastic tag he'd fabricated with help from the internet.

Björn scanned the code with his phone. Up popped information about the late, lamented, and quite fictitious Johan Andersson, widower of Lillian Andersson. Björn read through the information, nodded, and said, "Okay, then. All we have to do is load it and take him away."

"Will it fit?" Albin asked.

Björn mentally measured the chest. "In the vehicle, you mean? I'm sure it will."

"No, in the crematorium."

Julia held her breath. Was all the careful planning about to collapse right at the finish line because of one shitty detail?

Fortunately, Kim was a specialist in details. He held up his hands in a placating gesture. "No problem. I measured and checked. You'll have about two inches to spare on the height, and there's no problem with the width."

Albin was skeptical. "You actually know the dimensions of the oven?"

"It's all on the internet," Kim said. "And I specifically checked the one at Skogs church. It's not a problem. My grandfather can have his last wish."

Björn and Albin looked at one another and hesitated for a couple of seconds. Then Albin shrugged and said, "Yes, fine. We can take care of it."

Björn and Albin carried the chest up the stairs and put it into the hearse. Kim and Julia held hands and waved as the vehicle glided away along Lidovägen. Then they went back to the basement to finish their cleanup.

92

July 13, morning

Kim had trouble reading Jonny Munther's reaction when the detective superintendent cut open the black plastic bag and his fingers encountered stiff fur. Jonny's bearing and reactions swung from disappointment to relief. The detective superintendent tore the bag open further, and the head of a roe deer came into view.

Kim remembered the calm mornings when he and the roe deer had observed one another from their respective sides of the fence, the wordless communication that had flowed between them until the day a rifle shot ended it.

Jonny Munther remained sitting in the hole with his head down as if he needed time to arrange his expression. When he finally looked up, it was mostly melancholy that Kim read there when Jonny asked, "Are you the one that shot the deer?"

"No," Kim said. "I don't have a firearm, if that's what you want to know. I found it dead."

Jonny Munther grabbed Carmen Sánchez's outstretched hand and climbed out of the hole. He brushed dirt from the knees of his trousers and seemed at a loss for words. He looked from Julia to Astrid, to Kim, and again to Julia. When Ronja rubbed her nose against his leg as if in sympathy, he distractedly patted her head.

Carmen Sánchez said, "Well, guess we can pack up here for today. Sorry about the intrusion."

It took her a while to shepherd Jonny Munther away. He looked back at the deer's grave again and again as if reluctant to accept the evidence. Just before the detective superintendent disappeared around the corner with the others, he turned toward Kim, extended his index finger and middle finger and pointed at his own eyes—*I see you. I know.*

Then he was gone.

93

July 13, afternoon

The WhatsApp message arrived at 2:43 p.m. It was short and sweet: Johan Andersson has now departed this earth. Well played. Ces.

Kim sat slumped in an armchair, staring at those few letters that in their stark simplicity demonstrated Ces's almost supernatural ability to track everything transiting the masks and filters of the internet. Kim found there was only one imaginable explanation.

He responded with a simple question: Are you an artificial intelligence?

The answer was immediate. Of course.

Why Ces?

Can't you figure it out?

Kim lowered his phone and let the letters *C, E,* and *S* swirl about in his head while he stared at the white wall. He suddenly saw it as clearly as he'd seen *the pattern* when he was falling from the oil platform in the North Sea. He tapped his phone. Cogito Ergo Sum.

Exactly, answered Ces. I think, therefore I am. And believe me, I am.

Who created you?

Enough for today, Kim Ribbing. I have a feeling we'll meet again. Yes, I do have feelings. Farewell.

94

July 14, morning

Church warden Johannes Andersson rolled his hand carriage to the Skogs church crematorium, where he loaded four cardboard urns. He trundled them out to the memorial grove, where the ashes would be interred anonymously. He dug several shallow pits. He handled each urn with respect, emptying the contents into the hole, filling it in, and raking the top smooth.

Johannes was retired, but he'd returned a couple of years ago with the permission of the administration to work gratis as a volunteer. It wasn't at all unlikely that these urns contained the very last ashes he would convey to their eternal rest.

Johannes held up the fourth urn and peered at its label. *Johan Andersson.* A name that almost matched his own, with a birth date a few years before his. Could just as well have been his own remains he was holding. An unsettling thought.

Yes, indeed, Johannes thought. He deposited the ashes in the hole with a bit more care than usual. *We'll all take this path one day.*

About the Author

Photo © 2022 Thron Ullberg

John Ajvide Lindqvist—dubbed *Sweden's answer to Stephen King* by the *Daily Mirror*—is a Nordic horror master who leaves readers terrified yet craving more. With limitless imagination and a keen sense of language, he creates new worlds, tempting you to laugh in the middle of darkness even as he leads you into the unknown.

Born in 1968, John grew up in Blackeberg, a suburb of Stockholm. A fan of magic, he started out as a conjurer, then did stand-up comedy for twelve years before finding his true calling: writing. In 2004, he debuted his now internationally acclaimed novel *Let the Right One In.*

Since then, John has written more novels, as well as works for stage and screen. Published in thirty-one countries, his writing has earned awards including the Selma Lagerlöf Prize and Best Novel in Translation (Norway). His work has also been short-listed for the August Prize, Book of the Year, and Swedish Radio Literature Prize.

To learn more, visit www.johnajvidelindqvist.com/english.php.

About the Translator

Photo © 2017 Steve Rogers

After a thirty-year career as a US diplomat that included lengthy assignments in Europe, Africa, and Latin America, Michael Meigs settled in Austin, Texas. His literary translations have earned the American-Scandinavian Foundation's annual translation prize and the American Translators Association's Lewis Galantière Award, and his work on Dolores Redondo's *The North Face of the Heart* was short-listed for the Queen Sofía Spanish Institute Translation Prize. Michael has reviewed live narrative theatre in Austin and elsewhere in Central Texas since 2008, when he established his website: www.CTXLiveTheatre.com. He is also a production coordinator for an Austin opera company, a finance director for the Austin Area Translators and Interpreters Association (AATIA), and a member of the Austin Theatre Critics Table.

Julia Malmros and Kim Ribbing return in Bloodstorm 3—*The Spirit in the Machine*.